Portrait of
Charlotte

Portrait of Charlotte

Jessica Blair

PIATKUS

First published in Great Britain in 1999 by
Judy Piatkus (Publishers) Ltd of
5 Windmill Street, London W1

This edition published 1999

A catalogue record for this book is available from the British Library

ISBN 0-7499-0476-3

Set in 11/12pt Times by
Action Publishing Technology Ltd, Gloucester

Printed and bound in Great Britain by
Mackays of Chatham plc

for Joan with love

and with thanks to Geraldine and Judith
for their advice and criticism

and to Lynn
a sympathetic and first-rate editor

Chapter One

Stepping outside of his Chelsea home overlooking the Thames, Charles Campion glanced skywards and was thankful that the poor July weather of 1820 had turned better with the new month. It augured well for a good crossing of the Channel.

'Goodbye, Charlotte, my dear. I should be home in two weeks. Buying the wine and lace and arranging shipment shouldn't take any longer than that.' He kissed his wife on both cheeks and held her hands as they stood beside the post-chaise which would take him to Dover. He looked tenderly and admiringly into her eyes, expressing the love he had felt from the first moment he saw her two years ago.

It was a moment he would never forget. He had been invited to a small dinner party arranged by Francis Wakefield, Charlotte's father, for some business friends. He had had several contacts with him, which had turned out profitable to both men. He liked Francis, fifteen years his senior, recognised his shrewdness, and saw that future arrangements could be beneficial to his own commercial empire.

Francis on his part admired the business acumen of the younger man. Many a person, if they had inherited, at thirty-eight, estates in Lincolnshire, property in London, ships sailing out of Boston and London, would have sat back and enjoyed the wealth, but not so Charles. He was determined to expand and broad-mindedly saw that in doing so he was not only adding to his own coffers but was providing work for others not so well off as himself.

Suspecting that Francis might have a proposition to make he

1

had accepted the invitation, the first to Wakefield's home, and had come from Lincolnshire especially for it. That decision was one he did not regret, for the moment he walked into the parlour, where jovial conversation buzzed, and saw Charlotte, her face lit up with laughter at some remark which had been exchanged among her group of four, his heart was lost. His mind was transfixed and he had to forcibly direct his attention to the welcome from Francis. Even in that moment he wondered if he dare hope that he, a thirty-nine-year-old, could gain the love of someone who, at nineteen, filled that room with magic.

He went through the introductions with Francis, acknowledging those he already knew, making polite and charming exchanges with those who were new to him, but all the time eager for the second when he would be face to face with the girl who had captured his imagination.

'My daughter, Charlotte. Charlotte, Charles Campion,' Francis presented them and then turned to answer a query from one of the other guests.

Charles bowed but his eyes never left her. 'I am delighted to make your acquaintance.'

Charlotte gave a demure inclination of her head. She had been aware of the tall handsome man who had entered the room; now, close to, she saw that he was even more so. His dark hair, with its attractive sweep above a broad forehead, was thick around the sides and ran into two sidewinders which accentuated the squareness of his jaw. The laughter lines around his mouth proclaimed an enjoyment of life and relieved the firmness of his mouth. His steel-blue eyes were sharp, demanding attention, but she knew that at the same time they were shrewdly observant. He was immaculately dressed in a dark blue coat cut away square at the waist but dropping in knee length tails at the back. The large silk covered revers ran into a high collar. He wore the new fashion of trousers which Charlotte liked much better than the breeches still preferred by her father. His yellow waistcoat covered a white shirt, at the neck of which was a neatly tied yellow cravat.

'It is a pleasure to have you with us this evening, Mr Campion,' returned Charlotte. 'I believe you have come all the way from Lincolnshire especially.'

'I thought your father might have some business proposition to make.'

'And that was your only reason for coming?' There was a mild rebuke in her teasing tone.

'I knew no other when I received the invitation, but I do now. At this moment business is far from my mind and no doubt will be for the rest of the evening.'

'You flatter me, Mr Campion,' she protested demurely.

'Indeed I do not, Miss Wakefield.'

'But, you must have met many young ladies far more beautiful than I.'

He gave a slight shake of his head. 'None that captured my attention as you did immediately I entered the room.'

'Ah, maybe that was my dress.' She gave a knowing smile.

Charles raised his hands in protest. 'No you underestimate your charm and my judgement.' The pause was almost insignificant but it placed an emphasis on those words. Then he added, 'But of course your dress is most exquisite.'

His glance of appreciation slid over the pale blue silk dress with its Gothic V-neck trimmed with lace in the manner of Vandyke portraits. The puff shoulders gave way to the newer fashion of longer sleeves complementing the narrow skirt and natural waist-line. The design set off her figure and its colour matched perfectly the blue of her eyes. Her mousey-brown hair was curled and drawn up from the back of her neck making an alluring setting for her petite nose, full rosy cheeks, bowed lips and rounded chin.

Their conversation was interrupted by the announcement that dinner was served.

Francis quickly assessed the situation around the room and turned to Charles.

'Will you escort Charlotte?'

'It will be my pleasure.' He held out his arm which Charlotte took gracefully and, after a moment's pause, they followed the other couples to the dining room.

Charlotte smiled to herself. This had the signs of being engineered by her father and she thought that more so when she found that she was seated next to Charles at the table. She knew her father thought highly of him and realised that his assets and the way in which he conducted his affairs could be helpful to his own business. She suspected that her father was hoping that she would develop more than a pleasant relationship with Charles Campion.

Well, he would make a good catch even though he was twenty years older. He was rich with vast country estates and a London home. He was handsome and from the few moments she had been with him she thought he would be kind, considerate, gentle and attentive. So did age really matter if they were compatible? But, she wondered, why had he never married?

She found her judgements confirmed throughout the meal. He was all she thought he would be; not only to her but to everyone around the table. He was a stimulating conversationalist with a wide knowledge which was abreast of the times.

He was delighted to be sitting next to Charlotte for it enabled him to find out more about the girl whose sparkle had attracted him to her beauty. In closer conversation at the table he found that she did not conform to the set image of the daughter who was seen and not heard, waiting to be married off to some eligible man picked out by her parents. He suspected that Francis Wakefield might have had a match in his mind when he made the invitation, but he realised that Charlotte would definitely have her say in who she would wed. She would have to be won.

And win her he had done.

Now, Charlotte watched the post-chaise turn out of the short drive. Charles waved, and she raised a hand in return. He passed from sight. She stood, lost to her surroundings, her thoughts nowhere, her eyes unseeing. Then she sighed, turned and walked slowly back through the doorway where James, one of two footmen, waited patiently to close the door.

She paused in the centre of the hall.

'Will that be all, ma'am?' James's voice almost startled her.

'Yes, thank you, James,' she replied tonelessly.

His footsteps faded into the silence of the house.

Her gaze drifted slowly round the hall. A wide staircase curved gracefully to the first floor, its iron balustrade exquisitely shaped with roses, joining and intertwining two sets of the letters 'CC' spaced at intervals all the way up the stairs.

4

'The flower of love linking Charlotte Campion and Charles Campion together forever, my dear,' Charles had whispered when he had brought her to the house for the first time on their return from their month's honeymoon in Italy.

Italy! Oh, it seemed so long ago, yet so much was still vivid. Charles had been ever attentive, concerned for her comfort and well-being. Only the best was good enough for her, the travel, the accommodation wherever it was; on the journey, in Milan, Rome, Pisa, Florence, Venice. He showered her with gifts, tokens of his love, mementoes of their honeymoon. She had been happy, revelling in his attention, enjoying the sun, the new experience of foreign travel, the excitement of returning home to the estates in Lincolnshire, to this, their London home especially purchased and renovated by Charles as his wedding gift to her.

It had been decorated to the latest fashion by expert decorators. Curtains and drapes matched or contrasted in the best taste with the wallpaper. Furnishings, comfortable and practical, had been bought from craftsmen. Nothing had been spared and when he first brought her to this house she could do nothing but stare in wonder, lost for words. She had been used to a beautiful elegant home but that paled beside the luxury which now surrounded her. She knew any girl would give anything for the life of opulence which lay ahead of her. She had servants at her beck and call ever ready to do her bidding for they liked her as much as they did their employer, seeing him as a kindly, considerate man who paid them justly and would never think of exploiting them.

Everyone said how lucky she was to capture this most eligible of bachelors. Mothers who had been trying to match their daughters with Charles Campion tended to be cutting about his choice, their daughters envious.

As Charlotte walked slowly up the stairs to her room, and stood looking out of the window across the drive, she knew how lucky she was. Her mother and father had told her so, right from the moment when Charles had asked their permission to visit their daughter whenever he was in London, and Charles made that often, leading up to the day when he asked them for their daughter's hand in marriage.

By that time she had become convinced that it was the right

5

thing to do. She had told herself that life with this man would be happy. Love? Well, she liked him ... yes, she loved him. But did she really know what love was? She had dismissed the doubts. Of course she loved him. Did he not spoil her, lavish her with gifts, give her every comfort? She wanted for nothing. And plainly he was so in love with her.

She sighed. In love? Was that it? Was she in love with Charles? She loved him, but was that the same? She sensed a disturbing questioning in her mind. Had she discovered something lacking in her feelings? Was this why at times she felt a chill in the relationship? It did not emanate from Charles but from her inner self. She had always dismissed it as being something which had come with her new life, doubts about whether she could live up to Charles's expectations, but now she wondered if she had misinterpreted her reactions.

She stiffened and chided herself for such thoughts. They were the result of being parted from him for the first time. That was it. She was gloomy because he was not here, would not be coming in later in the day. It was not like her to be feeling depressed. Stupid to doubt her feelings. Of course she loved him.

She was about to turn from the window when she saw a carriage come through the gateway.

Her face broke into a broad smile. 'Mother and Father!' She raced down the stairs, and was out of the front door and reached the bottom of the steps just as the carriage stopped.

'Oh, it's good to see you,' she cried as she hugged them both.

They laughingly exchanged greetings with their daughter as she ushered them up the steps and into the house.

'You've just missed Charles.'

'We know,' smiled her mother, and Charlotte sensed some intrigue.

'We knew what time he would be going but did not want to intrude on your goodbyes.'

'You shouldn't have worried about that.' Charlotte pulled the bell sash. 'Take your coats off.'

'No, my dear, no need for that. We're not stopping.' Her father laughed when he saw disappointment darken his daughter's face.

6

'Francis! Don't tease the girl,' his wife frowned.

'Don't spoil the fun, Gertrude.'

'Fun? See the girl's face? Do you call that fun?'

A little bewildered, Charlotte looked from one to the other, but the arrival of one of her maids, drew her attention. 'Oh, Betsy, we shan't need you now.'

'Yes, ma'am.' The girl bobbed a curtsey and turned away.

'Wait!' Francis boomed, drawing Betsy up with a start.

She shot a questioning look at her mistress.

Before Charlotte could say anything Francis went on. 'Charlotte, you are coming home with us and tomorrow we sail to Whitby where we will spend ten days!' He delivered the words with a flourish.

Both Francis and Gertrude noted with glee the look of astonishment with which their daughter regarded them. They exchanged glances of pleasure at the way they had surprised her.

'Don't stand there gawking, lass,' laughed Francis. 'You'll need to pack a few things. We'll wait.' He shrugged himself out of his coat. Gertrude removed her cape and bonnet and handed them to Betsy who thought how lucky her mistress was to be taken on holiday. 'Betsy, do you think you could get us a cup of hot chocolate?' Francis asked as she took his coat and hat.

'Certainly, sir.' Betsy hurried from the room. She liked Mr and Mrs Wakefield; they were always pleasant and never put on airs and graces though he was a successful merchant, highly thought of in London trading circles.

Charlotte was still trying to take in her father's announcement. It was so unexpected and, coming at a time when she was feeling a bit low, it had taken her breath away. 'Whitby? On the Yorkshire coast?'

'Aye,' replied her father.

'But why Whitby?' she asked as she and her mother sat down on the bar-backed sofa, based on the designs of Hepplewhite, while her father, hands clasped behind him, stood with his back to the fireplace.

'Your father's been angling for a while to go to Whitby to revive childhood memories though why he should want to do that considering the circumstances he was in at that time I shall never know,' explained Gertrude.

Charlotte looked queryingly at her father. She knew nothing of his early days except that he had come to London from Yorkshire. She had only ever known him as a successful merchant living in the capital. It seemed that his origins were something that he never wanted to discuss. It appeared he had forgotten his roots though there were times, especially when he was excited, that his words were laced with the Yorkshire accent.

Francis shrugged his broad shoulders, hardened early in life by physical work, but softened as his mode of living changed and demanded less muscular exertions. His sharp mind had always been there, seeking opportunity to progress beyond the poverty he had once known. The seizing of those chances had brought money, a better way of life, a new social circle where he had met and loved the only child of a moderately successful merchant whose business only needed a nimble brain to take it to the forefront of the London trade, specialising in wine imports from the Continent.

The taste for his own goods was beginning to show in his florid complexion and the enjoyment of good food had started to show around his middle, a fact he did not deliberately attempt to disguise, though the superb cut of his clothes, in the best of cloths, channelled people's attention to the way he held himself – straight, commanding attention.

Though he exuded an air of authority when it came to business matters he was known for his friendliness and his easygoing manner. He did not see these as weaknesses but rather as positive attributes for they enabled him to get on well with people, not least his wife and daughter. He was well aware that they could twist him round their little fingers, but he did not let them know that, allowing them to imagine it was their lovable guile which had won him over.

'It's just something I feel I want to do,' he went on. 'I don't know why, but the urge is there. The business is running smoothly, my capable manager can take over for a few days.'

'I've been pressing him for some time to let Jack have more authority. After all, he's been with your father a long time and knows the business inside out,' put in Gertrude.

'Aye, your mother will have her way,' he flattered,

knowing it pleased her to think she wielded such influence, though he told himself he had decided to take that course some time ago but had only just got around to finalising it.

The chocolate arrived, and, though they settled down to drink it, Charlotte was all excitement inside. What she thought was going to be a drab time while Charles was away now held the promise of something new: a sea voyage, different sights and experiences, and a view of the place where her father was born.

She looked at him. 'What is Whitby like?'

'I doubt if he'll remember,' Gertrude put in. 'Your father was only ten when he came to London forty-six years ago.'

'With your parents?' asked Charlotte.

Francis shook his head. 'Alone.'

'What? At ten?' Charlotte was aghast at the prospect which must have faced him, for she had never known anything but the protection of loving parents.

He nodded. 'They both died when I was eight.' Charlotte was held by every word as he went on for now she was learning something about her father which she had never known. 'Father was lost on a whaling expedition to the Arctic, Mother went to pieces, never really recovered and was found drowned in the river.'

'Oh, I'm sorry.' Charlotte's voice was low with sympathy.

Francis gave a sad smile. 'It was so long ago, I hardly remember them.'

'How did you get to London?' asked Charlotte.

'I was put in a home after they found Mother. It was awful so I determined to run away but I didn't get the opportunity until I was ten. Stowed away on a ship bound for London.'

'You weren't found?'

'No. Got ashore. Lived rough. There were those who tried to befriend me but I was wary, reckoned they wanted me to thieve for them. I kept myself to myself. Got a job running messages for two brothers who had four shops. Worked my way up, bettered myself, met your mother and the rest you know.' He glanced at his wife and, before Charlotte could comment, said, 'And, Gertrude, I can remember something of what Whitby looks like. It's a place you never forget; the river flowing to the sea between high cliffs, up one of which there are layers and layers of red-roofed houses seeming to stand on

9

one another, reached by narrow alleys. And high on the cliff above them the old parish church and the ruined abbey. Quays line the river, busy with ships which sail to other British ports and to the Continent.'

'It sounds exciting,' said Charlotte enthusiastically. 'And interesting. I'm longing to see it.'

'Then finish your chocolate, lass, and away and get packed,' urged her father.

'Come home with us now and then we can all go to the ship together tomorrow,' explained Gertrude. 'I'll come and help you.'

Mother and daughter chose the clothes they thought would be most appropriate for their stay in the Yorkshire coastal town. While Gertrude and Betsy packed two bags Charlotte issued instructions to the housekeeper, Mrs Baines, knowing that everything would be taken care of conscientiously.

'Good morning, my dear.'

Her father's cheerful voice made Charlotte turn from the rail. 'Good morning, Father.'

Beneath her blue bonnet, held to her head against the strong breeze by a matching ribbon tied in a huge bow, he saw her eyes were shining so that he knew the answer to his question as he put it, 'You're up early. Enjoying the voyage?'

'Oh, yes,' she replied with such energy it was as if she were hugging herself with pleasure.

'Sleep well?'

'Once I'd got used to the motion of the ship. I woke early so thought I'd come on deck. Is Mother all right?'

'Sickly at first; had a fitful night; still a bit queasy. I told her some fresh air would do her good. She'll be here soon.'

They turned to lean on the rail. The sails, filled with the strong breeze, cracked above them. Ropes creaked and timbers squeaked, the sounds mingling with the swish of the water sent curling along the sides by the bow as it cleaved through the waves.

Charlotte breathed deeply of the brisk, crisp air, relishing its tang tingling her lungs. Her eyes beat through the distance towards the coast which had been in sight ever since she came on deck.

10

A movement behind them caused them to turn.

'Now, my dear, how are you feeling?' Francis stepped towards his wife to take her arm and steady her against the roll of the ship.

She gave a little smile which soured as she pulled a face.

'Take some deep breaths, Mother. You'll feel better,' advised Charlotte.

She did as her daughter bade her and had to admit that there was a wise head on her young shoulders. She came to the rail and gripped it tightly.

'Don't look down!' Charlotte's instruction was sharp and Gertrude obeyed instantly but not before her eyes had focused on the water rushing from the bow towards the stern. Even in that brief moment she had felt her head spin, but as soon as she followed her daughter's gaze towards the coast the sensation disappeared.

Within a few minutes she was enjoying the sail as much as her husband and daughter and kept up a flow of conversation until, ten minutes later, the sailor assigned to steward duties informed them that breakfast was being served.

They went to the saloon where the other four passengers had already assembled.

They were halfway through their meal when the captain appeared, bade them 'Good morning,' hoped they had had a trouble-free night, and announced that they were making good time with an estimate that they should arrive in Whitby about midday.

After breakfast the Wakefields spent the time on deck eager to take in the views as the ship beat its way northwards close to the Yorkshire coast.

'The abbey!' Francis's voice rang with excitement at being the first to glimpse the ruin as the ship rose to the crest of a wave. The vessel slid into the trough and the abbey was lost to sight.

Charlotte let her gaze follow the direction of his pointing finger.

'There!' he cried again.

'There!' Charlotte called at almost the same moment. 'See it, Mother?'

'Yes.' Gertrude was swept up by her daughter's enthusiasm,

11

and eagerly shared the exhilaration which gripped her husband at his 'homecoming'.

They watched the abbey come closer, a prominent sentinel high on the cliff, a 'welcome home' sign to Whitby sailors, a beacon to strangers seeking a safe haven from the trials of the sea.

Activity seethed around them as the crew raced about their tasks which would see the ship safely into harbour. Orders rasped loud and were passed on with equal vigour, men swarmed aloft to be ready to take in sails, the ship altered course, manoeuvring towards the narrow entrance between the two piers.

Charlotte's eyes widened. 'We'll never get in there,' she cried.

'Oh, my goodness,' gasped Gertrude, her voice charged with apprehension, and she grasped her husband's arm with a grip which made him wince.

He glanced at her and saw fright in her eyes; but they were not directed at the small gap through which they must sail. Instead they were focused on the wreck of a fishing lugger lying on the rocky scaur behind the east pier; its captain had evidently misjudged his run to safety.

'It's all right, my dear,' Francis reassured her with a gentle pat on her hand. 'Captain Moresby has entered Whitby harbour many times, I'm sure he'll do so safely now.'

They watched, fascinated, as the ship swept nearer and nearer the piers. Suddenly they seemed to rush at them. One moment they appeared far away, the next they were close. The captain held his order to furl sails until the last moment for he wanted to use the maximum wind power to enable him to make as much way up the river as possible before he need call on the oarsmen, standing by in boats on the river, to tow them to the berth beyond the bridge.

Orders rang out with a crispness which eliminated misunderstanding.

Charlotte was enthralled by the agility of the men on the yards, who seemed to have no fear of their precarious foothold on the footrope. The sails were furled with the dexterity of long practice. The ship slowed. Her attention was directed to the men on the deck who threw ropes to the waiting boats.

They were gathered, secured and then, at the command, the oarsmen, who had kept their boats in motion, now bent their backs with greater tension and hauled hard on the oars to tow the ship up river.

The intense activity had held Charlotte's attention, but now she turned her gaze on Whitby itself. On the east side of the river houses clung precariously to the steep cliff, climbing one on top of the other as if trying to vie for a sight of the sky. The whole area was a mass of red pantile roofs. Only a few of the maze of chimney pots belched smoke but it took little of her imagination, having come from London, to realise the pall which would hang over the town in the cold weather, though there was more chance of it being blown away by the wind.

Above them, as if keeping a watchful eye on everyone, stood an old church, a ruined abbey and what appeared to be a disused house.

'I remember that in use,' commented Francis, seeing the direction of his daughter's gaze. 'I wonder what happened?' He switched his attention to the west side. 'And there were no fine houses yonder,' he added indicating the newer buildings towards the top of the west cliff. 'And there's still a lot of space for development.'

'Now don't get that business gleam in your eye, Francis,' his wife warned. 'We're here on holiday.'

'Don't worry, my love, my money's tied up in London,' he reassured her.

'Were those older houses built at the same time as those on the other bank?' asked Charlotte.

'Yes, dear. Both sides of the river were developed together but the east side more so. Now with the wealth generated by the port, particularly the whaling trade, folk must see better prospects higher on the west cliff.'

Charlotte was drawn by the energy which emanated from this Yorkshire port. She had expected it to be quiet, sleepy in its remoteness. Instead she was witnessing a pulsating activity.

People were about their business everywhere, hurrying, with hardly a glance at the new arrival from London. They had seen it all before. Others, though used to the familiarity, paused and watched the passing vessel. Fishermen prepared their nets, sailors stowed ropes, children clung to the skirts of

13

their gossiping mothers, barefooted urchins ran in chase, clerks hurried from offices to deliver documents in some other part of the town.

'We'll never get through there,' observed Gertrude with just as much doubt as she had expressed on approaching the gap between the two piers. This time her comment was directed at the drawbridge which had been opened to allow the vessel to proceed to her berth upstream.

'The captain knows what he's doing,' replied Francis. He realised negotiating the passage through the bridge would need careful handling, for, apart from the narrow gap between the supports, the counterweight beams which opened the two halves of the bridge were set, when open, at topsail height. Precise manoeuvring would be required to avoid any entanglement.

Carefully, inch by inch, the ship was guided through the gap while crowds on either side of the bridge waited impatiently to cross the river.

Once the ship had cleared the bridge it was lowered and people swarmed over, hastening about their business.

As the ship moved towards the quay on the east bank, the sound of hammers from the shipbuilding yards mingled with the screech of the seagulls which had followed the vessel from the moment she had entered the river.

At other points along the quay, which ran alongside the roadway on the east bank, ships were unloading goods from the Continent, imports from the Americas or were taking on board local produce destined for major ports in the known world.

Charlotte was immersed in the bustling activity and knew she was going to find much of interest in Whitby.

'I'll go and see to our luggage,' Francis informed them. 'Is yours all ready, Charlotte?'

'Yes, Father,' she replied, and turned her attention back to the quay where people were gathering.

'What are they all about?' she mused.

'It is interesting to speculate,' replied her mother.

As the ship was taken nearer and nearer the quay they guessed: 'That young man, waiting to collect some package, maybe an important letter.' 'That young woman, waiting to greet her sweetheart.' 'That group ... ah, they are waving.' Gertrude glanced along the deck. 'It must be the relatives Mr and Mrs Snowdon said they were visiting.' She indicated the people they had spoken to in the salon last evening.

'Hi, there's a pickpocket!' cried Charlotte. 'See him, Mother? He just took something out of that elderly man's pocket.' Before Gertrude saw him he was lost in the crowd.

Amid their speculations they watched the gangway run out and the first passengers to leave the ship bidding goodbye to the captain who had come to the head of the gangway.

Francis appeared with two sailors who had been acting as stewards to the passengers throughout the voyage. They had all their luggage and moved towards the gangway.

'Good day, sir, ma'am, miss.' The captain saluted. 'I trust you had a pleasant voyage?'

'Admirable,' replied Francis.

'Oh, yes,' cried Charlotte.

The captain smiled. 'And you, ma'am?' he gave a slight inclination of his head to Gertrude.

'Once I had got used to the motion I found it most invigorating.'

'Good. I wish you a pleasant stay in Whitby.'

'Can you recommend a suitable hostelry?' asked Francis.

'The Angel in Baxtergate.' The captain glanced at the quay. 'Boy! Boy!' He pointed at two youngsters hanging around near the gangway.

They needed no second bidding. This was just what they had hoped for, and they were up the gangway in a flash.

'Sir!' snapped the taller of the two.

'Take these ladies and this gentleman to the Angel Inn.'

'Yes, sir.'

'And mind how you go with that luggage,' he ordered as the two boys took the bags from the stewards.

'Follow us, sir.' The youngster's wide-eyed glance included Charlotte and her mother.

Charlotte was amused by the zest of the two barefooted boys whose clothes were torn and ragged. She guessed the coins her father would give them would be the highlight of their day. She liked their open faces and felt that, in spite of their poverty, they did not let life get them down. They were

15

attentive to the pace of the adults and adjusted to the flow of people along the quay and over the bridge.

Reaching the inn, Francis quickly informed the landlord of their requirements and was pleased that they could be met. He received gushing thanks from the two boys when he tipped them generously and engaged them to report on the day of their departure to carry out a similar service.

As Charlotte washed and changed out of her travelling clothes she wondered about Charles and hoped his journey had been as pleasant as hers.

She eyed herself in the mirror. 'Come, Charlotte, is that all you think? Don't you miss him?'

'Of course I do.'

'Nothing more?'

Charlotte hesitated, her eyes never leaving the reflection which stared back at her. 'A little ...' her voice trailed away.

'What?'

'I like him.' She rushed on, not wanting to contemplate the next question. 'He's kind, generous, handsome, attentive, rich, I'm the envy of many a girl.'

'He's in love with you.'

'I know that.'

'And you?'

'I love him. Could I not?'

'Ah, but are you in love with him?'

The answer did not come readily. She stared at herself, seeking the answer in her expression, but it was not there.

She turned away from the mirror. Maybe this separation would provide the answer.

Chapter Two

'Whaleship! Whaleship!'

The cry of the youngsters racing from the cliff top, down the Church Stairs, the one hundred and ninety-nine steps from the church to the town, tore through Whitby like a fire through dry corn. It flew from lip to lip, along every street and alley, along the quays, across the river, through the shipyards, resounding wherever it was taken up.

It sent Whitby folk hurrying through the streets to welcome the town's own ships after five months facing the perils of whaling in the forbidding Arctic. Anxiety mixed with the euphoria and it would not be banished until the ships had been identified and there was joy in the knowledge that every whaleman was safely home.

Artisans left their work, clerks their offices, mothers, with children at their sides, ran from their homes, innkeepers saw customers ignore half-finished tankards of ale, housewives forgot their shopping, merchants broke off conversations and joined the streams of people flocking to the staithes and piers. Many climbed the cliffs on both sides of the river to get a sighting sooner.

At the first distant call, Richard Parker raised his eyes from the paper on which he was drawing. He caught the sound again. This time there was no mistaking it. He looked at the old, weather-lined face he was drawing and saw Joss too had heard. A gleam had come to his eye. Richard had seen it before when the whaleships returned and he knew Joss was reliving the times he had come home from such expeditions. His life at sea had added deeper character to an interesting face and Richard was capturing it on paper. He had only a little more to do and he would be satisfied, but that would have to wait. The whaleships were back!

Joss gave a knowing nod. Richard would be anxious to identify the *Phoenix*, for his father and two brothers sailed on her. 'Off with thee, lad. Wish I could run with thee.' The old man gave a wry smile of regret and started to push himself to his feet with his walking stick, wincing with the pain in his knees.

Richard was already stuffing his paper and pencils into the bag he used only for his art materials.

He jumped to his feet. 'See you tomorrow, Joss!' he cried, and was off. There was no need to make any more arrangement than that. If it was fine Joss always spent his time on the Burgess Pier watching the activities of the busy port.

People were coming on to the pier and Richard had to weave his way through them. He could have waited with Joss and had a good view of the ships as they proceeded up the river but he wanted news before that. He had to be on the cliff top. He ran through the narrow street to the Church Stairs and was impatient of the people already making their way up for they impeded his speed. Reaching the top he cut through the churchyard where gravestones and memorials were grim reminders of the unrelenting power of the sea. But Richard had no time to consider them; he wanted to make sure there would not be one recalling his father and brothers lost in the Arctic in 1820.

Reaching the edge of the cliff he searched the sea. Apprehension touched him for there were only three ships and he knew Whitby had sent five. Then he dismissed the worry as nonsense. Each whaleship sailed an individual course and so they did not necessarily all reach Whitby together unless they had rendezvoused in Shetland when they dropped off the islanders who had joined the ships on their way north.

'Hello, Richard. Thought we'd find you here.'

His concentration on the ships was broken. 'Hello, Sarah, Maggie,' he greeted his sisters. 'Where's Mother?'

'She decided to stay at home. She said the news would be soon enough when we returned,' replied Sarah.

'Is the *Phoenix* out there?' asked Maggie.

18

'Too far off to be certain,' he replied.

'How did your drawing go?' enquired Sarah.

'Soon have it finished.'

'Show us,' pressed Maggie with undisguised interest.

'Do.' Sarah added her own enthusiasm to the request.

Richard smiled as he opened his bag. He was always grateful for the interest in and encouragement of his drawing and painting shown by his sisters and mother for it was in marked contrast to the teasing and jibes he had to tolerate from his brothers.

They were whalemen, honed and tempered by the Arctic seas and the hunt for a creature which towered over their small open boat, a leviathan opposed by a small hand-held harpoon.

It was a contest and adventure they revelled in. To experience it they were willing to put up with the harshness of the voyage and the risk that they might not see Whitby again. They enjoyed the glamour which attached itself to whalemen. They were men apart, looked on with a certain awe, for not only were they sailors but they were hunters and explorers often sailing unknown seas to find the whale and boost the economy of their home port and line their own pockets with a share in the catch in addition to their wage.

John Parker had sailed every season with the whalers since he joined them as an eighteen-year-old in 1794. His aptitude was soon noticed and his promotion had been rapid; in six years he had become captain of the *Phoenix*. His success at catching whales soon earned him the tag of 'Lucky Parker' though everyone knew there was more skill than luck involved. He was pleased that his sons Will and Jim, now twenty-two and twenty-one respectively, had followed him into the whaling life and showed all his aptitude and skill. He tolerated their exuberance, especially when they were in port, for he remembered the day when he too attracted the girls with the charisma of a whaleman until he had fallen in love with Martha who in turn loved him for himself.

But he was disappointed in Richard who had no desire to find the same life at sea, though he did earn a little money from fishing with Joss's son, Mark, who owned a coble. He had sailed on his father's whaler when he was seventeen but had hated every minute of it. He was revolted by the cramped quarters in which he had to share a bunk, because in the cold Arctic it was warmer to do so. Rough seas brought sickness to some, Richard included, and the stench became nauseating. He was horrified by the blood and grease when the whales were flensed and the blubber cut up and stowed below decks for transport back to Whitby. After that voyage he swore he would never sail on a whaler again, much to the chagrin of his father and the jibes of derision from his brothers. They could not understand his reaction just as they had never recognised his true ability with a pencil and paintbrush, something which had come naturally from an early age.

They had mocked his desire to become an artist. Supported by his mother and sisters Richard had ignored them. He was sorry he had disappointed his father but this knowledge heightened his desire to succeed at all costs.

He became a familiar figure around the port sketching ships, people, activities in the shipyards and sights of Whitby. He tempted captains with portraits of their ships and the pence he received always went into helping with the household expenses. He insisted, for, though it did not match his brothers' contributions after a whaling voyage, he wanted to lessen their resentment. But it did not diminish their opinion that he was a weakling, afraid of a man's world, preferring what they regarded as the effeminate world of the artist.

'That's Joss to a T,' praised Sarah.

'How do you do it?' gasped Maggie with envy.

Richard smiled. He shrugged his shoulders. 'The lines just seem to come when I put pencil to paper.' He fished in his bag again. 'Like this?' he asked as he drew out a painting.

'The *Henrietta*,' said Sarah immediately.

'You recognise her?' asked Richard, delighted that his sister had made an immediate identification.

'Of course. No mistaking her, is there, Maggie?'

'No.'

'But you both were always good at recognising whaleships, you had an eye for them.'

'Don't belittle your work,' said Sarah.

'Did Captain Kearsley commission it?' asked Maggie.

'No, but I thought after doing twenty-one voyages in her he

might buy it now that she's been sold to Aberdeen.'

'I'm sure he'll be delighted with it,' agreed Sarah.

A murmur ran through the crowd gathered on the cliff top drawing their attention back to the sea.

'The *Esk*!' Sarah confirmed the word which was being passed from lip to lip identifying the first whaler.

Richard narrowed his eyes, beating at the distance, wanting to recognise the next vessel before his sister.

'The *Mars*!' They said together.

Their eyes were riveted on the next silhouette, far out to sea. The tension between them grew as their concentration deepened.

'The *Phoenix*!' cried Richard.

'Father's back,' announced Sarah at the same moment.

The three of them hugged each other, knowing their father was safely home.

'There's bone at the masthead!' announced Richard with an excited tremor in his voice, for a whale's jawbone, hoisted high, indicated a full ship and that meant extra money to see families through the winter.

They watched, filled with pride, as the three ships approached and then, with commands being obeyed instantly, reached the calm river to proceed upstream towards their berths.

The Whitby folk gave them a tremendous welcome. Their men were safely home from the terrors of the Arctic. The crowds cheered and waved and the crews responded with equal enthusiasm. Word soon came from the ships that the rest of the Whitby fleet were a day's sailing behind and the whole of Whitby was relieved that there had been no losses this year.

As the *Phoenix* passed between the piers Sarah said, 'Come on.' She turned and, with Maggie and Richard, hurried through the churchyard, down the Church Stairs, and along Church Street to reach the quay where they knew the ship would dock.

People were already thick along the quay, wives, eager to feel their husband's strong arms around them again, mothers pleased their sons were safe, fathers equally delighted but with the added interest of wanting to hear about the voyage, something they had once been part of. Girls slipped through the

21

crowd, anxious to make contact with their sweethearts, hoping that five months' absence had heightened their ardour. Owners, eager to know the quality and quantity of the catch, pushed their way to be near the gangway when it was run out.

Ropes were thrown out. Folk dodged them as they slammed on to the quay and were gathered by shoremen to be wound round bollards so that the *Phoenix* could be manoeuvred into its berth and tied up.

The gangway was run out and the crew swarmed ashore, to be swamped in the overwhelming greetings of their families and loved ones.

'Will! Jim!' Sarah jumped up and down, waving her arms.

Her brothers straightened from the rail and hurried down the gangway, with laughter filling their voices as they hugged their sisters.

Richard exchanged broad grins with them and gripped their hands in a warm welcome.

'Full ship,' he observed.

'Aye. Great voyage,' enthused Will. 'Should have been with us.'

Richard made no comment. Instead he asked, 'Father all right?'

'In good health. He got four whales himself.'

Maggie turned her attention to the ship. Her father stood, a tall, broad-shouldered figure, with his hands clasped firmly behind his back, surveying the homecoming from the deck while informing the owner, who had gone on board, of the catch they had made. He was a man who was not demonstratively expressive in public. He had seen his family on the quay and had waved. He had not expected his wife to be there, for she preferred to wait at home and make her welcome in private. It would be no less intense for that, and the family kept out of their way, for they respected the deep love which existed between their parents and knew that homecoming from the Arctic was a special time for them.

Maggie watched him. She loved him very much for he was a kind and considerate father, a handsome man who held himself erect, exuding an air of authority which had the respect of his crew. His face was marked by the wind and sea. His greying hair had the hint of a wave along his temples. She was sorry he was disappointed that Richard had not followed him aboard the whaleships, but she admired his understanding though at times he could not help but make a teasing probe at Richard's chosen life. Sometimes she wished he would curb her brothers when they started on to Richard, and how she wished they could recognise a talent which needed encouragement, but they saw nothing but the tough life of the sea.

'How's Mother?' Jim's enquiry broke into her thoughts.

'Very well,' Richard replied. 'At home as usual.'

'Come on, Jim, we'd best be back on board, see to the unloading.' Will gave his brother a slap on the back.

Will bunched his fist and aimed a gentle blow at his brother who ducked and weaved and then turned for the gangway with Jim after him.

'Will they ever grow up,' remarked Sarah with a smile of approval. She loved her brothers who, in this playful mood, it seemed would remain ever youthful, but she knew they had their serious side. They were men, with the glamour of the whaleships about them. They were big, broad-shouldered, their muscles hardened by heaving at oars, flensing whales, cutting up blubber, hauling at ropes and furling sails high on the yards.

Will at twenty-two and Jim a year younger already had the weatherbeaten look of sailors. They were very much alike, so much so that some people took them for twins. Their angular jaws jutted with confidence; their blue eyes, sharp and clear, were full of restless vitality, as if they would make sure they wrested all they could from life.

Richard, while of similar build which could match them strength for strength, possessed a much quieter nature but behind this lay a steely determination. His brown eyes were gentle and gave the impression that to whomever he was speaking they were the only person worth considering at that moment. They were observant eyes which befitted an artist and he had a retentive memory so that sketches could be filled with detail later.

His hands also set him aside from his brothers. His were thin, long-fingered with a delicate touch, theirs were broad with thick-set fingers, marked and scarred by a rough life. Richard feared damage to his which could lead to the inability to draw

23

and thwart his secret ambition to become a noted painter.

'Are we going to greet Father?' asked Richard.

'He's busy,' Sarah pointed out. 'He's seen us. He knows he has our love and welcome.'

The three of them caught his eye and waved. He returned their gesture and watched them until they were swallowed up in the crowd as they made their way home.

When the cry of 'Whaleship! Whaleship!' swept through Whitby the Wakefields were strolling towards the west pier.

They were overwhelmed by the upsurge in activity as people appeared from everywhere and thronged to the piers and quays or climbed to the cliff tops.

'What is it?' asked Francis, halting a man who was hurrying past.

'Whaleships have been sighted,' he cried, surprised that here was someone who did not know what was happening.

It stirred something deep in Francis's memory and when Gertrude and Charlotte looked queryingly at him he was able to explain. 'Whitby's whaling fleet is returning home after five months in the Arctic. It's something special and folk are anxious to see if all are safe and to welcome them home.'

'Can we watch?' asked Charlotte.

'Of course. It is something we should not miss.'

They found a vantage point on the west pier and were swept up in the euphoria of the homecoming of the whalers.

Francis chatted to an old man who had served on the whaleships and who parted with first-hand knowledge with enthusiasm. His descriptions were graphic, especially those appropriate to the homecoming.

'What a painting that would make, Gertrude,' he remarked. 'The ships heading for the gap between these piers, the background of the cliffs, the houses and the old church and the ruined abbey.'

'Might you find one?' she asked, knowing the place he would hang it among his collection.

From the time when Francis found he could afford to indulge himself he had started to collect paintings, not in a big way but those which he particularly liked. He had developed an eye for a picture and deeper guidance came when

24

he made the acquaintance of Jacob Craig.

He was a man of about his own age whom he had met at Old Slaughter's Coffee House in St Martin's Lane, a convivial meeting place for artists. Francis had been taken there by a friend on the periphery of the art world. He had been introduced to Jacob, and the immediate rapport between the two men was such that when Francis's friend had to leave, Francis stayed on chatting to Jacob. By the time they parted he knew Jacob's life story.

He came from a well-to-do family and had always dreamed of becoming an artist. He had talent but that was suddenly cut short when in a coach accident his hands were badly and permanently damaged. He could no longer hold a pencil or paintbrush. Determined not to let this destroy him he directed his attention elsewhere in the art world. He made himself a connoisseur and dealer in art and opened a salon, which he eventually extended to include a studio. Here he would take four artists, whom he personally would choose, to enable them to develop their abilities under his supervision and guidance. He brought in several master painters to instruct, so that his artists never came predominantly under the influence of one person. His system avoided the pupil being apprenticed to one master which, though it had its merits, could stifle the pupil's special aptitudes.

'I might,' replied Francis. 'Or commission one. I don't know if there is any talent in Whitby but it will give me something to look for during the rest of our stay.'

'I hope you can, it will make a nice memento of our visit,' said Charlotte.

'Going to pursue that dangerous trade of yours this morning, little brother?' Will asked with a wink at Jim across the breakfast table. There were only the three of them in the kitchen. Their father had already gone out and their mother and sisters were upstairs making the beds.

'Mind your pencil isn't too sharp, it might harpoon you,' Jim added to the teasing.

'The blubber yards will be a good place for you,' grinned Will, knowing how nauseating the smell could be when the blubber was being boiled.

'Give you sixpence if you'll go,' offered Jim in a tone as if making a dare to a child, and then added, 'little brother,' knowing full well that Richard hated being addressed that way.

Richard laid down his knife and fork on the plate of bacon he had just started. He eyed his brothers with some contempt. 'Can't you two grow up?'

Jim let out a harsh laugh. 'Grow up? Listen who's talking.'

'I'm good enough to knock your heads together,' snapped Richard. 'And I'll just do that if you call me little brother one more time.'

'What? And risk hurting those delicate hands?' mocked Will.

'Aye, think on that, little brother,' grinned Jim with a challenge in his eye.

Richard stiffened. His eyes narrowed. He would have flung himself at the pair of them but their words made sense. 'Aye. You're right. Thanks for reminding me that it's not worth risking my career to teach you a lesson.' He grabbed his bag of artist's materials and stormed out, knowing there were grins on the faces of his brothers which he would have loved to knock off.

A few moments later Martha Parker came into the kitchen. 'Was that Richard I heard go out?'

'Yes,' the brothers replied together.

She eyed Richard's unfinished breakfast and knew immediately what had been happening. 'Have you two been at him again?'

They shrugged their shoulders and looked blameless.

'And don't play innocent with me. You two are too bad with your brother.'

'But, Mother, it's time he got a real job even if he does a bit of fishing. He contributes practically nothing to ...'

Martha set herself to face her sons. There was a gleam in her eyes and the brothers knew they would get a lashing from her tongue. 'You leave him be. You know very well he gives me something from the drawings he sells.'

'A pittance,' muttered Jim.

Martha set her lips tight in exasperation. 'Maybe it is now, but you might like to know that after you docked yesterday he sold a painting of the *Henrietta* to Captain Kearsley. You mark my words, one day he'll be earning more than you two put together. And there'll be a day when you'll look up to him. If your teasing puts him off what he wants to do you'll have me to answer to.' She gave them both a withering look. 'And don't you forget it!'

Anger had tightened Richard's muscles and it took a lot of determination to keep his temper under control and stop himself from turning back to confront his brothers with his fists.

But gradually the pleasure of anticipating a morning's sketching calmed him and he saw his surroundings with his artistic eye, taking note of possible viewpoints for future work. There was so much of Whitby and its life he wanted to record, but he wanted to finish the drawing of Joss for he felt sure that his daughter would buy it when she saw how he had achieved likeness and the underlying character.

He made his way to the Burgess Pier. Joss was not there but he knew he would not be long. He sat down on a bollard and started to sketch two colliers unloading coal. They had been left beached by the receding tide, a ploy employed at the stretch of sand between Burgess Pier and East Pier known as Collier Hope, so that the coal could be unloaded into carts pulled by horses. The sketch was shaping well when Joss arrived and took his seat in the way that Richard wanted. All altercations with his brothers were forgotten as he immersed himself in putting the final touches to his drawing.

With Whitby bathed in warm morning sunshine Francis decided to take his wife and daughter on the east side of the river. Church Street was thronging with people about their daily business. Gertrude and Charlotte paused to examine wares on offer in a variety of shops and were particularly enchanted by the jet work, eyeing some pieces for purchase before they left Whitby.

Having seen the east side from the river as they sailed into Whitby, Charlotte was now fascinated to see it close to. She was amazed at how the houses climbed the cliff side to be reached by narrow alleys running from Church Street. How people existed in such crushed conditions with, she imagined, the ever-present threat of cliff falls, she could not envisage. She knew there were crowded conditions in London though she had never seen them, protected as she always had been from the harsher side of life, but here the houses almost stood on top of one another. Even from the entrance to the alleys she could see that some were unkempt, with rubbish and slops littering the rough pathway, while further on there were those in which the inhabitants took pride.

Life bustled around them and Charlotte was gripped by it. Shopkeepers called their wares, housewives bartered, others chatted, fishermen greeted each other on their way to their boats to prepare for sailing, carpenters hurried to the ship-yards, sailors were already making their way to the inns for a last drink before they sailed on their merchantmen bound for the Baltic, France and Spain. The whole town was busy. Seeking a little respite from the flow of people and seeing a point from which they would get a different view of the town, Francis led them on to the Burgess Pier.

He took little notice of the two men who appeared to be sitting talking near the end of the pier. Halfway along he stopped and looked back. Gertrude and Charlotte did likewise and were taken aback by the impression of the cliff towering over them as if it was about to send its houses tumbling down on them. This sensation gradually assumed normality and they turned their attention to watch the coal being unloaded from the colliers.

Slowly they made their way towards the end of the pier, pausing every now and then to admire the different perspectives of the town and the river.

Francis leaned on his walking stick and cast a casual glance at the two men who had taken no notice of their arrival. He received a jolt of surprise. One of them was drawing. He straightened and stepped casually closer so that he could see what the young man was doing.

A face. A portrait of the other? Francis glanced at the older man. Yes. It was. And it was good. Francis's attention was riveted. He moved a little closer so he could watch the deft stroke of the pencil. By jove, it was more than good. The like-ness was perfect but there was more. The artist had probed depths of character. The man on the paper had been a sailor, he had seen distant horizons and he still dreamed about them. There had been a determination to cope with anything life threw at him and he had done so. Now in his later years he had the satisfaction of having won and found peace in his home port. Francis looked at the sitter. Yes, it was all there on the human face as well. This artist was talented.

Aware that someone stood slightly behind him, Richard glanced over his shoulder. He received a friendly smile. 'Good day, sir,' he said tentatively.

'Good day, my boy. An artist, I see.'

'If you can call me that. No, sir. I draw because I like to.'

'I would put it more strongly than that. I would say because you love to. And I would also say you desire to capture more than you see on the surface.'

'You are a judge of such matters, sir?'

Francis pursed his lips. 'Well, I have cultivated an eye for art and I have friends who are more knowledgeable than I.'

'And you really do think this is good?' asked Richard cautiously.

'As I say, it is better than good. If you have never been taught you have a natural gift.'

Joss, who had remained silent, puffing at his pipe during this exchange, cast a shrewd eye at Francis. 'Thee ain't from these parts, sir, but I detect a touch of Yorkshire in your speech.'

'Aye, thee's reet,' said Francis thickening his accent deliberately. 'I left Whitby when I was ten and have lived in London ever since. My wife and daughter are here on holiday. My first time back.' He turned and called, 'Gertrude, Charlotte, come over here.'

They turned their attention from the view of the drawbridge.

'What do you think of that?' Francis asked them, indicating Richard's drawing.

He jumped to his feet and acknowledged them with a slight inclination of his head.

They looked at the drawing and then at the subject and immediately approved the skill which had created a notable portrait.

'Do you do landscapes, seascapes?' Francis asked.

'I do, sir, but my real love is portraits.'

'Any more in that bag you can show me?'

Richard withdrew a pad of paper and passed it to Francis. He flicked over the cover and saw the sketch of the colliers unloading coal. The next two drawings were of Whitby ships and the third a view of the east side of the river.

Francis nodded approvingly. He had seen confirmation of his judgement. This young man had talent. As he handed the pad back to Richard he said, 'I've had an idea of what could make a splendid picture: whaleships entering Whitby harbour. Think you could do it?'

'Yes, sir,' replied Richard with confidence. A commission! Though he had sold a few pictures this was the first time he had been asked to do a specific painting.

'Good,' smiled Francis. 'What's your name?'

'Richard Parker, sir.'

'Right, Mr Parker, come to the Angel Inn tomorrow morning at ten. We'll discuss the project in more detail.'

'Yes, sir. I'll be there. Who do I ask for?'

'Mr Wakefield.'

Richard watched them as they walked from the pier, hardly able to believe his luck. Might Mr Wakefield want more paintings? Was this a turn in his fortune? Wait until he told his family, it would be one in the eye of his brothers.

Joss broke into his thoughts. 'She's a bonny young lass.'

Richard started. 'Oh, is she? I hadn't noticed.'

Chapter Three

Richard, excited by the prospects which might await him, had a sleepless night. He had received a commission! Well, almost. He tried to temper his elation. Nothing definite had been settled. But surely Mr Wakefield would not go back on his word. If he hadn't been really interested he wouldn't have asked to meet him at the Angel.

He had hurried home, eager to break the news to his family. His mother and sisters had been thrilled by his announcement and vowed that his talent was bound to be recognised one day and that maybe this was it. His father expressed his congratulations but said little more than that. His brothers made reluctant compliments but then dampened his enthusiasm with their observations that there was nothing definite about Mr Wakefield's interest and even if there was it might be the only commission he would ever receive.

Their comments had annoyed him but he was determined to ignore them and, with the idea of doing just that, he had left home in the afternoon to do some preliminary background sketches which he could show Mr Wakefield.

Although he had seen Whitby from the sea on a number of occasions when he had been fishing he wanted to refresh his impressions. He got Mark to take him out to sea from where he made three rough sketches of backgrounds for his subject. He had put a few finishing touches to them before he climbed into bed.

He was kept awake by a confusion of thoughts centred on what had happened that day. Scenes of Whitby mingled with portraits of Joss and then merged into the smiling face of Mr

Wakefield. He floated in and out of imaginary drawings, of exhibitions, of paintings sold, of throwing money on to a table in front of his brothers, seeing their eyes widen in amazement at the amount. Words echoed in his mind, Mr Wakefield's praise, his request, Joss's comment about Mrs Campion. Yes, he was right, she was a bonny lass. Richard was not aware that he had noticed. It must have been the artist in him who had subconsciously noted her striking features and sparked a desire to interpret them on paper.

Determined not to be late, he arrived at the Angel with a few minutes to spare and, on enquiring for Mr Wakefield, was shown into a small room which the gentleman from London had requested be set aside for his meeting.

Richard sat uneasily, fingering his bag in which he had his sketches and pencils. He jumped to his feet when the door opened and Mr Wakefield walked in.

'Hello, my boy,' he greeted Richard amiably with a broad smile.

'Good day, sir,' returned Richard. He felt a little flutter inside for he realised that he was facing what could possibly be a great chance for him. Satisfy Mr Wakefield with his depiction of whalers entering Whitby and there could be more commissions, maybe from people who would see this picture hanging in the house in London.

'Sit down, sit down.' Francis gave a little wave of his hand and pulled out a chair beside a small table.

'I've done some preliminary sketches for a background, sir.' Richard plunged in, not wanting to get involved in every-day talk.

'Ah.' Francis stiffened and gave a momentary pause. 'I've changed my mind.'

Richard's face fell with disappointment. Frozen by the abrupt end to the elation he had been experiencing, he stopped taking his sketches from his bag.

Francis reacted quickly. He threw up his hands in a gesture of despair. 'My boy, I've put that badly. I will still want a painting of whalers entering Whitby but there is something else first.'

Relief flooded over Richard. His spirits were lifted once again. 'Anything, sir, anything.'

'Hold on, young man,' said Francis. 'First a little information. I realise you have a natural talent, but have you had any training at all?'

'Well, not exactly, sir. There are several artists in Whitby, one of whom, Mr George Chambers, a painter of nautical scenes, has given me tips and advice, but no more than that for he said he did not want to inhibit a natural talent.'

Francis nodded. 'Quite right. But no doubt his words have proved valuable.'

'Yes, sir. And he enabled me to get materials – pigments, brushes, canvases and so on.'

Francis looked thoughtful, rubbing his lips with his forefinger. 'Now, let me see what you've been doing.'

Richard drew his three sketches from his bag and laid them on the table in front of Francis who leaned forward to examine them with great interest. His eyes were sharp, intent and he pursed his lips as he gave an approving nod. 'Admirable,' he commented. 'Have you just done them?'

'Yesterday afternoon after I had seen you. I got a friend to take me to sea in his coble.'

'Good, good.' He liked the young man's enterprise. 'That's the one I would like you to use when you do the painting.' He stabbed his finger at the third picture.

'You have an eye, sir. That is the one I think would make the most suitable background to the ships.'

'Good, then that is settled, but first, I was so taken with your portrait of the old man that I decided I would like you to do a portrait of my daughter.'

Richard swallowed hard at this unexpected request. He was breathless.

'Well?' Francis prompted a reaction.

Richard started. 'Are you sure you want *me* to do it?' Even as he put the question he was hoping the answer would be yes for he relished the challenge.

Francis smiled at the Whitby man's caution. 'You think I could have gone to eminent artists?' He nodded. 'Yes I could, but let me tell you that I have not seen in their work the depths which you drew out of that portrait you were doing on the pier.'

'Those are kind words, sir. I hope I can do justice to your daughter.'

33

'Then you'll do it?'

'Yes, sir, and thank you for your patronage. You wish me to do it in oils?'

'Yes. You have worked in oils before?'

'Yes. But to be frank with you, only small paintings of Whitby.'

'No matter. I am sure you will succeed.'

'Thank you for your confidence, sir. How long are you going to be in Whitby?'

'Another week.'

Richard's heart sank.

'I realise that you cannot possibly complete the portrait in that time. So what I suggest is this, a couple of sittings for you to do some sketching on which you can enlarge and work. No more than two for this is my daughter's holiday and I want her to have every opportunity to enjoy it. Then, when we return to London you come with us to complete the painting.'

'London?' Richard gasped. 'But ... but ...' he spluttered.

Francis laughed. 'Does the thought of London frighten you?'

'No, sir. It's just so unexpected.'

'I know nothing about your family, will they object?'

'My father is a whaling captain, my two older brothers serve with him on the *Phoenix*. I have two sisters. My mother encourages me to follow my artistic desires, my father tolerates it, my brothers ridicule it. You can be sure, I'll come to London.'

'Good. Your fare will be paid, and you will have a room in my house.'

'Sir, you are too generous.'

Francis waved the thanks aside. 'Just do me a good portrait. It is important to me and to my wife. I must explain. Charlotte is our only daughter, in fact our only child. Now that she is married we miss her and we want a reminder – your portrait to hang in our home.'

'Sir, it may not come up to your expectations.' Richard's cautious tone was matched by his doubtful expression.

'From what I saw on the pier yesterday and what you have just shown me I think it will.' He raised a finger and looked intensely at Richard. 'Let me give you a piece of advice.

34

Never underestimate your ability and talent and always have confidence and faith in yourself. If I had not done so I would not be where I am today.' He relaxed and leaned back in his chair. 'Now, I think I should explain a little further. My daughter is married to Mr Charles Campion, a successful merchant with ships sailing out of Boston in Lincolnshire where he has a fairly substantial estate. At the moment he is in France on business and that is why we have our daughter with us. When he returns he will be coming to their house in London. How long they will be there I do not know, for none of us know his plans when he gets back. It may be, therefore, that he and his wife will be going to Lincolnshire as soon as he returns and if that is so I will ask for you to go with them in order to finish the portrait. Would you be willing to do that?'

'Of course,' replied Richard. The more he heard about the social status of the people with whom he was dealing the more he was determined to make a success of his chance. He was willing to do anything to further his ambition to become a respected artist. He saw an even greater opportunity as Francis went on.

'I have a friend, a Mr Jacob Craig, who is well known in the art world. He encourages young artists, has a studio for them, and I'm sure he will be interested in your work.' He raised his hands as if to dampen the sparkle he had seen come to Richard's eyes. 'I can't promise anything. But I don't want him to meet you or see your work until the portrait is finished. My feeling is that it will make more impact.' He gave a little chuckle. 'Besides, he prides himself on discovering talent; I want to show him that he isn't the only one who can do that and that it can be found outside of London. He was going to Italy sometime, about now, doing a grand tour steeped in art, and won't be back for maybe six months. Perhaps you can have the portrait finished by then?'

'I would hope so, sir.'

'Admirable.'

They fell to discussing Francis's specific requirements and an hour later Richard left the Angel knowing that his mentor wanted a head and shoulders portrait, the background being left to Richard's discretion. It was to be oil on canvas, the size to be determined when Richard saw the position in which it was to hang. He was to be formally introduced to his subject at three o'clock that afternoon, would probably do some preliminary sketching and then have one more session before leaving with the Wakefields for London the following week.

Richard's spirits were high when he left the Angel and hurried along Baxtergate, crossed the bridge, cut through Grape Lane to Church Street where he was oblivious to the activity on the quays as he quickened his steps to reach Prospect Place.

The family had moved to a more salubrious dwelling in pleasanter surroundings when these stone houses, up a flight of steps at the southern end of Church Street, had been built four years ago. His mother had never really settled, being apprehensive about living on a ledge cut in the cliff, and was already visualising finding a better site on the other side of the river.

Richard climbed the steps two at a time and burst into the house.

His mother looked up sharply from the dough she was mixing. Sarah stopped peeling potatoes and Maggie was pleased that the interruption brought a break in washing up.

'Thee looks mighty pleased with thissen,' commented Martha, raising her eyebrows at her son.

Words poured from his lips and they brought elation to the faces of his mother and sisters.

'London? Oh my goodness.' Martha's tone was full of misgiving as, with her hands still covered in dough, she sank on to a wooden chair beside the table at which she had been standing.

A flash of disappointment crossed Richard's face even though his sisters were eager with their congratulations.

'Mother, I thought you'd be pleased,' he said.

She suddenly realised what her reaction must have sounded like. 'Oh, I am, Richard, I am.' She stressed her words, hoping to alleviate his disillusion at her initial attitude. 'I am pleased. I always said thee had a gift and that someday it would be recognised.' She gave a slight pause. 'But London? It's so far away.'

'Not so far, Mother. It's easily reached by ship. And I'm not going forever.'

Martha nodded. 'I know. It's only a mother bemoaning the fact that she's going to lose one of her children.'

He knelt down beside her and put his arm lovingly round her shoulders. 'I'll be coming back.'

'You might be tempted to stay when you see what it has to offer an artist.'

Richard laughed. 'I'm not that, Mother. Well, not yet.'

'You will be,' she said quietly. She looked into his eyes. 'Whatever happens, remember us and be a credit to us.'

'I will, Mother.' He kissed her on the forehead.

She stood up, the bustling mother abroad in the kitchen. 'Now girls, this isn't going to get our work done,' she said, deflating the excitement they had shown throughout the exchange between mother and son. She plunged her hands into the dough and experienced the beneficial value of giving vent to her feelings in the kneading.

His news, broken to his father and brothers when they returned from the *Phoenix* for their midday meal, was given a mixed reception. His father grunted his congratulations without enthusiasm for even this success did not mitigate his disappointment that his youngest son had not taken to the sea. He still held a hope that this would be reversed one day and, though secretly he admired his son's persistence in pursuing his ambition, he held grave doubts about the viability of the career he sought.

His brothers made half-hearted congratulations then mimicked the imagined forgery of their illusion of the art world. Richard refused to rise to their teasing. His sisters came to his defence but were immediately hushed by a sharp glance from their mother who knew it was best to ignore her sailor sons unless things got out of hand.

'Will thee ever get a man's job?' said Will, his mimicking turning to ridicule.

'Frightened he'll hurt his hands,' added Jim.

'Or slip on the deck of a rolling ship,' laughed Will.

'Sea too rough for thee?' asked Will, derision in his voice.

Richard eyed his brothers. 'I'll stand on board ship alongside both of you any day,' he snapped coldly.

Will gave a grunt of disbelief. 'Thee didn't when thee came whaling with us. Scared stiff thee was.'

'That was three years ago, and you two weren't any help. You both made it hard for me. You're both to blame for making me loathe the job. You wouldn't get away with it now.'

'Then prove it,' challenged Jim. 'Sail with us to the Arctic in March.'

'And give up the chance I've just been given? Not likely.'

'Scared,' Jim taunted.

'No. Wise.'

Jim looked at Will and they both put on an effeminate air.

'Paint my portrait, Will, darling?'

'Any time, my sweet.'

Both roared with laughter.

'Enough!' The sharp command cut the air. The laughter stopped abruptly. Martha's dark, angry scowl was not one to be defied. Jim and Will knew they had gone too far. They withered under an imperious gaze.

'All right, boys, that will do.' John's voice was quiet but it carried the authority of a man backing his wife.

The meal continued in silence except for the occasional comment on the latest piece of Whitby gossip.

Richard arrived at the Angel five minutes before the appointed time. He knew he was going to be early but he wanted to create a good impression on the first step of his assignment.

He waited impatiently at the foot of the stairs but composed himself when Francis and his daughter appeared.

His first impression was that here was a girl who was approaching this meeting with some reluctance and that maybe he would have to break it down to find the real person.

'My daughter, Mrs Campion,' said Francis proudly. 'Charlotte, this is Richard Parker.'

Richard acknowledged the introduction with a slight inclination of his head.

Charlotte's response was expressionless with only a slight nod.

'I've arranged for you to use the room we were in this morning,' said Francis.

'Thank you,' replied Richard. 'I would prefer to do some preliminary sketching outside; the light is better and it is a nice day.'

'Oh.' Francis appeared to have been caught off guard by this request. 'I hadn't planned to go out until Mrs Wakefield was ready. She is resting at the moment.'

'I see,' started Richard but before he could say any more Charlotte cut in.

'I'll be perfectly all right, Father. I'm a married woman, no longer a child, remember.' She glanced at Richard. 'I'll get my bonnet and cape.' Without waiting for approval from her father she turned and hurried back up the stairs.

Francis showed no sign of the rebuff when he turned to Richard. 'Where will you go?'

'Along the west pier, sir.' He smiled to himself at the concern of a protective father.

'Very well. Mrs Wakefield and I will be along later.'

When Charlotte returned she was wearing a small bonnet tied under her chin with a blue ribbon. Her red cape, fitting to the waist, emphasised the cream colour of her ankle-length dress.

Richard felt a little uneasy. He had never walked with anyone as elegantly dressed as Mrs Campion, but if this was to be the pattern of his life then he must push his embarrassment aside.

'Shall we go, Mr Parker?' She started for the door.

'Sir.' Richard offered his goodbye to Francis and followed her.

'Where are we going?' she asked.

'I thought the west pier, Mrs Campion.'

'Very well.'

She set a gentle pace and he matched it. He needed to find out more about her to try to get something of her inner self which could be expressed in his drawings and eventually on the canvas. He knew any results today would not be enough and revelations he might be able to use would emerge as the picture developed.

He had, even in the few moments they had been together, seen that there would be no difficulty in transferring her evident beauty to a canvas. Her smooth skin was delicately rosy, a texture and colour he would find challenging. Her bowed lips gave her a sensual character but it was through her blue eyes that he visualised, at this stage, capturing the inner person. Those eyes had in these few moments held a variety of expressions all of them revealing something of the girl he was to paint. Even now he knew that to capture her eyes in the proper relationship to the expressions of her other features would be to make her live on the canvas. He was already looking forward to trying to do justice to his subject. Now he needed to know more about her personality.

'Is this your first time in Whitby, Mrs Campion?'

'Yes.'

'Do you like it?'

'Yes.' Her eyes twinkled teasingly as she looked coyly at him and saw the disappointment on his face. 'You want me to say more than yes so that you can get to know more about me for your painting, don't you?'

'It would help,' replied Richard, annoyed that his intention had been obvious.

'Well, then. What shall I tell you?' She paused in mock thought. 'I'm twenty-one. That surprises you – a lady admitting to her age! But then I'm not really at the age where we are particular about disclosing it. Now I've told you that, what about you? I think you are of a similar age to me.'

'Twenty.'

'And you think you have the experience to tackle a portrait of me?'

'No. I certainly haven't the experience, but I believe I can do it.'

'So confident,' she mused.

'Your father must think I have the ability from what he has seen.'

'Ah, Father, well he would think that. He always expects to discover an unknown artist who, one day, will be great.'

'He has done this before?' Alarm came to Richard's voice.

She gave a short laugh. 'Don't worry, Mr Parker. He has never commissioned a portrait of me but I am sure you will do me justice.'

'Oh, I shall, Mrs Campion.' Richard had learned something about his subject in this brief discussion. There was a touch of frivolity about her nature, a willingness to oblige, but he guessed that would be if the proposal suited her. Mischievousness had touched those blue eyes and though some

40

people might get the impression that she was laughing at them he had received no such feeling from her.

'What is it you like about Whitby, Mrs Campion?' Richard asked to get back to his original enquiry.

'It is so much alive.'

'Isn't London?'

'Oh, yes, but it's different. So much bigger and you can be separate from the activity. Where we live is quiet, away from the bustle of the city.'

'There are quiet parts in Whitby.'

'Oh yes, but within a few minutes' walk you can be among it. Just look around you now, we are embraced by everything, people going about their work, fishermen tending their boats, merchantmen at the quays. Listen.' She inclined her head. 'The hammering.'

'In the shipbuilding yards.'

'See what I mean, we are part of it. You'd have to cross London to hear such a sound, but here it is. There's so much going on close by.'

He saw her eyes were alert with the enthusiasm of someone involved. She was a person who observed and would remember.

'And the nature of the place. The river, the cliffs, the houses seeming to jostle for position on precarious footholds. And above them all the serenity exuded by the ruins of an abbey which must have witnessed peace and tranquillity as the monks prayed and sought God.'

He had learned more. 'You're a romantic, Mrs Campion.'

She smiled a pleasant smile. 'I suppose I am.' This young man is perceptive, she thought, Charles has never judged me this way.

As they moved from the roadway on to the pier and left the protection of the cliff they felt the breeze, but it was not unpleasant for it was gentle and warm.

He chose a position a short way along the pier and, getting her approval, started to sketch. His pencil moved swiftly over the paper. First an overall impression then, on succeeding sheets, details. As he was drawing he chatted pleasantly and established an empathy between himself and his subject. He derived satisfaction from this for he realised it was a big step

41

towards achieving the desire to interpret this attractive young woman on canvas. And he was pleased that she had not thrown up a barrier. There had been no resistance to the psychological interplay between them.

Charlotte also learned and wondered. He was from a whaling family yet he had an inborn ability and desire to be an artist. From where did it come? He was agreeable to talk to and interesting to watch as his hands moved across the paper. Those long fingers would be gentle. His brown eyes were always observant and particularly intense when he was sketching. His build, broad shoulders, rugged yet attractive features, were more whaleman than artist.

He looked up from his paper and saw her watching him with an intent interest. She glanced away. He saw her frown and set her lips in momentary annoyance. He followed her glance and saw Mr and Mrs Wakefield coming on to the pier.

So Mrs Campion regretted the arrival of her parents. She must have been enjoying herself, and he realised that he too was annoyed at the interruption.

'Ah, now, how's the drawing going?' cried Mr Wakefield heartily as he reached them.

Richard turned the pages so that his work could not be seen. 'Very well, sir.'

'Show me.'

'Sorry, sir. No one sees my work until I think it the right time,' Richard said firmly.

Francis drew himself upright and glared at Richard. 'But I want to see what you have been doing.'

'I'm sorry, sir. Not yet.'

'But ...' Francis spluttered, taken aback by Richard's attitude. 'Don't you forget, young man, that I commissioned this portrait and can just as easily cancel it.'

'If you do, sir, you will regret it, for you will lose a painting you will love and which all your friends will admire.'

Francis bristled. This young man was not only defiant but he also felt sure of himself.

Richard shot a glance at Charlotte and saw a twitch of amusement on her lips and a sparkle of admiration in her eyes. He knew that as much as she loved her father she was revelling in seeing him opposed in this way.

42

Francis glanced at his wife. 'What do you think to that, Gertrude?'

'Well, I agree with him. I don't want to see any of his work until it is finished. It might spoil my surprise when I see the completed picture,' she replied.

'But it may not be coming up to expectations,' protested Francis.

Richard detected weakness in the protest. 'I don't think you believe that, sir. After seeing my work yesterday you know that you won't be disappointed.'

Francis grunted. Not only had this young man confidence in himself but he had also seen through him. 'Very well.' His snap accepted defeat.

'Sir, I did not say that I will not show it to you. I will do so at some stage, in case there are alterations you want making, some aspect you prefer.'

'Very well,' Francis nodded curtly, irritated that he had been outdone. 'Now, are you finished for today?'

'Another quarter of an hour, sir.'

'Mrs Wakefield and I will take a walk along the pier and collect my daughter on the way back. Come, Gertrude.' He held out his arm for her.

After they had taken a few steps, Richard flicked open his pad of paper. He looked up at Charlotte and saw amusement dancing in her eyes, and laughter lines running from the corners of her lips.

'Not many people better my father,' she said. 'Well done.' She gave a little trill of laughter. 'May I see your drawings?'

Richard read teasing in her request. He eyed her steadily. 'You may not. Not even when your father does. You will not see the work until it is finished.'

'Oh, come now, Mr Parker, I insist.' There was challenge as she met his gaze unflinchingly.

'No.'

She knew his firmness would brook no attack. She admired his resolve and succumbed with a shrug of her shoulders, a small coy pout and acknowledgement of his victory with a wisp of a smile.

When Mr and Mrs Wakefield returned, Charlotte was ready to go with them.

'May I do some more sketching the day after tomorrow?' he asked politely.

'Yes,' Francis agreed. 'If that is convenient to Mrs Campion.'

'Certainly,' agreed Charlotte.

'The same time at the Angel?' Richard asked.

She nodded and Mr and Mrs Wakefield approved.

'Then I'll bid you good day,' he said and with a slight bow he turned and strode away.

As she sauntered from the pier with her mother and father, Charlotte was lost in her thoughts as she watched Richard until he disappeared among the people on the promenade beyond the Battery. He was a likeable young man, full of confidence in his ability but not overbearing with it. His voice was softer than she had imagined it would be and there was a certain gentleness about him, though she reckoned he could be stubborn when necessary.

He was younger than Charles and from a very different background, but she saw much of her husband in him, and she wondered how he would take to life in London.

Chapter Four

As the London packet made steady progress up the Thames, Richard was on deck, his energy directed at taking in every sight and experience. This was a new world to him. His knowledge of port activities was confined to Whitby. He had always thought that was busy, but here he was almost overwhelmed by so many ships lying at quays and plying the river. The variety of craft spanned the biggest ships he had ever seen, four-masted merchantmen that would sail the distant oceans, to the smallest boat propelled by the power of one man at the oars.

He had enjoyed the voyage. There had been a strong sea running, nothing too rough, but sufficient to confine the ladies to their cabins. Mr Wakefield had ventured on deck and Richard had admitted to him that he had an affinity for the sea. 'After all, sir, coming from a family of seafarers it's in my blood.'

'And your artistic ability?' Francis had queried.

'Must come from somewhere on my mother's side.'

'Do you think you might go back to the sea?'

Richard gave a wry smile. 'I'll never forsake it, but it won't be my career, that lies with my pencils and paints. And one thing is certain, I'll never go whaling again.'

He knew from Mr Wakefield's grunt of satisfaction that he had given the right answer, and that, knowing his true ambition, he saw him as his protegé and would do all he could to help him.

Now, in the warm sunlight, he saw a London of infinite possibilities for an artist. There were interesting subjects

45

everywhere. The gift from Mr George Chambers, an oak box containing pigs' bladders which held oil paints, would be well used. He was determined to widen his talent and seize every opportunity he could while doing Charlotte's portrait. He had no doubt that variety could only help his main commission.

'How do you like the look of London, Mr Parker?' Charlotte asked, she and her mother having come on deck as the ship was being manoeuvred to its berth.

'Interesting, Mrs Campion. Big and so much bustle.'

She smiled. 'You haven't seen it yet. We have to drive to my parents' home in Russell Square. There's our carriage coming on to the quay.'

'Well timed,' commented Richard.

'Nicholas, he's the coachman, and Harold, he's one of the footmen, are very efficient.'

Within a matter of minutes after the ship had been tied up, the Wakefields and Richard were in the carriage leaving the quay.

Mesmerised by the activity, Richard said little. He visualised his pencil recording street-traders shouting their wares, entertainers, jugglers and clowns, striving hard for a penny, beggars seeking a copper from the well dressed going about their everyday business. Carts, costers' barrows, cabs and carriages vied with the crowds forcing the flow of people to part so that they could proceed. Buildings crowded one on the other with little space between any of them and smoke rose from what appeared to be a thousand chimneys.

Gradually the crowds thinned, the buildings were given more space, and Richard felt some relief from the overcrowded City when they turned into tree-lined Russell Square. It took little of Richard's imagination to realise how their inhabitants relished the fresh air and peace after the smoke and hubbub of the crowded areas he had come through.

The coach pulled up and another footman came from the house to assist the ladies and help with the luggage.

Francis stretched, driving the stiffness from his limbs. He looked around as his wife and daughter went into the house.

'It's good to be home, Mr Parker. I'm glad to have seen Whitby again, but London is really where I belong,' he said with a note of satisfaction.

'A very pleasant position, sir,' Richard commented, glancing round the square.

'It is, but I can see us moving again as London expands. Oh, by the way, see that house across the square?' He indicated one. 'Sir Thomas Lawrence, the well-known portrait painter, lives there and Captain David Fernley* lives three houses along.'

'The famous whaling captain from Whitby?' There was a note of awe in Richard's voice.

'The same.'

'Firm of Fernley and Thorseby?'

'Yes.'

'My father is captain of one of their whaleships.'

'Captain Fernley might be interested in meeting you.' Francis gave a little chuckle. 'He might even want his portrait painting.'

'That would be an honour,' gasped Richard, now all the more determined to make a success of Charlotte's portrait.

'Apart from his interests in Whitby, Captain Fernley runs the London firm of Hartley Shipping with whalers going to the South Seas and the Arctic, as well as controlling a fleet of merchantmen. Now, come along in.'

When he stepped inside Richard stopped, stunned by the size and opulence. He had never been in a place as big as this. The hall was three times the size of their living room at home. A staircase with a carved oak banister climbed in two stages to the next floor. As he looked up he saw that there were two more floors beyond that.

The hall was a hive of activity. The footmen were carrying the luggage upstairs. Two maids, neatly dressed in ankle-length black dresses with white aprons and mob-caps to match, were taking the outdoor clothes from Mrs Wakefield and Mrs Campion. A third came forward to take Mr Wakefield's coat, hat and cane and then turned to Richard. He started at the unexpected attention, but slipped out of his coat and handed it to her together with his hat. Words of welcome and snippets of household news passed between owners and servants.

*See *The Red Shawl* and *A Distant Harbour*

Richard waited uneasily, noting that his two bags had been placed at the bottom of the stairs.

Mrs Wakefield perceived Richard's bewilderment and immediately took charge as mistress of her house.

'Jean, leave those coats on a chair, see to them later. Mr Parker will be staying with us. He can occupy the second guestroom on the second floor. Slip up there now and see that everything is as it should be.'

'Yes, ma'am.' The maid bobbed a curtsey, placed the clothes carefully on a chair and tripped quickly up the stairs, following Charlotte who was already on her way to her room.

Gertrude turned to Richard. 'We'll show you your room and round the house in a few moments. I'll go and let cook and the kitchen know that you will be staying here.'

'Thank you, ma'am,' he replied.

'Francis, take Mr Parker into the drawing room, I'll be there in a few minutes.' Gertrude left the hall, holding herself erect, gliding across the floor with no apparent haste but covering the ground as quickly as anyone with a hurried stride.

In the drawing room, Richard once again was speechless. All the items of furniture were obviously specially chosen to complement each other, with nothing dominating. There was a comfortable, homely feeling about the room which was enhanced by the flickering fire lit for the homecoming.

'You've a beautiful house, Mr Wakefield.' The words came drily as Richard found something to say.

'I have, my boy. Shrewd dealings but especially hard work have done it,' he replied proudly as he positioned himself with his back to the fire. 'Apply yourself with your talent and there's no reason you cannot achieve the same.'

Richard's mind whirled. He laughed to himself. As if he would ever be in this position!

Francis noted the flick of doubt in Richard's eyes. 'It's true. Be determined to achieve something and there is no reason why you shouldn't.'

He gave a little nod. Maybe Mr Wakefield was right. If he ...

All further speculation was driven from his mind by the arrival of Mrs Wakefield.

'Now, that's all settled,' she said with an obvious note of

satisfaction that things were to her liking. She crossed the room and stood beside her husband. Her glance took in both men. 'What I suggest is that Mr Parker takes breakfast with us at eight o'clock. That will provide the opportunity to plan for the day. I suppose a lot of the time you will be working in the room my husband says he will set aside as a studio for you?' She raised a querying eyebrow at Richard.

'Yes, ma'am.' Richard registered delight at the thought of a room of his own to work in. 'I may also take myself outside somewhere to make a change from the portrait and enable me to come back to it with fresh eyes.'

'Very well, you work your days as you wish. I also suppose that if you are in the flow of work you may not want to interrupt it to sit down at table with us so I have arranged that your midday and evening meals are served to you in your studio and then you can partake of them when you wish.'

'That sounds admirable, Mrs Wakefield. You have gone to so much trouble.'

'It is no trouble. I just like to have things organised. Now, if you are going out and want some refreshments with you just inform our cook in plenty of time.'

'This does not mean that you are cut off from us completely,' put in Francis.

'Of course not,' added Gertrude. 'I hope I did not create that impression. Certainly there will be times when we dine together and social evenings which might be of interest to you.'

'Thank you. You are both so kind.'

'Now should we show him his room, Gertrude?'

She nodded and led the way.

Richard picked up his bags and followed them upstairs.

'Will you be comfortable in here?' asked Gertrude as she opened the guestroom door.

Richard hardly knew what to say. He had expected nothing like this. The mahogany bed was big and covered with a colourful patchwork quilt. A chest of drawers with a swivel mirror standing on top was placed centrally on one wall. There were two small tables, one on each side of the bed while further along to the right of the bed there was a dressing table with a bowl and ewer and two towels over a rail. An

49

easy chair was placed near the long window which gave a view across the square.

'Mrs Wakefield, I ... I don't know how to express my thanks. This is much more than I expected.'

'Enjoy it, my boy, be comfortable and you will work much better,' said Francis.

'Sir, you said that Mr Campion may be returning to Lincolnshire ...'

'That's true,' Francis cut in. 'We do not know his plans and the arrangement may have to be altered accordingly. But we have four more days before he returns to London. We have discussed the situation and my daughter is to stay here until the day he is due back so you can get started right away. If she and her husband are going to be in London a while she has agreed to sit here for you whenever you want. Lincolnshire? Well, we'll deal with that if and when it arises.'

'Thank you, sir. Where would you like Mrs Campion to sit for me?'

'I'll show you the studio. There's a small room on the ground floor with plenty of glass on one side looking on to a walled garden. The light should be good. I'll have the footmen arrange it for you. You tell them how you want it. There is a piano in there, which my daughter plays, but it shouldn't be in your way.'

'I ordered some tea,' put in Gertrude. 'Let us go to the drawing room and then we'll show you round the rest of the house and introduce you to the servants.'

Charlotte was already in the drawing room and two maids were placing trays on a long low table close to the couch on which she was sitting. As the maids left the room Charlotte poured the tea and her mother handed round a plate of freshly baked scones.

'So, Mr Parker, when do you start on my portrait?' asked Charlotte as she passed him a cup of tea.

'Tomorrow morning immediately after breakfast, if that is convenient to you, Mrs Campion.'

'Certainly.'

With the arrangement agreed she glanced at her mother. 'After tea, I'll slip to see Marietta.'

Her mother nodded. 'Very well. Be back and ready for a

six-thirty meal.' She turned to Richard. 'We'll all eat together then, Mr Parker.'

'Good day, ma'am.' The butler who had answered the door greeted Charlotte with a smile which befitted his position, yet reflected his pleasure at seeing her.

Charlotte was popular with the Kemps and their household. They had watched her grow from the moment she became friendly with Marietta when they had moved into Russell Square fifteen years ago. Of the same age, the girls had shared their joys, sadnesses, and secrets.

Though she had seen Charlotte's growing interest in Charles Campion it still came as something of a shock when her friend had announced her betrothal. Marietta had been happy for her, not envious like so many others of their acquaintance, for, though she knew he was a 'good catch', she hoped for someone nearer her own age.

She had been an attractive bridesmaid and, before Charlotte was whisked away on her honeymoon, the two girls had sworn to maintain a lifelong friendship which would never be broken and that they would always remain in contact. It had been so throughout this first year. Whenever Charlotte was in London she visited Marietta, and Marietta had twice been to the Campion home, Reed Hall, in Lincolnshire.

The butler crossed the hall to a door on the right. 'Mrs Campion,' he announced.

Charlotte hurried past him. Marietta was already jumping to her feet from the chair by the window where she had been reading.

'Charlotte!' she cried with delight as she ran across the room, arms held wide.

The two girls embraced and whirled each other round in the joyous rapture of reunion.

'It's good to see you again, Charlotte, come, sit down and tell me all about your holiday. Did you enjoy the sea voyage? What's Whitby like? Where did you stay?' The questions poured from Marietta.

Charlotte put on an air of mock superiority and said, 'I'm going to have my portrait painted.'

Marietta stared wide-eyed at her friend. She flopped on to a chair as if the news had struck her a blow.

With her head held high, Charlotte twirled in front of her and repeated her information. Then she looked down at her friend and both of them burst out laughing in a way they used to do when, in girlhood days, they shared exciting, unexpected information.

Charlotte settled herself into a chair opposite Marietta. 'It's true. Father's arranged it.'

'Not Sir Thomas a cross the square?' Marietta asked, doubt in her tone.

Charlotte gave a little laugh. 'Oh, no,' she answered and then added quickly so that Marietta did not get the wrong impression, 'not that Father couldn't afford him. You know Father, he's always looking for an artist to promote. Well, he says he's found him.'

'Before you went away?'

'No, silly. In Whitby.'

Marietta, not grasping the significance, frowned. 'What's the use of him being in Whitby?'

'He's not there. Father brought him back with us.'

'What?' Marietta stared incredulously at Charlotte.

Charlotte laughed at her friend's disbelief. 'He's in our house. He's going to live there while he does my portrait. Possibly in six months.'

'You're going to be there that long? What does Charles say?'

'He doesn't know. He's not back from France for another four days.'

'He'll get a surprise.' Marietta raised an eyebrow.

'If we go to Lincolnshire then Mr Parker will go with us, I expect.'

'Mr Parker? What's he like? Some old ...'

'No, he's twenty,' Charlotte broke in. Her eyes widened a little. 'And he's rather handsome. But you'll see for yourself.' She went on to tell her what she knew of Richard's background, making it mysteriously intriguing to capture Marietta's imagination.

'And is he a good artist?' she asked.

'Father thinks so.'

'But he's so young. He can't have had the experience.'

'Father says he has a natural talent. And remember Sir

52

Thomas Lawrence painted Queen Charlotte when he was only twenty.'

The two friends chatted ceaselessly until Charlotte had to make her excuses. Otherwise she would incur her mother's displeasure for not being punctual for their evening meal.

'When do I see him?' asked Marietta when she was seeing Charlotte out of the front door.

'Tomorrow,' replied Charlotte. 'Come over shortly after breakfast. Mr Parker wants to start then. Maybe he'll let you sit in so we can chat while he works.'

'Oh, I hope so.' She kissed Charlotte on the cheek and watched her as she made her way lightly across the square.

Richard lay in his bed staring unseeingly at the ceiling. His mind was filled with the images of the day on which his ambition to become a renowned artist could be said to have taken firm root. He had Mr Wakefield to thank for his chance; he would always be in his debt, and he hoped he would fulfil his faith in him.

So much had been promised over the evening meal. And that was a revelation in itself. Never before had he sat down to splendid food in such elegant surroundings, with glistening glassware and an array of shining cutlery. When he had entered the dining room with its high ornate ceiling, heavily curtained windows, and mahogany furnishings and had seen the servants standing by he had been nervous in case he did anything wrong. But throughout the meal he was always careful to be that slight moment behind the others so that he could do what they did.

He had noticed Charlotte's occasional twitch of amusement but he was thankful that there was nothing derisive in her observing eyes, rather there was a touch of sympathetic understanding.

As they ate, Francis had enlarged on the presence of Captain David Fernley and Sir Thomas Lawrence in the square. He had suggested that, while Richard was in London, it would be advantageous for him to see other work and he felt sure that Sir Thomas would oblige privately and in his capacity as the new President of the Royal Academy.

Richard could hardly believe what was happening. Less

than a week ago he was earning a few coins from fishing, and from selling paintings locally in Whitby, but now he had the chance of meeting one of the most exalted artists in the land, renowned for his portraits.

Tomorrow was going to be a busy day. In the afternoon Mr Wakefield was taking him to buy equipment and materials to supplement the few that he had brought from Whitby. They were sufficient for him to make a start after breakfast when he was going to have the first sitting with Charlotte. He was not looking forward to her friend being there but it would not have been polite to refuse Charlotte's request. He had insisted however that she would not be able to see his work until he said so.

Breakfast was a less formal meal and as soon as it was over Charlotte asked Richard when he would like to start work.

'As soon as you are ready, Mrs Campion,' he replied politely.

'Ten minutes,' she replied, then excused herself and left the table.

'Would you like to arrange the seating before Charlotte returns?' Francis suggested.

'Yes, sir.'

Taking their leave of Mrs Wakefield the two men crossed the hall. The soft morning light flooded the room, and Richard saw that a mahogany throne chair with a graciously curved frame, stout arms, and green leather padding had already been brought in.

'Move things around to your liking, Mr Parker,' said Francis. 'Set it for your convenience.'

Richard studied his surroundings and assessed them quickly. 'The piano will be all right where it is. I will work from the centre of the room.'

From there the door was in the right-hand corner. Almost opposite the door was a large window with another further along the same wall. To take the best advantage of the light he moved the sitter's chair close to the first window and set it at a slight angle towards it, rather than have it directly facing his working position.

'I believe a friend of Mrs Campion's is coming to keep her company while I work.'

'So she tells me. Miss Kemp is a pleasant person. She'll be no bother but I hope you can cope with their chatter.' He chuckled. 'And remember, don't let her have one peep of your work. She'll try.'

Richard smiled. 'I won't, sir. You will be the first to see anything. She won't even get a chance this morning as I will be working on my sketching paper. The easel and canvas will come this afternoon. No doubt this won't be Miss Kemp's only visit?'

'I'm sure it won't,' agreed Francis.

'Then we'll sit her between the two windows. She'll be near enough to Mrs Campion and she won't be able to see my canvas from there.'

Francis nodded his approval.

Richard surveyed the room and, satisfied, said, 'I'll go and get my materials before Mrs Campion returns.'

He was waiting when Charlotte arrived a few minutes later. The light streaming towards the door from the window highlighted the white muslin dress with an ethereal glow. It was cut perfectly, dropping with only a narrow flare from a high waist. The hem was embroidered with a flounce, the pattern of small yellow flowers matching exactly that of the whole dress. The neckline and high-shoulder sleeves were similarly edged, leaving the neck bare except for a thin gold chain and pendant.

Her hair, carefully brushed, emphasised the perfection of her features. She smiled not only with her mouth but with her eyes, which were observing Richard carefully without seeming to do so.

'Will this be suitable, Mr Parker?'

Richard had jumped to his feet and though he tried to hide his reaction to her appearance he had not been entirely successful.

Charlotte knew she had made an impact and it pleased her just as it always delighted her to impress those around her.

'I brought this, which you might think will enhance the portrait.' She held up a small bright red silk shawl. Before he could express an opinion she swirled it round her shoulders. It dropped perfectly into position, meeting just below the neck then parting to reveal the neckline of her dress.

Richard almost gasped at the change, for now her smooth

55

delicate rosy skin was accentuated by the reflection of the new colour and her hair was given copper tints which added an extra dimension to the character of her features.

He knew she had noticed his reaction and he was embarrassed that she had done so. 'It's perfect and will enhance the finished picture.'

'Good. How would you like me to sit?' She went to the chair which had been placed for her.

'I want to do a three-quarter view. I will be working from here.' He took up the position he estimated would be best for him. He summed up the angles and then came to her. 'I'll move the chair a little if you don't mind, Mrs Campion.'

She stood and he turned the chair slightly towards the window.

'We'll try that.' He went back to his place and she sat down. 'Just a fraction towards me, please.'

Charlotte adjusted her pose. 'Is that better?'

'Yes, if you are comfortable.' She nodded. 'Look towards the chair on which your friend will be sitting.'

She did as he asked. He studied her, then asked her to turn her head slightly so that the light cast revealing shadows on her features. Satisfied, he started to sketch. His pencil moved quickly across the paper. He rushed on, absorbed, his eyes flashing from the subject to the pad, from the drawing to Charlotte. Then she was there smiling at him from the paper. He stared at the drawing – so quickly executed yet he had captured the very essence of her as he saw it, no, as he felt and experienced it.

A distant bell sounded.

'That will be Marietta!' Charlotte rose from her seat and ran from the room.

The spell was broken. He started and stared disbelievingly at the sketch. What had he done? Had he really had the feelings he had revealed in the drawing? Not only had he captured her likeness but there was something of himself there. He slipped the paper between two sheets of the pad.

He heard happy exchanges and laughter from the hall. Charlotte came into the room accompanied by her friend.

'Marietta, please meet Mr Parker. Mr Parker, this is Miss Kemp.'

56

He felt her dark eyes appraising him with a curiosity which wanted to know more about him. She held out her hand which he took gently as he made a slight bow. 'I am pleased to know you, Miss Kemp.' Their eyes met when he straightened and for a moment he felt distrust of himself knowing what he had expressed in the sketch which lay out of sight.

'And I you, Mr Parker.' Marietta's eyes held a genuine warmth. Her immediate reaction on seeing Richard was one of liking, for she sensed someone different to those in her usual circle of friends.

She had never met a man from the north of the country and she laughed to herself that she could have thought he would be no different from the young men she knew around London, aristocrats, army officers, sons of successful businessmen, rich, mostly sure of themselves, among them some gamblers, drinkers, party-goers who liked a continuous round of pleasures. Even in this brief meeting, and as the morning wore on, she sensed the growing feeling that this young artist was none of those things. For sure, he had little money, his clothes, though good, were not of the fine material she was used to seeing. He was handsome with a ruggedness which she found attractive. His brown eyes were gentle yet she felt beneath that there was a turbulence which could draw her into a whirlpool of desire.

Richard was wondering if there might be another commission forthcoming. Would Marietta resent being outdone by Charlotte and want her portrait doing? She looked a promising subject. Her oval face had a gentle jawline, her mouth was attractively shaped and her nose sharp. Her thin eyebrows arched only slightly and were dark like the hair which this morning she had piled and pinned neatly on the top of her head giving her that extra appealing height. Her chintz dress was a mass of small leaves in blue, yellow, brown and green on a dark red background. A white bodice with a frilled neck showed above the curved neckline of the dress.

'You are to sit over there, between the two windows, Marietta,' Charlotte indicated. Then she added with a knowing glance at Richard, 'From there you won't be able to see what Mr Parker is drawing.'

Marietta turned a teasing pout at him. 'But you will show me, won't you, Mr Parker?'

Richard gave a slow smile as he shook his head. 'I'm afraid not, Miss Kemp.' Her eyes met his with a challenge. 'Mr Wakefield, as the commissioner, has to be the first. Maybe I will let you look after him, but if I do you will have to promise me that you will not say anything about the portrait to Mrs Campion. She must not see it until it is completely finished.'

'And that may not be for six months,' sighed Charlotte as she sat down again and resumed her pose.

Richard, ready to suggest an adjustment, was surprised to find she had adopted the exact position she had taken before the interruption. He started to sketch.

'Well, what's been happening while I've been away?' asked Charlotte, eager for the latest gossip.

'Leo Kenyon's joined the Army.'

'What? He'll never survive.'

'Seems Gerry Hilton and Ben Winstan dared him.'

Charlotte nodded. 'And poor old Leo didn't want to appear a coward.'

'Claude Potter's been banned from two clubs. The two d's – drink and debts.'

'I expect his father will dig into his pocket again.'

'He won't. He told Claude to get a job or he won't even get an inheritance. Claude's been to see Father.'

'No doubt through you.'

Marietta gave a wan smile and nodded. 'I like Claude. I couldn't but try to help.'

'He'll be proposing to you next,' chaffed Charlotte only to have the teasing expression change to one of alarm when Marietta replied.

'He did!'

'And?' asked Charlotte, her eyes wide with horror at what the answer could be.

Marietta laughed. 'I turned him down!'

Charlotte relaxed and realised Richard was staring at her. 'Oh, I'm sorry, I've moved. But, with what might have proved devastating news ... oh my goodness, Marietta, you frightened me so.' She fluttered a hand in front of her face and then resumed her pose.

'Forgive us our gossip, Mr Parker,' Marietta apologised

and in order to include him added, 'Is this your first time away from Whitby?'

'Yes,' he replied, 'if you do not count a whaling voyage I did when I was eighteen.'

'Whaling? Like Captain Fernley across the square?'

'Yes. My father is master of a whaleship belonging to Captain Fernley's Whitby firm.'

'And you had no desire to follow the same trade?'

'Marietta, he's an artist,' put in Charlotte.

'Are you missing home?' asked Marietta.

Richard gave a little laugh. 'So much has happened I really haven't had time to think about it.'

'He'll be so absorbed in doing my portrait he won't miss Whitby,' trilled Charlotte teasingly. She shot him a glance to try to assess his reaction but saw only concentration on what he was doing.

'What will happen when Charles returns?' Marietta asked.

'I don't know,' replied Charlotte. 'If we return to Lincolnshire then Mr Parker will accompany us. He'll have to otherwise how can he complete the portrait?'

Marietta nodded. Secretly she hoped that Charles would choose to stay in London awhile for not only would she be able to spend time with Charlotte but she could get to know the young man from Whitby better.

Chapter Five

Charlotte hastened down the stairs. From her bedroom window she had seen the chaise. Charles was back!

For one moment she had experienced mixed feelings. Excitement at his return was mingled with regret that now she would not be spending as much time with Richard. Their routine would be altered. She would sit for him when possible but now life with Charles would be resumed. There had been moments when she had looked forward to it, for her social life would start again. Theatres, balls, dinner with friends, parties, were all part of the life of a vivacious young woman and she had realised that, much as she had enjoyed the holiday in Whitby, London was really the place she liked, provided she had the chance of escaping to the country life of the Lincolnshire gentry with its whirl of social gatherings in a different mode to those of London.

Richard, hearing the crunch of wheels, had gone to the window of his room. Knowing that Charles Campion was to arrive today he sensed that this chaise was bringing him. He pulled himself up short when he found himself wishing that Charlotte's husband had stayed away. Annoyed with himself for entertaining such a thought he turned sharply away from the window and grabbed the pad on which he had been sketching.

Charlotte, in three different poses, looked out from the paper. He stared at her. A longing welled inside him. He scowled. His lips tightened, and he flung the pad across the room.

'Fool!' he hissed, and slammed his clenched fists hard on the wall. 'Fool. Don't ruin your chances!'

Even in these last four days he had seen the enormous opportunities there could be to hone his talent and attract influential people with his work. In Mr Wakefield he had a patron eager for him to display his ability. He had not only taken him into his household, but, along with the commission for a portrait of Charlotte, had spared nothing in fitting him out with the best equipment.

He had arranged for him to meet Sir Thomas Lawrence who, on seeing his sketch pads, had encouraging words to say as well as offering some advice, pointing out the advisability of studying the works of the best portrait painters.

He had been greeted warmly by Captain David Fernley and had seen a wistful longing come into his eyes when they talked about Whitby. Richard sensed that here was a man contented with his lot, happy with his family, but felt a yearning for a life which was gone. He looked long at the sketches of Whitby characters and as he did so Richard had the chance to study the face beaten by the winds of the Arctic and scorched by the heat of the Pacific. And there was about the eyes the distant look of a whaleman ever searching for his quarry.

Captain Fernley nodded as he handed the sketches back to Richard. 'When you have finished your portrait of Mrs Campion come and see me. I think I would like a portrait of myself, a present for my wife.' His face wrinkled into a smile of intrigue. 'Think we can do it without her knowing?'

'We can that, sir,' Richard had replied, and he had left the house elated and eager to tell Charlotte the news.

He recalled that moment. She had been delighted for him and in telling him so had used his Christian name for the first time. Suddenly realising what she had done she apologised and in doing so reverted immediately to the formality of 'Mr Parker'.

'Please,' he had countered, 'Richard.'

She had nodded but had not offered Charlotte in return. He understood. After all she was a married woman. He was content to hear his Christian name come from gentle lips.

Now he tried to banish the emotions which had tugged at his heart. He must or he could ruin himself. Charles was home and that might help.

*

61

'Charles!'

Campion stopped in the doorway and stood watching his wife race down the stairs. He smiled, delighted at seeing her again, admiring every facet as she ran across the hall. She flung herself into his arms and hugged him, feeling some comfort and solace in his strong arms to counteract the thoughts she had entertained in her room.

He laughed at her excitement and enthusiasm, seeing the exuberance more associated with a daughter than a wife. But he did not mind. He liked her the way she was, at times the high-spirited girl, at others the sophisticated wife. She had brought joy to him, opened new horizons, widened his social life, and shared his own interests, especially those associated with his estates in Lincolnshire.

'You'll never guess where I've been?' she cried, her eyes sparkling with the expectation of surprising him.

He put on a mock air of puzzled thoughtfulness. He frowned for a moment, then banished all his doubt. 'Whitby!' he exclaimed.

The shock of his knowledge startled her and she gave a small pout. 'You knew!' Disappointment clouded her eyes.

He gave a low amused laugh. 'Your father told me what he had in mind the day before I left. He swore me to secrecy, not to give even a hint, as he wanted to surprise you.' He gave her an extra hug to ward off her chagrin.

'So that's how you knew I'd be here rather than in Chelsea?'

He nodded. 'Your mother said you might as well stay here on your return.' He looked at her curiously for he had noticed a glow of satisfaction coming mischievously to her blue eyes. He knew she had something to tell him.

'Ah, but I do have a surprise for you.' Laughter trilled from her lips. She was not going to be outdone after all. She slipped from his arms and twirled in front of him.

He laughed at her excitement as he grabbed her hand and stopped her. 'What is it?' he asked eagerly.

'I'm having my portrait painted!'

There was no disguising his astonishment. 'Splendid! Sir Thomas?'

She shook her head and went on to explain quickly the

events which had led to the commission.

He listened intently as he shed his outdoor clothes and walked with her into the drawing room.

'And where is this young man whom it seems your father recognises as an artist whose work will be sought after?' Recalling Francis's aspirations, he gave a little chuckle.

'In his room, working, I expect,' Charlotte replied. 'You'll meet him later. Now, how was your visit to France?'

He was about to reply when they heard the front door open and close. Brisk footsteps approached the drawing room and the door opened with a flourish. Francis swept into the room followed by his wife.

'Charles, how pleasant to see you back!' Francis held out his hand. His grip was firm and expressed friendship and regard.

'It's good to be here,' replied Charles then turned his attention to Gertrude. 'Mrs Wakefield,' he bowed as he took her hand. He kissed her on both cheeks. 'You look well after your holiday.'

'I am, Charles. It was a welcome change from London, but I'm glad to be home again.'

'Has Charlotte told you her news?' asked Francis eagerly.

'The portrait?'

'Yes. I've found a new talent. I've set him up with a studio here in order to do Charlotte's portrait. Of course I realise there is a problem when you return to Lincolnshire. And I would like the work finished and hung before Jacob returns from the Continent.'

'Ah,' Charles smiled knowingly. 'You want to astound him with talent *you* have discovered.'

'Well ...' Francis spread his hands in a gesture of agreement.

'There's no difficulty about Lincolnshire,' Charles reassured him. The artist ...'

'Richard Parker,' put in Charlotte.

'I look forward to meeting him and seeing some of his work.' Though no expert, Charles knew enough to say what he liked and why he liked it, but beyond that he was perfectly willing to accept Francis's judgement and the expertise of Jacob Craig whom he had come to know through his father-in-law. 'He can come to Reed Hall with us. In fact he must, otherwise he won't get the painting finished in time. But we are not able to go north yet.' He caught Charlotte's questioning look. 'I'm sorry, my dear, but I have to return to France and possibly Germany in four days, and I might be away a month.'

Charlotte looked downcast, but her mind was a confusion of thoughts, the absence of Charles, the presence of Richard. 'Oh, Charles, so soon and so long?' she said to bring some equilibrium to her tumult.

'I'm afraid so,' he replied with regret.

'Nothing wrong with your negotiations?' asked Francis anxiously.

'No,' replied Charles. 'Everything went well. A shipment of wine will be made into London next month.'

'Good,' said Francis with relief, for he had invested in Charles's enterprise.

'We'll discuss the storage and disposal later. It is as a result of this deal that further opportunities have arisen which necessitate me returning to the Continent. I think you will be interested. We'll not bore the ladies now.'

Charlotte rose from her chair and went to the bell-pull beside the fireplace. 'I'll get Jean to bring Mr Parker. You can meet him, Charles, and I can tell him I won't be sitting for him until you leave again.'

'No don't do that,' Charles hastened to advise her. 'Your father and I have things to discuss, so when we come over tomorrow you may as well have a sitting.'

'Very well,' Charlotte agreed, pleased that the suggestion had come from him.

Richard realised the request brought by the maid was for him to meet Charlotte's husband. This man could help his future or break it. During these few days of preliminary work he had felt deep down that he would more than do justice to his subject and that, in achieving the portrait he visualised, he would be making certain of his future as an artist. But if Campion disapproved of her sitting then his career could be set back or even destroyed forever.

'Ah, Mr Parker,' cried Francis heartily, as Richard entered

the room. 'We want you to meet Charlotte's husband, Charles Campion.' He turned to his son-in-law, 'Charles, this is the artist we told you about, Richard Parker.'

'Pleased to meet you, sir,' said Richard firmly, hiding any expression of the surprise he was experiencing. He had expected a younger man, someone about Charlotte's own age. Though not old, Campion was obviously much older than his wife, maybe even twenty years. But he still cut a fine figure. Undoubtedly he looked after himself, taking the necessary exercise to keep himself trim. He held himself erect but there was no air of superiority in the pose. And he was handsome. Oh, the ladies would swoon over him and undoubtedly Charlotte had made a good catch in that respect.

'I am pleased to know you, Mr Parker.' His voice was soft, warm, his grip firm and friendly.

Richard sensed that there was no animosity in this man but knew he had come under careful and searching observation from his sharp steel-blue eyes.

'I hear you are doing a portrait of my dear Charlotte. How is the work proceeding?'

'Very well,' replied Richard. 'Though, of course, I am only working on preliminary sketches at the moment.'

'May I see them?'

Richard hesitated, confused as to what his answer should be. He did not want to offend Campion, nor did he want to upset Francis by agreeing to this request.

He was relieved when Charlotte sprang to his help in his moment of reluctant hesitation.

'Oh, no, Charles. You can't do that,' she cried with laughter in her voice. 'Father commissioned the painting, he has to be the first to see the complete work, though he may get a glimpse of it halfway through. No one else, not even I, can see anything connected with it until it is hung.'

'But ...' Charles started to protest.

'No,' she cut in firmly, as she came beside him and linked arms with him. She smiled a smile which was for Richard alone for she had seen relief and gratitude directed at her in his glance.

'But you'll show him some of your other work?' queried Gertrude.

'Of course,' replied Richard without hesitation.

'Then join us for our evening meal.' She looked questioningly at Charles. 'You will stay and eat with us?'

'Nothing I'd like better,' he replied. 'If that is all right with you, my dear?' he added with a querying look at Charlotte.

'Splendid,' she replied. 'You can see Mr Parker's work and get to know him. Oh, by the way, Mr Parker, you might as well know now, my husband has to return to the Continent in four days and will be there for a month. I will stay here while he is away, so your painting needn't be interrupted.'

Richard nodded. 'Very well.' This was better than he had thought. He had expected with Campion's return they would be leaving for Lincolnshire and he had really wanted to stay in London for a while. In the few days he had been here he had seen the opportunities to study paintings and drawings on display as well as the chances of enlarging his own work with London scenes and characters. Now, knowing the broad timing of Campion's schedule, he could do some planning.

'And I will be available for a sitting tomorrow,' Charlotte informed him. 'Charles is coming over to discuss some business with my father.'

'Very well.' He gave a little nod of acknowledgement and then, not wanting to intrude any longer on the family's privacy, added to them all, 'Until this evening.'

'A pleasant young man,' commented Charles when the door had closed. He had expected to see someone much older, someone with experience. 'Talented?' He glanced at Francis.

'He wouldn't be here if I didn't think he was.'

'Of course,' said Charles quickly, wishing he had not doubted his father-in-law's judgement.

'You'll realise that when you see his drawings this evening.'

It proved to be so. Charles was impressed. He liked the bold lines which expressed the vibrant life of Whitby and was taken by the delicate touches which, in other drawings, drew out the character behind the faces of fishermen, housewives, merchants and children.

The meal passed off in a pleasant flow of conversation and Charles was conscious of knowing Richard much better. Any doubt which had initially come to his mind that someone of Charlotte's own age should be undertaking this work, and thereby spending so much time with her, was banished by Richard's sensible approach to life and his intense desire to become a well-known artist. Charles felt that this young man from Whitby would let nothing block the road to that ambition.

Richard, already aware of the wider world beyond Whitby which awaited him if he fulfilled his dream, was drawn more towards it by the talk which flowed around the table.

Charles enthused about *Frankenstein* though he doubted if the ladies should read it. Francis had taken to Walter Scott and had read *Rob Roy* and *Ivanhoe* with enthusiasm while Gertrude was reading *Emma* for the second time.

'Do you get much opportunity for reading?' Charlotte asked Richard, not wanting him to feel out of the conversation.

'I prefer my pencils, but I have read tracts devoted to the sea.'

'And plays? Do you have a theatre in Whitby?' Charles asked.

'Oh, yes,' replied Richard. 'The present one is the second. The first closed in 1784, a new one was built on another site and was opened in 1785 and can take about five hundred people. I've been a few times but not regularly.'

'You must cultivate the habit while in London,' boomed Francis with benevolent enthusiasm. 'We'll all go to Drury Lane the night after next and see Sheridan's *School For Scandal*.'

'Please, don't include me,' Richard said in half-hearted protest.

'Nonsense, my boy,' returned Francis with an aplomb which would brook no refusal. 'It will be good for you and your artistic eye will be aware of London's delights.'

'What a marvellous idea,' said Charlotte enthusiastically. 'May I invite Marietta, then Mr Parker won't feel the odd one out?'

'Splendid,' her father agreed.

Richard looked a little embarrassed but made no comment. He did not want to raise any objections which would appear as if he was throwing their kindness in their faces. He realised that Mr Wakefield had the best intentions, seeing this widening of his protégé's outlook as a help to furthering his artistic talents.

Marietta kept her excitement strictly to herself when Charlotte invited her to join the party. She showed her appreciation and extolled her knowledge of the play but her real, though stifled, exuberance was for the fact that she saw herself as Richard's female companion. She was even more delighted with Charlotte's news that Charles was to return to the Continent leaving his wife to stay with her parents so that the painting could continue without interruption. Now she could see more of Richard.

Marietta, sitting next to him in the theatre, kept up a flow of conversation without making him feel that she was being condescending towards a stranger on his introduction to the theatre in an unfamiliar city so different to the small town on the Yorkshire coast.

Richard, apprehensive about this outing, was grateful to her for her friendliness and open approach when a reserved awkwardness could have proved a disaster. He appreciated her interest in his Yorkshire home, his life there and his art. He, at first a little shy, was drawn by her easy manner and gradually decided he was pleased to be in the company of a pleasant and attractive young woman.

They were a relaxed party who returned to Russell Square and everyone discussed the play at length while enjoying a cold supper. When Charlotte and Charles left for their Chelsea house, Richard accompanied Marietta to her home across the square.

'Thank you for a very pleasant evening, Miss Kemp,' he said when they reached the gate.

'It is I who should be thanking you,' she returned quietly. 'I have enjoyed your company.'

'I would have felt a little out of place had I been on my own, so it is I who should be grateful to you.'

'Maybe we should both be grateful to Charlotte for asking me.'

'True, Miss Kemp.'

She met his look as she said, 'Please, may we not be so

formal? I have a Christian name and would not object to you using it. And as Charlotte will be in London for another month we will no doubt meet on more than one occasion.' A slight pause was followed quickly by, 'Unless you object to me visiting when Charlotte is sitting for you?'

'No, Miss Kemp, er, Marietta. As far as I am concerned you are welcome whenever you want, but I am ruled by Mrs Campion's wishes.'

Marietta gave a little laugh. 'Charlotte won't raise any barriers. She likes to gossip as you will no doubt have noticed.'

So it proved. Charlotte welcomed her friend, and the two girls, while enjoying their private exchanges about acquaintances unfamiliar to Richard, were also pleased to include him in their conversations. The painting sessions often became lively with chatter but Richard never let them intrude too much on the serious work at hand.

His painting went well and he was highly satisfied with the way the portrait was developing, though, as yet, there was a lot more to do to capture the hidden depth of his sitter. As time passed he found that exclusivity he wanted to capture changing. With each brush stroke he began to feel an empathy developing with Charlotte that he really ought to curb or rather dismiss altogether.

He was not helped by the social outings arranged by Francis and Gertrude for he was nearly always included. More visits to the theatre, to musical concerts, dinner with the Fernleys, the Kemps and other friends of the Wakefields took place. Charlotte was always there, and more often than not, as Charles was away, he was seated beside her. He sensed that she was pleased and knew about the effect she was having on him. At first he thought she might be cultivating it in a teasing way but he began to realise it was more and that there was within her a similar feeling to what he was experiencing.

It came to the fore at the end of one painting session. They were alone. Marietta had had another engagement. Pleasant conversation had passed between them, the atmosphere was light and easy but when Charlotte held out her hand to be helped from the chair it became charged with a different meaning. It was as if the whole world was in this room and was theirs alone. Nothing beyond these four walls existed. Only they mattered. Their hands met and in that touch there was an intimacy expressing more than mere friendship. Their eyes, intent on each other, expressed feelings that needed no words. They knew they should not entertain them but in that challenge there lay the daring to express themselves.

'Mrs Campion ...' The huskiness in his voice betrayed what he wanted to say.

'Charlotte, please,' she whispered. Her searching look showed she wanted to hear him use her Christian name.

He could not escape her eyes. They held him, drew him into their enticing blue depths. Her sensuous touch tingled down his fingers. Her grip closed around his wrist. 'Say it,' she whispered.

His mind swirled at the tempting encouragement.

'Charlotte.' There was little strength in his voice.

'Again.' Her damp lips parted in a gentle smile.

'Charlotte.' Her name came louder, charged with feelings previously held at bay in his inner heart.

The tension was broken. The barrier between them was shattered. Their relationship would never be the same again. And it moved on to a more intimate plane as they came closer together, knowing they should turn away but succumbing to the overwhelming power that drew them towards one another. Their lips met, gently, firmly then passionately as his arms swept around her, crushing her close. That moment was theirs forever, indelibly, seared into their memories, never to be forgotten.

Suddenly Richard turned away, with the enormity of what he had done exploding in his mind. His eyes were troubled. Full of apology, they searched for forgiveness.

'Mrs Campion, I'm sorry. I shouldn't have ...'

'I wanted you to.' Her voice, soft, broke into his distress.

The silence between them seemed to stretch endlessly.

'This shouldn't have happened,' he muttered with a shake of his head.

'You regret it?' she asked.

'No!' he protested at her implication.

'Nor do I. I'm in love with you.'

'You shouldn't be. You are married. You love your husband?'

'Yes.'

'Then there is no more to be said. We should forget what has just happened.'

'But we never will. I do love Charles but I am not *in* love with him as I am with you. There is a difference.'

'The situation is impossible, Charlotte. I'll not have your name sullied by scandal. I'd return to Whitby and forget my career in London before I'd let that happen.'

'Then you must love me to consider that sacrifice.'

Biting his lips, he made no comment but she could see from the look in his eyes that she was right.

'You'll have to stay, you've a commission to fulfil. If you leave, Father will want to know why and there would be no satisfactory explanation without the truth, and that would destroy us both.'

'Then we must not let this happen again.' Richard left his clipped words hanging in the air as he hurried from the room.

Charlotte stared at the closed door. 'You did not mean that,' she whispered.

As he crossed the hall to the stairs, Francis came in by the front door.

'Ah, Mr Parker,' he called, 'I wanted to see you. Have you a moment?'

As much as he desired to go to his room to try to come to terms with his confused thoughts, he could not refuse his sponsor's request.

'Yes,' he replied. 'I've finished working on the portrait for the day.'

'Good.' Francis had removed his coat and hat. 'Come into my study. I have some news for you.' He led the way into a room panelled in oak with bookshelves along one wall. A large oak desk was placed so that the light from the tall sash window came from the left. Francis indicated to Richard to take a seat as he went behind the desk and sat down.

'You are happy with the way things are?' asked Francis.

'Yes,' replied Richard, knowing full well that he could not reveal the turmoil in his mind.

'Our visits to the Royal Academy and the Picture Gallery at Dulwich have been beneficial?'

'Yes, sir,' Richard replied quickly.

'Good. I would advise you to visit them again. Study the paintings.'

'It is my intention to do so. I know I can learn a lot from them.'

'And your expeditions to paint London scenes?'

'They help my portrait work.'

'Good. You'll do more?'

'As time and work on the portrait permit.'

'Excellent. I'd like you to have a presentable portfolio when Jacob Craig returns from Italy. You remember I mentioned him as someone I feel sure will be impressed by your work. Well, tomorrow, I'm going to take you to his studio.'

'But I thought you said he was in Italy.'

'He is but that does not mean that his studio closes down. Oh, no, the artists he has under his wing must continue to work and, as a supervisor and someone to keep the place running, he has a friend who knows what he wants and how to entertain clients. You'll see what could await you if your work impresses Jacob. I thought of taking you there so that you will have something to aim for.'

'I appreciate your thought and kindness, sir. And also the faith you have in me. I hope I won't let you down.'

'I'm sure you won't.

Those words haunted him as he lay in bed that night. Sleep would not come. So much was before him. The chances to develop his artistic ability were being offered. Though he was never fully satisfied with his work and always saw there was room for improvement, he knew that perfection was a goal that could never be achieved, but he felt that he could, one day, come close to it if only he did not put a foot wrong. And everything would come to ruin if he persisted in an illicit relationship with Charlotte.

In the darkness of his room he whispered her name and felt a sensuous thrill on his lips and the music of the word in his ears. He could not escape the love he felt for her though he tried hard to cast it from his mind, telling himself that no good

72

could come of it and that to persist in it could bring disaster for them both and ruin other lives as well. But the enormity of what could happen was overwhelmed by the haunting vision of the expression he was trying to capture on a piece of canvas, the expression of a girl in love, but inescapably, to his eyes, in love with him.

'You won't be required for a sitting today, Charlotte,' Francis announced at breakfast. 'I'm taking Mr Parker to see Mr Craig's studio.'

'Very well, Father,' she answered quietly. 'Maybe tomorrow.' She shot a glance at Richard but could read nothing in his face.

She took heart from the fact that he was going to Mr Craig's. It meant his talk of leaving in order to break off their relationship had meant nothing. She had worried during the night in case she lost him. She would be devastated if he left. She had tried to curb the growing feelings of love and admiration which had culminated in yesterday's kiss but it had been to no avail. Even as these thoughts pressed their case she confounded her mind by reminding herself that she was a married woman with a husband who loved her dearly, who spoiled her, who only had her happiness at heart. She liked and respected him, indeed she loved him, but it was not the same as being in love and that experience had come and persisted the more she saw of Richard.

The following morning Richard was in awe of the elegant row of stuccoed houses when he and Mr Wakefield turned into St Andrew's Place. The unified style and colour of the terrace exuded a feeling of solid well-being and spoke of affluence.

They stopped before a gate in the iron railings, from which a short path led to a door painted dark green. The arched fanlight of simple geometric design was repeated in the upper portion of the sash windows in the four bays to the right of the door. Between each bay a column attached to the wall rose to a decorated capital supporting an entablature of a simple architrave which ran the full length of the terrace, at first floor level. The first and second floors each held four double-hung sash windows of three over three glass panes. Above the topmost architrave ran a series of short, gracefully shaped balusters. Richard could just make out the slates of the attics held back a little so as not to mar the effect of the top facade of the terrace.

'This is Mr Craig's?' he asked, rather overawed by the prospect of what promised to be an experience of stepping into another world, one of opulence.

'Yes,' replied Francis.

'He actually owns this house?' Still bewildered, Richard put his questions tentatively.

'Oh, yes,' Francis reassured him. 'He comes from a very rich family. They were able to help him with his venture. He had a great desire to be an artist and he embarked on such a career and went to Italy to view and study the masters. There he suffered a terrible accident which damaged his hands permanently and he could not hold a pencil or a brush to do the work he demanded of them. Many a young man would have given up, become a recluse, but Jacob had a powerful determination. He did not let his love of art waver and he channelled his interest two ways. He became a dealer in paintings and drawings, and set up a studio where he could develop talent. He generally has four or five young men whom he encourages, instructs and advises, and because of his dealings with clients looking to buy paintings he can gain commissions for his artists. This is the world I want you to see.' Francis opened the gate.

'His studio's here? In this fine house?' Amazement still held Richard's mind.

'Yes,' laughed Francis. 'I expect it will be different to what you imagine.'

They had reached the door and Francis rapped hard with the brilliantly polished brass knocker.

A few moments later the door swung open without so much as the faintest squeak.

'Good day, Mr Wakefield.' Recognising Mr Craig's friend, the footman stood to one side and allowed them to enter.

'Mr Tizard?' asked Francis.

'I'll tell him you are here, sir,' replied the footman as he closed the door. 'Will you come this way?'

He led the way across the hall to a door on the right.

74

Richard was still staring round the hall. A wide staircase with one turn rose to the next floor. The delicate iron work of its banister was an intertwining of leaves and fish. Light came not only from the fanlight above the front door but from a large window at the turn of the stairs. There was little furniture in the hall but what there was Richard sensed would be of the best and he saw it was set with the occasional figurine so placed to emphasise its artistic merit and to create an impression for art connoisseurs that they were stepping into the world of an expert.

When he followed Francis into the room, he saw it had just the right amount of furniture to remove the feeling of sparseness without giving the impression of overcrowding: a small table, two straight-backed chairs, two comfortable armchairs and a sideboard on which stood six wine glasses and two decanters of Madeira.

'A glass of Madeira, sir?' asked the footman.

'Thank you,' replied Francis.

He knew Richard was being impressed. He was pleased, for he expected his protegé's work to make such an impact on Jacob that, when the portrait of Charlotte was finished, Richard would be moving into this house. He hoped that by seeing it now the young man's ambition would be focused even more sharply.

They were comfortably seated and enjoying their drinks when the door opened and a small thin man bustled in.

'My dear sirs, I am so sorry to have kept you waiting, but those two clients I have just seen out could not make up their mind about a sunset by Mr Turner.'

Richard gulped. Mr Turner? Could it be the Joseph Turner? Was Mr Craig selling Mr Turner's paintings?

Francis had risen from his chair. He threw up his arms in protest at the apology. 'Think nothing of it, Benjamin, we were most comfortable and you keep exceedingly good Madeira.'

Benjamin gave a little bow of acknowledgement at the praise, then turned sharply to confront Richard. 'Now who have we here?' He was aware from Richard's dress, which, though decent enough, was not of such quality that it would mark him out as a purchaser of art works.

'Benjamin, I want you to meet Richard Parker.'

Before Francis could say any more, Benjamin effusively greeted Richard. 'Ah, young man, welcome to this humble abode. You are in the good hands of Mr Wakefield, and any friend, acquaintance or protégé – and I guess, knowing him, that you are the latter as well as now the former – is welcome here.'

Richard was overwhelmed by the flow of words and the exuberance of this small man, whose thinness belied an abundant energy. His brown eyes appeared to be darting everywhere whereas in reality they were taking everything in with shrewd judgement. His hair was thick and straight and his eyebrows matched it. His nose was thin and pointed. In some men it might have given a ferret-look of unfriendliness but not in Benjamin. His hollow cheeks gave way to a pointed chin and small goatee beard which conferred a distinguished look on him and seemed to add to his aura of an art connoisseur.

'Thank you, sir,' replied Richard.

'Polite as well as good-looking.' Benjamin's smile, as he looked at Francis, revealed a row of perfect teeth.

'He is that,' grinned Francis. 'Are you still looking for a husband for your daughter?'

Benjamim raised his eyes heavenwards in despair. 'I am that. Men court her and run away. I don't know why. I've thrown artists at her feet but she is adamant that she'll never marry an artist.'

'Then you're safe, Richard,' laughed Francis.

'Ah, I thought so, young man, Mr Wakefield's protégé.' Benjamin seized on Francis's remark and his daughter was forgotten. 'Where's your work?' He glanced around expecting to see a portfolio somewhere. Perplexed at not seeing one he glanced sharply at Richard. 'Work? Work? Where is it?'

Richard, at a loss for words, looked at Francis.

'I've not brought him here for judgement. In fact I want your strict promise that you will not mention him, nor this visit, to Jacob until after I do. No one is seeing the painting he is doing for me until I say so. I have brought him here so that he can see what opportunity awaits him.'

Benjamin pulled a face. 'Well, now ...' he started doubtfully.

76

'It will be finished by the time Jacob returns. When he sees it he will instantly bring Richard under his wing.'

'You've seen this painting developing and are willing to make a judgement on that?' Benjamin looked horrified and there was touch of mockery in his voice.

'I've not seen any of it,' replied Francis.

'Not seen ...' Benjamin gasped.

'There are some other ...'

'How many?'

'Not many, sir,' put in Richard.

Benjamin threw up his hands in hopeless disgust. 'Francis, you shouldn't raise Mr Parker's hopes this way.'

'Benjamin, I'll bet you a hundred pounds that Jacob will take him on when he sees this work.'

Richard gaped at Francis. What was he thinking about to wager a fortune on him like that?

Benjamin saw Richard's distress at the faith that Mr Wakefield had in his ability. He saw him wondering if he could fulfil what was expected of him. He shot him a look of comfort. 'Don't worry, I'll not take his wager.' He turned back to Francis. 'So, why have I the honour of your visit?' he asked smoothly.

'I would be grateful if you would show Richard round the studio and explain what happens here.'

'Very well. I see you not only want to widen his education and knowledge of life but you want him to see what can be gained by studious devotion, application and dedication to his art.' He looked solemnly at Richard. 'Before we set out on what for you will be a voyage of discovery can I ask you one question?'

Richard nodded, a little in trepidation of what was coming.

He need not have worried. The question was a simple one. 'What do you want to be?'

Without hesitation he replied, 'A great artist.'

Benjamin looked at him for a moment, weighing up the sincerity and conviction in Richard's voice. Then he nodded. 'A very commendable ambition. So I will take you on your voyage.'

He led the way into a large room which was lit by the four windows Richard had seen at the front of the house. The plain light blue wallpaper was covered with framed paintings each placed with care so that when viewing a particular picture the client was not distracted by its neighbours. Two large easels were positioned so that when they were used to display a particular painting for a potential buyer they took the right light from the windows and enabled the customer to view from the comfort of strategically placed armchairs. The rest of the furnishings and the curtains reflected good taste and conveyed a sense of wealth, the whole creating a convivial atmosphere befitting the type of client Jacob Craig encouraged to visit his showroom.

The painting viewed by the customers who had just left still stood on one of the easels. Its vivid colours of yellow, orange and red, mingled with subtle touches of blue and brown, created a vibrant picture, a turbulence through which there was peace. Richard was drawn into it and felt a sense of warning – there could be peace for him if he chose the right path and avoided the upheaval which threatened him. His world could be here, in this studio. He sensed it. He knew it. And yet ...

'Some of the paintings on this wall, those three and that, and that and those four are by young artists whom you will see working in the painting room.'

Benjamin's words broke into Richard's mind. He started and turned his attention to the pictures indicated. He moved closer and gave the impression of examining them more closely but his mind was on the thoughts which had just occupied him.

Benjamin led the way to a smaller room in the centre of which was a mahogany dining table polished to perfection. Five places were set with exquisite silver cutlery and the best crystal. A sideboard against one wall was laid with serving spoons and forks and two wine decanters.

'Obviously, our dining room,' Benjamin announced. 'If Jacob had been here there would have been another place set. He would be at the head, my humble self at the bottom. But as he's away I take pride of place.' He straightened and puffed himself out with a degree of satisfaction. 'Our artists on either side with, of course, room for guests or visiting masters.'

'Your pupils eat here with you?' asked Richard, a little surprised at this possibility.

Benjamin looked horrified. 'My dear boy, they are not pupils. We don't teach. We give them the facilities to pursue their own ideas and develop their own talents. Mr Craig is very careful to vet would-be artists before bringing them here and I might tell you if they do not show that they will fulfil his expectations they are gently told to leave, but it is not very often Mr Craig is wrong.'

'So there is a lot of freedom of artistic expression here,' put in Francis.

'My word yes. We will offer advice and encourage. Jacob brings in master artists to lecture and demonstrate. This gives our artists a chance to see a variety of abilities and techniques and widens their outlook and experiments. Of course, you do know that there are those who prefer to be apprenticed to master painters. That system has merit but Jacob takes the view that the method we run here is better. He feels that the master apprentice system can turn the apprentice into a drudge doing just what the master wants or the apprentice becomes stifled by the limitations of the master he is with. This cannot happen in our studio.'

'I can vouch for it being an admirable system,' said Francis. 'I have seen so much talent encouraged here.' He glanced at Benjamin. 'And there is a ready-made outlet for work.'

'My goodness, yes,' enthused Benjamin. 'We are always looking to sell our artists' work as well as paintings from outside our studio. Jacob looks out for commissions and maintains an exclusive clientele. The person in that category expects to be entertained in luxury, which is why Jacob has furnished and decorated the studio to the high standard you are seeing. And he believes that because his clients expect this standard his artists should be used to it too.'

Richard was almost overwhelmed. This was an aspect of the art world he had never envisaged. Mr George Chambers's studio in Whitby seemed a very humble abode compared to the luxury here. This world in London was tempting, something to aim for. Here he could develop his talent without restriction, only heeding advice, and instruction from the visiting masters, as he saw fit for his own work.

On the next floor Benjamin took them into a large room

where four young men were busy at their easels. Each had ample space without distractions. Identical elegantly shaped painter's cabinets of three drawers standing on curved legs stood close to each easel. The walls were papered in light green with a tiny flower motif. Two tables held small easels, hinged on box-shaped stands which housed the paints and brushes for those wishing to do miniature work.

When he stepped into the room Richard was met with curious glances. They were only momentary, for the artists had little desire to break their concentration. He felt the intensity of a workroom and yet there was a relaxed atmosphere, both conducive to production of good work. He noted that three artists were working on portraits and the other was intent on a large historical work. Immediately Richard wondered if there was an opportunity for him to concentrate on portraits and if there was the possibility of an opening for seascapes.

He watched quietly for a moment or two until Benjamin broke the silence with a request. 'Edgar, do you mind if I show this young man your room? I'd like him to see the accommodation we give our artists. He may join us after Mr Craig returns.'

The young man whom Benjamin had addressed raised no objections. He smiled at Richard and as he turned back to his canvas he gave Richard a huge wink.

They moved upstairs and Richard realised they must have reached the roof space covered by the slates he had seen outside. Though the room had a sloping ceiling it was not cramped. There was a bed, a wardrobe, a table, a highbacked chair and two easy chairs with still plenty of floor space to give a feeling of roominess.

'All our artists have rooms like this. We have maids to keep the rooms clean and make the beds. Our artists are not here to do that sort of work but are here first and foremost to develop their talents.'

'Well, Richard, there is a great opportunity with Mr Craig if you want it,' said Francis as they left the house in St Andrew's Place.

'I appreciate you taking me,' replied Richard. 'It was most interesting. But it will depend on whether Mr Craig likes my work sufficiently to offer me a place.'

Francis stopped, a look of astonishment on his face. 'Like your work? Of course he will. He can't do any other. When he sees Charlotte's portrait he'll be eager to take you.'

Richard gave a little smile at Francis's enthusiasm. 'But you haven't seen it yet. It may not come up to expectations.'

'From what I saw in Whitby, I know it will.' There was every confidence in Francis's tone as he fell into step again.

Francis had a call to make at the house of a merchant importing furs from Canada and left Richard to make his own way back to Russell Square.

By the time he reached there he had considered the faith that Francis had in his ability. He would not have taken him to see Jacob Craig's studio if he had not thought him capable of impressing Mr Craig. He saw the opportunity that Francis was offering him. It was something many an artist would dream about. He should not jeopardise his chances, and that kiss had brought him close to doing just that.

Chapter Six

With the sight of the house in Russell Square all thoughts of the opportunities which could be his with Jacob Craig were challenged by those haunting moments with Charlotte. His mind became a torrent of confusion taking him to the brink of despair.

Closing the front door quietly behind him he made straight for the stairs intending to seek the seclusion of his room. He needed to think in the reassurance of his own private world, the world he had created within the confines of four walls. There, surely he would find the solution to his dilemma, there he must sort out his future. But he must not compromise Charlotte. His own feelings must be as nothing. Should he complete the portrait or forget it? Should he return to Whitby now and renounce his ambition to become a renowned painter?

He was halfway to the stairs when the quiet notes of the piano came from the studio. They drew him up short of the first step and swirled in his mind. Charlotte! He did not know the tune but it mesmerised him with its haunting tone. It was as if it held a specific meaning, meant for him alone. He stood listening allowing the music to move deeper and deeper until it possessed his very soul.

He turned, glanced towards the half-open door and then moved slowly towards it, drawn by the enticing repetition of the theme, frightened that any sharper movement would break the spell which lured him on.

He reached the doorway and stopped. He stifled the gasp of admiration which sprang to his lips. Nothing should disturb the enchantment of this moment.

The light caught Charlotte's face, highlighting her features into a beauty which entranced him. The artist in him desired to capture it as it was at that moment, in which she appeared lost to only the gentle music. But that desire was overwhelmed by the love which wanted to burst from him. It threw into confusion all the thoughts he had had on the way home from Jacob Craig's. Lost in a love for the beautiful girl who drew magical, haunting notes from the piano, he wanted this moment to go on forever.

She looked towards the door. Their eyes met and held each other and read each other's thoughts.

'Hello, Richard,' she said, scarcely above a whisper.

He nodded. 'What is that piece of music?' he asked hoarsely.

'It is part of Beethoven's Sonata number fourteen.' She could see that that meant little to him. 'You like it?'

'Yes.'

She started to play it again. 'Then I shall always play it for you.'

'Our tune,' he whispered.

She smiled in a way as enticing as the music. These were their moments and theirs alone. They shared them, their eyes on each other.

The front door closed. Footsteps crossed the hall. The magic was broken. She stopped playing.

'Did your visit to Mr Craig's premises go well?' she asked.

He did not answer immediately. The question had reminded him of the resolve he had made that his art should take precedence. Should he fight for that or should he succumb to the moments he had just experienced?

'Mrs Campion.' He bowed with over-emphasised formality. 'It did indeed.'

Light laughter escaped her lips. 'So formal?' Her eyes teased him. She kept her voice low as if to emphasise the secret they held. 'Surely after what we have just shared, and after yesterday ...?' She left the suggestion unspoken.

'I think we should forget yesterday,' he replied gravely.

'You do?' She raised her eyebrows in surprise. 'Was it so unpleasant?'

Richard's face reddened with confusion. 'No, no, I did not mean that,' he spluttered, 'but you are ...'

83

'Married,' she finished for him. She inclined her head coyly while holding his attention with enticing eyes. 'Surely that is for me to worry about?'

'And for me. No scandal should touch you. You are too fine a person to be tainted.'

'Then you do think of me. I was right in reading certain feelings in your kiss?'

'Please, Mrs Campion, go no further,' he pleaded. Then, wanting to bring this line of conversation to an end, he added quickly. 'You must excuse me, I have things to do.' He turned away.

With her gaze intent upon him she asked, 'Are we to have a sitting this afternoon?'

'No. I think not. There are some aspects of the portrait I want to explore and settle before we have another sitting.'

'Very well,' she replied making no attempt to hide her disappointment. 'Tomorrow then?'

'We shall see. It depends how I get on today.' He left the studio and took the stairs two at a time as if he wanted to put distance between them as quickly as possible. He was breathing heavily as he flung open the door of his room. Closing it quickly behind him he sank back against it with a sigh of relief, imagining these four walls could protect him from the turmoils which faced him. But he knew it was not so. Peace and comfort could only come from his own determination.

Peace? He gave a short silent laugh of derision. Would he ever find peace again? Wouldn't the vision of Charlotte's beauty, the tenderness of her lips, the smooth touch of her hands, always haunt him? Could time ever be a healer?

He pushed himself from the door and walked slowly across the room to the window. He looked out but his brain did not register what his eyes saw. It was filled with the delicate face he was exploring on a canvas, a face which tormented him with its wistful beauty. He bit his lip and stiffened his determination to see Charlotte only as a person whose likeness and character he was trying to capture with paint to fulfil a commission from her father.

He glanced down. A sketch pad and pencil lay on a small table beside the window. The lines on the paper hit him. They formed a rough outline of a London skyline dominated by the dome of St Paul's Cathedral. It was of little consequence, only a practice drawing, a test of perspective. But the pencil marks screamed at him. Art! This is what you wanted! This is your talent, your gift. Are you going to destroy it and yourself for an encounter with a married woman in which there could be no certain future?

His lips tightened as rage surfaced, his face set grim as he snatched up the paper and pencil. He would purge himself of his illicit feelings by submerging himself in his art to the exclusion of everything else. He swung round, grabbed his hat as he strode across the room and out on to the landing. He moved so quickly down the stairs that his feet hardly touched them; he hoped he would not meet Charlotte again but if he did he would not stop. Thankfully he met no one and was quickly across the hall to the front door which he let swing closed as his footsteps took him away from the house.

Marietta, her attention drawn to a figure who strode across the square, stopped and let the front door of the house click gently behind her. Richard. A flutter of disappointment touched her. He was going out. He would not be painting Charlotte this afternoon. She had been on her way, expecting to chat through another sitting. She had been a frequent visitor and enjoyed her friend's companionship, but to her inner self she had to admit that she was beginning to use it as an excuse to be in Richard's company.

She always found him pleasant, amiable, never intrusive on the conversation between her and Charlotte but ever ready to join in when it merited. She had helped him relax at social functions and she knew he appreciated that. Never once had he gone beyond the bounds of friendship but her feelings towards him brought a hope that one day he might see her as more than a friend.

She frowned. Something was wrong. There was anger in his step and frustration in the set of his shoulders. She felt an urge to help, to try to put right whatever had upset him. She noted the pad in his hand and recalled his sketches of London scenes and people. Maybe he was going to do some more. But what troubled him?

Keeping at a discreet distance, she followed him. It soon became obvious to her that he was making for the river and she recalled that from a certain spot it presented his favourite aspect of the London skyline. He did not let his pace slacken even when the flow of people about their daily business became thicker. Fearful of losing sight of him she closed the gap and only slowed down when he emerged on the embankment and it became obvious that he was looking for a position from which to test his artistic skill.

Not wanting it to be obvious that she had followed him she made a detour so that she could approach him from the opposite direction.

She brought her pace to a stroll when she saw him intent on his drawing. She kept stopping as if interested in the activity on the river, but all the time her real attention was on Richard. Though he was concentrating on his work she could tell from the scowl on his face that his mind was elsewhere, as if he was fighting some troublesome thoughts which had had the temerity to intrude. If they were private then there was nothing she could do except maybe take his mind off them, at least for a while.

His attention had been so intent on the distant scene that she was close before he realised she was there. He sprang to his feet even as she was saying, 'Hello, Richard.'

'Marietta!' He greeted her with pleasant surprise.

'Another of your London landscapes?'

'Yes.'

'May I see?'

'I haven't got very far. I haven't been here long.' He held out the pad for her.

She took it and let her gaze alternate between the paper and the panorama of the city. 'Very good,' she approved. 'I like your sketches in which you capture a scene with few lines.'

He smiled and she was glad to see his frown had disappeared and the scowl had been replaced by the calm, gentle look that she associated with him. 'Then if you'll wait you shall have this. My gift to you for being such a pleasant companion whenever social occasions have brought us together. You have no idea how much I have appreciated your help in a world which was strange to me.'

'I have done nothing,' she blushed, but was pleased at the flattery as well as the fact that she seemed to have had the effect of lifting Richard's gloom.

'You'll wait?' he asked but before she could reply he added quickly, 'That is presumptuous of me. You may have another engagement?'

She shook her head. 'No. I've been visiting a friend and was on my way home.'

'Then we could walk together, if you'll permit me?'

'It will be my pleasure.'

She watched, intrigued, as the pencil swiftly and deftly made lines on the paper and an image of London, as he saw it, unfolded. Beyond the mere representation she saw emerge his feelings for the view. She spoke little, allowing him to concentrate on his art. As he became absorbed she sensed the tension she had witnessed earlier drain away and leave behind the Richard with whom, she now admitted to herself, she was falling in love.

Dare she ever reveal that to anyone else especially when Richard had never openly given her any cause to feel as she did? Could she share that secret with Charlotte? So close a friend might advise her what to do, but with deeper thought she decided, for the time being, to keep her secret to herself.

With her mind so occupied she wandered a little way to stand gazing across the river, leaving Richard happily to his drawing.

Ten minutes later a voice broke into her thoughts. 'Marietta, Marietta.'

She started and turned to see Richard raise his hand.

'Have you finished?' she asked as she approached him.

He did not reply but held out his sheet of paper to her. She gave a little gasp. Her glance at the sketch came sharply up to Richard then quickly back to the drawing.

Her attention was fixed on a picture of herself with the London landscape as the background. She realised he had captured her wistful attitude of that particular moment as well as a delightful representation of her features.

'Oh, Richard,' she whispered, moved by what she saw. 'You have a gift which must never be allowed to die. Such skill, so quick.' She gazed at the picture a moment longer and then held it out to him.

'It's yours,' he said quietly.

'Mine? Oh, thank you. I will treasure it all my life and remember today with pleasure.'

'You flatter my poor effort.'

'Poor? Don't underestimate your talent. I believe you have a great future as an artist.'

'Thank you for your faith. Shall we walk home?'

As much as she did not want to break up the moment she could do nothing but agree.

He matched his pace to hers and she made sure it was no more than a stroll.

'Is the portrait of Charlotte going well?' she asked casually.

'I'm satisfied,' he replied.

'You're on schedule?'

'Oh, yes. I'll have it finished as agreed with Mr Wakefield.'

'Then you'll have to go to Lincolnshire to complete it when Charlotte's husband returns?'

'Yes.'

'And that will be soon, he'll be back next week.'

He nodded.

'Are you looking forward to it?' she added.

He screwed up his face. 'I don't know. I think I'm getting used to life here.' His thoughts troubled him, for this turn in the conversation had made him realise, more markedly than before, that he and Charlotte would be thrown into each other's company much more in Lincolnshire. But he recalled Marietta's comment, "You have a gift which should not be allowed to die." She was right. He must not let anything prevent him from fulfilling that gift. And that could be achieved here in London with Jacob Craig. He must keep that constantly in mind to the exclusion of all those feelings which could jeopardise his future as an artist.

By the time they reached Russell Square he was in a more determined frame of mind as well as feeling calmer and rid of the earlier turmoil. He knew that Marietta had contributed to this and when they paused to say goodbye at her home he said, 'I have enjoyed your company. It turned what had promised to be an unpleasant day into something convivial.' He waved his hand to dismiss the query mixed with concern he saw on her face. 'It was nothing really. Something troubled me and I let it grow out of all proportion. But you put it into perspective and made me see I had been foolish to entertain such thoughts.'

'I am pleased if I was of some help though I wasn't aware that I had done anything.'

'I know, but you did.'

'Will you be working on the portrait tomorrow?'

'Yes, in the morning.'

'With Charlotte sitting?'

'Yes.'

'Then I'll come over. I think talking to me makes it less of a chore for her.'

'You will be most welcome,' he replied, seeing her presence preventing Charlotte from bringing up their relationship. 'Goodbye, and I'm glad you saw me sketching.'

'Goodbye, and thank you for this.' She indicated the paper she had carried with care. 'I will always treasure it.'

He crossed the square to the Wakefield residence. Even as he reached the front door to let himself in he felt a little needle of apprehension. Would he be strong enough to resist any overtures from Charlotte? He must be if he was to be true to himself.

As the door closed behind him he felt an iciness wrap round him and his skin come out in the goose-pimples he had experienced earlier, on hearing the magic notes drifting from the piano. There they were again. They held him riveted. His mind was mesmerised by the music as it flowed smoothly through the same tune which since that first time he had heard it he had regarded it as their tune – his and Charlotte's.

The music drew him. It created a spell he could not resist. He crossed the hall slowly towards the open door, knowing what he would find when he reached it.

He stopped in the doorway. Charlotte sat at the piano. The music swirled around him, saturating his senses, taking him into a vortex of her creation from which there was no escape.

She played on as if unaware of his presence. Then she looked up and, with her gaze fixed firmly on his eyes, she smiled. It was a smile which mixed love, admiration, pleasure, the smile of a temptress who knew without any doubt that the sounds she was creating had woven a bewitching spell around the man who stood watching her.

She played on. He did not move. The notes were repeated. Her eyes never left his. Then the music, so heart-capturing, drew him forward. His steps were slow. Their eyes were locked in an understanding. Then he was close, looking down at her, aware of her hands moving across the keys extracting a haunting melody which he knew would never leave him. Suddenly he leaned forward, grabbed her hands, cutting the music off in mid-note, and pulled her roughly to her feet. His arms swept around her and his lips sought hers with a fearsome passion which she returned.

'Richard! Richard, I love you!' The whispered words stormed his mind, but they had broken the spell and returned a little reality back to him.

'Don't Charlotte, don't.' It was a cry of torment. He swung on his heel and strode quickly from the room.

She half reached out as if to stop him but she held back. Instead she watched him and said to herself with a knowing smile, 'You do love me.' She turned to the piano and as she heard him crossing the hall towards the stairs her fingers idly crossed the keys playing the tune which she knew would be ever theirs.

The notes reached Richard. His footsteps faltered. He knew they were deliberately being played to remind him of what had just happened. His mind was pounding as he ran up the stairs two at a time and ran along the landing to his room. He flung the door shut behind him but could not eliminate the notes completely for they, and the vision of the beautiful young woman sitting at the piano, were reverberating in his imagination.

The following week was not easy. He wrestled with the two desires in his life, one of which could only lead to ruin and scandal but one which he found almost overpowering in its attraction. He fought it by reminding himself of Marietta's advice that he should not let his talent die. And die it would if encouraged by an affair with Charlotte. And what else had he to offer her? He would not only be able to earn a pittance for they would be outcasts and he would never be able to match the affluence she was used to.

He tried to avoid being alone with her but that was not easy. Though she was not aware of it, he deliberately used Marietta as a foil, encouraging her to come to the sittings, saying it relaxed Charlotte and made it easier for him. Charlotte dared not countermand his request for fear of raising suspicion in her friend's mind. They had been so close all their lives that they could read each other's feelings and attitudes unless they were heavily disguised.

When Charles returned from the Continent Charlotte made a strong outward show of pleasure and Richard seemed to have been forgotten. Was his dilemma solved for him? He felt some relief that he might not have to make a choice, but he found himself jealous of the fuss she made of Charles.

The five days after Charles's arrival were a whirl of activity, social meetings with friends, two visits to the theatre when Richard was pleased at Marietta's company but unaware of the pleasure she derived from being with him, and preparations to leave for Reed Hall in Lincolnshire. Very little was done to the portrait and it was carefully crated for shipment north.

'Make sure you have all the materials you want,' Francis advised. 'They won't be so easily come by in Lincolnshire. Reed Hall is a little isolated but that might be to the good – fewer distractions to interfere with painting.'

I wonder, mused Richard to himself.

With sailing at ten o'clock in the morning there was early bustle in the Wakefield household. As Francis and Gertrude had arranged to say their goodbyes at the dockside they were to take Richard from Russell Square to join the ship.

Marietta had said her farewells to Charlotte the previous evening but now in the morning sunlight she crossed the square with a little sadness in her heart. Though she had known that one day Richard would have to leave for Lincolnshire, saying goodbye to him was no easier.

The carriage was already at the door. Mr and Mrs Wakefield emerged from the house, she pausing to give some last-minute instructions to one of the servants, he turning to say something to Richard who followed close behind them.

'Ah, here's Marietta,' cried Gertrude. 'Are you come to say

goodbye to Mr Parker?' she asked with a slight twinkle in her eye.

'Yes,' replied Marietta, breathless with her haste. She turned to him and held out her hand. 'Goodbye. I hope you have a pleasant voyage and enjoy Lincolnshire.'

'Thank you,' he returned politely. As Francis helped his wife into the carriage, Richard took Marietta's hand and added, 'It has been a pleasure to know you. Thank you for your companionship.'

'I have enjoyed our meetings,' replied Marietta, a little dignified while her heart was wanting to cry out her real feelings and to tell him how much she would miss him. 'I hope we will see each other again when you return to London.'

'I'm sure we shall.'

'I look forward to seeing the finished portrait.' She made a slight pause then added in a tremulous whisper, 'And thank you for that sketch of me.'

He smiled. 'That was a pleasant meeting. One day I will do a much better one of you.'

'But that will always be my favourite. It has special meaning for me.'

Richard tried to fathom the look in her eyes but before he could query her remark Francis shattered his thoughts. 'Come along, my boy, we must not miss the sailing.'

Richard started. 'Sorry, sir,' he blustered. 'Goodbye, Miss Kemp.' Richard felt he should address Marietta formally in front of other people.

'Goodbye.'

He climbed into the coach and, even as he settled himself, Francis called for the coachman to get underway.

Marietta watched, her thoughts dwelling on the young man it was taking away and wishing she knew if he had any feeling towards her apart from companionship.

There was much activity on the deck of the schooner, *Lindsey*, when the Wakefields and Richard arrived on the quay. Charlotte and Charles were already on board, anxiously watching for the arrival of the carriage from Russell Square.

The *Lindsey* was one of two vessels which Charles had had at Calais for the shipment of wine to London and Boston. The

Lincoln had sailed straight to Boston with its cargo and messages from Charles for his housekeeper and head butler at Reed Hall about the date of his homecoming and instructions about the rooms to be prepared for the artist he was bringing to Lincolnshire. The *Lindsey* had brought him to London where it had unloaded half its cargo and then prepared to convey him and his wife to Boston.

'All shipshape?' asked Francis as he bustled on board and shook hands with Charles.

'As far as I can see,' replied Charles. 'I leave all such matters to Captain Burgess. He's one of my most competent captains. All that concerns me is that he has sufficient opportunities to keep this ship busy along with the *Lincoln* and the *Imp*.'

'You are certainly doing that. These last two forays to France and Germany are paying off handsomely.'

'You are sure you have all the information you want about the next shipments I arranged?'

'Yes. You have nothing to worry about. I will see that everything goes according to plan here in London.'

'Good man.' He smiled and gave Francis a friendly tap on the shoulder. He glanced towards Richard who had wandered along the deck and was taking an interest in the last-minute preparations to sail. He turned to Mrs Wakefield, who had been in earnest conversation with her daughter, telling her of Marietta's visit to say goodbye to Richard and adding that she thought Marietta rather liked the young man. Charlotte had made no comment and was relieved when her husband intervened to end further speculation by her mother. 'Sorry, ladies, I had some business to attend to.'

'It's always the same with you men,' teased Gertrude. 'But we wouldn't have it any other way.'

'The weather is set fair. You'll have a good voyage,' commented Francis.

'I'm sure we shall,' agreed Charles.

'Have you any idea when you will be bringing my daughter back to London?' Gertrude asked.

'I have no immediate plans,' Charles replied. 'It depends on how things are in Lincolnshire but now that your husband can see to the London end of our arrangements it may not be too soon. In fact I don't know whether it will be this side of Christmas.' He saw disappointment cloud Gertrude's face, and to halt any protests added quickly, 'I've an idea. Why don't you come to Reed Hall for Christmas? And we'll follow it with a New Year's Eve party with all my local friends.'

Gertrude's eyes brightened but a regretful tone came to her voice. 'But we wouldn't know anyone.'

'You soon would,' said Charles. 'If you would feel more comfortable with someone you know, bring the Kemps with you.'

Charlotte tensed. After what her mother had suggested about Marietta, she was about to object but thought better of it. Knowing her mother's ability to unearth information, she wanted no probing.

'Well, if you're sure,' replied Gertrude.

'Splendid,' cried Charles. He turned to Francis. 'Will you extend an invitation on my behalf? I will send a formal one from Boston.'

'Certainly. A splendid idea,' beamed Francis. 'And a generous gesture.' He looked at Charles knowingly. 'I have no doubt Christmas in Lincolnshire can be special.'

'We'll try to make it and New Year something to remember.'

Chapter Seven

'Well, Mr Parker, are you glad to be leaving London?' asked Charles.

They had left the bustling river with its surging sounds and were watching the coast grow smaller. The bow cut through the sea, sending water speeding and hissing along the hull to mingle with the vastness of the ocean.

'It has been a big change for me but I have enjoyed it,' replied Richard.

'That is good. From what Mr Wakefield tells me about your ability, I'm sure Jacob Craig will want to take you under his wing.'

'Mr Wakefield is flattering. How can he feel so sure when he hasn't seen the portrait?'

'He's seen some of your other work and he has faith in that. Would you want to return to London and Craig's gallery?'

'It would be a great opportunity for me and, as my ambition is to be a noted artist, it would be foolish of me to turn down the chance should Mr Craig offer it.'

'There could be clients in Lincolnshire. We have frequent visitors to Reed Hall who might be interested. I think it would be as well to have a portfolio to show them.'

'Yes. I have been doing other drawings in London and I would like to do so in Lincolnshire. I find it not only expands and tests my talent but it is a relaxation after concentrating on the portrait, and I believe that helps the portrait itself.'

'I certainly look forward to seeing it.'

'Seeing what, my dear?' asked Charlotte.

They both spun round on hearing her voice.

'Mr Parker's portrait of you.'

'Ah, you will have to wait. Mr Parker, remember Father has to be the first. Charles no doubt will try to persuade you otherwise when we are in far-away Lincolnshire.'

Charles held up his arms in protest. 'That I should ever think of doing such a thing!' he offered with seeming innocence.

'He'll try it, I promise. Resist him.'

'I want a word with Captain Burgess. Enjoy the sail.' Charles moved towards the stern where Captain Burgess was keeping an expert eye on the actions of the crew as they paid out more sail to catch the fresher breeze away from the coast.

She sensed tension in Richard when Charles left them alone and realised that he still remembered those two shared kisses.

Since Charles's return from the Continent there had been no opportunity to be alone together. Work on the portrait had been suspended amid the preparations to leave for Lincolnshire and Charlotte's determination to fill the time with as many social occasions as possible before she left the capital for the quieter surroundings of Reed Hall.

She knew she would miss London society and the whirl of city life but for Charles's sake she had cultivated a liking for the country life he led in Lincolnshire. She had felt it not only a duty but right to do so. Although his business interests took him to London he was a countryman at heart and had not really entered society in the capital until he had met Charlotte. He knew she enjoyed it so he had fostered a liking for it knowing it would please her. He believed that sharing interests would draw them closer together, for he was always conscious that he might have to counter their age difference.

She had come to like living at Reed Hall and had soon realised that there could be a social life among the Lincolnshire gentry and Boston merchants which could compensate her for the loss of life in the capital.

With Charles back, attentive, kind, considerate, spoiling her, she had begun to look at her life again and to consider the consequences of encouraging her feelings for the young man who stood beside her now. Maybe she could cope with the scandal even though they would be ostracised by everyone she knew. Not only would her life be changed dramatically but

Richard's too. There could be no Jacob Craig's for him, no commissions from the circle of friends in which her father moved. Instead he might earn some coins from drawing and painting Whitby scenes and ships. But could they even settle in Whitby? When it became known that she had left her husband would Whitby folk be just as shocked as those in London or Lincolnshire?

'Are you pleased to be at sea again?' Charlotte asked with a glance at Richard.

'Yes. It's a world of its own but I don't want to make my living from it.'

'You never wanted to be a whaler like your father and brothers?'

'No.'

'Nothing but an artist?'

He nodded. Why did she ask that? He knew if he allowed his feelings for her to dominate, his life as an artist would be jeopardised. The forces against him would be too strong no matter how brilliant his work. Did he want to risk that for the love of this married woman? And yet the thought of never being with her again tore at his heart. Could he ever cope with life without her?

But how did she feel? There had been little opportunity since Charles's homecoming to exchange anything more than a few polite words. But she had never hinted by a look or gesture that she still thought of those two stolen moments. Maybe Charles's return had made her see things differently and she now looked upon those moments as mere flirtation. The coming months might be difficult for him but he would have to cope, for he must finish the portrait.

'Have you ever sailed into Boston?' she asked.

This conversation was far from the thoughts he had entertained. Was she telling him to forget what had happened between them or was she being exceptionally cautious because of Charles?

'No,' he replied, resting his hands on the rail.

She leaned forward and her hand brushed his. Though the touch was slight, yet the sense of joyous pleasure which swept through him was almost overwhelming. His thoughts raced in confusion but the demanding question was, had she meant it?

97

Did she want him to read into it something about her feelings for him?

Then the moment vanished and the ecstasy was replaced by the mundane when she went on.

'It was once a thriving port but it began to silt up. Nothing was done about it and fewer and fewer vessels used it. A few years ago my husband, together with a number of the town's merchants and some local landed gentry, thought of opening up the river once again and restoring the port to some of its former commercial success. The river has been widened and the silt is constantly removed. Vessels are beginning to return but access limits the size of ship, which is why Charles uses small schooners.' She gave a little laugh. 'I see from your expression that you are surprised at my knowledge and that a girl raised in London has taken an interest in such matters.'

'Well ...'

His words remained unspoken, for at that moment she turned to lean with her back on the rail. The movement caused the silk shawl to slip from her head to her shoulders. Richard was transfixed by the beauty silhouetted against the blue sky and enhanced by the shimmering light which gleamed in her hair.

She was aware of Richard's reaction and it pleased her, but she was also conscious of her husband talking to Captain Burgess. She drew the shawl across her head and fastened it more tightly at her throat.

'As you should know by now, I am not one for tea parties and idle gossip. So many women in my station of life see no further than that, content to run the household for their husband and taking no interest in how he makes his money so long as it is there to keep them in comfort. Not for me. I determined when I married that my husband's interest would be mine, as I hoped mine would concern him. They do and as a result we share life together more fully. Also, I calculated that if I knew something of his business affairs I would be in a position to maintain my way of life should anything happen to him, for he has no relatives who could take over the business and estate.'

'Very commendable,' said Richard. He admired her attitude but the information disturbed him. Was it a subtle way of telling him that those exchanged kisses were best forgotten, and that her future lay with Charles?

'That is one thing about the wives of the landed gentry in Lincolnshire: they assert a certain amount of independence and are much more relaxed socially. Oh, they have their tea parties and exchange gossip but there is more to their lives than that. I'm getting used to it. Though there are aspects of London that I miss terribly there are compensations in Lincolnshire. Maybe my marriage gives me the best of both worlds.'

Before Richard could make any comment they were joined by Charles. Richard made his excuses and went forward to do some sketching.

Charlotte's observations kept intruding and breaking up his concentration until he gave up. He sat staring at the sea, wondering what life would bring at Reed Hall.

The weather held fine, the wind set fair and the *Lindsey* made a good run north. As they swung into the Wash, Captain Burgess was even more attentive to manoeuvring the ship. Sand banks could be treacherous and had claimed many a vessel through careless seamanship. He took her through Lynn Deeps and with caution ran between Long Sand and Roger Sand into Boston Deeps. He kept everyone alert as they ran along the west side of Buoy Sand to the Haven, where they began the five-mile run to Boston docks.

'Those are my wharves,' Charles indicated the long quay at which two schooners were tied up. 'The *Lincoln* came straight to Boston from France. The other, the *Bicker*, should be loading with local produce for London.' A proud gleam came to his eyes. 'Trade is reviving here and one day you'll see the port back to its former glory.'

Men were carrying goods from the warehouses lining the quay and the *Bicker*'s deck sounded to the tramp of their feet as they hastened to have the vessel ready to sail that evening. The *Lincoln* was seeing activity of a different kind as the crew with onshore helpers got the vessel shipshape for her next voyage. She was being washed down, her sails repaired and some of her ropes replaced.

Shouts of welcome came from both vessels to greet the

Lindsey and the families of her crew waved excitedly from the quay at which she would berth.

'All this activity never ceases to thrill me,' commented Charles. 'There's something fascinating about a port and its ships. But I expect you realise that, being a Whitby man.'

Richard nodded, recalling the numerous times he had watched ships leave and return to Whitby. 'There's always excitement, sometimes sadness, and we get this especially so when Whitby's whaleships return. That is really something to see.'

'I can vouch for that,' Charlotte put in. 'I wondered what was happening when the streets suddenly filled with people after the cry of "whaleship" passed through the town. Everyone stopped what they were doing to welcome the whalers home.'

'Maybe I'll see it one day,' said Charles. 'Ah, there's Sam now.'

A coach was turning onto the quay and was brought to a halt close to the point at which the *Lindsey* would tie up.

Orders were yelled and instantly obeyed. Ropes were thrown from the ship to be gathered quickly by the waiting men on the quay. Swiftly they were coiled around the nearest capstan and the ship was brought gently alongside the stout wooden quay built of huge timbers. The gangway was run out and, as soon as it touched the quay, sailors, who had already brought the passengers' belongings to the deck, were quickly at the coach where Sam Kyme saw that the luggage was stored properly for the journey to Reed Hall.

Charles, Charlotte and Richard bade farewell to Captain Burgess and were soon seated comfortably in the coach.

It rumbled away from the quay leaving the noise and bustle for the streets of the town itself. People hurried about their business; clerks with messages, butchers calling their wares, a knife grinder making sparks fly from his grinding stone, carpenters repairing the woodwork at the front of an inn while, a few yards further on, a mailcoach was preparing for its run to Louth.

They left the town and the dominant Stump, the tall tower of the parish church, a landmark for travellers in the flat fen country, behind and moved out into the open landscape.

Sam quickened the pace but not so much that it would make the journey unpleasant for his passengers. The two horses were lively but they answered readily to his control.

Richard was interested in the whole scene. Apart from being at sea, he had never travelled far from Whitby. Occasionally he had explored the moors in the vicinity of the port. He was used to hills but here there wasn't a hill in sight. The flatness surprised him and when he mentioned it both Charlotte and Charles were amused by his comment.

'I can understand how you feel, having been to Whitby,' said Charlotte. 'There are hills in Lincolnshire though not on the scale of those we saw near Whitby. Ours are much more gentle and lie further north in the county.'

'My dear, don't forget Reed Hall is on a hill,' said Charles, amusement twitching his lips.

Charlotte gave a shrill laugh. 'A hill. Twenty feet! Can you imagine that being called a hill?'

'Well, my ancestors built it on that east-west ridge to give them a view to the south. And you must admit it gives us a better view than that which some of our friends have.'

'You'll soon be able to judge for yourself, Mr Parker.'

A few minutes later they were turning on to a drive which ran north. Only when they swung right was he able to look in the direction they had come and see that they had climbed away from the flat country which ran all the way back to Boston and beyond. Looking out of the other side of the carriage he was surprised to see a large copse for so far he had been amazed by the absence of trees.

Sam guided his horses beyond the copse and along the drive which swung round the trees and assumed a northward track. It brought in view Reed Hall lying a little to the left a mile ahead.

'There it is!' Charlotte cried out like some excited schoolgirl.

Charles smiled at her exuberance. 'Mrs Campion always reacts like that on seeing home,' he said.

Richard could not be absolutely certain but he thought he detected an emphasis on the word 'Mrs'. Whether it was as a reminder to him that she was married, though he could not see that Charles had any grounds for suspecting what had passed between himself and Charlotte, or whether he was drawing her attention to her schoolgirl reaction, and preferred her to react in a more ladylike manner, he wasn't sure.

The thoughts were instantly dismissed in the moment of seeing Charlotte's country home for the first time. This would be his abode until he had finished the painting.

The gradual ascent, though not great, had taken them above the flat and sometimes marshy ground of the low country. Now they were riding through what he would describe as parkland. There were trees, oak, ash, elm and beech, older than the house itself.

'My grandfather built the house,' he heard Charles telling him. 'And drained a lot of the land between here and Boston. He placed it on this little ridge to gain the best view and face south.'

'A wise man,' Richard commented.

'And astute one,' Charles went on. 'He was an excellent farmer, as was my father, but he saw that by widening the drains and keeping them open they could be used as waterways to transfer local products into Boston. There he handled them as a merchant on the Boston market or used a ship he had purchased to transport them to London.'

'And you still follow the same pattern?'

'Yes, expanding on what my father had developed from what his father had done.'

Glancing at Charlotte, who was still peering from the window of the coach, he saw the sparkle in her eyes which told him that in spite of her town upbringing she loved this place.

He turned his eyes on the house. It was not as big as he might have expected. There was solidity in its compactness, a sense of permanence which even the winds from the Wolds to the north or the blasts coming from the sea to the east could not disturb. The plum-coloured bricks gave it a warm look, a haven in what could be a bleak countryside. It appeared to be of two storeys but beyond the low balustrade there were dormer windows giving a third storey in the roof space. The two storeys each had four large sash windows on either side of the front door set in an elegantly curved wide central segmented pediment.

102

The crunching sound of the wheels and the clop of the horses' hooves must have been heard, for as the coach swung round and came to a halt in front of the house a man, whom Richard presumed must be the head butler, accompanied by two girls, neatly dressed in black dresses, short white aprons and matching caps, appeared. The girls stood to one side while the butler came forward to open the carriage door.

'Good day, ma'am,' he said amiably as he helped Charlotte from the coach. 'I trust you are well?'

'Yes, thank you, Thomas. And you?'

'Very well, ma'am. Everything at Reed Hall is ready for you, I hope to your satisfaction.'

'I'm sure it will be.' Charlotte passed on to instruct the two maids about the disposal of their luggage.

Charles and Thomas exchanged greetings and Charles introduced Richard.

Thomas greeted him politely, hiding his surprise that the artist should be one so young.

'I got your message sent on the *Lincoln*. The room you suggested has been prepared for Mr Parker.' He turned to Richard. 'I hope it will be to your satisfaction, sir, and also the room which Mrs Campion instructed us to make available as a studio.'

'I'm sure they will be,' said Richard.

'Don't make judgements until you see them,' smiled Charles. 'Come along in and we'll soon see what you think.'

When they entered the house, a formidable-looking woman who held herself erect with her hands neatly crossed in front of her was standing to one side of the doorway. Two more maids, similarly dressed to those outside, and a footman holding a tray of steaming punch, stood beside her.

'Mrs Gregory,' Charles greeted the woman pleasantly. 'Ah, punch, how thoughtful of you.'

'Sir, ma'am.' She made a little bow to them both. 'Welcome home. I thought something warming after the cold journey.'

'Thank you, Mrs Gregory,' said Charlotte. 'It is good to be back.'

'Everything has been done according to Mr Campion's instructions from France. I hope it will all be satisfactory.'

'I'm sure it will,' replied Charlotte, 'and thank you for looking after things while we have been away.'

'My pleasure, ma'am.'

Charles half turned to Richard. 'Mrs Gregory, this is Mr Parker. He will be our guest as well as being here, as you know from my message, to paint Mrs Campion's portrait. Mr Parker, Mrs Gregory is our most efficient housekeeper.'

'Sir.' Mrs Gregory greeted him with a friendliness which was laced with the solemnity befitting one who, while enjoying her position of authority, realised she could still be regarded as an employee.

Richard saw that behind his first impression of a formidable woman there was also a considerate, kind person. He saw it in her eyes which were of the softest shade of pale blue. She would rule her staff with a rod of iron but without harshness, and, being aware of their problems, would be considerate and fair.

He was aware that it would be best to keep on the right side of the housekeeper. She would be a better friend than an enemy. 'A pleasure to know you, Mrs Gregory.' His tone was light, friendly. 'I hope my stay here will not be too much trouble for you.'

'I'm sure you will be no trouble at all. If there is anything you need or want to know please ask.'

'That is very kind of you.'

While they had been talking Mrs Gregory had signalled to the two girls and they had helped the arrivals to take off their outdoor clothes.

The footman handed round the cups of punch and Charlotte, Charles and Richard relished the warming effect.

'I told Mrs Todd that dinner would be at the usual time. I hope that is all right.'

'Perfect, Mrs Gregory,' replied Charlotte. 'It gives us a chance to familiarise Mr Parker with the layout of the house.'

They finished their drinks and, as the staff went about their duties, Charlotte moved towards a door on the left.

The judgement which Richard had made when he walked into the house confirmed that which he had made outside. The house had been designed on a grand scale but grandeur had been toned down for comfort and homeliness.

The hall was spacious without being over-large. It ran the full length of the house with a door, predominantly glass, opposite that through which they had come. On either side of it there were windows which, apart from adding to the lightness of the hall, gave views of the distant Wolds.

The door which Charlotte opened led into a magnificent room which ran the full length of the house. Windows on the west side would allow the setting sun to fill the room with a glow which would be ever-changing in its colours. Lightness was added by the windows to the north and south. There was just sufficient furniture for comfort, so that the style of the individual pieces could be appreciated. At one end stood a piano.

They returned to the hall and Richard was shown into a room half the size of the one they had just left. It was cosy, comfortable and he guessed that when Charlotte and Charles were here on their own this was the room they used. A door in the north-west corner led into the dining room, where the oak panelling was matched by the six dining chairs placed round a table in the centre of the room. A second door led back into the hall.

'To the kitchen.' Charles indicated a further door from the hall towards the rear of the house. 'Mrs Todd is our cook, second only to Mrs Gregory.'

If Richard was impressed by the ground floor he was even more so when they came to the first floor via an elegantly curved staircase.

The large windows gave the six bedrooms a light airy atmosphere. They were all of similar size except one which was twice as big as the others. Each was decorated differently, appropriate to its orientation. As with the rooms downstairs there was sufficient furniture without overcrowding. A seventh room shared a connecting door with the main bedroom. It was of similar size, its walls lined with bookshelves, with a desk across one corner and two comfortable armchairs placed on either side of a fireplace. This no doubt was the room from which Charles Campion conducted his business affairs and ran his estate.

'There is another floor, as you will have guessed from seeing the dormer windows,' said Charles. 'The servants' quarters are up there and they are reached by a staircase from the kitchen. Now there are two more rooms to show you. They are at the southeast corner of this floor.' Charles led the way. The first one they entered was a bedroom similar to the others. 'Will this one suit you?'

A little taken aback at being offered such an attractive room, Richard hardly knew what to say. 'It is more than I expected. Are you sure ...?'

'Of course we are,' put in Charlotte. 'You must continue to regard yourself as one of the family as you were able to do in my father's house.'

'Then I am most grateful for your generosity.'

'You must have a comfortable room in which you can escape the task of painting. I'm sure there are times when you will want to,' said Charles.

Richard gave a little smile. 'There certainly are.'

'Very well. Now your studio. I sent word for the room to be prepared. If it is not to your liking then say so.' As he was speaking Charles led the way to a corner room with windows in its east and south walls. It contained a table, two high-backed chairs and a mahogany 'throne' chair, its arms and supports beautifully curved. The brocade covering was patterned with brown leaves and the legs were finished with small brass castors.

'A sitting chair for me,' cried Charlotte with excited surprise. 'Oh, Charles, how thoughtful of you.'

'In that note I sent on the *Lincoln* I told Thomas to find such a chair in Boston.'

'Thank you so much.' She kissed him lightly on the cheek and ran across the room to the chair. 'There, how do I look?' she asked taking up her pose for the portrait.

Richard noted how easily she had slipped into the exact position.

'Wonderful, my dear. If Mr Parker can capture you like that on canvas then indeed he will have a great future as an artist.' He turned to Richard. 'Will this room be suitable?'

'Indeed it is. I cannot thank you enough.'

'Your thanks will come in delivering a good portrait to Charlotte's father. He sets great store by you.'

'I will get settled in, arrange my easel and materials and

then maybe start tomorrow, if Mrs Campion is agreeable?'

'Certainly,' she replied, with a glance at her husband for his approval.

'It will suit me. I have a lot of work to do.'

'Good,' said Charlotte. 'Now, I'm sure Mrs Todd will have that meal ready for us. After that I think a walk within the vicinity of the house will help Mr Parker to get his bearings.'

'A good idea,' agreed Charles. 'If you will take him, my dear. There are things I must see to.'

'Will you be happy here?' Charlotte appeared to put the question lightly but there was seriousness behind it.

'Who wouldn't be? I am indeed fortunate that I have the opportunity to paint in such surroundings.'

They had walked a short distance from the house, Charlotte taking him to the point from which she loved to view her home.

'With nothing to distract you?'

'I hope not.'

'Do you really mean that?'

'If you refer to what happened between us . . .'

'If?' She raised her eyebrows. 'You know I do.'

'Yes.' He hesitated. His eyes locked on hers and she held his gaze, defying him to be honest.

'Well?'

'Charlotte, we know little of each other. Your life has been so different to mine. I was not used to the life you had in London, I am not familiar with it in these surroundings. It was all beyond my wildest dreams. Then painting you . . . that situation drew us together in a way we should have resisted.'

'Should we? Wasn't it destiny that brought my father to Whitby, that took him to the place where you were drawing?'

'If you believe that then you believe that we were meant . . .'

'For each other,' she finished for him when he left his thoughts unspoken. 'Yes, I do.'

'But you are a married woman.' From the anguish in his voice she deduced that he loved her.

'Then our love will have to remain our secret.' She saw he was starting to protest but did not allow him to speak. 'I know you love me. That last kiss told me so.'

He knew how true her words were but he also knew he should resist them. Discovery of their feelings would spell ruin, hers by the scandal and ostracism, his by dishonour and the devastation of his opportunities to become a brilliant, sought-after artist.

But the magic in the girl beside him was overpowering. Maybe they could love each other, enjoy each other's company and no one need ever know if they were careful and guarded in their attitudes to each other when in the company of others.

They had walked into a little hollow. Their hands brushed, lingered and their fingers entwined. Conscious that they were out of sight of the house, Richard stopped and turned her to him. There was no need for words. Their feelings were in accord and each knew it. He drew her close. She did not resist but tilted her face. He was lost in the depth of her blue eyes which in their expression of love for him reassured him that everything would be all right, that their love could not be harmed. His lips met hers in a passion which she felt equally.

As their lips drew apart she whispered, 'Oh, Richard, I love you. No! Oh, yes I do, but I'm also in love with you.'

He looked down at her and smiled. 'But not with Charles?'

'I love him, but I am not in love with him as I am with you.'

Chapter Eight

The following morning Charles announced that he was going into Boston on business and would not be back until late afternoon. Richard arranged for a sitting for the portrait to start at ten o'clock.

He was waiting when Charlotte came into the room set aside for his studio. He had arranged it so that the angle of light which would fall across her was the same as that he had used in London. His easel was set at the same angle to the sitter's chair and his paints lay readily to hand.

When she closed the door she came straight to him. She placed her hands gently on his arms but with a telling touch of love. She looked up into his eyes. 'Yesterday I believe we were honest enough with each other to enable us to handle, in spite of all the obstacles, a love which must never die.'

He raised his hand lightly to her shoulder. 'And I believe that too.'

She kissed him gently on the cheek, whispered, 'Dear Richard,' and did not linger for a reaction but turned and crossed to the sitter's chair.

He watched with love and admiration. If only they had both been free! Now he was lost in her beauty as she assumed her pose and he concentrated on interpreting her complete being, hidden depths included.

They chatted idly about Lincolnshire, Boston and Whitby. The morning passed quickly and after a light lunch, for they would be dining substantially that evening when Charles had returned, they wandered in the grounds close to the house. Relaxed after the morning's concentration they were perfectly happy to be in each other's company.

They strolled through gardens laid out and looked after with tender loving care by five gardeners, who were now busy weeding and planting. The southwest corner of the garden ran down to a small lake created by diverting water from one of the dykes without affecting its use as a navigable waterway for farms to the northwest.

The air was warm and they sat on a seat which gave them a view across one corner of the lake to the house.

Richard studied it for a moment then drew out of his pocket a pad of paper and pencil, which he always carried with him. The lines he drew on the paper soon gave a picture of the house as they saw it. Charlotte watched fascinated as he filled in the details. She admired the skill which not only put the replica on paper but captured something of the atmosphere of that moment. It was a moment that she would recall for she saw that here was a talent which should be nurtured and developed. She saw what her father had seen in Whitby and knew why he was so keen for Richard to come under the influence of Jacob Craig.

Finished, he tore the page carefully from the pad and handed it to Charlotte. 'For you,' he said.

'My thanks,' she acknowledged. 'It will always remind me of this time.' She left it unsaid but she knew it would always bring to mind her thoughts about the advancement of his skill and his desire to become an artist of renown.

'May I do one or two rapid sketches of you?' he asked. 'They could help in the development of the portrait.'

'Of course.'

Richard sketched quickly, not so much with the portrait in mind but in order to capture Charlotte in these moments so that he would always be reminded of the time when they had declared their love for each other.

For the next four days the weather stayed bright and sunny with high white strands of cloud only occasionally hazing the sun. Each day Charles went to Boston, leaving Charlotte and Richard to a morning's work on the portrait and an afternoon in the open air. Life seemed idyllic. Two lovers together, talking as lovers do or sharing silence as only those in love can. They accepted the intertwining of their lives without any intention of hurting anyone. Yet each knew that at some time this situation would change.

They were sitting by the lake when Charlotte broke the tranquillity.

'What will happen when you finish the portrait?'

'A position with Mr Craig, I hope.'

'But what about us? If you go to him we'll be parted. I don't know whether I could bear that.'

'It's what must happen if I want to achieve my ambition. You'll visit London.'

Charlotte brightened a little. 'And you'll have to come to Lincolnshire.'

'But I won't have a reason.'

'Oh yes you will. I'm commissioning you now to do a painting of Reed Hall. I'll commission others and I'm sure our friends will want your work. There's no need for Jacob Craig.'

Richard was silent, thoughtful.

'Well?' She was surprised that he had not immediately reacted with enthusiasm to her idea.

He turned his gaze on her. She frowned, for she sensed a troubled mind.

'But your father will expect me to go to Mr Craig if he offers me a place at his studio. Your husband will expect it too. Maybe we should put an end to this. It can have no satisfactory conclusion. It could lead to you getting hurt and I wouldn't want that. Other people would be badly hurt too.'

'No, Richard! No!' she cried, putting a pleading hand on his arm.

'Maybe I should return to Whitby for good.'

'Forget your career? You can't!'

'It will be ruined if we are found out.'

'We won't be if we are careful. Oh Richard, I couldn't bear life if I was not to see you again. Please promise me you won't do anything rash.' When he hesitated she made her plea again. 'Please!'

'Very well,' he said slowly.

'And we go on as we are?'

He nodded.

111

But their afternoons and some of their mornings together came to an end six days later when Charles announced that all the business which had piled up while he had been away had been dealt with.

'Now I can spend more time with you, my dear,' he concluded. 'I am sorry I have neglected you but I'm sure it has afforded Mr Parker the opportunity to get on with the portrait.'

'Indeed it has,' he agreed. 'I have been grateful for that time.'

'But now I must claim my wife more often,' said Charles. 'You must say when you need a sitting and we will try and arrange it to suit everyone.' He turned to Charlotte. 'I met Henry Sedgebrook in Boston and he has invited us to Westland Hall for the weekend. Just a small party, the Ashtons, Bells and Cravens. I accepted, so I hope you are agreeable, my dear.'

'Of course,' replied Charlotte without hesitation, though regretting the ensuing separation from Richard. Days without seeing him. 'I have always enjoyed Westland Hall gatherings. It will be good to see old friends again. And we must think about inviting them back here.'

'Good.' Charles smiled, satisfied that his acceptance of the invitation had met with instant approval. 'I'm sure you'll find plenty to do here, Mr Parker.'

'Of course.'

On Friday after a light lunch Richard heard the bustle at the front of the house and from his window he watched luggage being loaded into a carriage, the servants rushing about, heard last-minute instructions from Charles to Thomas before Charlotte was helped into the carriage. A maid handed her a rug, then Charles got in beside her, Thomas closed the door and the carriage went on its way.

Disappointed, Richard watched it until it was lost to sight behind the small copse – Charlotte had not even glanced up at his window to see if he was watching. He thought she would for they had not had an opportunity to exchange a private word that morning.

Downcast and morose he flung himself into a chair. Was she not bothered? Was her love beginning to wear thin?

112

Would this weekend show her the way of life which was really hers? Would it show her that Charles's love was more than his? That her husband could give her a social position that he couldn't? Would the intimacy that there must be between them overpower the depth of pure love which he and Charlotte shared?

Such thoughts made him uneasy. He must be rid of them. Drown them with work. He hastened to his studio, jerked the cover from the portrait, grabbed his brush but stopped with it midway to the canvas. He cursed. The portrait was not the way to cast the image of Charlotte in Charles's arms from his mind. He threw the cover back over the portrait, snatched up his pencils and paper and stormed from the house.

Throughout the weekend there was a fury to his strokes as he committed scene after scene to paper. By the time the weekend had passed he had come to regard it as alien, a place which belonged to Charlotte and Charles in which he had no part. Seeing it as hostile he told himself to finish the portrait and be gone. Yet the overwhelming thoughts of the beautiful girl he had kissed, with whom he had shared idyllic moments, poured into his mind and he saw vividly her reassuring, loving smile. Could he ever give her up? Was there no way they could be together without the scandal? Would he always be content to love a woman who was in a marriage which could never be broken?

'Charles tells me you are having your portrait painted.' Freya Sedgebrook, sitting at the end of the dining table opposite her husband at the head, put the statement to Charlotte.

The other guests looked at Charlotte with surprised interest.

'By whom? Some well-known London portrait painter no doubt,' asked Lawrence Bell sitting on her left.

Charlotte smiled. 'Oh no, he's an unknown.'

'Unknown?' Bella Ashton raised an eyebrow.

'Yes. When we were on holiday in Whitby my father discovered him and commissioned him.'

'Bit risky, wasn't it?' blustered Bernard Ashton, leaning against the back of his dining chair and savouring his wine with the thought that you could always be sure of a good wine at the Sedgebrooks'.

'My father trusted his judgement about the work he saw in Whitby.'

'And is he right?'

'I can't tell you,' replied Charlotte, a tinge of mystery in her voice.

'What she means,' put in Charles with a laugh, 'is that no one is allowed to see the painting until it is finished, and then Charlotte's father as the commissioner will be the first.'

'Oh my goodness, your father is taking a chance,' cried Naomi Craven.

'Not from the sketches I have seen.'

'Of yourself.'

'Yes, but from what Mr Parker tells me the portrait will be different.'

'Richard Parker,' put in Charles. 'Young man about Charlotte's age, from Whitby. His father's a whaling captain.'

'So young?' said Patricia Bell. 'I thought he must be someone with experience.'

'Charlotte's father assures me that he has a natural talent,' explained Charles.

'We'll all look forward to seeing some of his work.'

The heavy curtains had been drawn back to let the silvery moonlight shaft its light into the bedroom. It seemed to bring with it a peace and tranquillity in marked contrast to Charlotte's troubled thoughts.

Charles was asleep beside her. He had been attentive and gentle in their satisfying love-making which she had had no thought of refusing. He was her husband, he needed her and she needed him. She knew she could never betray him in a physical way even though at times her body had yearned for the intimacy of Richard's. But now, remembering his kindness, his generosity, the way he worshipped her, his answer to her every need and whim, she wondered at her betrayal. Shouldn't she call a halt to it? If it carried on wouldn't it only lead to disaster, hurting deeply the kindly man who lay beside her in contented slumber? Could she really hurt him, which was what she would do if ever her relationship with Richard was discovered? He didn't deserve that. She loved him, she had to admit, but he didn't make her feel the same way that

114

Richard did. Her love for him went further. She was in love with him. She wanted to be with him always but she did not want to shatter Charles's life.

She was no nearer making a decision when she rose the next morning.

Charles lay back on his pillow watching her, finding sensuousness in the way she brushed her hair. He realised how lucky he was to have been accepted by such a lovely person so much younger than himself. Younger? He envied Richard, the same age as Charlotte. Could there ever be an emotional relationship between her and the painter? After all they were being thrown together, and his wife was attractive and beautiful. Then Charles chided himself for such thoughts. Could he ever doubt Charlotte? No!

Charlotte turned and smiled at him.

His thoughts tumbled. How could he ever have entertained such ideas? Was there not love in that smile?

She stood up from the stool in front of the dressing table, stretched, and drawing her nightdress tight across her small breasts, came to the bed. Sitting down on the edge, she kissed him. Her lips lingered even as she whispered, 'I love you.'

His arms came around her tantalisingly. She threw back the bedclothes and rolled close to him.

Richard rose before her mind and was dismissed. For ever? She did not answer herself.

A young man floated in Charles's thoughts to be banished as he lost himself in the arms of a wife in whom he had implicit faith.

The painting sessions were the only time over the next two weeks that Charlotte and Richard were alone. Charles was free to devote himself to the pleasure of his wife's company and, even on his business visits to Boston and his perambulations of his estate, he expected her to accompany him as she had done in the first year of their marriage. He had seen then she was prepared to cultivate an interest in such things, unlike so many of the young women he could have married, and he encouraged her to do so.

Their friends were invited to Reed Hall three weeks after they had stayed with the Sedgebrooks and Richard knew he would come under scrutiny. They were charmed by his manner and affability and impressed by his talent when Charlotte insisted that he show them some of his work.

By the end of the weekend he had been commissioned to do a painting of Westland Hall and the Bells wanted sketches of their eleven-year-old twins. He had been delighted to receive their approval in this way, and as well as seeing it as a compliment, he saw it as an opportunity to widen his skill while still keeping the February deadline in mind.

The day after the guests had departed, Charlotte came for her sitting.

'Forget the painting, there was a message from the estate manager for Charles at breakfast. He wanted him to go to see one of our tenant farmers. He won't be back until late afternoon. Apart from the painting sessions we have had no time together, and I would like to walk.'

'Very well,' he agreed. He could not refuse the searching look for agreement.

Ten minutes later they were out of sight of the house enjoying the sharp air, their fingers entwined, the feeling of love between them needing no other expression than being together.

'I have always felt like this when we are alone in the studio, Richard, but now I can tell you, so much more appropriately, that I love you so much and I'm so proud of your talent and so pleased that other people recognise it.'

He stopped and she turned to him, her fact tilted. He kissed her lightly.

'And I love you, Charlotte. Oh that you had come to Whitby unmarried.'

'How many times I have wished the same. But there is nothing we can do about it.'

'But we cannot go on as we are.'

'It is the only way.'

'But we'll be found out one day.'

'No. Not if we are careful. Meetings will be easier when you are in London under Jacob Craig.'

'We're not sure if he will want me.'

'I'm certain he will. You are better than some of the artists he's had.'

116

'But if I'm in London and you are here in Lincolnshire ...'

'Not all the time, Richard. Charles has business interests with my father. He has trips to the Continent. Besides, you will have to come here. Remember, I commissioned you to do a painting of Reed Hall and now you have commissions from the Sedgebrooks and Bells. It can all work out very nicely and no one need ever know the love we share.'

'That all sounds so neat but if Charles should find out ...'

'How can he if we are careful?'

'Accidents, a little carelessness, the unexpected, someone putting two and two together. So many things can happen to make him suspicious.'

'I am in love with you and that is all that matters.'

'And I am in love with you. Don't think I am not, but is it all that matters? If we were found out the scandal would ruin you. Your reputation would be as naught.'

'I know there is always a risk but that will make us all the more cautious, careful to act normally in company and ...'

'That is difficult,' he put his own finish to the sentence.

'I know, my darling, but if you are as much in love with me as I am with you you will want us to go on as we are.'

'Oh, I am and I do.' He swept her into his arms and their tremulous lips moved slowly together with a passion which sealed their love.

The year moved on, October bringing the last of the autumn days and November seeing the first touch of winter with some sharp frosts.

Richard saw the changing moods of the countryside as an opportunity to test his ability to capture them with his paints, and to do his studies of Westland Hall and Reed Hall. He spent every day with pencil or brush in his hands. The mornings were devoted to the portrait and during the afternoons, if weather permitted, he would wander the countryside endeavouring to enlarge his portfolio to show Jacob Craig when he returned to London. He was included whenever visitors came to Reed Hall and was sometimes invited on the occasions that Charlotte and Charles visited friends. Life seemed good to him, his one regret being that he could not openly profess his love for Charlotte.

She too had the same sorrow, but with no other alternative, except to leave her husband, she was content to love in the realms of secrecy.

The physical contact of their kisses was almost overwhelming but they realised the destruction they could cause, not only to others but to themselves, if they went further. The love between them strengthened on this final denial. There was no need for a touch, nor even a word, for the shared silences were charged with deep love and respect and they were happy in the times they were able to spend together.

One morning at the beginning of December they were just finishing breakfast when Richard, who had been a little uneasy during the meal said, 'The portrait is progressing to my satisfaction so, if you are agreeable, I would like to go home for Christmas.'

Charles, who had been concentrating on buttering a piece of bread, looked up and only just missed the regret mingling with surprise which flashed across his wife's face. The caution she had exercised all these months took command.

'I see no objection, my dear, do you?' asked Charles amiably.

'No,' she said quietly as she shook her head. 'We are having Mother and Father and the Kemps for Christmas, and there's the New Year's Eve party. I expect Father will want to see Mr Parker.'

'Oh, I'll be back for New Year. Christmas is always the special time at home, New Year is secondary. If I'm not there it would be the first time the family has not been together.'

'Then you must go,' said Charles. 'Giles Craven has the occasional ship sailing to Whitby. I'll see if he has one going about then.'

'Thank you. That would be a great help,' said Richard, preferring that to the tedious journey by coach.

'Why didn't you warn me about Christmas?' demanded Charlotte a little haughtily when she came for her sitting an hour later. 'The shock nearly betrayed us.'

'I know, I saw that look you gave me. I'm sorry, I did not think of what your reaction might be,' apologised Richard sincerely.

'I'm going to miss you, Richard. I had expected you to be here for Christmas.' There was a catch in her voice. 'I did so want to share the first Christmas of our love with you.'

'I'm sorry. I hope you understand. I have not been home since August.'

'I do, my love.' She took his hand and with tear-dimmed eyes looked directly into his. 'I'm only being selfish. I never want you to be far from me.'

'Nor I from you, but there are times ...'

'I know,' she cut in quietly.

'I will be back for New Year.'

'Promise.'

'I promise.' He kissed her lightly on the lips. 'I'll be thinking of you all the time.'

'And I of you.'

Two days later Charles informed Richard that Giles Craven had a ship sailing to Whitby on the twenty-first of December to collect a cargo of hams and whale oil. The Christmas fare of Boston and the surrounding district would be supplemented by the best Yorkshire hams and the feasts would be lit by oil from the Arctic.

'Regrettably he will not have another ship in Whitby until after the New Year,' Charles added.

'That can't be helped, but thank you for arranging the passage north. I might find a Whitby ship which will put in to Boston on its way to London. If not then I will return by coach.'

'You'll be sailing on the morning tide so you'll miss Mr and Mrs Wakefield and the Kemps. The *Lincoln* will be bringing them from London later that day.'

'I'll see them when I get back.'

'Certainly. They are staying a month.'

At breakfast the morning before Richard was due to sail Charles asked, 'The portrait, do you need Mrs Campion today?'

'No. I can get on with my landscape of Westland Hall.' He regretted having to agree but he had to be careful and could not very well refuse Charles's request for he obviously had something in mind for his wife.

119

'But, Charles ...' Charlotte started to protest. She let her words trail away when she gained a grip on her disappointment and realised what he might think if she went against his wishes.

'Mr Parker has no objection,' Charles interrupted. 'And I want to take you into Boston to have a dress made for the New Year's Eve party. With your family and the Kemps arriving tomorrow it will be the last opportunity.'

'Oh, Charles,' she exclaimed. 'How kind and thoughtful of you.' The excitement of choosing a new dress overwhelmed all other thoughts at that moment.

He smiled across the table at her and in that smile there was the admiration and love he felt for her.

Charlotte's conscience pricked her at the thought of the betrayal she was committed to through her love for Richard. She realised that even if ever Richard achieved the wealth to provide her with similar gifts he would never be able to do so, for even secret gifts would be fraught with discovery and denunciation. There was regret in her heart as she went to her room to prepare to leave for Boston to choose the material for her dress.

After the evening meal Richard excused himself in order to make his final preparations for his voyage to Whitby. Charlotte and Charles went to the drawing room where a blazing fire sent out a cosy warmth. Settling himself in his favourite wing chair, a glass of port to hand on a small table, Charles took up his copy of *Northanger Abbey*. Charlotte settled herself with her embroidery on the opposite side of the fireplace.

After a few minutes Charlotte felt irked by the scene of tranquil domesticity in which the silence was broken only by the spluttering of the fire. Tomorrow Richard would be gone. With family and friends she would have to act as normal when all the time she would be aching for him, wanting him near, longing to share the joy of Christmas with him.

She looked across at her husband. He was deep in his book. The light from the oil lamp heightened one side of his face, throwing the other into deep shadows. It enhanced his handsome features but it also emphasised lines which, though she had noticed them before, she had never interpreted as giving him an older look. She immediately found herself comparing his face with that of Richard, young and fresh. There was an eagerness for the future about the young man from Whitby whereas Charles, at this moment, made a picture of satisfied contentment in which he was pleased to remain. Was this what the future would have held for her if she had not met Richard? Her lips tightened. The needle took the thread into the pattern she was creating but she had little enthusiasm for it. Charles sipped his port. He went on reading.

The clock in the hall struck eight. He did not respond with his usual, 'Eight o'clock already?' Surprised, Charlotte glanced at him, then her gaze returned to linger on him. She peered at him. Was he asleep? The book, no longer held by his fingers, lay on his lap. His head had dropped forward, chin on chest. She watched him closely for a moment. He did not stir.

She laid her embroidery down and rose slowly from her chair. Watching him she moved silently to the door. Carefully she turned the knob, eased the door open and paused to look back. Charles was breathing deeply in a sound sleep. She slipped into the hall, closed the door quietly behind her and slipped quickly across the hall to the stairs. She glided up them, feet scarcely touching the carpet. Her heart was racing. What if Charles woke and came looking for her? The thought brought a falter to her step, but almost in the same moment it was gone. He was sound asleep and even if he did wake he would give her a few minutes to return.

She reached the top of the stairs and hurried to Richard's room. Her gentle tap on the door brought no answer. She went to his studio, paused and cast a quick anxious glance back along the corridor. It was still, and the silence of the house seemed to hang a cloak of mystery and intrigue around her, daring her to step over the boundaries of convention. She turned the knob slowly and pushed at the door. It swung open and she stepped inside, closing it with the faintest of clicks.

Richard looked up from sorting some pencils and brushes to take with him to Whitby. He looked dumbfounded. 'Charlotte, what ...?'

She was quickly to him, silencing his words with her own,

121

'I had to see you, my love, to say goodbye. I may not get a chance in the morning.' Her arms went round him, holding him tightly. She wanted to remember the feel of his strong body and when he embraced her she snuggled close.

'But, Charlotte, it's dangerous. Where's Charles?'

'Asleep. Good food, a warm room, his book and port have taken their toll. So I took my chance.' She looked up at him with a smile as if she was enjoying the sense of danger.

'But suppose he wakes and finds you gone?'

'He'll think the obvious.'

'Then you shouldn't be long.'

'Ever the cautious one.' She reached up and kissed him tantalisingly. She let their lips separate for a fraction of a moment, teasing him with their parting, then adding more sensuality when she kissed him again.

His arms tightened around her and she thrilled to the feel of the power he exerted, yet in it there was tenderness and consideration.

'I love you,' she whispered hoarsely.

'And I love you.'

'Don't go. Stay for Christmas.'

He looked down at her, his eyes revealing the desire to agree, but behind that she saw caution. He shook his head slowly. 'I must go. How would it look if I cancelled after Charles had arranged a passage for me? Besides, I have my family to think of.' She pouted. 'Please understand, Charlotte.'

'I'll miss you.'

'And I you. Now you must go to Charles.'

She clung to him for a moment and then, realising he was right, she said with all the sincerity and hope she could muster, 'Come back soon, my love. Have a happy Christmas.'

'And you too.' He kissed her.

She moved reluctantly away from him, her hands sliding across his until, with arms at full stretch, only their fingertips touched, conveying their love and regret at parting.

'Goodbye, Richard.' She was at the door. With longing in her eyes, expressing the desire to stay with him, she opened the door and was gone.

She glided swiftly along the corridor, tripped lightly down the stairs, cast a furtive glance around the hall and in the direction of the servants' quarters, and entered the drawing room to find Charles still asleep. Tension flowed from her and, with contented relief, she sat down and picked up her embroidery.

'You're quiet, my dear,' commented Charles as they drove to Boston to meet her father and mother and the Kemps.

'Just thinking of all that there is to do,' she replied, though her thoughts were with Richard.

'It's all taken care of,' returned Charles lightly. 'There's nothing for you to worry about. You've issued your instructions. Mrs Gregory will see to everything.' He patted her hand reassuringly and pulled the rug closer around her to stave off the sharp December air.

She made a forced attempt at brightness. 'I suppose I'm worrying unduly.'

'Of course you are, my dear. Now forget all the mundane things and look forward to having your mother and father and seeing Marietta again. I'm sure you'll have a lot to talk about.'

As they neared Boston they became ever more aware of the magnificent medieval tower of the great parish church which seemed to hang over the town from where it stood by the river. Charles was lost in admiration of the craftsmen who built such splendour. It was from the tower that he had viewed the town and the river and had been inspired to suggest plans for widening and straightening the river and bringing trade back to a revitalised dock area.

The coachmen guided the two carriages to part of the new development – the quay where the *Lincoln* would tie up.

The ship was in sight and Charlotte, having apparently thrown off the gloom of the early part of the ride, was eager to be at the quayside.

Charles laughed at her new-found enthusiasm and, although there was a chill wind swirling from the water, he did not detain her but accompanied her. Her enthusiasm would counteract the cold and he had seen that she put on her warmest clothes.

'There they are!' Her cry was joyous as she raised her arm and waved at the group of people standing at the rail amidships. Her parents and the Kemps responded with equal delight and she could sense the excitement of her dear friend from the broad smile on Marietta's face.

Once the gangway was run out they were ashore quickly, exchanging hugs, kisses and welcoming words in a whirl of greetings.

Charles, Francis and Simon Kemp saw the luggage brought ashore by two sailors who stored it on the carriages. Charles quickly arranged who should travel in which coach and, a little less than ten minutes after the arrival of the ship, they were heading on the north road out of Boston.

'How's that young fellow getting on with the portrait?' asked Francis.

'Very well, Father,' replied Charlotte.

'You haven't seen it?' There was a touch of alarm in his voice, fearing that Richard might have succumbed to his daughter's persuasive powers.

'No. He is very strict about covering it up before I leave a sitting. And I can't sneak back to take a peep for he keeps it under lock and key.'

'Good for him. Has he done any other work?'

'Oh, yes. He's for ever at it. He's been commissioned to paint Westland Hall and sketch the Bell twins.'

'Good. The more practice he gets the quicker he'll improve and the more he'll have to show Jacob. I put great store in that young man and I look forward to seeing what he has done and having a long chat with him.'

'That will have to wait until after Christmas. He sailed earlier today for Whitby to spend Christmas with his family.'

She did not notice the disappointment which flicked across Marietta's face.

'But he will be back for New Year's Eve, when Charles has planned a party.'

Relief at that news came to Marietta but she still wished Richard was going to be at Reed Hall over Christmas.

Chapter Nine

The sky was grey and overcast as the ship edged nearer the Yorkshire coast north of Flamborough Head. In spite of the dull wintery sea and the cold northeast wind, Richard was relishing the voyage.

On leaving Boston he had been disappointed that he had not seen Charlotte again, but he recalled the risk she had taken to visit him the previous evening. When he returned he must warn her again to be careful, and with that thought he threw off introspection about their relationship. Now, he was heading home for Christmas and a full family reunion.

He leaned on the rail, breathing deeply of the clean sharp air, identifying familiar landmarks. Waves driven by the wind were crashing right over the low mile-long ridge of rock known as Filey Brigg, which stretched like a breakwater from the headland. They were pounding the cliffs at Scarborough where, high above the sea, the ruined Norman castle still defied the driving wind as it had would-be invaders. The towering cliffs stretched northwards. The fishing village of Robin Hood's Bay clung tenaciously to them, its red roofs muted under grey clouds. Richard felt a tinge of excitement as the marker for all Whitby sailors returning home came in sight – the ancient abbey perched high on the cliffs had always been a landmark, a sign that the port awaited its ships from all corners of the world.

He watched it come nearer and nearer and marked, with approval, the captain's handling of the ship as he brought her between the piers and into the river. Home! He hadn't expected to miss Whitby as much as he was feeling it now.

He went ashore among the bustle and activity which was only Whitby's. Folk, recognising him, shouted a greeting and in their friendliness it seemed as if he had never been away.

He hurried along Church Street and climbed the steps to Prospect Place, smiling to himself as he imagined the surprise he would give his mother.

The front door was unlocked as it always was. He walked straight in and through to the kitchen.

'Hello, Mother. Still at it?' he said with reference to the fact that she was preparing a meal.

She dropped her knife and swung round from the table, her eyes wide in amazement. 'Richard!'

He flung his arms round her, kissed her on the cheek and hugged her tight. She in turn held him as if she wanted to make sure he was no ghost. Tears of joy came to her eyes.

'Oh, Richard, are you really here?' There was a catch in her voice.

He laughed and shoved her gently away. 'See for yourself.'

She had to laugh with him through her tears. 'It really is you.'

'Yes, Mother.'

'But how? Aren't you happy in London? Is the portrait not going right?' The questions poured from her.

Richard laughed at her troubled expression. 'Everything's all right, but I couldn't miss Christmas at home.'

Martha sank on to a wooden chair beside the table looking at her son with relief. 'Oh, is that all.'

'All! Isn't that most important?' he grinned, knowing how his mother played things down at times.

'No, no, I didn't mean it wasn't important for you to be here.' She spluttered her apology. 'I meant I was glad there was nothing wrong, no trouble.'

'I know.' He gave her another hug of reassurance and let her know once more that Christmas at home meant a lot to him.

'How did you get here?' Before he could answer she added, 'You must be ready for something to eat.' She jumped to her feet.

'No, Mother. Just a cup of tea now. I'll wait until your meal.'

'But—'

126

'Just a drink of tea,' he broke in firmly. 'Where's everyone else?'

'Your father and brothers were out fishing this morning so are no doubt laying the boat up until after Christmas. The girls are visiting Jane, but they'll all be back for the meal.'

She busied herself getting his cup of tea while he told her he had sailed from Boston.

'Boston?' she was puzzled. 'I thought you were in London?'

'I was.' He went on to explain how he came to be in Lincolnshire and to tell her all that had happened to him.

'So it will be good for your painting?' She had listened intently with a mother's deep interest in the welfare of her son.

'It's a golden opportunity if this Jacob Craig thinks highly of it.'

'I'm sure he will, and I'm sure you are improving all the time. Have you brought anything to show me?'

'I've brought a sketching pad. There are a few drawings in it.' He reached in his bag and passed the pad to his mother.

She looked through it, spending a little time on each drawing. Though she was no expert she was thrilled by her son's work.

'They're scenes of London,' he explained, pointing out any prominent landmark.

She was halfway through the pad when the door opened and Sarah and Maggie came in. Their astonishment at seeing their brother changed to squeals of delight as they hugged him and cried their welcomes.

'Come and have a look at Richard's drawings,' said Martha. As the girls crowded behind her to look over her shoulders, she glanced at him. 'I thought you were doing portraits?'

'I am. These landscapes provide a change and help me develop in a different direction. I hope to concentrate on portraits but, if these landscapes are liked, I hope to find a market for Whitby seascapes.'

As he had been speaking Martha had continued to turn the pages. She came to a blank page and believing that there were no more she flicked the rest of the pages over quickly to make absolutely certain she was missing nothing. The action moved a loose leaf at the end of the pad. As she started to move it back into place she saw there was a drawing on it. She withdrew it completely.

She stared at it, transfixed by the sketch, then remarked, 'A beautiful girl. Who is she?' She glanced up at Richard and saw that a slight flush had come to his cheeks. She made no comment.

Richard cursed himself. He had forgotten that those first sketches of Charlotte were still in the pad. 'That's Mrs Campion, whose portrait I am doing for her father.'

Martha nodded, looked a moment longer at the page, then passed the pad to her daughters. 'You missed the beginning. Now I must get on with the meal, your father and brothers will soon be here.' She pushed herself to her feet. 'Your room is always ready for you.'

'Thanks, Mother.'

Richard picked up his bag and went upstairs. Inside his room he stood for a moment looking round. So different from the rooms he had in Russell Square and in Reed Hall. This was so small that the furniture seemed to be crowding in on him. He never remembered it being as small as this, but then he had never had anything bigger with which to compare it, nor had he experienced luxury until he went to London.

He pulled himself up sharply. He shouldn't compare. He had seen the home of a highly successful London merchant and the seat of a wealthy Lincolnshire landowner. This was the home of a Whitby whaling captain, with a grown-up family still living there. And home it was, and always would be. Here was warmth, comfort and love, a feeling of belonging. It was only now, back among the familiar with the prospect of soon leaving it again, that he was suddenly homesick. Here he felt cushioned from the dilemma which faced him. If he stayed in Whitby he would not have to meet its challenge. But that would mean an end to the portrait. He would let Mr Wakefield down and lose all the aspirations he had to become a successful artist.

His thoughts were interrupted by the sound of the front door opening and his father's voice booming, 'We're home, Martha.' The laughter which was ever on the lips of his two brothers filled the house.

He flung open the bedroom door and raced down the stairs.

'Father! Will! Jim!' he cried as he burst into the room.

They were hardly able to believe their ears.

'Richard!' There was pleasure in his father's greeting as he held out his hand and took his son's in a strong grip. 'It's good to see you.' He slapped his son on the shoulder.

'Will, Jim.' He turned to his brothers and took their outstretched hands in his and amid their laughter exchanged mock sparring punches.

'What brings you home?' asked Will.

'Christmas,' replied Richard.

'Not for good then, little brother?' queried Jim.

'No.'

'Still like their fancy ways down in London?' There was a slight tone of mockery in Will's voice as if he believed the only life was the tough northern one of a whaleman.

'He's not in London now,' said Martha.

The rest of the family turned enquiring eyes on Richard but his mother went on with the explanation.

'He's at Reed Hall in Lincolnshire. Big place from what he tells me.'

'Oh, landed gentry now? What next? Little brother will be getting too high and mighty for the likes of us,' said Will.

Before Richard, who bristled at the last remark, could counter it, his father stepped in. 'Never forget your roots, lad. Never forget us.'

'I won't.' There was such conviction in his voice that it silenced any retaliation by his brothers.

'The meal's ready so let's all sit down. Richard can tell you all about what has happened to him while we eat.'

They all listened intently, his sisters with the excitement of hearing about a different world, his brothers looking for openings to tease him, his father concerned for his son's welfare, and his mother recalling the portrait of a beautiful young woman which had been placed at the back of a sketching pad as if it should not be seen.

Time passed quickly in the pleasure and happiness of a family Christmas. Not one of them would have missed any of the celebrations.

The house buzzed with activity as Martha and her daughters

129

prepared the food for the meals, sending the menfolk out of the way or finding them repair jobs which had been neglected while they were away whaling in summer followed by voyages to the Baltic for timber before the severe winter weather set in.

But all gathered together on Christmas Eve for the traditional evening meal of frumenty. Martha had had the wheat in a pan simmering for a whole day and had then supervised Maggie while she added sweetening, spices, currants and milk before thickening it with a little flour. All appreciated its warmth as they ate it by the light of the Yule candle, with the sound of the Yule log spitting on the fire. Afterwards Christmas cake, gingerbread and cheese put them in the mood for telling ghost stories by the light of the flickering flames.

Christmas Day was fine but cold with a raw wind blowing from the sea making them wrap up well for the walk to the parish church high on the cliff close to the ruined abbey.

On the way home the men made a call at the Black Bull where Richard was greeted by friends as if he was a prodigal son returning home for good. A Christmas dinner of Yorkshire pudding, roast beef and plum pudding awaited them when they arrived home.

Earlier in the month Martha had bought three geese from among those brought by local farmers into Whitby for sale. She and her daughters had made all the preparations so that Captain Parker could keep up the tradition, which he had started when he first commanded a whaleship, of giving a goose pie to each member of his crew on the twenty-sixth of December.

That occupied a great deal of the day for him and his sons and it seemed to slice into the time Richard had left. He was due to take the diligence to York on the twenty-eighth and there change coaches for one heading for London, which he would leave at Stamford and then take another across Lincolnshire until he reached Boston.

The day before he was due to leave Richard took himself off to do a rough sketch of a particular aspect of one of the quays, a view he wanted to work on when he was back at Reed Hall, for he thought it could add to the portfolio to show Jacob Craig.

His sketching went well and he returned home earlier than

anticipated to find his mother sitting alone thoughtfully by the fire.

'You'll be off tomorrow,' she said sadly, as he sat down opposite her. 'I'll miss you.'

'And I'll miss you too,' he replied. 'I've had a wonderful Christmas, one I'll never forget.'

'I'm pleased.' She paused slightly as if deciding whether to express her thoughts. 'But Richard, there have been times when your mind has been elsewhere.'

'No there—' he started to protest but she cut him short.

'A mother's intuition.' She gave a wan smile. 'We mothers can sense when something is troubling one of their children. I've sensed it in you. Oh, you've been happy with us, I know you've enjoyed yourself, but sometimes your mind has been elsewhere as if you were taken up by some problem.'

He was silent.

'Richard, I'm here to help if I can. You aren't in trouble?'

'No, Mother.'

'You wish you hadn't accepted Mr Wakefield's offer? You don't want to be an artist?' There was a little alarm in her voice as if she feared an answer which would shatter her ambitions for her son.

'Oh no. I want to be an artist.'

'Then what is it?' she pressed. 'You didn't say that with the conviction you would have done once. Is there something happening which might thwart your ambition?'

Richard tightened his lips. His thoughts were in a turmoil trying to decide what he should tell his mother.

'A girl?'

He looked up sharply and knew from the intent gaze in his mother's eyes that his sudden reaction had told her the truth.

He nodded.

'You're in love?'

'Yes.' His voice was scarcely above a whisper.

'So what is wrong with that? Why should that stop you being an artist? Is she nice?'

'Beautiful.'

That word, suddenly linked with the thought of his cheeks colouring when she found the portraits in his sketch pad on the day of his arrival, told her the truth. 'The girl in those sketches?' There was an incredulous note to her query as if she did not want it to be the truth.

'Yes,' he replied huskily.

'But that's Mrs Campion! A married woman! Does she know how you feel?' Martha's voice was strong, wanting to emphasise the enormity of the situation.

'Yes, she does.'

'And what does she have to say about it? Hasn't she told you ...?'

'She loves me!' he blurted.

'What? But the situation's impossible. You must stay here. You cannot return.'

'But I've got to. I've a portrait to finish. If I don't then my career as an artist is doomed.'

'It will be doomed if this affair comes out.'

'Mother, it is not an affair. We love each other deeply. We are in love.'

'Does anyone else know? What about her husband?'

'No one knows. Her husband is a nice, kindly man, and that makes it worse. We don't want to hurt him.'

'What do you expect will happen? You cannot keep such a thing a secret forever.' Her voice rose with indignation and passion. 'Haven't you thought of the consequences. There'll be scandal. Your career as an artist will be wrecked. You'll both be outcasts, but it will be worse for her than you. Society, at whatever level, will shun her. Her own family will in all probability disown her. She'll be on the streets to fend for herself. Think what that will mean, and could she do it?' Martha knew she was running on, she had never said as much before, but she had to make a desperate bid to save her son. 'Think hard on it, Richard. Think of what might happen if you don't stay with us now. But if you are determined to return to finish this portrait, tell her immediately that this love between you can only destroy you. Stop it, be strong enough to resist even the slightest hint that it could start up again, throw yourself into your work, live for it and it alone and you might have a chance to pursue the career that you've always wanted. You'll have to be strong and so will she. Weaken once and your lives will lie in ruins without any hope of revival.' Tears had come to her eyes. 'Son, heed your mother's words.'

132

He came and knelt before her and hugged her. 'Mother,' he whispered. 'I am determined to finish the portrait. It is my passport to an artistic future, so I will heed what you say.'

'You won't stay here now?'

'If I did, I wouldn't be true to myself and I would never know if I could become the artist I want to be.'

She pushed him gently away from her so that she could look deep into his eyes. 'Then you will have to be very strong, for love can be very destructive. God help you. You will always be in my prayers.'

Richard said his goodbyes to the family at home with a promise to visit again as soon as he could. His father wished him well, and he detected behind the words a pride in the fact that his youngest son was resolute in the pursuit of his ambition. His brothers teased him, cajoled him to come back to a 'man's life' but he knew it was all in good fun now that they had seen how his ability with a pencil had developed. His sisters bade him farewell with tears in their eyes and his mother made a whispered, 'Remember what I said,' as she hugged him.

He took the diligence from the Angel Inn having paid the extra to ride inside. Even so it was a cold, draughty and uncomfortable journey with the road across the moor roughened by the winter frosts. The horses pulled hard, urged by a driver determined to keep to his schedule. They struggled up the steep and winding hill at Saltersgate before settling down to the steady run from the moors to Pickering. Away from the hills the road to York was some improvement, affording a little less discomfort. Nevertheless the passengers, who had kept up a lively conversation to alleviate the monotony of travel, were glad to disembark at the York Tavern in St Helen's Square.

He was the only passenger staying overnight at the inn and ate a meal of game stew followed by apple pie washed down by a good-bodied ale. Conveniently a coach by the name of the Edinburgh Mail arrived on its way to London and Richard was able to book a seat as far as Stamford where he would have another night's stop to await the London to Boston mail-coach. Its recent route extension to Louth enabled him to alight from it only two miles from Reed Hall.

It was late afternoon as he approached the Hall and with it in sight his mind was beset by his mother's words. His future was in his hands.

His tug at the bell was soon answered by a maid.

'Welcome back, sir,' she said pleasantly.

'Thank you, Alice. Did you enjoy your Christmas?'

'Yes, sir,' she replied with a smile which told him that all had been well during the festive time. 'I'm sure all the people from London were more than pleased.'

'Good.' He started towards the stairs but was only halfway to them when a door on the right opened and Francis came striding into the hall. He had shared a joke with someone for he was smiling broadly and laughter came from the room he had just left.

'Ah, Mr Parker,' he boomed. 'You're back. You missed a splendid Christmas. No doubt you'll enjoy the New Year's Eve party. I hear your painting and sketching are going well. Good man. You'll prove to Craig I can discover talent! I'll have a look at what you've been doing when I get back.' He gave Richard a slap on the back and headed for the door at the opposite end of the hall.

Richard started for the stairs again but was pulled up short once more. The notes of the piano floated gently through the open door on the left. Their tune! It mesmerised him. Charlotte! She must have heard her father greet him and was now making her own special welcome, reminding him of their love for each other.

He dropped his bag at the foot of the stairs and walked slowly to the open door, drawn by the lilting notes. He paused in the doorway. Charlotte sat at the piano at the far end of the long room. The late afternoon sunshine streamed through the windows and highlighted her rosy cheeks and tinted her hair with its warm glow.

'Welcome back.' She smiled a smile reserved only for him.

It went unnoticed by Marietta who, on hearing Charlotte's words, had turned away from the piano, where she had been standing. Her face lit up with a broad smile. 'Hello, Mr Parker. How nice to see you again.'

'And you, Miss Kemp.' He inclined his head in greeting as

he crossed the room to take the hand she had extended to him. He felt warmth in the pressure and saw pleasure in her eyes, and he knew she remembered their meeting by the Thames. 'I hope you have had a pleasant Christmas.'

'Wonderful.' She made no effort to suppress her delight. Though she would have liked to add that it would have been better had he been here, she dare not. 'Charlotte and Charles have been marvellous, and their staff have catered for our every need. Nothing has been too much trouble for them. It's a new experience to spend Christmas away from London but one I have greatly liked.'

Charlotte had been deliberately playing their tune, making the notes soft and sensuous with her gentle touch, knowing the effect it was having on him.

'I trust your Christmas passed agreeably too?' she asked. Her eyes, fixed on him, were wanting to know if the images she had held while he had been away were true.

'Yes, thank you. Our usual family Christmas.'

'Good. And are your family all well?'

'Yes,' he nodded.

'Do you feel sorry to return?'

He knew she was testing him, wanting an answer to the question she would have put if Marietta had not been present.

It amused him to give her an oblique reply. 'I have a portrait to finish.'

She pursed her lips at him in mild rebuke, raised her eyebrows in query and felt her desire to know just what he felt deepen. Had his break from her, his return to his home, altered his attitude?

She was not to know that, the moment he heard the piano and walked through the door and saw her, his mother's warning, which had kept worrying him on his journey, had been completely banished. He could not live his life without seeing Charlotte.

'But there'll be no painting tomorrow, Mr Parker,' put in Marietta. 'There's the party.'

He smiled. 'I haven't forgotten.'

'It's as well we have no snow. The guests will be able to get here.'

'The Sedgebrooks, Ashtons, Bells and Cravens, whom

you've met before, will all be here and staying overnight,' Charlotte explained. 'A couple of more local families, the Bonners and the Soulbys, will also be here for the evening and to see the New Year in.'

'And Charles has engaged four musicians from Boston,' Marietta informed him excitedly. 'You must save a dance for me.'

'I certainly will, but I'm no dancer.'

'Oh, you'll soon pick it up,' she replied lightheartedly.

'I have no doubt you will be a splendid tutor,' replied Richard. 'I look forward to it.'

Charlotte had watched them closely during this exchange. Her lips tightened, annoyed with herself for experiencing a pang of jealousy.

'Maybe Charlotte knows a few steps I don't,' said Marietta, turning to her friend.

'I doubt it,' she replied. 'After all we learned together.'

'I really must let Mr Campion and Mrs Gregory know that I'm back.' He made a slight bow. 'Please excuse me.' He caught Charlotte's eye as he turned and he knew she had been irritated by his attention to Marietta.

As he reached the door Charlotte played a few notes to remind him of their love.

New Year's Eve dawned with a hoar frost draping dark branches and drooping grasses in a fairyland of white. Though the sun was bright there was little heat to contest the frost and the countryside was clothed all day in an entrancing cloak.

Seeing it from the window of his room Richard felt the urge to capture it on paper. He knew just the place, a short distance from the house, where a dyke was diverted to take water to the lake.

Breakfast was an informal meal and when Richard arrived in the dining room Marietta was alone.

'You're up early,' he commented.

She smiled. 'So are you.'

'I saw beauty out there and want to capture it on paper.'

'I wish I had your ability to do that, but I haven't so I can only walk, observe and hopefully remember.'

'You are going to walk now?'

'Yes.'

'Then come with me, if you wish.'

'That would be a pleasure.' Marietta's heart raced, silently thanking him for creating this opportunity for them to be together.

They had almost finished their breakfast before anyone else appeared. Francis, keen for Richard to impress Jacob Craig, was pleased to hear that the young man was about to leave on a sketching expedition.

Five minutes later, Marietta and Richard, suitably clothed against the sharp air, met in the hall and left the house by the front door.

Charlotte, who had just finished dressing, looked out of the bedroom window and was startled to see them walking away from the house. Her eyes narrowed. Had this been arranged or had it evolved from a chance meeting, maybe at breakfast? She was furious with herself for not being down sooner, but what could she have done? She was going to be engaged all morning, seeing that everything was ready for their guests, though she had every faith in Mrs Gregory. And in the afternoon she would have to be available to meet the visitors on their arrival. When would she get Richard to herself? Marietta would be here another three weeks, and, having just seen them together, she was beginning to think that her friend rather liked the young man from Whitby. Hadn't she exuded excessive pleasure when Richard arrived yesterday? Or was this her imagination playing tricks with her?

She tried to interest herself in everything that was happening, and there was plenty going on as Mrs Gregory discussed the preparations, recalling the days when Mr Charles's father gave parties at Reed Hall. But her mind kept wandering to Richard and Marietta and wondering what they were doing.

'Is this your first time at Reed Hall?' asked Richard as he courteously directed Marietta along the path to his chosen place.

'No, I came shortly after Charlotte returned from her honeymoon and Charles was going to be away on business.'

'It's a beautiful place,' Richard remarked.

'Yes, and I didn't expect it to be so attractive in winter. I look forward to seeing your interpretation.'

137

'I'll never be able to do it justice.'

'You're too modest. You shouldn't be. You should have faith in your talent.' Marietta's voice strengthened with purpose. 'You can achieve so much through your art. I know it.'

Richard smiled. 'Thank you for your belief in me. I hope I can live up to it.'

'I'm sure you can.' She paused slightly and then added, her voice soft, full of sincerity, 'If ever there is anything I can do to help, you only have to ask.'

'Thank you. You are so kind.'

'I want to see talent and ambition fulfilled.'

They walked in silence.

Though he had cast aside his mother's warning when he had seen Charlotte at the piano, he found himself remembering it now. He needed time to think, time to get the portrait finished without becoming too deeply involved with Charlotte. Maybe Marietta was the answer. Maybe he could arrange it so that she unknowingly, acted as a chaperone.

'Here we are,' he said.

The path had dipped between some bushes to the side of the dyke. Low, frost-painted willows hung over the frozen water. Tall grasses and reeds, heavy with hoar frost, arched from the banks. The frozen water glistened diamond-like in the cold sunshine.

'It's beautiful,' whispered Marietta as if anything louder would shatter the picture into a thousand pieces.

Richard took off his heavy coat and spread it on the stump of an old tree, felled when the dyke had been drained to facilitate a better flow of water.

'You'll be cold,' protested Marietta.

'I knew this was here so I came prepared. I've plenty on to keep me warm.'

They sat down beside each other. He started to paint. She watched in silence, admiring his skill and concentration. She followed every line, matching it with the real thing. She saw the picture grow and take shape. She saw the colours glow and sparkle, with the white portraying the hoar frost as he saw it. On the paper the frozen water shimmered with a light which captured the magic of this winter's day.

Marietta knew these moments she shared with Richard would always live in her memory, as would that day by the Thames. She would like nothing better than to be with him on many, many more of his drawing expeditions.

Richard made one last stroke of the brush, leaned back and held the paper at arm's length.

'That's wonderful,' she said with deep admiration.

He gave a little grunt of satisfaction. 'Not bad.'

'Not bad?' she cried indignantly. 'The touch is expert.'

He gave a small laugh. 'You like it?'

'I adore it.'

'Then it shall be yours.'

'Oh, Richard, I couldn't. You've spent so much time.'

'Good practice time. It would please me if you had it.'

'I am most grateful. It will be a memento of a very pleasant morning spent with you.'

'There is only one thing I would ask.' He hesitated.

'Then ask it,' she encouraged him.

'I would like it to be in the portfolio I show to Jacob Craig.'

'Of course you must have it. Just let me know and it shall be yours.'

'Only a loan,' he reminded her. 'It is my gift to you.'

'I said if ever there is anything I can do to help your career you only have to ask.'

'Thank you,' he said. 'And may I say how much I have enjoyed your company both here and beside the Thames.'

'It has been my pleasure too.' Her dark eyes searched his and saw his were warm with a friendship which she secretly hoped might turn into love.

'Should we be getting back?'

Reluctantly she had to agree.

'If this dyke is frozen then maybe the lake will be suitable for skating. Let's go back that way and see,' she suggested.

He nodded his agreement as he put his coat on. 'You skate?'

She laughed at his surprise. 'Oh, yes. Charlotte and I learned together.'

'But where?'

'The lake in St James's Park. We both became quite competent. I take it you don't skate.'

139

He shook his head. 'I never had the opportunity.'

'Well, if the lake is frozen we will rectify that,' she said with a determination which would not be challenged.

The ice on the lake shimmered in the sunlight, and when Marietta tested it carefully she was able to pronounce it suitable for skating. 'So long as the cold keeps the sun's temperature down,' she added cautiously.

Richard examined the sky with the eye of a sailor. 'I would say that the frost will continue for a few more days yet.'

His pronouncement brought an excited clap of her hands from Marietta. 'Good, good. Then I'll teach you to skate.'

When they reached the house they found it a hive of activity. Lunch was being set in the dining room. Maids were making the last-minute preparations for the visitors. Charlotte and Charles were discussing the seating arrangements for the evening meal with Thomas and Mrs Gregory.

Charlotte saw Richard and Marietta return, their faces glowing from the exhilarating walk in the frosty air. Charlotte found herself resenting what they had shared, but outwardly she kept her reactions under control.

'Welcome back, you two,' she called brightly.

Richard made no reaction to her greeting but Marietta did not disguise her glee.

'We came back by the lake. It's frozen. Suitable for skating, Charlotte. I'm going to teach Mr Parker.'

'Good. Tomorrow afternoon, when everyone's recovered from tonight, we'll have a skating party.' Charlotte made her enthusiasm sound genuine though she was inwardly annoyed that her friend had commandeered Richard for the ice. 'Charles, dear,' she called over her shoulder, 'that will be all right, won't it?'

'Of course, anything you wish,' he replied.

'And look what Mr Parker has done for me,' said Marietta, her eyes bright as she held out the painting for Charlotte to see.

'Beautiful,' Charlotte agreed, though she shot Richard a glance which put the question, 'Why for her and not for me?'

He gave an almost imperceptible shrug of the shoulders which he hoped she interpreted as meaning, 'I could do nothing else.'

Charlotte handed the painting back to Marietta who said, 'I must show it to Mother and Father.'

'They're in the drawing room,' she replied. As Marietta hurried away Charlotte turned her attention back to her husband. 'Are we satisfied with the seating for tonight?'

'I think it is all settled.'

'Good.'

'And you know the wines to use, Thomas?' Charles asked.

'Yes, sir. I have them laid as you instructed.'

'Luncheon in half an hour, ma'am?' asked Mrs Gregory.

Charlotte knew it was more a statement than a question seeking her approval. Mrs Gregory was a stickler for timing and Charlotte knew that the housekeeper was certain everything would be ready in half an hour. 'Very well,' she replied.

Charles had already started towards the drawing room, but Charlotte, aware that Richard was making for the stairs, called quietly after him. He stopped on the second step at the sound of his name and turned. She paused, her hand on the rail.

'I've not seen you alone since you returned yesterday,' she whispered, her tone containing a plea for him to put that right as soon as possible.

He was so startled by her making this statement now that he glanced in the direction of her husband, half expecting him to have heard and to turn and demand to know the meaning behind her words.

'There has been no opportunity,' he replied coolly.

'You make your own opportunities,' she said. Her eyes were restless, searching his face for his feelings. 'I was frightened that your visit to Whitby might have changed what there was between us, but I realised I was foolish to entertain such an idea when I saw your reaction on hearing our tune. Yet you sought to go painting this morning accompanied by Marietta.'

'We have to be careful, especially now there are more people about.' He could not hold back from the love expressed in the blue eyes which challenged him to meet that love head on. 'Our chance will come,' he said with an expression which indicated he would create an opportunity.

'Thank you,' she whispered. 'I must go.' Her smile reflected her feelings for him, but she changed it to one of

141

mere enjoyment of life as she turned to follow her husband to their guests in the drawing room.

Luncheon passed off lightly and quietly as if everyone saw it as a lull before the gaiety which would come later. They seized on the following hour as a time in which they could relax until the new arrivals demanded their attention.

Richard retreated to his studio and awaited the result of whispered information to Charlotte as they left the dining room.

He had been idly passing a pencil across a sheet of paper for ten minutes when the door opened and Charlotte hurried in, with a furtive glance back along the corridor as she quickly closed the door. He dropped his paper and pencil on the table beside him and stood up to meet her rush into his arms.

'Oh, Richard, I missed you so. Don't ever leave me again.' She pressed herself close to him looking up pleadingly into his brown eyes which gazed back at her with admiring tenderness.

'I missed you too,' he whispered.

Their lips met in a deep expression of love, driving away both their fears that something might mar the love they felt for each other. That love was almost overwhelming, needing only a spark for them to throw caution away and proclaim their feelings to the world. They only drew back when she remembered her husband, a man she loved and did not want to hurt, and he recalled his mother's warning of the consequences of not controlling his feelings for a married woman.

'I love you, Richard. Oh why was I married when we met?' She half turned away as if in desperation she could find an answer.

'And I you.' He kissed her gently. 'But what is, is.'

She grasped his arm. 'Unless we risk scandal and are prepared for people to shun us, we can do nothing.'

'I won't have your name dragged through all the bitterness there would be.'

'Then we go on as we are.'

He frowned and could do nothing to hide the trouble reflected in his eyes. 'But the risk to you?'

'And what about you? Your career would be in jeopardy.'

'It's your reputation which matters most.'

142

She pressed both his arms tight. 'I am willing to take the consequences if ever our love for each other is discovered, if you agree to go on as we are.'

He gave a wan smile. 'I must match such love. My career as an artist will be bound by what happens in the future.'

'And if we are careful neither of us should suffer and no one else either. Now I can go on knowing how much you are in love with me. But I could not go on not knowing that.'

He bent forward, whispering 'sweet Charlotte,' and kissed her.

For two lovers lost in each other the next hour passed all too quickly and they were drawn back to the New Year's happenings by the sound of hooves, the grind of wheels and the creaking of leather. They went to the window and saw the first guests arriving.

'I must hurry,' Charlotte cried. She kissed him and as she turned for the door she noticed the sketch on the table. It only required a glance for her to see Marietta's likeness. She was startled but she said nothing, for, with guests arriving, there was not time.

As she sped along the corridor to the stairs her mind dwelt on the picture. Had Richard feelings for Marietta? Why else would he sketch her? She chided herself for letting jealousy raise its head. Artists will draw anything and anyone. And hadn't he just declared his undying love for her?

By the time she reached the bottom of the stairs her thoughts were composed again with the reminder that Richard was hers.

Chapter Ten

Richard stood at the window watching Freya and Henry Sedgebrook alight from their carriage, helped by two footmen with maids waiting to escort them inside. Charles greeted them gracefully and with obvious delight at welcoming two friends of long standing to his home.

He saw a smiling Charlotte burst on the scene with an effervescent spirit as if everything at Reed Hall was perfectly normal. And so it would seem to everyone; only he and Charlotte knew of the secret kept below the surface which if exposed would shatter the idyllic scene for ever.

He waited at the window while another carriage turned on to the final portion of the drive which curved past the front of the house. He saw Patricia and Lawrence Bell greeted with the same cordiality which had been afforded the Sedgebrooks.

He liked both these families, not because they had given him commissions, but he had found them exceptionally friendly, with none of the snobbery he had half expected from the Lincolnshire landed gentry. He could see why Charles encouraged their friendship, and that of the Ashtons and Cravens, for they all had the same demeanour and inclinations. He had no doubt that the strangers whom he would meet later, the Soulbys and Bonners, would be of the same mould, people who had the same views as Charles about the management of the land and the trading possibilities out of Boston.

So it proved, for he felt at ease with them as soon as he was introduced when he arrived in the drawing room, where drinks were being served prior to the evening meal. They were interested in his art, particularly Norman and Elsa

Bonner who were collectors of seascapes.

'You must see Mr Parker's seascape which he did during his Christmas visit to his family in Whitby,' insisted Charlotte, who, knowing of the Bonners' interest, had made the introduction.

As she moved away to circulate with the other guests, the Bonners asked him about his connections with Whitby. On hearing that his father was a whaling captain they enquired if he had any painting of whaleships either in port or preferably with an Arctic background. On hearing that he had some drawings and sketches which, though not complete, could be developed, they became even more interested.

As people moved around he found himself alone for a moment. He was considering the possibilities of his art work developing here in Lincolnshire and wondering if there was any need to go to Jacob Craig, when Charles came to him.

'Mr Parker, would you please escort Miss Kemp to the dining room? Everyone else is paired off, you are the only two alone.'

'Certainly, it will be my pleasure,' he responded. Glancing round the room he saw Marietta just finishing a conversation with her mother, who moved away to her husband.

'Marietta, Mr Campion has asked me to be your escort.' He bowed with a pleasing smile.

'I am more than delighted, I am flattered,' she replied gracefully, her eyes conveying the impression that she regarded him as more than a mere escort.

A gong sounded in the hall and the head butler appeared in the doorway to announce, 'Dinner is served.'

Amid the buzz of conversation escorts sought out their partners and in twos followed Charlotte and Charles into the dining room. There were admiring glances at the elegant silver and crystal sparkling in the light from the candelabra and oil lamps. Places were quickly found from the names on the place cards so neatly written in Charlotte's exquisite copperplate hand.

Richard found himself with Marietta on his left, a positioning insisted on by Charles outreasoning Charlotte with the fact that, apart from herself, they were the two youngest and had known each other in London. To his right he was pleased to have Elsa Bonner for he liked this bright-eyed woman whom he judged to be maybe only ten years older than himself. Her lilting voice was captivating and he had been astonished at her knowledge of the sea. Now he thought he could learn where she had acquired it and if this was the reason for her interest in seascapes. Opposite him was Mrs Kemp with Francis Wakefield on her right and Bernard Ashton on her left.

As he glanced around the table, with Charles at the head and Charlotte at the bottom, he realised how carefully the seating had been arranged for no one could feel isolated or unable to converse with those near them, even though they might only have met for the first time. Footmen and maids were stationed strategically around the room, ready in an instant to pander to the wishes of the guests.

As soon as everyone was seated, bowls of steaming vegetable soup were brought in and each guest was served individually at the table. Entrées of cutlets and tongue, with a variety of sauces and pickles, followed. The principal dish of the main course, a succulently cooked sirloin of beef, its aroma teasing the palates of the diners, was paraded round the table for all to see before being placed on the sideboard to be carved. A leg of lamb was put to one side of it and to the other, geese and partridges. As these were being served to each guest, choice dishes of vegetables, carrots, spinach, cabbage, all boiled and buttered, were brought to the table and placed beside dishes of beetroot and red cabbage, both in vinegar, which added a red colour in contrast to the greens. Roasted potatoes were served either plain or sauced with sack and sugar. Pork pies, with tempting browned crust, were sliced and placed for the guests to help themselves.

The meal was leisurely with a short break between courses so that everyone's palate was given time to enter into the right mood for the next one.

There were cries of approval when dishes of plum pudding, flamed with a touch of brandy, were brought in to go alongside colourful jellies, syllabubs, and fruit tarts, with whipped cream available for those who wished to make the dish even richer.

Appropriate wines, both home-made and those imported by Charles from France, were served with each course.

146

Though he had a good appetite, Richard was amazed at the capacity of those around him. But he was even more taken by the luxury of it all and compared it with the much simpler meal, though just as enjoyable, he had shared at Christmas with his family in Whitby. His mother would have been astonished at the quantity and variety of food which graced the table in Reed Hall this New Year's Eve.

The meal had started at five o'clock and finished at eight after which the hosts and their guests adjourned to the long west room where the musicians from Boston, having partaken of their meal in the servants' dining room, where already playing quietly.

Marietta took Richard's arm as he dutifully escorted her from the dining room. She had learned more about him during the meal and she was pleased that he had adapted so well to his new life and surroundings without forgetting his roots. She felt even more drawn to him and she hoped that when he returned to London she would see him more often.

An area had been cleared for dancing but the guests waited for their host and hostess to take the floor first. They, knowing their guests would rather like their meal to settle somewhat before taking more vigorous activity, allowed time for conversation. People sat in groups or circulated, but Marietta made sure she held Richard's attention by displaying her knowledge of London and offering to show him subjects which she thought would be suitable for his pencils.

Richard noticed Charlotte, who was talking to Elsa Bonner, glance in his direction. Catching his eye, she beckoned him over. He made his excuse to Marietta, who wondered why Charlotte should want him. When he joined the two friends, Charlotte suggested that this might be the appropriate time to show Elsa his seascape.

He escorted the two ladies to his studio where he placed his seascape on an easel for better viewing. Elsa studied it without speaking, and Richard and Charlotte respected her wish to make no immediate comment. Then, when she nodded slowly, they both felt relief, for they read that she approved of the painting.

'It is truly wonderful. The dark sky against the white of the foaming waves is really atmospheric but the thing that makes the picture for me is the fact that in those distant cliffs you have shown a break and that, together with the hint of a building on the cliff top, speaks of home. I am drawn into the picture as if I was sailing for that gap beyond which there is home and safety from the brewing storm. And that to me symbolises that there will always be a haven somewhere from the troubles of life.' She paused, still looking at the picture with a concentrated and admiring gaze.

Richard waited a moment then broke the silence. 'Thank you for those kind words, Mrs Bonner. I am so glad you like it.'

She waved a hand as if to dismiss his thanks and, still looking at the picture, said quietly, 'I must have it, Mr Parker. I really must. I have a place where it will hang perfectly and always remind me that there is hope in the future.' She looked up. 'May I bring my husband to see it?'

'Certainly.'

She nodded and started for the door.

'You can find your way?' Charlotte queried.

'Yes.' With that she was out of the door.

As soon as it clicked shut Charlotte turned to Richard. 'You have enjoyed the evening so far?' The questions came a little tentatively.

'Yes.'

'I caught you looking thoughtful a few times and I thought maybe ...'

'Oh, yes, it all made me think of what you would lose if ever our love was discovered, all the opulence, the luxury, those friends, this house, this land, your home in London, but, more than anything, you would become estranged from your father and mother, and lose the love of a kindly and considerate husband. I can't let you risk all that.'

'I thought something was troubling you.'

'I could never give you the same standing, the same wealth, even if our relationship was accepted, which of course it can never be. And even if we went far away I could never provide this sort of life.' He imbued his words with feeling, trying to make her see their relationship in this light.

'Richard, you must never think like that again. My love for you in strong enough to withstand any adversity.'

148

'It is easy to say that now, in the comfort of your home with only the two of us sharing the secret, but what would it be like in the light of discovery?'

'It would be as strong.' She grasped his arms and looked deep into his eyes. 'Believe me, it would.'

He looked down at her upturned face and saw it fill with pleading for him to believe her. The look shattered his reason. This was the girl he loved. All rationality was drowned in their blue depths. He drew her closer and kissed her.

'We were meant to be together,' she whispered as they drew apart on hearing voices in the corridor.

Norman Bonner followed his wife into the room. 'Now where is this painting that's taken my wife's fancy?' he said breezily. He moved to view it from the most advantageous point. He made his assessment quickly, grunted and said, 'And mine too. Mr Parker, I'll buy that painting.' He held up his hands to stop any word from Richard. 'Price? We'll not talk of mundane things on this night of enjoyment. That delightful Miss Kemp has told me that there is to be skating on the lake tomorrow.' He turned to Charlotte. 'May we invite ourselves?'

'Of course,' she agreed. 'I was going to extend the invitation to all later.'

'Splendid,' cried Norman heartily. 'We'll talk money tomorrow, Mr Parker. You said you had some others, have we time to see them?'

'We shouldn't delay Charlotte from her guests,' said Elsa.

Norman raised his eyebrows at Charlotte. 'Just a quick look?'

Charlotte laughed. 'A few moments.'

Richard flicked his sea pictures over quickly. Though they would have liked to look at each one for longer they knew they must not at this particular time. Having seen the ten Richard had brought with him from Whitby, they were impressed and arranged to have a longer look at a later date. With the possibility of a sale Richard agreed not to sell any of them to anyone else.

They returned downstairs where Marietta, taking Richard to one side, was eager to learn if he had made a sale. She was delighted at his news and passed it eagerly to Francis who was equally warm in his congratulations, seeing it as a confirmation of his judgement.

The rest of the evening passed with enjoyment. Pleasant conversations, joking laughter, dancing, when Marietta seized the chance to teach Richard, charming music which Charlotte took up at the piano while the musicians had a break for more food and drink. Throughout the evening there was a continuous flow of sweetmeats, biscuits and chocolates and drinks of every kind.

There was momentary hush as the grandfather clock in the hall boomed the first midnight note, then hilarity broke out as everyone wished everyone else a happy new year and the married couples exchanged kisses.

When Marietta faced Richard she added, 'May this new year bring you everything you want.'

Richard smiled. 'Oh that it would. And may you have every happiness.'

'A happy new year you two,' Charlotte interrupted gaily. She and Marietta hugged each other. She turned to Richard and with Marietta out of hearing, merrily accepting someone else's good wishes, Charlotte whispered, 'May 1821 be a year of our growing love.'

As he lay in bed two hours later Richard reflected on the good fortune which had come his way in 1820 and hoped it would continue in 1821. He had sold pictures, he had gained commissions, he was promised an introduction to Jacob Craig, one of the leaders in the art world. Everything he had ever dreamed of was moving his way and the only way he would jeopardise it would be if the love he and Charlotte shared was discovered. He recalled his mother's words and knew that he should follow her advice, but, even as he was starting to make a resolve to do so, his love for Charlotte forced its way more strongly into his mind. Then he reminded himself that he could never give her the life she was used to. But hadn't Francis Wakefield started out with nothing? Hadn't he been in a worse position? Hadn't he succeeded in spite of life being stacked against him? If he had done it so could he. But, he recalled, no scandal had touched Francis as it could him.

With these troubled thoughts he fell asleep.

Only a short distance away Charlotte lay with her husband. In the feeling of well-being and contentment at a successful party they had made love, gentle, then demanding and passionate. Charles was now asleep but Charlotte had found a conscience. She knew how much the man beside her loved her. She knew how much he appreciated the change their marriage had brought to his life. She knew he wanted nothing more than that she love him. 'Yes, I do.' The words were formed convincingly on her lips. She didn't want to hurt him. He didn't deserve that. But that is what would happen if her love for Richard was ever revealed. She couldn't bear to think how Charles would be devastated, and how he might be ridiculed even by some people who respected him now. That would wound him terribly. She couldn't let that happen. But could she give up the man with whom she was in love?

That conscience was still with her the next morning, but it did not help to see Marietta teaching Richard to skate. She should have been teaching him, she should have been holding his hands, supporting him, been close to him. Her mind was jerked from the scene when Charles skated up to her to stop with a flurry as his skates flaked the ice.

'Come on, my love, don't look so glum. The ice is perfect for skating.' He held out his hands to her.

She started out of her reverie. 'Oh sorry. I was miles away.'

'Anywhere particular?' He smiled his query as she took his hands.

She gave a little laugh. 'I really don't know what I was thinking.'

They pushed off, moving into a graceful rhythm as they glided across the ice. The harmony of their movement struck Charlotte. They were perfect on the ice together, just as that harmony seemed to stretch into all their life. But, even as that came upmost in her mind, she recalled the kisses of the man who had filled the niche which she had felt had always been empty in her life. She had loved but when Richard came into her life she had experienced a new sensation and knew that she was truly in love.

151

Laughter filled the frosty air as everyone, suitably clad against the cold, circled the lake. Experts showed their talents and helped the less experienced or the outright beginners like Richard. They all drank the hot punch brought from the house, and welcomed the Soulbys and the Bonners who arrived with their skates and were soon gliding on the ice.

The spirit of enjoyment continued throughout the luncheon after which everyone was left to their own devices. Some went for a rest, others for a walk and those not inclined to do either played cards or relaxed in conversation. The Bonners seized this time to look at Richard's unfinished sea paintings and sketches. After a lot of careful consideration and discussion they chose, to Richard's utter delight, three unfinished pictures of whalers in the Arctic and one portrait of a harpooner about to dart his harpoon at his quarry. The Bonners paid him a price which satisfied both parties for the finished seascape they had purchased yesterday, and Richard promised them they would have the others completed in the manner discussed.

When he came downstairs, Charlotte, who had been keeping an eye open for his arrival, excused herself from the Sedgebrooks with whom she was talking.

'Well, were the Bonners interested?' she asked.

'Four,' he replied, his eyes bright with excitement.

'Very good,' she commented. 'Father will be pleased. Something for him to tell Jacob Craig. The Sedgebrooks were asking me about the abbey at Whitby, come and tell them what you know.'

Disappointment that her reception of the news of his sale had not been more enthusiastic, he followed her to her guests.

During the conversation with them he noticed that Marietta, who was talking to the Soulbys, kept glancing in his direction as if she was awaiting the moment he would be free. Five minutes later Charlotte and the Sedgebrooks left him to have a word with Charles. Marietta seized her chance, made her excuse to the Soulbys and came to Richard before his time could be monopolised by anyone else.

Her eyes were bright with query as she asked, 'Did you make a sale to Mr and Mrs Bonner?'

'Yes. Three unfinished paintings of whalers, one of a

harpooner and we agreed a good price for the one they were interested in yesterday.'

Her face beamed with pleasure as if the sale had been her own. 'Oh, I'm so glad. I made enquiries from Charles about their interest in seascapes and he told me they have quite a collection, so they must think highly of your work. I'm delighted for you. You deserve success.'

Richard was overwhelmed. 'Thank you. I don't think I'm entitled to such praise.'

'Of course you are. And I know Mr Craig's sure to be enthusiastic about your work. You will be a great painter.'

'I hope I can live up to your faith.' He gave a wry smile. 'And may I thank you for the dancing and skating lessons?'

'They were my pleasure,' returned Marietta. 'There may be other opportunities before we leave.'

'I hope so but I do have to finish the portrait to take back to London.'

Three days later Charles approached Richard. 'I have a ship bound for France on the first of February and could arrange for it to take us all to London if the portrait can be moved then?'

'That will suit very well,' he replied. 'It is to be framed by the picture-frame makers who have done all Mr Wakefield's collection. He leaves it to them, trusting their judgement as to the most suitable frame, and they in turn know what he likes.'

'Splendid,' said Charles. 'Then we'll work to that date and I'll arrange passage for us all.'

As he started to turn away Richard stopped him. 'I must thank you for allowing me to continue the portrait here at Reed Hall and also for your hospitality. And I should thank you for the opportunity that it gave me to show my work to interested people.'

'Think nothing of it, Mr Parker,' he said with an expression of bonhomie. 'I am only too pleased that things turned out so well. And I'm sure that Mr Wakefield is too, for it puts the stamp of approval on his faith in you, unknown, except in Whitby, until he saw you.'

'I'll be eternally grateful to him.'

'And he had a beautiful daughter for you to paint. I am just as eager to see the finished work as he is.' He paused and then added in an almost conspiratorial voice, 'If I like it I'll commission you to do a full-length portrait of my wife. There is just the place for it in that long narrowish section of wall at the foot of the stairs.'

Richard felt his heart beat faster. Everything seemed to be conspiring to throw him and Charlotte together. He really must put a wedge between them even if it meant marring their love, for he could not wound this generous and kindly man, who, though he could be a tough negotiator in business, appeared to see no wrong in anyone.

'An ideal place,' Richard muttered in agreement.

'She is a beautiful woman,' said Charles. 'I am a lucky man. I hope you have done justice to her, but we shall see.'

When the Campions, Wakefields, Kemps and Richard left Reed Hall they carried with them happy memories of their visit.

In the midst of all the activities of the last weeks in Lincolnshire Charlotte and Richard had little opportunity to be alone together. He had to devote his time to his paintings while she could hardly ever escape from her husband and their guests.

The day was bright, the sea running well, the breeze filled the sails and there was a genuine feeling of well-being on the voyage south. Everyone had enjoyed Lincolnshire, now everyone was looking forward to their London homes, and Richard to unveiling the portrait.

Three days previously messages had been sent via one of Campion's other ships to the Wakefield and Kemp households informing them of the date of their return and instructing their grooms to have carriages waiting at the quay on their arrival.

They were there now, the horses restless, but under control, among the bustling activity as the ship tied up. The two families were quickly ashore, with Simon Kemp and Francis supervising the transfer of their luggage from the ship, and Charles giving instructions for the Campion belongings to be taken to the Wakefield house as he and Charlotte were to stay there for the night. Richard, who had packed the portrait against possible damage and had kept it near him throughout the voyage, now saw it suitably positioned on the coach.

When all was satisfactorily arranged the carriages left the bustle of the quay for the congested streets. After the quietness of Lincolnshire the din of London sounds burst upon them. There was a constant movement of people hastening to complete their tasks before the onset of darkness which, though still two hours away, was hastened by the pall of smoke curling from a thousand chimneys.

The occupants of the carriages were pleased to clear the crowded streets and move to the more salubrious conditions of the suburbs. In Russell Square the Kemps offered their heartfelt thanks once again to Charles and the two families parted with a reminder from Simon to let them know when the portrait of Charlotte would be unveiled.

The following morning Francis took Richard with the portrait to the frame-makers. They were about to remove some of the packing when Francis stopped them.

'Not until after I've left. I am not to see the picture until it is hung. But I do want to know when you will deliver it?'

'A week today, if that is suitable.'

Though he was eager to see the portrait, Francies knew better than to rush them. 'Very well. Deliver it by ten o'clock.'

'You shall have it at half-past nine.'

'Splendid.'

As they headed for Russell Square, Francis set his timetable. 'Delivery at half-past nine. You should have it unpacked and hung by ten o'clock. Jackson will help you.'

'Then he'll see it before you.'

Francis smiled. 'My head butler knows when to keep a discreet silence. He'll make no comment to me nor anyone else until after everyone has seen it. So ten o'clock it is hung. Quarter past I'll see it, and the rest of the family and the Kemps at half-past.'

A week later Richard was impatiently waiting in the hall casting anxious glances at the grandfather clock. It had been rather an uneventful week. Charlotte and Charles had returned to their home in Chelsea but would be here for the unveiling. He had been able to get on with his commissions and was thankful that he had something to keep his mind occupied.

155

The minute pointer moved close to the Roman numerals representing six. He glanced round when he heard the measured footsteps coming from the direction of the kitchen.

'Hello, sir.' The head butler's deep voice brought with it a sense of immediacy.

'Adam.' Richard nodded. 'You don't expect them to be late?' He commented on the butler's appearance so close to the delivery time.

'No. They never are, sir. Mr Wakefield is such a good customer they know not to let him down.'

The clock chimed half-past. In a distant corridor, close to the servants' day rooms, a bell rang. The butler opened the front door and stood back to allow two men to bring in a carefully protected package.

'Good day, sir,' said the tall thin man, who was obviously the one in charge as the other was little more than a youth.

'Good day to you,' returned Richard. 'In here, please.' There was an eagerness in his voice as the moment he was awaiting drew closer. He opened the door to the drawing room.

He stood to one side, his fingers twitching, wanting to help, as the two men carefully peeled away the paper and dismantled the timber protection. They stood the portrait against an armchair to one side of the fireplace.

Richard's heart beat faster, then any apprehension that the frame would not suit the picture disappeared. Francis's faith in his framers was justified. The frame was heavy enough to give substance, ornate but without overwhelming the portrait, and gilded to the right intensity to add to the glow of the colours and not swamp them.

'Highly satisfactory,' he exclaimed.

'Would you like us to help with the hanging, sir?' asked the thin man.

Richard glanced at Adam.

'If they do that then you can stand back and direct the positioning,' said the butler.

He had already seen that a pair of steps was available, and the younger man, eager to oblige, brought them from where they had been placed to one side of the fireplace.

Adam nodded his thanks and mounted the steps while the

men from the framer's carefully lifted the portrait to him. In a few moments the picture was hanging from the hook above the fireplace.

Richard stepped back to view the position as the butler glanced over his shoulder with an enquiring look.

'Not quite straight,' said Richard. 'The right side wants raising.' Adam made the adjustment. 'Perfect.'

Adam came down the steps and the young man folded them and awaited instructions.

Adam came beside Richard and viewed the portrait. 'I think that is all right, sir.'

Richard nodded. 'Yes.' His glance took them all in. 'Thank you all for your help.'

The two men from the frame-makers touched their foreheads in acknowledgement.

'And may I say, sir, what a fine portrait.' Adam turned away and ushered the two men from the room, leaving Richard gazing at the portrait.

Beautiful Charlotte was there before him. His heart and mind were awhirl. His love for her was overwhelming. He could not give her up. The resolve to do so, which he had made so many times this past week, was dismissed once again. He could not deny the love he felt. And here she was, her eyes fixed on him, filled with a love for him, daring him to deny that he loved her, daring him to forsake her. 'Oh, Charlotte,' he whispered. 'I cannot.'

The clock in the hall struck quarter past. He started. With the unpacking, the hanging, and then lost in his love for her, he had not noticed the passing time.

The last note died away and the door opened. Francis strode in. Richard swung round. Francis had stopped in his tracks and was staring wide-eyed in amazement at the portrait. The door swung slowly behind him to close with a click.

Francis did not move. Richard stayed still, searching his mentor's face for some clue as to what he was thinking, but he could not read it. His mind put doubt to him. Was Mr Wakefield shocked to disappointment? Richard began to feel uneasy. The moments passed with Francis's gaze still on the portrait. Then he moved slowly forward. After three steps he looked at Richard.

157

'Truly amazing. Absolutely beautiful. Far, far better than I expected.' He put his arm round Richard's shoulder, adding to the relief that his words were bringing, and they both moved nearer the portrait. 'Wonderful. Not only have you captured a likeness but you have brought out Charlotte's character. And she is alive. I'm expecting her to speak to me at any moment.' He slapped Richard on the back. 'Wait until Mr Craig sees that, he'll know I've made a discovery.'

'I don't know that it's worthy of such praise,' rejoined Richard, feeling a little embarrassed by such enthusiasm.

'What? Don't talk nonsense. Don't play your ability down. Your talent is there for all to see. Look at the brushwork, look at the delicate blending of colours, but, more than anything else, this is not just a representation of a person: you have brought out personality and character. My boy, you've got a great future. Take it. Grasp it while you can. If I had let go for one moment when things turned my way I would not be a highly successful merchant, living in one of the best parts of London, able to indulge myself and my family. You can do the same through your art.'

Footsteps crossing the hall interrupted them. They heard the front door open and then voices.

'Charles and Charlotte,' said Francis. He started towards the door then stopped. 'Can we hide our response? Better the surprise for them if we give nothing away.'

'We can try, sir,' he replied with a smile.

'I ordered some warming punch to be served in the hall as people arrived. That might help us.'

He started for the door but Richard stopped him. 'Sir, I'm so pleased you like it. And thank you for the opportunity you have given me.'

Francis waved his hand, dismissing the thanks. He opened the door and stepped out into the hall.

A maid and footman were taking the outdoor clothes away while others were serving the hot punch.

Charlotte rushed to her father. 'Well, what's it like?'

Francis frowned. 'You'll have to wait and see.'

'Oh, Father.' She kissed him on the cheek and linked arms with him.

'And you'll not get round me like that, my girl.'

158

Charlotte let go of his arm. She turned to Richard. 'What did he say?'

'Your father will give you his opinion when you've seen the portrait.' replied Richard stiffly.

'Oh you're as bad as he is.' She turned and took the punch proffered by one of the maids.

'I told you you wouldn't get to know,' laughed Charles teasingly.

'You should know your father,' Gertrude pointed out, taking the punch passed to her by her husband.

The bell rang again and the front door opened to admit the Kemps. Once greetings were exchanged and outdoor clothes were discarded and punch served, everyone eagerly awaited Francis's lead. It amused him to keep their excited anticipation mounting until they had all finished their drink. Then he quietly opened the door to the drawing room.

They flowed in only to be halted by the impact the portrait made on them. An intense silence had come to the room. No one wanted to utter a sound or make a gesture which would shatter this particular moment when they first saw the portrait of Charlotte.

Richard stood to one side, hardly daring to breathe yet wanting to know each one's opinion.

Francis knew how they all felt but someone had eventually to break into their thoughts. 'Well?' he said. His voice was scarcely above a whisper but it was sufficient to bring them all alive again.

Immediately everyone started talking together.

'Magnificent.'

'Wonderful.'

'That's my Charlotte!' gasped Charles.

'And my Charlotte,' said Gertrude, for she could see her daughter whereas Charles had seen his wife. Both were there.

'Beautiful.'

Marietta, who was standing near Richard, turned to him and said quietly, 'I knew it would be wonderful for I saw the expertise in those two drawings but this displays a truly singular talent.'

He smiled at her. 'Thank you.' But he was wondering what Charlotte thought for she had not yet spoken.

159

It seemed everyone else had realised that she had not voiced her opinion for silence descended on the room, as everyone looked at her.

'Well, Charlotte, are you pleased?' asked Francis.

She started. 'Oh, silly me.' She fished for a handkerchief from her sleeve and dabbed at the silent tears which had flowed as she had gazed intently at the picture lost to everything else.

'I'm sorry if it made you cry,' apologised Richard. 'I didn't intend it to.'

'Oh, no, these are tears of joy. I am so pleased with it. It is so wonderful. Thank you so much, both to you for doing it and to Father for making the commission and for recognising your talent in Whitby.' She could not say what she wanted to say but she would tell Richard later for she had seen in the portrait not only her expression of love, which any individual viewer could interpret was for them, but his love for her.

'I must have a portrait of my daughter,' broke in Simon. 'You can take that as a definite commission. Mr Parker.'

'Thank you, sir. I will be pleased to paint such a charming subject.'

'Mr Parker, I am envious that this portrait should hang here,' said Charles. 'Please consider that proposal I put to you before we left Lincolnshire as firm.'

'What was that, Charles?' asked Charlotte, curious about the secret the two men had shared.

'I want him to paint a full-length portrait of you for that narrow section of wall at the foot of the stairs at Reed Hall.'

'Oh, Charles, how wonderful. Thank you so much.' Her thoughts were already entertaining the possibilities this raised, for now she and Richard would have more time together.

Chapter Eleven

Richard lay on his bed staring at the ceiling. He had doused his lamp leaving his room moonlit, hoping that the soft silvery glow would soothe his turbulent mind.

This had been an eventful day. He still felt the impact of the enthusiasm and praise for his portrait, followed by the two firm commissions. They would keep him in London and he saw danger in that. Charles's commission would throw him closer to Charlotte. To refuse that commission would only raise awkward questions which he could never answer satisfactorily. Besides, he wanted the challenge of a full-length portrait, and he had the insatiable desire to repeat his success with a head and shoulders portrait of Marietta. Francis was even keener for Jacob Craig to see his work and if Craig took him into his studio he would have to stay in London.

If he did could he quell the love which burned in him and pursue his career? Charlotte's face swam temptingly before him. As much as he tried to thrust it from his mind he failed. Was this a sign that his love for her was too consuming and would not be denied? He eventually fell asleep with these questions unanswered.

The question of when he should start the full-length portrait had not been raised, so he decided to do some sketches of Marietta as a preliminary to starting her portrait.

He found her a willing sitter, eager to oblige with different poses until he found the one which satisfied him. She was good company, easy to talk to, and showed a deep interest in his work and his life in Whitby.

As he became more and more immersed in drawing, he wondered if absorption in his work would solve his dilemma.

The answer came two days later in the form of a letter. It was delivered by a shabbily clad boy who after handing it to the maid who answered the door, ran off before she had time to peruse the envelope or question him.

She gave a grunt and raised her eyebrows in exasperation. After she had closed the door she saw that the envelope was addressed to Mr R Parker so placed it on a small table in the hall where he would see it when he returned.

Pleased with the way the sketching session with Marietta had gone, he was whistling to himself when he saw the letter. Curious as to who could be writing to him, for he did not recognise the hand which had printed his name, he took it to his room.

There in seclusion he opened the envelope and withdrew a sheet of paper. Unfolding it, he glanced at the signature and was startled to see Charlotte's name.

He read:

My dear one,

I am missing you so terribly. My heart aches for the sight of you. I long to hear your gentle voice. I desire to feel your touch to know that you are close, that you are there. I need to be in your presence to know that you are real, that you are no ghost, a figment of my imagination.

I know you are not. If you were how could I be so in love with you?

Please think of me until we are together again.

My love is no less for Charles but my strength for you lies in being IN LOVE with you.

Yours forever,
Charlotte

Sensations raced through him. This profession of love for him served to make him realise that his love for her had not diminished either. He felt ecstatic at receiving such a letter. His heart was overwhelmed by her ardent love, but there came, following sharply upon all other feelings, alarm clouds, thunderheads which threatened the future.

She had committed her love for him to paper. Here was sufficient evidence of what they felt for each other to condemn them in the eyes of the world. The letter must be destroyed.

He bit his lip and shook his head. No, he could not do that! He must keep this token of her great love. He stared at the paper for a moment then carefully folded it and thrust it deep into an inside pocket of his jacket. Safe for all time.

A week later when he returned from the Kemps he noticed some luggage in the hall, and was halfway to the stairs when the drawing-room door opened and Francis appeared.

'I thought I recognised your footsteps,' he said breezily. Richard sensed he had some news to tell him. 'Charlotte and Charles are here. During the last week he has made some business deals which require him to go to the Continent for twelve weeks. Charlotte is not keen to go; she says she would rather move in with us and let you get on with the portrait that Charles commissioned. He's leaving in a few minutes. Have a word with him before he goes.'

Richard made no comment but followed Francis into the room.

Charlotte was standing beside an armchair speaking to her mother. The light, angling from a window on her right, highlighted the silky texture of her hair and the delicate rose tint of her skin. Her blue eyes shone with pleasure but Richard saw them take on a new look when he walked into the room. He saw that they confirmed the love which she had expressed in the letter. He also knew from the sensation which gripped him that he was lost and that no matter what happened in the future, whether decided by themselves or by others, he would always be in love with her.

'Ah, Mr Parker,' Charles greeted him, rising from his chair. 'A timely arrival. In ten minutes I shall be leaving for the Continent – business. Can you do some work on my wife's portrait while I am away?'

'I can do preliminary sketches, to decide stance, pose, probably dress, but I won't start work on the canvas for a while.'

'We may go to Reed Hall for the summer when I return and you could do canvas work there.'

'There may be a snag, Charles,' put in Francis. 'Jacob

163

Craig will have returned before you and, after seeing the portrait of Charlotte, he may want our artist to stay in London.'

'I'm sure we'll be able to arrange something with him. We'll meet that problem when it arises.'

Richard said nothing. It seemed as if other people were in charge of his destiny.

He wished Charles a good voyage and successful negotiations abroad and then went to his room. From the window he saw Charlotte make her farewell to her husband and watched the carriage drive away.

A few minutes later he wandered downstairs to partake of some tea and found Charlotte alone in the drawing room.

'Hello, Richard.' Her voice was soft, sensuous. 'I've missed you.' She watched him cross the room. Here was the man who had entered her life less than a year ago, and then insignificantly. She had taken little notice of him on that stone pier in Whitby. But before long she had realised that he was the person who filled the void she had felt even when she married – she wanted to be in love. Then Richard had come into her life and her life was full. She knew it even more now as he sat down opposite her. 'I've missed you so much,' she said again as if to make sure he really knew.

'And I you,' he replied quietly. 'Thank you for your letter. It was dangerous to write and I dare not acknowledge it.'

'I just had to let you know how much I missed you. And I thought you would keep it safe.'

'It is and will always be with me.'

Their eyes met in an expression which needed no words. Being in love with each other was of such magnitude that it transcended all other feelings. It challenged the future. It defied opposition. It would only be satisfied if they were together. But in that knowledge came the caution, the wariness which they so much wanted to abandon but dared not.

He noticed there were only two cups on the tray. 'Your mother and father?'

'They had an invitation to friends. There is only you and me.' She held out her hand to him, an invitation for him to sit on the sofa beside her. He accepted, never taking his eyes off her.

His touch closed off the rest of the world. No one else existed, only she and the man with whom she was in love. Her love for Charles was as nothing. This feeling of being in love overwhelmed everything. The world and everyone in it vanished. There was only themselves.

He leaned forward and kissed her. She trembled at the touch. There was love and desire in the contact. They merged as one expression, not separately as they did with Charles, one leading to the other. There was also a deep respect which lifted their love on to a different plane, a place which no one else could reach. No matter what the future held, their love for each other would never die.

As their lips parted, Richard whispered, 'I'm sorry.'

She looked into his troubled eyes. 'Sorry? For what?'

'That I have got you into this impossible situation.'

'I was a willing participant.'

'But I should have stopped it, shouldn't have let it happen.'

'I didn't want you to.'

'And I didn't want to. I love you deeply, Charlotte.'

'And I you.'

'But what can we do about it?' He frowned.

'Charles?'

He started. 'You can't tell him about us. You mustn't.'

'It might be the answer.' She bit her lip.

'You can't,' he protested even more strongly.

'It might be the best thing in the long run. But it would mar one of the two things I want most.'

'What are they?'

'For us to be together always, and for no one else to get hurt.'

'But Charles would.'

She nodded and said slowly, 'I know and I don't want that. He is so loving and so kind and he's told me what a difference I have brought to his life. I wouldn't want to shatter all that.'

'Then you can't tell him.'

'That will mean we go on as we are.'

'And run the risk of discovery.'

She looked hard at him. 'I am willing, if you are.'

He hesitated, then holding her gaze said, 'Maybe if I—'

'No,' she cried, cutting him off before he even had time to

165

make his suggestion. 'I know what you are going to say. But I could not live if I was never to see you again.'

'You could, and you would.'

'No! No!' She flung herself into his arms with tears rolling down her cheeks. She held him tight as if to relax her hold would be to lose him forever.

Throughout the next nine days, as he sketched Charlotte and Marietta, Richard pondered the situation. His mind became more and more enmeshed in turmoil. He cried out for a solution to the love he and Charlotte shared. He recalled his mother's words. Dismissed them. Brought them back. He read Charlotte's letter over and over again, only to have the conflict in him deepen. He remembered Marietta's words of encouragement for his art, and her indubitable belief that he could be a great artist and her words of advice that if Jacob Craig made him an offer he should take it.

But if he did that and stayed in London could he resist seeing Charlotte? Only if she agreed. He was certain she would not, for he knew she believed seeing each other in secret was a solution. But he was not happy with that. Discovery would mean scandal and ruin for them both. It would be better if only one of them lost and yet ambition gnawed at him.

The twenty-fifth of February was a date which would always burn in their minds. Knowing that Francis and Gertrude had been invited to a business friend's for dinner on that date, Richard planned to confront Charlotte with the decision he had made.

'You were quiet during the meal,' she commented as they went into the drawing room. 'Is something worrying you?' When he did not immediately answer, she added in a voice which tried to lighten the situation, 'Come on, serious face, tell Charlotte.' She smiled teasingly at him.

They had reached the sofa beside the fire. Still looking at him she was about to sit down when his words stopped her.

'I'm going home to Whitby.'

'You're doing what?' She gasped in astonishment at this cold announcement. 'But you can't. I stayed here especially for you to consider the commission Charles gave you. Go later on by all means but you can't go now.'

His face was serious as he looked straight at her so that she would not misunderstand. 'I'm going to Whitby and not coming back.'

She stared at him, her mouth open, not able to say a word. Then the impact of his clinical statement burst upon her. 'You can't!' she cried, her voice full, afraid that he meant it. She had always known his eyes to be soft and kind; today they were still that way but they were also tinged with a hard determination that she had never seen before. 'You mean it, don't you?' she gasped incredulously.

'Yes.'

The one word bit into her mind. Her eyes widened in distress. 'Richard don't leave me! I won't be able to go on without you!'

'You will. You'll have to. You have Charles. You've got to forget me.'

'I never will. How can I with that portrait hanging there? Oh, I know it's me, but there is you in it too. Don't deny it, and I'll see you every time I look at it. Don't torture me, please don't let me live a life like that!' She grasped his arms and looked pleadingly up into his face.

It churned his insides to be hurting her so. 'Charlotte, it's for the best.'

'How can it be when we are so in love?'

'It's because I love you so that I've made this decision.'

'If you loved me you'd stay.' There was desperation in her voice. She wanted him here. 'We can keep this a secret, no one need ever know.'

'I doubt if we can do it forever,' he returned quietly yet with some force to try to impress her. 'We might be exposed sooner than you think.'

'What do you mean?' She frowned, unable to comprehend what he was getting at.

'I think your mother has suspicions.'

'Nonsense.'

'I've noticed her cast one or two glances in your direction.'

'Those could have been anything,' she put in quickly, trying to disarm him before he elaborated.

167

He shook his head. 'I've noticed them after a look you have given me, after a remark you have made. They have been a mother's intuition.'

'You don't believe that.'

'Oh, I do. I've seen it with my own mother, especially where my sisters are concerned. And she has nearly always been right.'

'She has said nothing to me.'

'And she won't until she is absolutely certain and then it will be too late. She'll try to keep it quiet, but there'll be an ultimatum to you. As far as she is concerned, your name will be sullied and if ever it went further there would be scandal. I won't have that for you. That is why I am going.'

Charlotte knew he was right. She had noticed some odd looks from her mother but she was not going to tell Richard that. She wanted him to stay, but seeing his determination to leave she tried a different approach.

'But you have two commissions ...'

'Nothing has been started. I've only been doing preliminary sketches. If I had put brush to canvas then that would have been different. I would then have got a bad name for not fulfilling a commission.'

'Then put some marks on a canvas.'

He smiled and shook his head. 'No. I must go.'

'But what will you tell the Kemps? What am I to tell Charles? What excuse will you give my father, who has helped you so much and is certain you will get a place with Jacob Craig? Are you going to give all that up? Throw his kindness in my father's face? Ruin your career?' Her words came fast, wanting to bombard him with reasons for staying.

'My excuse will be that my family need me in Whitby.' His voice softened, his eyes took on an intent look. 'But, my dear Charlotte, you know the real reason – I love you too much to see you get hurt.'

'But I'm hurting now. And always will.' Her eyes dampened but she fought to hold back tears.

'You won't. You will be strong enough to face the future without me. You have a loving husband, he will help, though he will never know how or why. But you will have to make a conscious effort to succeed. Only by doing so will you win

168

through what I know will be a trying time. Face the problem of our parting and you will realise that we were right. You will never forget our love for each other, I know I won't, but I think it will become stronger for the parting.'

She saw he was right. She knew how hard it would have been for him to make this decision, a career thrown away.

'You're sacrificing yourself for me.' Silent tears flowed, accepting the overwhelming love he was showing her. 'When will you go?'

'I have a passage booked on the *Amelia* sailing to Whitby the day after tomorrow.'

Her eyes widened. 'So soon? You had all this planned.'

He nodded. 'I had to be determined for your sake. I will make my excuses to your father and to the Kemps tomorrow. As far as they are concerned I will be returning in three weeks.'

Chapter Twelve

The following morning Richard strode across Russell Square with a spring in his step. Coming to a decision about his relationship with Charlotte seemed to have cleared his mind and settled the future.

Francis had received his intention of going to Whitby with understanding when he had explained that he had always been there for his mother when his father and brothers left for the whaling season in the Arctic. It was a traumatic time for her, knowing the dangers her menfolk faced, and he wanted to be there to ease the burden which always seemed heaviest during the days immediately following the sailing.

Charlotte had been absent from the breakfast table and had only been coming down the stairs as he had crossed the hall to the front door. Frightened that he might weaken his resolve if he stopped to talk to her he kept walking.

She stopped on the stairs, her heart beating faster. She wanted to reach out and hold him back, to tell him she did not want him to sacrifice himself for her sake, but she had seen the determination set to his face and knew it would be useless. With an aching heart she watched the door close behind him.

Admitted to the Kemp household he was greeted with the usual warmth and pleasure by Marietta.

'More sketches?' she asked.

'Sorry, not today.' He saw disappointment cloud her face and deepen when he added, 'I'm going home to Whitby.'

'For how long?' She could not hide the desire to see him back in London.

'Possibly three weeks.' He hated lying to her but he could not betray Charlotte. He went on to explain his reason for going and she gave him her understanding.

'I'll miss you. I've always enjoyed your company when you have been sketching and I have fond memories of our time together in Lincolnshire.'

'So have I,' he agreed. 'Your father and mother?'

'They are out but I'll tell them. I look forward to your return. Have a good voyage and I hope you will find everyone at home in good health.'

When he returned to the Wakefield house the coachman, on Francis's instructions, was already waiting for him. He lost no time in putting his luggage on board, and left quickly. Though it hurt not to see Charlotte again he was pleased she had not come to say goodbye. The parting might have been too much for them to hide their feelings.

He sat in the carriage morose and downcast that he was leaving a beckoning future as an important artist behind. There was nothing else he could do. He realised the position would have become impossible if he had stayed.

From an upstairs window Charlotte watched the carriage drive away. Her eyes filled with tears. Already she felt an emptiness which she knew would never go. She had wanted so much to see him and speak with him once more but she knew if she did she would not be able to suppress her love for him.

She watched the coach out of sight. Richard hadn't even looked back but she had seen him lean forward and wave to someone on the other side of the square. As the carriage moved on and cleared her view, she saw Marietta standing at the gate of her home, her hand raised, her eyes on the carriage. Charlotte turned from the window, sank on to her bed and cried.

Richard left the coach at Whitby's Angel Inn. The sky was overcast, and the wind, blowing from the sea, rippled the waters of the river, funnelled between the two cliffs and swirled its way through Whitby's narrow streets.

The arrival of the coach brought activity to the hostelry as stablemen scurried to attend to the horses and servants hastened to see to the needs of the passengers.

Richard ignored them all and entertained no thought that this was the place where he had first been introduced to Charlotte. He turned up the collar of his coat and with a brisk step headed for the bridge. The life of this thriving Yorkshire port went on around him. It was as if he had never been away. The Whitby he knew seemed to send a message: 'This was your home, it can be again. That unfamiliar world you have experienced was not for you. Forget it. Dismiss Charlotte from your mind. She can never be yours. Purge yourself forever of dreams that can never be realised.'

As the river came in sight and he neared the bridge, his eyes searched for only one thing – the whaleships. Had they already sailed? Was the *Phoenix* still in port? Or was he too late? Had the fact of taking a ship to Boston, delivering his Lincolnshire commissions and then having to make the onward journey by coach, delayed him too long? His gaze moved quickly along the river and across the quays. Relief gripped him. The *Phoenix* was there at her usual berth beside the east bank.

He quickened his pace almost to a run. He cut down Grape Lane and out on to Church Street. He took little notice of the activity around him as he threaded his way through the stream of people, dodging round sailors loading a vessel with local produce bound for London, and sidestepping the men stacking timber on the quay. He had eyes only for the *Phoenix* and even before he had reached her he could sense that preparations for the Arctic had been completed.

He paused at the foot of the gangplank. 'Jeremy!' he called, attracting the attention of the young man who had shared his first and only voyage to the Arctic. Jeremy had taken readily to the life of a whaleman in contrast to Richard and had continued to serve on the *Phoenix*.

'Richard!' Jeremy, surprised to see a friend, whom he thought had long gone to London, ran to the gangway.

'Is Father on board?' There was an urgent tone in Richard's voice.

'No. Nor your brothers. Only me. I'm shipkeeper. We're ready to sail tomorrow. We're boiling the kettle later today.'

He was just in time. His father altered this usual custom a little to suit his own needs, always lighting the fire in the galley the evening before sailing rather than a few days earlier before the preparations to sail. The crew and their families would come to share the first food on board and his father would pay his men a month's wage in advance to help their folk while they were away.

'Then they'll be at home.' Richard turned away.

'You back for good?' Jeremy shouted after him.

'Aye,' he called over his shoulder with a firmness which made his friend wonder where the ambition for an artist's life in London had gone.

Richard was soon climbing the steps to Prospect Place and did not stand on ceremony by knocking at the door. He know it would not be locked and he still regarded this as home, even more so now that he had broken his ties with Charlotte, London and Lincolnshire.

His mother, father, brothers and sisters were seated at the table having a meal. It was a sight he remembered, a setting he had shared and it tugged at his heart. They looked up sharply at the sudden intrusion.

'Richard!' His mother, hardly able to believe her eyes, was the first to react, and was rising from her chair almost before his name was out.

'Son! What brings you home?' John's gaze searched his son's face for an answer. If something was wrong he wanted to know. If Richard was in trouble and needed help he was prepared to give it.

Sarah and Maggie, startled by the unexpected, voiced his name with delight.

'Little brother!' Following their surprise, Will and Jim raised questioning eyebrows at each other before waiting for an explanation for his return.

Martha held her arms wide in welcome. She hugged her son with a mother's affection for the return of a prodigal. Tears of pleasure began to run silently down her cheeks. She sought a handkerchief in her pinafore pocket and dabbed her eyes.

'Father, I want to sign on with you!'

The unexpected request, delivered in a no-nonsense fashion, brought incredulous looks from those around the table.

173

'What did you say?' John screwed up his face in disbelief.

'I want to sail on the *Phoenix*,' replied Richard just as firmly.

This second delivery made the others see he was not fooling.

'Not you?' gasped Maggie and Sarah.

'Little brother's decided to become a man,' commented Jim.

'Remember last time?' warned Will. 'It'll be no different this voyage. Might even be worse.'

Richard ignored these remarks. His attention was focused on his father.

'I've a full crew of Whitby men.' John's eyes never left Richard as he made this announcement. He saw the momentary disappointment vanish with the arrival of an idea.

'You'll be finalising your crew at Lerwick with some Shetlanders. Make it one less and take me.'

Will and Jim gave a little snigger of derision at this suggestion. 'Those men are real whalemen, which you certainly aren't.'

Richard disregarded their objection. 'Well, Father?'

A whaleman's life was hard in the Arctic seas. Danger was never far away. A captain could not afford to have a weak link in his crew. Every man must be able to fulfil his role and more, for situations could arise which might stretch his ability to breaking point. Witnessing death and maiming, he would have to hide his true feelings. All this would be overlayed with the gory slaughter of the whale and the nauseating stench when it was flensed and the blubber cut up.

The captain was wary.

'Father, you've got to take me!' pressed Richard.

'You hated it last time,' his mother reminded him. 'What has happened to bring you back here wanting to sail with your father?'

'I realised an artist's life in London was not for me.' He was aware that his explanation was weak but he was not going to offer anything else.

'What happened to that burning ambition to be a famous artist?' she asked with a quiet firmness. 'Has that gone?'

He knew his father was watching him, knew his ability to

174

judge a man by his answers. He had to be careful.

'I recognised that the subjects I want to draw and paint are here in Whitby. I can feel them in here.' He pressed his hands to his chest. 'These are my people, my scenes. It's through them that my work will find its true expression. Oh, it may not be world-shattering, I may not become a great artist in the sense I thought I could but I will be true to myself and my subjects. If I become known along this coast for my marine paintings and my portraits of Yorkshire folk then I will be satisfied.'

'But why do you want to sail on the *Phoenix*?' asked his father. He had liked his son's explanation for his return. If he had said he no longer wanted to draw and paint he would have been deeply suspicious of his motives, but it seemed that, having seen and tasted the life of an artist in London, he had found the true role for his ability.

'The whaleships, the life on board, the men who brave the Arctic seas, the people they leave behind are an important part of Whitby life and if I want to portray that aspect then I have got to sail on a whaleship. If it is not the *Phoenix* then I'll find another! But another captain might not take kindly to one of his crew spending some of his time sketching. You would understand.'

John kept a serious face while smiling to himself. His son had put his case well.

'Father, you can't sign him on. If he's drawing he won't be doing his share,' protested Will. Jim grunted his support.

John, seeing further objections springing to Will's lips, held up his hand for silence.

He looked hard at Richard. 'You know what the life is like. I'll have no shirker on board my ship. You will have to do your share of the work and maybe more if the men see you taking to your drawing. They'll not give you an easy ride. But I'll tolerate your paper and pencil now you seem to have realised where your gift should be exploited.' He glanced at his wife. 'Another plate, Mother. There's plenty of stew left.' He looked back at Richard. 'Better fill up good, lad. You'll get nothing like this aboard the *Phoenix*.'

Richard's face broke out in a wreath of smiles. 'Thanks, Father. You'll not regret it. I won't let you down.'

175

'See you don't.'

Later when John, his two sons and daughters were about to leave to partake in boiling the kettle, Martha contrived for her and Richard to follow in a few minutes.

'Son, you are sure about sailing on the *Phoenix*?' she asked, her gaze intent upon him. She did not want to miss even the smallest reaction to what she had to say.

'Certain.'

She could not deny the determination behind his expression.

'There's more to this than the explanation you gave your father.' She made her statement warily. 'You hated that previous voyage. Is this something to do with—'

He did not let her finish the sentence, for he knew it was no use trying to hide anything from this shrewd woman. 'Yes. I remembered your words and I came to realise that there was no future in my relationship with Mrs Campion. Better for me to give up my chance in London than to ruin her and myself by scandal.'

Martha gave her approval. 'You chose well, my son.' She paused then added, 'You still love her, don't you?'

He nodded.

'So you think you will purge yourself of that love if you sail to the Arctic?'

'I hope it will help me to forget her, forget what I might have achieved as an artist, and show me that I can live a man's life in the style of Will and Jim but still use my artistic talent around Whitby.'

She came to him and hugged him. In that gesture there was a mother's love, a mother's support and it said 'I am here if you need me.' She brushed away a tear as she stepped back and said, 'Now, let's gan and boil that kettle with the rest of them.'

The *Phoenix* slipped down the river, passed between the two piers and met the first swell of the sea.

From the moment she cast off and eased gently to midstream, she received the shouts and good wishes of Whitby folk who crowded the staithes, piers and cliffs to watch her leave her home port for the Arctic.

176

It was always the same whenever one of her whaleships left to hunt whales, at great risk, in order to bring back blubber and whalebone, important products contributing to Whitby's economy.

They knew the dangers their menfolk would face and, though no one would mention it for fear of tempting fate, there was always the thought in the back of their minds that the ship could be lost in the icy wastes of the north.

The whalemen deserved their exclusive send-off. They were special. There was an aura about a whaleman which set him aside from other sailors. He was a hunter, an explorer sailing into unknown waters in search of whales. There was a glamour about him that stirred the imagination and Whitby folk were not going to let him sail without making the occasion something to remember.

Richard knew the esteem in which whalemen were held and he hoped that he could forget his first voyage and this time live up to that reputation. Now he was swept into the enthusiastic send-off as much as the next man. He laughed, waved and shouted, and strengthened his determination not to let his father down.

As the *Phoenix*'s bow, strengthened to combat the Arctic ice, cut into the first wave and sent it hissing along its hull, Richard looked back at his home town. As it did with all whalemen, it would remain indelibly printed on his mind throughout the long Arctic days and throughout the entire voyage until they returned in six months' time.

He had regrets at leaving. The qualms about what faced him among the ice floes were drawn stronger by the horrors of the hunt and the gory flensing. He had known that when he had chosen to sign on but he hoped the world into which he was sailing would expel all thoughts of Charlotte.

With Whitby lost below the horizon, Richard set about coiling some ropes, determined he would not shirk any task given to him. He knew he would get no special privileges from his father and no concessions from his brothers. He wanted none and he did not want the crew to get the impression that he did.

The crew was a good one. Most had sailed with his father before. He knew them all, but was especially pleased that

Jeremy was on board. As new hands they had sailed together on Richard's first and only whaling voyage and he had found Jeremy a friend indeed when he showed his revulsion at the results of harpooning a whale.

The crew settled down. The *Phoenix* ran north; its first and only stop would be the Shetlands where the crew's full complement would be made up from men born to the sea who made some of the best whalemen in the world. The weather was fine, the wind in the right quarter and with confidence running high all seemed well for a successful season.

About the time the *Phoenix* was setting sail from Lerwick, having been there but a day, Jacob Craig was being admitted to the Wakefield residence in Russell Square.

Having been informed about the visitor, Francis came hurrying into the hall where a maid was already taking his overcoat, his hat and walking stick.

'My dear fellow,' Francis greeted him heartily as he took Jacob's hand gently, for he knew the old injury could still be painful. 'How nice to see you. I did not know you were back.'

'Only yesterday,' replied Jacob, showing equal pleasure at seeing his friend.

He was a man of medium height with a rounded face which, though bearing the marks of early problems and disappointments, still had an attractive openness to which people easily responded. It matched his friendly manner, his quiet demeanour, though these did not take away his enjoyment of life in which he was always eager to share a joke. He wore a navy, double-breasted frock coat. It had a small collar and revers, showing his desire to keep to the latest fashion as did his acceptance of the return of the flowered waistcoat revealed by wearing his coat open. His white shirt had a yellow cravat tied neatly at the neck, and his trousers, exquisitely cut, matched its colour.

'Then I am flattered that you should look me up so soon,' returned Francis.

'Ah, my good man, I think you expected me to.' His blue eyes twinkled in merriment and there was the twitch of a smile on his lips.

'Well ...' Francis gave the impression of disagreement.

'Oh, come now, my dear friend, you don't bring a young man to my establishment unless you are at your old tricks again – trying to spot an artistic genius.'

Francis did not reply but made towards the drawing-room door. He opened it and allowed Jacob to precede him. Jacob stepped into the room and stopped. He stared straight ahead. Francis closed the door quietly in case the faintest click disturbed Jacob's concentration. He moved to his side, stood still and waited for a reaction.

A few moments later Jacob took four paces further into the room, then stopped again, his eyes still on the painting above the fireplace. He waited a few more minutes, his concentration unmarred. Then he turned quickly on Francis. 'Who is he? Where is he? There's a great talent lurking beneath that paint. Where did you find him? How old is he? When can I meet him?' The questions poured excitedly from Jacob's lips. His eyes were bright with enthusiasm.

Francis laughed, pleased at his friend's reaction. 'Calm down, Jacob. Come, sit down and have a glass of Madeira.' He started towards the sideboard on which stood a decanter and some glasses.

'No, no, Francis. I can't be bothered with such a trivial thing as wine. I want to know all about that picture.' He pulled an armchair from its position by the fireplace so that he could view the portrait better while they talked.

Francis shrugged his shoulders, raised his eyebrows and smiled to himself. Jacob must be impressed to turn down a glass of Madeira. He liked good living, good food and good wine. Francis sat down opposite him.

'That is a particularly good likeness to Charlotte, you almost expect her to speak. But there is more to that painting. The artist, whoever he is, has been clever enough to avoid aiming for the full likeness, for that would have established the portrait as a good work, but no better than many others that float around the art market. Here there is character in the face, we know Charlotte, not just what she looks like but something of her personality. In those eyes there is expression which is meant for the person who is looking at the portrait. Each one of us will see it differently, will take a different message from it and it will be a message for that person only.'

179

He stood up and moved to the picture and examined it closely for a few moments before returning to his chair. 'There are some aspects of his painting technique, his brushwork, which could be bettered, which would benefit from him being attached to my studio. Francis, whoever painted that portrait can become one of the leading artists of his time, indeed maybe of all time. To see more of his work will help me judge that but certainly on the strength of that picture I must have him under my wing. If he escapes me I would regret it for the rest of my life.'

Francis had never heard Jacob react so strongly about anyone before. It delighted him to think of the great future Richard could have and of course it pleased him that he would be able to say, when Richard was famous and sought-after as an artist, that he was the discoverer of this talented man.

'Now, Francis, keep me in suspense no longer. Tell me all about him and where you found him.' Jacob snuggled back into his chair and settled to hear the story.

'His name is Richard Parker, and he's twenty-one next month.'

Jacob nodded approvingly. He liked to catch talent young.

'I found him in Whitby.'

'Whitby?' Jacob raised his eyebrows in surprise. 'What on earth were you doing in Whitby?'

Francis went on to explain how he came to be there and of his chance discovery of Richard. He told him of bringing him to London and of the completion of the portrait in Lincolnshire.

'I hope that his entire time has not been devoted to the portrait.' Even as he made the statement he waved his hands dismissing it. 'Of course it was not. I could see that in the portrait. If he had concentrated on it and nothing else there would be times when he would be stale. The parts executed then would not be as good as the rest. It would show, well, certainly to me.'

'He did some drawings of various aspects of London and London life. When he was in Lincolnshire he did some landscapes and I know he had with him some unfinished seascapes which he completed for one of Charles's friends.'

'Good, good. Splendid. He sounds to be a young man

engrossed in his art. Now Francis, let me meet him.'

'I'm sorry, Jacob, I can't.'

'Can't?' blustered Jacob, sitting upright in his chair and staring disbelievingly at Francis.

'Sorry. He's gone home to Whitby.'

'Home? But I thought you'd keep him here until I got back.'

'Don't worry, he's only gone to see the whaleships sail. His father is captain of one of them, his two brothers serve on the same ship. He's always been there for his mother when they leave. It's understandable. He'll be back in three weeks.'

'Three weeks?' Jacob raised his eyebrows as if in despair. Then he laughed at his own expression of dismay. 'I'll look forward to meeting him as soon as he's back.' He relaxed in his chair.

'Now that glass of Madeira?' Francis offered.

Jacob gave a little smile. 'Might I be so presumptuous as to ask for a cup of tea? I haven't had a decent one since I left England.'

'Certainly, my dear fellow.' Francis pulled the bell sash beside the fireplace and fifteen minutes later he was pouring out the tea.

They had settled with their cups when the door opened and Charlotte walked in. She stopped on seeing the room occupied. 'Oh, I'm sorry, I didn't know—'

'No, no, come in,' her father cut in as he made a gesturing wave. He went to the bell sash and when the maid appeared ordered another cup and saucer for his daughter.

She nodded to Jacob who had sprung to his feet. 'Mr Craig, so nice to see you and welcome back to London. I hope you had a pleasant time on the Continent.'

'Mrs Campion.' Jacob made a small bow. 'It is indeed a pleasure to be home, particularly to see such a magnificent portrait of yourself.'

'It is good, isn't it?' she said as she sat down.

'Good?' Jacob raised his hands as if in horror of the word. 'That doesn't express the talent it reveals.'

'Jacob is absolutely delighted with it and wants Richard into his studio as soon as he returns in three weeks' time.' Francis enthused.

Charlotte said nothing. Her father and Mr Craig were destined for a big disappointment.

'You'll be missing Mr Parker.' Marietta's statement raised a shiver of alarm in Charlotte. Did she know something? Had she suspected a relationship? Almost at the moment she was dismissing the answers as impossible, Marietta went on, 'It's always the same when someone has been around for some time and then leaves. And Mr Parker has been here since last August.'

'Yes, it was strange at first, particularly as I expected him to be working on the full-length portrait. If I'd known he was going to Whitby I might have gone with Charles.'

It was only four days since Richard had left and Charlotte was missing him terribly. As her best friend she had sought Marietta's company each day. Those moments when she had seen Richard and Marietta together, when little pangs of jealousy had surfaced, she cast aside. Richard could not have declared his love for her so strongly if there had been anything between him and Marietta.

Her friend gave her some feeling of stability. This world of theirs was the one she had known before either Charles or Richard came into her life. Being with her showed her that life must go on. It brought comfort after the seclusion of her bedroom where silent tears had flowed each night and her emotions had been torn apart. Each day became a trial as she tried to assume normality with her parents and the people around her. She had seen her mother cast questioning glances at her and the accompanying query was always passed off as, 'I've a headache,' or 'I feel sickly, it must be something I ate.'

'A shame you missed a holiday on the Continent, but Mr Parker will be back soon and he'll be able to resume work on our portraits,' said Marietta as they decided to take another stroll around the square.

'It couldn't be helped. I understood his reason for wanting to go at this particular time.'

If only she could confide in her friend, tell her the real reason and that Richard would never be coming back, that he had sacrificed his career for love. But he would not want her to do that. Eventually everyone would know that he had forsaken London forever.

Four more days passed and instead of coming to terms with the situation Charlotte found herself longing more and more to see Richard. Her thoughts battled through the fog of false perspectives. Maybe she had not been strong enough in trying to persuade him to stay. Maybe with a new more determined resolve she could make him see that they need not be apart, that they could continue to meet. She would go to Whitby and see him. She would tell him how much Jacob Craig wanted him in his studio, how highly he spoke of his work. She could tempt him with the prospect of becoming a great artist and fulfilling his dream, and that she would be there, with their love remaining a secret.

Charlotte made her preparations to go to Whitby. She booked a passage on the London packet sailing to the Yorkshire port on Monday, in two days' time, knowing that her father and mother would be visiting friends at Hatfield House for a few days.

When she announced that she was going to Reed Hall, as there were a few things she wanted to attend to in preparation for her and Charles's summer residence, her father pointed out that, as he and her mother would be using their carriage, he would hire a coach to take her to the docks. Charlotte smiled to herself for her timing had worked out as she wanted. Which ship she took would be of no consequence to a hired coachman.

The deceit began to weigh heavily on her and she felt the deep need to tell someone where she was really going. Mother? Father? No, they would stop her. But she desperately wanted to confide in someone

The day before she was due to sail, her mother and father having left for Hatfield House, she hurried across Russell Square. She waited impatiently on the doorstep of the Kemp House until the door was opened by a maid.

'Is Miss Marietta at home?' she queried anxiously.

'Yes, Mrs Campion.'

The maid stood to one side and Charlotte stepped into the hall. The maid closed the door and said, 'If you'll wait in the drawing room I'll tell her you are here.' She hurried towards the stairs.

Those words, 'Mrs Campion', suddenly gave Charlotte a conscience. What was she doing? She would be wrecking Charles's life if ever her relationship with Richard was discovered. He didn't deserve that. And yet here she was going to tell Marietta the whole truth. What if she refused to keep her secret? Could Marietta be so unfaithful to their long friendship?

Charlotte almost cried out to tell the maid to forget the request, but the vision of the man with whom she was in love exerted itself. She had to see him. Make one more effort to persuade him to see things her way. The maid reached the top of the stairs and disappeared from sight. Charlotte walked to the drawing room.

Nervous apprehension began to fill her. How should she begin to tell Marietta? She heard footsteps tripping quickly down the stairs and a moment later Marietta burst into the room.

'How nice to see you,' she cried as she rushed forward to hug her friend. As she stepped back her face became serious. In their contact there was not the usual warmth and ease from Charlotte. She sensed all was not well. 'Something is worrying you?' she queried with concern.

'Are we likely to be interrupted?' asked Charlotte.

'Now I know this is serious.' said Marietta, her face clouding with anxiety. 'We won't be disturbed. Father is in the City on business, not expected back until this evening. Mother is lunching with some ladies wanting to raise funds for repair work on a church. So we will be all alone. Now do sit down and compose yourself. Would you like some hot chocolate?'

Charlotte shook her head. 'Not now, thank you.'

She sat on the sofa with Marietta beside her, each half turned towards the other.

'Well?' Marietta prompted when her friend hesitated.

'Where to begin?' Charlotte half whispered to herself.

Marietta caught her words. 'The beginning is generally the best place,' she advised.

Charlotte looked up with doleful eyes. 'I'm not sure it is in this case.'

'Well, you know best.'

A moment passed. Marietta waited.

'I'm going to Whitby!' The words, though quiet, were shattering.

'What?' Marietta gasped, then stared aghast as the real significance sank in. Her mind was in a turmoil. There was only one reason Charlotte would be going to Whitby and that was to see Richard. There must be something deeply serious between them for her, a married woman, to do that. At the same time as these thoughts hit her, her own feelings surfaced. She was experiencing jealous antagonism towards her friend of many years and realised something she had suspected – she herself was in love with Richard and had nurtured the hope that he loved her. He had never given her any sign that he did but she knew he liked being with her and enjoyed her company. Hostility rose sharply. Why should Charlotte fall in love with him? She had Charles. What had she been thinking about to let this happen? She should have stopped it right at the start no matter who had made the first move.

'I am in love with Mr Park – Richard.'

'But ...' Marietta was bewildered, not knowing what to say.

'I know it's all wrong but it has happened. I must go and see him.'

'He'll be back before long. Maybe by that time you'll have seen things in the right perspective. Remember if you pursue this love so many people are going to get hurt and you and Richard will never be accepted in society, even middle-class society. You could face a life of poverty.' The words poured from Marietta as she tried to emphasise a case for calling a halt to this affair.

Charlotte raised a hand to stop the torrent, and said, 'He won't be coming back.'

The statement so coldly put was like a bombshell in Marietta's mind.

'That can't be true. What about his career? Why, only the other day you told me Mr Craig was keen to have him.'

'Richard left because he said there was no future for us in our relationship. He did not want to go but he saw how difficult things might become if he stayed. He did not want me to suffer scandal so he said he would give up his career and return to Whitby.'

Marietta felt numb. This told her with no uncertainty that Richard was in love with Charlotte. She fought back the tears which threatened to expose her own feelings for him. Charlotte must not know that she loved him.

'Who else knows you are going?' she asked.

'No one. After I had made my decision I timed my leaving for when I knew Mother and Father would be away for a few days.'

'Charles?'

Charlotte shook her head. 'He knows nothing. I hope none of them ever will.'

'But if Richard is not coming back are you intending to stay in Whitby?' Marietta was appalled by the possibility and its consequences.

'I am hoping I can persuade Richard to return to take up his career. We can continue to meet in secret.'

Marietta was amazed that her friend should think this way. Charlotte could not hope to keep the secret forever. There would be ruination for them both. If she knew Richard he would not agree to return for he would remain steadfast to protecting Charlotte's life from scandal.

'If you believe he will come back with you why tell me?'

'Since Richard left everything has weighed so heavily on my mind. I just had to tell someone what was happening and what I was doing. You have been a lifelong friend. You were the only person I could turn to.' She looked hard at Marietta, sadness in her eyes. She reached forward and took her hand in hers. 'Please Marietta, keep my secret.'

Marietta met Charlotte's pleading gaze, a look which she could not deny, even though these revelations had pierced her heart. She bit her lip and nodded. 'Very well, your secret is mine.'

The sense of relief on Charlotte's face was overwhelming. 'Thank you,' she whispered and flung her arms round her friend.

'When do you leave?' she asked.

'Tomorrow by ship.'

'Before your mother and father return?'

186

'Yes. I told them I wanted to go to Reed Hall to do some preparations for the summer.'

'So I will be the only one who knows where you are?'

'Yes, but I'll be back in a few days, with Richard.'

Marietta thought Charlotte's certainty was ill-founded but she kept that view to herself. With troubled brow, she asked, 'I don't suppose there is anything I can say to dissuade you from doing this?'

Charlotte's shake of her head was emphatic. 'No.'

Chapter Thirteen

As the ship slipped between the piers and found the tranquillity of the river, Charlotte had a strange feeling. Though she had spent those few days here with her parents, when life had been stable and the future with Charles looked set to fall into a pattern, one she was content with but felt lacked something, this return assumed a move into a different life. Now she was in love and was here seeking to keep alive an experience which fulfilled every need.

The nip in the air recalled that spring had only just gone, while the sunshine and the blue sky, dotted with small banks of white cloud, spoke of nearby summer. Charlotte was content that the weather was benign for she saw it as a good omen for her return to Whitby.

With the ship moving slowly up river to her berth, Charlotte searched the staithes and quays hoping she might catch sight of Richard with his pencil and paper drawing the sights of Whitby. Surely he would be out on such a day? Her heart sank a little when she did not see him but she chided herself for taking such a view. He could be anywhere.

The activity on the quay as the ship tied up brought her back to a more pressing need. She had to find somewhere to stay. The only place she knew was the Angel Inn where she had stayed on her last and only visit, nearly nine months ago. She had decided to avoid the hostelry in case someone there remembered her, even though she had, as a precaution, taken a false name.

People were milling on the quay, dockers tying up the vessel, sailors running out the gangway, Whitby folk shouting greetings to passengers they had come to meet and then welcoming them with hugs and kisses, onlookers merely interested in the arrival of the ship from London. The whole quay was alive. Charlotte spotted a group of young boys jostling for places near the gangway, eager to offer their services to carry passengers' luggage. Maybe her answer lay with one of them.

She picked up her two bags and immediately she was on the quay she was bombarded with requests to carry them. She smiled at the group of six gathered around her and looked them over with a shrewd eye. Two, so much alike that they must be twins, were a little better dressed than the others. Their trousers and jerseys had the signs of a mother's care, their faces looked as though they had been scrubbed clean in contrast to others which had already accumulated the dust of the day.

'Right,' she said firmly, 'You and you.' She pointed at the twins.

Their eyes lit up while the other four groaned and then, quickly forgetting their disappointment, spun away to offer their service to other passengers.

'Where to, miss?' asked one of them.

'First, what are your names?'

'We've become known as Billy One and Billy Two. Folk thought that would help to tell us apart,' replied one of them. He gave a little grunt of derision. 'But it didn't help.'

'I don't suppose it did,' Charlotte smiled. 'So, who are you?'

'Billy One. Whenever anyone is speaking to us we generally hold up one or two fingers so that they know who they are talking to. If we used our proper names folk would get us mixed up. So, where do you want to go miss?'

'Well, now, I was hoping you might be able to help me with that?'

The boys shot each other a querying look as much as to say, 'Who have we got here who doesn't know where she wants to go?'

'I'm new in Whitby,' Charlotte went on.

'The Angel Inn,' suggested Two as he held up identifying fingers.

'Well.' Charlotte looked doubtful. 'I'd rather thought I might find somewhere a little more private, maybe someone who might have a room I could rent for a while.'

The two boys looked at each other again. Two mouthed a word silently to his brother and received a nod in reply. One looked at Charlotte who had been unable to decipher the exchange.

'Two thinks our ma might help.'

'Oh?'

'We'll go and ask her.' The two boys picked up a bag each. 'Follow us.'

They threaded their way between the people standing in groups or going about their business along the quay. They kept their pace to suit Charlotte who looked about her with a questioning expression when they turned into a narrow street which she judged to be heading back towards the river. Houses crowded in on both sides and rising three storeys seemed to be attempting to cut out the light. She had a feeling of claustrophobia having been used to the openness of Russell Square and the big sky country and vast spaces of Lincolnshire. But if this was where she would find a room so be it. They came to the last house on the right and mounted some steps to the front door.

One of the twins, she did not know which, hurried into the house shouting 'Ma! Ma!' The second one stood back and said, 'Go in, miss.'

Charlotte stepped inside, taken by the boy's politeness. She found she was standing in a passage which ran to the back of the house with a narrow staircase on the right.

The first twin came hurrying back followed by his mother who was wiping her hands on a hessian apron. She wore a worried expression of having been caught unawares.

'Ma, this is the lady I told you about. I said you might help her.'

'I hope these two haven't been pestering you, miss. I've told them not to worry passengers coming off the ships, but they will be with a gang who, I might say, are not the most desirable of Whitby lads.'

'Aw, Ma, they're all right,' protested Billy Two, holding up his fingers so that their new acquaintance would know who was speaking.

'I don't want them leading you into any scrapes.'

'We can look after ourselves, Ma, there's two of us.'

His mother smiled. 'Aye, there are, and don't I know it.' She looked at Charlotte. 'Sorry about that, miss. I'm Liza Brodrick.'

'And I'm Grace Mann. I've newly arrived from London and, wanting to find a lodging, I asked your sons if they knew of anywhere.'

'And they suggested here.'

'Oh, no. They said you might be able to help.'

Liza smiled. 'I'm sure they meant here. They must like you otherwise they wouldn't have made such a suggestion.'

Embarrassed, the two boys ran off to the kitchen to satisfy their mid-afternoon hunger. Charlotte saw how much they had inherited from their mother. She was of medium height with brown hair drawn tight to her head and fastened in a bun at the nape of her neck. Her eyes held warmth and friendliness and Charlotte was certain there was love between mother and sons. There was about her an air of confidence which comes from the fact that a woman has to be both mother and father when a husband is away at sea. She wore a plain brown dress, the only relief being a white lace collar. Charlotte judged her to be about forty and thought she would have been pretty in her younger days, but her face now bore the worry marks of a wife whose husband wrests a living from the sea and knows what a merciless enemy it can be.

'They are two fine boys, Mrs Brodrick,' commented Charlotte.

'Aye, they're grand lads but they miss their father. And it's Liza, please.' She wouldn't have made that concession of her Christian name if she hadn't taken to Charlotte. She could see she was a young woman of some breeding. She carried herself well. Her hands, well cared for, had never been employed in rough work of any kind. More than likely she could have had servants. Her clothes, practical for a journey, were of good quality. Her eyes held a sparkle and there was about her the aura of one who was interested in everything around her. Liza liked her attitude towards the boys. Yet she detected a touch of sadness about her, and wondered if that had brought her to Whitby. But it was none of her business and she would not

191

probe. She liked what she had seen and knew the boys did, so she would offer her the room. It would be nice to have some company in the house.

'I do have a spare room and the money will come in useful when my husband is laid off after the whaling season. Let me show you the room.' She led the way up the narrow stairs.

They reached a small landing and Liza opened a door on the left. The room was spotless with a double bed, a chest of drawers, a wash-stand with basin and ewer and a wardrobe. The bed was neatly made with snowy white sheets turned over at the head onto a patchwork quilt. After the size of rooms she was used to this one seemed to close in on Charlotte but she fought against the overwhelming feeling and saw it as suitable to her immediate needs.

'This will be right for me.'

'But we haven't fixed a price,' protested Liza.

'I'm sure it will be agreeable to me. I don't think you are one to overcharge.'

'How long will you want the room?'

'I'm not sure at this moment. Can I let you know later?'

'Yes. Do you want me to provide your meals?'

'Please. And let me have them with you and the boys.'

'But we generally eat in the kitchen.'

'Then let me as well.'

'I have another room downstairs which you can use.'

'Thank you, but let me eat with you unless you would rather I didn't.'

'Oh, no it's not that,' Liza hastened to reassure her. Her serious express changed to a wry smile. 'It might do the Billy boys good. They'll have to be on their best behaviour.'

'How do you tell them apart?'

'Well, I'm used to them but even so I still sometimes make a mistake. Their father is always confused for a time when he returns home.' Liza turned her attention back to the room. 'I think there is everything you'll need. I'll put some towels in later. Now let me show you downstairs.' As they stepped on to the landing Liza indicated a door opposite. 'That's my room. The boys sleep on the next floor in the roofspace. They have a similar view across the river to you.'

Once Charlotte had been shown the rest of the house the

boys took her luggage to her room where she unpacked her few belongings.

After putting the last item away she looked round the room and stepped to the window. Below, the river flowed sluggishly by. Across the water the shipbuilding yards were busy. The old houses beyond the quays, on the other side of the river, sent smoke curling into the air. Two four-masted ships were moored in midstream and several small craft plied their way across the water. The strange surroundings, so far from home, gnawed at her. She felt the sickness of unease in the pit of her stomach and she began to doubt the wisdom of coming here. The call of home was strong. She must counteract it quickly. She must see Richard.

Her troubled thoughts were interrupted by a knock on the door. She opened it to find Billy holding up one finger.

'Ma says would you like to come down for a cup of tea.'

Charlotte smiled. 'Indeed I would.' She closed the door and followed him to the kitchen.

Charlotte found herself in a square room with one window over the stone sink which was positioned with a view down-stream towards the bridge. A black-leaded grate held a red fire which also heated the oven beside it. A table and four chairs occupied the centre of the room. The flagged floor was neatly swept and two clip rugs added a little comfort. Charlotte was aware that Liza was a neat person who prided herself on keeping a good home and did her best out of what money was forthcoming from her husband.

As they were drinking their tea Charlotte put a query. 'You said your husband served on a whaleship, would that be with Captain Parker?'

Liza shook her head. 'No. He's with Captain Witham on the *Bird*. Do you know Captain Parker?'

'No, I don't, but I would be grateful if you could direct me to where he lives.'

'Certainly. Prospect Place. Rather than tell you how to get there, the boys can show you.'

'Thank you that would be kind.' She glanced at them. 'Is that all right with you two?'

With their mouths crammed with bread and jam, they both nodded eagerly.

'Captain Parker is away whaling,' Liza pointed out.

Charlotte thought quickly. She did not want to reveal her real reason for being in Whitby. 'I know. It's Mrs Parker I want to see.'

Liza was curious but she dared not press any questions. 'Martha's a nice person.'

When Charlotte made no comment Liza concluded that she did not know Mrs Parker either. So what business had this young woman, recently arrived in Whitby on the ship from London, with Martha Parker? Liza drew herself up short. It was no concern of hers.

'This is the house, miss.' Holding up one finger Billy indicated the building in Prospect Place.

'Thank you,' smiled Charlotte. 'You needn't wait. I'll find my own way back.'

The boys ran off and Charlotte, her heart beating faster, turned to the door. She hesitated a moment, trying to think what she should say, but that would depend on who answered the rap of the doorknocker.

A few moments later the door opened and Charlotte was confronted by a woman of medium height whom she reckoned was in her forties. Her round features were motherly and lined with friendliness. Her brown eyes, sharp, probing and alert, were now asking questions. Who are you? What do you want?

'Mrs Parker?' asked Charlotte tentatively.

'Aye,' said Martha, eyeing this well-dressed young woman with curiosity.

'I'm Grace Mann. You haven't met me before.'

You're right, lass, I haven't, thought Martha, but she was puzzled. There was something familiar about this stranger. Her mind struggled to find an answer but couldn't. 'What can I do for you?'

'It's really Mr Richard Parker I want to see.'

'I'm afraid he isn't at home,' Martha replied. She saw a flash of disappointment cross Charlotte's face and immediately said, 'Will you step inside.' Something about this person niggled at her. She wanted a few moments to try to identify what it was.

'Thank you.'

194

After Martha had closed the door she led the way into a room on the left.

'My daughters, Sarah and Maggie. This is ...' she hesitated. 'What did you say your name was?'

'Grace Mann,' she replied firmly.

As Charlotte repeated the name, recognition flashed in Martha's mind but she kept a tight hold on her feelings. You aren't Grace Mann, she thought. I recognise you from Richard's sketch. You're Mrs Campion, the young woman with whom he told me he was in love and for whom he left London so that no scandal besmirched your name. Now what are you doing here?

'Sorry the room is upside down, as you see we are busy sewing, and you can never keep a room tidy when you are doing that.'

'What are you making?' asked Charlotte, wanting to appear friendly.

'Dresses for these two,' replied Martha. She turned to her daughters. 'We'll leave this for the time being. You two run along and do that shopping for me.'

The two girls hurried from the room.

These few moments had made time for Martha to decide what to do, but first of all she wanted to know why this married woman was here. 'You want to see Richard?'

'Yes. I heard that he paints portraits. I'm interested in having mine done and wondered if he would take a commission.'

'I have no doubt he would be interested,' replied Martha. 'But I don't know when he will be back.'

'Oh, dear. That's a pity.'

'He came home from London. Said he was going away. He had some things he wanted to see to,' explained Martha. 'He said he would let us know where he was but we haven't heard from him yet. If you leave your address I'll tell him to get in touch with you.'

'I had better try again,' replied Charlotte.

Martha smiled to herself. So you have come after Richard. Well, better you don't know that he's gone whaling. If you did you would know approximately when he would be coming home. Now, maybe you'll return to London and see things in their proper place as befits a married woman.

'Very well, if you prefer that.'

'I think it's probably best. Thank you for your time. I'm sorry I troubled you.'

'That's all right. I'll pass your message on to Richard when I hear from him.'

Martha watched Charlotte for a few moments after she had left the house. She could see why Richard had fallen for her. She was pretty and those blue eyes were so enchanting. Not only that, she seemed a nice person, one who wouldn't normally lie about her name, but Martha could understand why she had done so. She would probably have done the same in the circumstances. Hopefully Mrs Campion would have time to think, get tired of waiting and return to London, not to be seen in Whitby again.

Charlotte was downcast as she walked away from Prospect Place. She had expected Richard to be in Whitby. Her disappointment was sharper because she had been in Richard's home, been in the rooms in which he had lived, met his mother and sisters and, brief though all that had been, she felt close to him, as if she had stepped into some tiny portion of his world.

What should she do now? If his mother did not know when he would be back was there any point in remaining in Whitby just on the off chance that he might return soon? When he did return his mother would tell him about Grace Mann and it would mean nothing to him, but when she described her visitor Richard would immediately know Grace Mann's identity. That might bring him hastening to London to find out why she had visited the Yorkshire port. It made sense to return south.

She had almost reached Tin Ghaut, where the Brodricks lived, when she saw Sarah and Maggie heading home with their shopping.

'Hello, you two,' she called pleasantly. 'Did you get everything you wanted?'

'Yes and a bargain, the cod,' replied Sarah, pleased that they had done well.

'Used our charm and he gave us a couple of crabs as well,' put in Maggie.

'Mark's a friend,' explained Sarah. 'Richard goes fishing with him.'

'A pity your brother wasn't home, I wanted to commission a painting,' said Charlotte casually.

'I'm sure he'll be glad to hear that when he gets back from the whaling. Mother will tell him.'

Whaling! The news stunned her. Richard had said he hated it! So why had he gone? She kept her emotions outwardly under control. 'Yes, she said she would let him know.'

Charlotte made her goodbyes before any more was said. Now she had information which needed considering. But what was behind it? Had Richard seen whaling as a new aspect of life in which she would have no part, something completely foreign to the art world in which she had been involved? Why had his mother lied about where he was? Why hadn't she said he was whaling? That puzzled her but it was of no immediate consequence.

It was a thoughtful Charlotte who reached the house in Tin Ghaut.

During the meal that evening she cemented her relationship with Liza even more when she readily answered the twins' questions about London. She saw no reason to hide the fact that that was where she had lived for she had arrived on the London packet. She liked their bright curiosity and admired their intelligent questions.

'Now,' she said when their mother was packing them off to bed, 'Sixpence each if you'll show me round Whitby tomorrow and answer my questions. Would you like that?'

Their assent erupted in shouts of excitement.

With the boys settled in bed Liza and Charlotte sat down to enjoy a little peace and quiet.

'You saw Mrs Parker?'

'Yes. Really it was her son Richard, the artist, I wanted to see but thought it might be best to approach him through his mother. But he's away with the whalers.'

'Is he?' Liza showed a little surprise. 'I thought he was the one son who didn't like whaling.'

'Yet he's gone this time.'

'No doubt he'll be on the *Phoenix* with his father.'

'When do the whaleships return?'

'July, August, depending on how the whaling has gone. If it's been good they could be early, bad and they might be late. Some of them run risks if they haven't a full ship and stay, hoping for one more catch.'

Charlotte wondered whether to return home or not.

Awakening to the early morning light filtering reluctantly through the net curtains, Charlotte had a feeling that a decision to stay had been made in her subconscious mind. But, as she stood looking out of the window watching the mist rise from the river, she realised there were practical things to think of. Charles – he would return from the Continent and be told she was at Reed Hall. Arriving there he would find out that she had never been there. But would he ever surmise she was in Whitby? That was a risk she would have to take if she stayed, and then face the situation if he came. Money – well, she had what was left of the generous sum Charles had made available for her while he was away, and she had brought some jewellery which she could sell. Staying was a possibility, and that was strengthened when she was out with the Billy boys touring Whitby.

They had obviously given some thought to what direction they should take.

'Had a good look at Whitby, Miss Mann?' Liza asked when they returned, red cheeks glowing with the effort and the tang of the wind.

'Grace, please,' she said, desiring to be on first-name terms and be part of the household. 'Yes, we've been everywhere and I've had two good guides.'

The boys grinned at the praise.

'I hope you didn't rush Miss Mann – Grace – too much.'

'They didn't. They were very considerate.'

'Good.' Liza turned to her sons. 'You two get thissens washed. Ten minutes and be sitting at this table.'

The boys scampered off and climbed the stairs to their room to use the basin and ewer, as their mother had instructed they should do, rather than use the kitchen sink while Miss Mann was with them.

'And you'll be wanting to freshen up too?' said Liza.

'Yes,' returned Charlotte, 'But first. Your sons are very

198

knowledgeable and bright. They showed me their school.'

'Teaching is limited. Jem and I know they want to learn so we help them whenever we can.'

'That's what they told me and it gave me an idea. I've decided I'll stay in Whitby and I'll open a private school. I've had a good schooling and I think I could pass most of it on. There must be merchants, shopkeepers, ship's captains and so on who would pay to have their children well educated.'

'There are already two or three ladies doing just that but I'm sure there is room for another.'

'Good,' said Charlotte with firm satisfaction. 'The two Billy's will be my first pupils.'

'But I couldn't pay ...' started Liza.

'I wouldn't expect you to,' Charlotte reassured her. The excitement of the experience of a new venture charged her voice as she went on. 'I'll need some premises. Maybe you could help me find somewhere suitable tomorrow and then maybe you would like to help keep the place clean and tidy. I would pay you a small sum.'

'No,' replied Liza. She rephrased her meaning quickly when she saw surprised disappointment cloud Charlotte's face. 'Oh, Grace, please don't misunderstand. Of course I'll help, but I won't take any money. Educating my two boys will be enough.'

'That is very kind and thoughtful of you, but I insist I give you something. We'll talk about that tomorrow when we find somewhere for my school.'

'Very well. Now off you go and freshen up. The potato and onion pie will soon be ready.'

'I'm looking forward to it, it smells so good.' With a smile Charlotte hurried away.

Liza stared at the closed door. She liked Grace but who was she? Why had she left London? Why had she decided to settle in Whitby? How did she know Richard Parker was an artist? Grace had offered no explanation and Liza did not want to pry. Maybe she would tell her in her own good time; in the meantime Liza would take things as they came. So far, even in this short time, they had been good. Grace was friendly. She had taken to the boys. There was the chance of a little extra money, which was not a bad thing when Jem's wage would depend on how good the whaling was. But more than that her boys would get some education and she had no doubt, from the way Grace conducted herself, the way she spoke, it would be wider than anything she and Jem could give them.

The following morning over breakfast Liza informed Charlotte that she had been giving some thought to a suitable property for her school.

'There are some houses for sale in Cliff Lane on the other side of the river. It would be quite a good place to be, with more and more of the better-off moving to the west side.'

'Then we shall go and see them together and the boys can come too if they want to,' pronounced Charlotte.

There was no denying the two Billys and they were eager at the thought of being taught by Miss Mann.

In the course of the day they looked at five properties and decided on one in Cliff Lane. It had three storeys. The front door opened into a small hall with a staircase directly ahead. On the right were two rooms, one of which was ideal for a schoolroom, while the other could act as Charlotte's study and double as an extra schoolroom if any individual tuition was needed. At the rear of the house was the kitchen which surprised Liza with its size after her own small compact room. The first floor contained two rooms, one of which Charlotte visualised as her drawing room with the other as her bedroom. The third floor also had two good-sized rooms and one smaller one. These Charlotte decided would remain empty until she was able to judge if they were needed.

The house had been decorated throughout only a month before the owners decided to leave to be nearer their daughter in Scarborough who had recently been widowed. With nothing to spend on decorating Charlotte was able to indulge a little more in furnishings.

Ten days later with carpets, tables, chairs and other necessary items installed, Charlotte was ready to interview parents and prospective pupils. She had put advertisements throughout the town announcing the opening of a new school with pupils offered education in reading, writing and arithmetic together with art, needlework, geography and history, deportment and etiquette under the guidance of Miss Grace Mann, recently arrived in Whitby. Interviews would take place on the thirty-first of March and the school would be open on the sixth of April.

Charlotte was apprehensive on the thirty-first but Liza did everything possible to reassure her that she would do well. Charlotte had left Tin Ghaut the day before, insisting that she would be all right alone in Cliff Lane. That night had brought doubts to her mind and she had to fight hard to convince herself that she was doing the right thing. In all the excitement of preparing the school her personal problems had faded somewhat. But in the quietness of the night they had resumed enormous proportions again. If only Richard was here: but he was far away in dangerous waters. Charles would soon be back in England. What then? What did the future hold? Had she been foolish? Should she give all this up and return to her family? No one would ever know where she had really been, only Marietta, and she trusted her friend to keep her secret.

Daylight brought an easing to her mind. Now there was activity and other things on which she had to concentrate. Liza came early. Her presence was like a rock to Charlotte and the ghosts of the night receded to the distant corners of her mind.

'You'll be all right, lass,' said Liza, putting a plate of bacon and fried bread before Charlotte and pouring her a cup of strong tea. She had interpreted Charlotte's paleness as doubt about facing probing parents. 'Just be yourself. Let them see what you have to offer their children but show that you can be firm and fair at the same time.'

'What if no one comes?' said Charlotte doubtfully.

'Of course you'll have customers.'

Liza was right and by the end of the day Charlotte had enrolled six children apart from the two Billys.

By opening day she had gained another five pupils.

Charlotte was delighted with the way things developed. Finding she was teaching responsive children heightened her interest in the venture and kept her mind focused on her new life.

That was only disrupted on the twenty-third of April, the

201

day she knew Charles was due back from the Continent. Now the whole enormity of what she had done reared its head again and she realised she faced a disruptive and agonising future.

'Sir, a sailor from Mr Campion's ship said that immediately they docked in London he was to bring this message here.' The maid held out two envelopes to Francis.

He and Gertrude were entertaining Adeline and Simon Kemp together with Marietta to tea.

He thanked her and, as she left the room, he glanced down at them. He looked up sharply at Gertrude. 'One is addressed to Charlotte, the other to me.'

'Then we had better send hers on. Is Charles's ship going on to Boston?'

'In a couple of days' time.' He stared at the envelopes. 'I wonder what these are about?'

'Well, my dear, there's only one way to find out. Read yours,' said Gertrude with a sly smile at Adeline as much as to say: 'These men never take the obvious line.'

'I suppose so.' Francis tore the envelope open and pulled out a sheet of paper. He glanced at it quickly, muttered 'Oh my God,' and then read:

My dear Francis,

It is with great regret that I write to tell you I am laid low with a fever. It may delay my return but hopefully not too long. There is nothing to worry about. I am in good hands and being well looked after. I have been told that this type of fever takes some time to clear so I cannot give any certain date when I will be home.

In the meantime, dear friend, I enclose some documents connected with business interests. There are several items which will need attention in the next four days some of which involve you, the others, my chief clerk, Bellamy, you know him, will tell you what needs authorisation. Please take care of them all.

I hope this fever will soon pass.

I am, sir, your faithful servant and son-in-law.

Charles

'Oh, poor Charles,' said Gertrude with concern. 'Oh my goodness, Charlotte should have that letter. It no doubt tells her of his misfortune. She'll want to come back to London, be here when Charles gets home. Francis, you must go to Lincolnshire.'

The suggestion brought panic to Marietta. Charlotte wasn't at Reed Hall and something had detained her in Whitby. She should have been home by now. She had expected to persuade Richard to return with her within a few days, yet a month had passed. Should she tell Mr and Mrs Wakefield where their daughter really was? But that would betray the trust of a very dear friend. She couldn't do that no matter what. But if Mr Wakefield went to Reed Hall ...

A sense of some relief came with Francis's reply. 'Gertrude. I cannot do that. You heard Charles's letter to me. There are business interests which must be seen to and by the time I have done that the ship will have left.'

Gertrude held back her annoyance. She could see her husband's dilemma. He would be concerned about his daughter yet he could not let down a business partner. 'Then we must get that letter back to the ship and instruct the captain to see that it is delivered into Charlotte's hands.'

Marietta's mind had been moving swiftly through the situation. She broke into the conversation. 'Mr and Mrs Wakefield, Charlotte invited me to visit her at Reed Hall. This might be a good opportunity, so I could take the letter.' She glanced at her mother and saw doubt about her travelling alone. 'I'll be perfectly all right. Our own coachman will see me on to the ship. The captain will be responsible for me and will no doubt see me safely on to some conveyance for Reed Hall.'

Her generosity and eagerness to help friends convinced her mother and father that it was a good idea.

'Well, if you are sure,' said Gertrude when Adeline had given her approval. 'It will be a weight off my mind and we'll be sure Charlotte knows of Charles's illness.'

'Jenkins, take me to the Whitby ship,' Marietta instructed her coachman when they reached the docks.

'But, miss, I thought ...'

'The Whitby ship,' she insisted.

'Very well, miss.' He turned the carriage away from the Campion vessel bound for Boston.

Marietta's heart was all of a-flutter though outwardly she had a firm grip on her emotions. Tension had been heightened by the order she had given, for that moment signified the start of this underhand venture.

Prepared to take the ship to Boston and there find an onward sailing to Whitby, or even complete the journey by coach, an alternative she did not fancy, she was relieved to ascertain that the London packet was sailing for Whitby on the same tide.

She felt a certain relief as she stepped down from the carriage, but was aware of curious looks from dockers and sailors who paused in their work to eye the female about to embark.

Jenkins tossed a coin to an urchin who, eagerly looking for a possible source of income, offered to look after horse and carriage, while the coachman carried Marietta's bag and escorted her on board.

'Thank you, Jenkins,' she said as he placed the bag on the deck.

'My pleasure, miss,' he returned. His face was impassive, though Marietta knew he would be wondering why she had altered ships when her father had instructed him to see her safely on board Mr Campion's ship.

As he touched the brim of his hat he turned to go but she stopped him. 'Jenkins, not a word to my father, nor anyone else for that matter, about my change of vessels. It is important that no one knows I have taken the Whitby ship. Just say you saw me safely on board.'

He nodded. 'Very well, miss.'

She was a favourite with all the staff loyal to the Kemp family. They saw her as a lively, kindly person who always had a word for them, someone who brought a bright active atmosphere to the house. She knew she could trust him to keep her secret.

'You can see Whitby Abbey, miss,' The mate of the London

packet pointed out the ruin which had just come into view, a mere dot as yet. 'A welcoming landmark for all sailors coming into Whitby.'

Marietta's interest was aroused. She had never been to Yorkshire before and was a little apprehensive about being alone in a strange town, knowing no one, with no knowledge of where Charlotte would be and with no idea where Richard lived. She banished her misgivings. She was a resourceful young woman and she could make enquiries. She would deal with matters as they arose. It was not in her to anticipate the future and any problems it might have.

For now, she concentrated on the unfolding scene as the ship plied the last few miles to Whitby. She took an interest in things around her and liked the experience of seeing new places.

She wondered how they were going to find a harbour on this coast dominated by towering cliffs, yet she knew there was one, for Richard had told her of the River Esk flowing between high cliffs and affording vessels a natural sheltered harbour with quays lining the banks upstream.

Then she saw the break in the formidable coast, with the piers guarding the entrance to the river and tempering the breaking waves to the tranquillity of the river. She was drawn by the houses clinging tenaciously to the cliffs on either side of the river, with the greater concentration on the east side below the abbey and the ancient parish church. Sunlight pierced the smoke, rising from the multitude of chimneys, to inflame the red tiled roofs. Richard had told her Whitby was a thriving port, and she guessed that, with the wealth attained through its many trading facets, there were those who were moving to the new buildings she could see high on the west side overlooking the town and river.

After the extent of the Thames and the port of London this was small but here there seemed to be much more activity for it was concentrated in a smaller area. The whole place was alive and Marietta indulged in speculation as to what everyone was doing and where the vessels at the quays would be going when they left port.

She was so drawn in the whole panorama that she had to jerk herself back to the reality of her purpose at being here.

She cast her eyes across the warren of streets, over the houses which hung on the cliff sides; each climbing upwards, standing on the one below, vying for a place nearer the open sky. Where in all those buildings, among all those people, was Charlotte? The task of finding her hung heavily on her mind. She was beginning to wish she had told Mr and Mrs Wakefield the truth, but she drove that thought away as loyalty to her friend prevailed.

It was a month since she had expected Charlotte back in London. What had happened? The possibilities troubled her. Charlotte might not be in Whitby. But if not, why had she not returned home? Surely she and Richard had not gone elsewhere, risking scandal and ruining a career which she herself wanted to encourage and see blossom?

The town seemed to take on an air of hostility towards her as if protecting its own. She feared the worst but now she was anxious for the ship to dock so she could confront the truth whatever it might be.

Chapter Fourteen

When Marietta reached the gangway, the mate, who had been supervising the disembarkation, wished her a pleasant stay in Whitby.

She thanked him and added, 'I do not know the town, can you recommend me somewhere suitable to stay?'

'I'm a Whitby man so I have never stayed at the Angel Inn but I can vouch for its reputation. It's second to none.'

'Good, then the Angel it is. Can you direct me?'

The mate eyed a group of boys seeking to help passengers at the foot of the gangway. 'Hi, you.' Youthful faces turned towards him, each hoping that the call was directed at him. 'You, Sweep!'

One of them detached himself from the group and raced to the gangway with a triumphant gleam in his eye.

'Appropriate name, miss, as you can see,' smiled the mate.

The youngster's face was black with smuts as if he had just come down a chimney. His hands and clothes were no cleaner. His bare feet were just as grubby and his trousers and jersey were in need of repair.

'He's as clean as a new pin first thing in the morning, but within half an hour he's like this,' the mate explained. 'Take no notice of his appearance, he's a good lad.'

The boy had reached the deck. He looked eager-eyed at the mate. 'Sir?' His voice was crisp.

'Sweep, take this young lady's bag and escort her to the Angel.'

'Sir!' grinned Sweep. 'Miss!' He turned his bright eyes on Marietta. 'Please follow me.' He picked up the bag and was about to start down the gangway when the mate stopped him.

'Report back to me.'

'Aye, aye, sir.' Sweep, with a serious face, did a mock salute, then let his expression dissolve into a broad grin.

Marietta followed the boy on to the quay. He kept two paces in front of her, frequently glancing over his shoulder to make sure he kept to that distance. She smiled to herself at his meticulousness and was thankful for it as it meant that she did not lose sight of him among the people thronging the quays and Church Street.

Flour and sailcloth were being loaded ready for tomorrow's departure, knives flashed, gutting a late arrival of fish, ropes were being taken on board a vessel in need of repair, while curious idlers watched the activity and old sailors pined for the days when they were part of the hustle and bustle of the port.

Sweep led the way across the bridge, weaving through the flow of people, and turned into Baxtergate. As he entered the Angel Inn he was stopped by an elderly man, whose stooped shoulders and hunched back were signs of long years of portering. His jowls drooped in a melancholy way matching the look in the grey eyes. 'Out,' he croaked and pointed to the exit with long skeletal fingers. 'Thee can't come in here.'

Sweep stopped in a defiant stance, legs apart, eyes fired by the curt obstruction.

'Here I is and here I stays, Charlie. I bring thee custom, this young lady.' He inclined his head with a glance over his shoulder. 'Now off with thee, I'll deal with no one less than Mr Griffiths, the landlord himself.'

The old man scowled at the impudence and would have responded with a clip round Sweep's ear if he had dared, but custom was custom and he had no desire to incur Mr Griffiths' ire by turning it away. To confirm the truth of Sweep's statement he glanced at Marietta who, though trying to suppress her amusement at Sweep taking his escort duties so seriously, nodded to him.

The old man pulled a face at Sweep and shuffled away, his feet scuffing across the floor.

Sweep turned and grinned at Marietta as much as to say, 'I told him,' but instead said, 'We'll soon have you fixed up, miss.'

A few moments later a large man, with a round rosy face and bright eyes beneath bushy eyebrows the colour of which matched his brown hair, appeared. His trousers were tight round the protruding stomach of a well-fed man who also liked his ale. He wore an immaculate white shirt, with a neat cravat at his neck, the shirt partially covered by a fine embroidered waistcoat. His smile was broad and friendly.

'Good day, miss. Abraham Griffiths, landlord of the Angel Inn, at your service.' He bowed slightly and when he looked up he winked at the boy. 'Hello, there, Sweep. You had no trouble escorting this charming young lady?'

'None, sir.'

'Good, lad. And thank you for doing so. Away to the kitchen, there'll be some pie for you there.'

'Thanks, sir.' His eyes were bright with the thought of the feast as he turned to Marietta, who held out a sixpence to him. He wiped his hand down his trouser leg as if that would clean it before he touched the silver coin. 'Thanks, miss.'

'I might have some calls to make in Whitby. I have never been here before. Will you be my guide?'

'Yes, miss,' he replied gleefully.

'Ten o'clock in the morning.'

'I'll be here, miss.' He turned and ran deeper into the building.'

'A good land, in spite of his appearance,' the landlord informed her. 'Now, you require a room?'

'Please.'

'How long for?'

'I don't really know. I've come to find someone who came to Whitby about a month ago. Have you a Mrs Campion staying here?' Marietta's hopes were high that she might have to look no further.

'No, miss. We have no one of that name staying here at the moment.' When he saw disappointment cross Marietta's face he said, 'But let me check the register to see if Mrs Campion was here recently.' He looked thoughtful as he flicked the pages of the book. 'Ah, here's something, a Mrs Campion stayed here last summer.' He clicked his fingers. 'A nice young lady. She was here with her father and mother.'

'That's her,' confirmed Marietta excitedly.

Abraham shook his head. 'That's the only time she has been here.'

Marietta's heart sank. She would have to start her search tomorrow.

By the following morning she had made up her mind that the first thing she would do was to try to locate Richard. At ten o'clock she left her room only to find that Sweep was not waiting for her downstairs, but seeing Charlie hovering around she went outside.

Immediately she appeared a figure jumped up from the ground where he had been sitting near the entrance to the hostelry.

'Morning, miss,' Sweep cried brightly.

'Hello,' Marietta smiled. She saw that the mate of the London packet had been right. There were signs that Sweep had been scrubbed clean but he was already attracting dust and dirt.

'Where to, miss?'

'Do you know where the Parkers live?'

'Captain Parker, sails the *Phoenix* whaleship?'

'Yes.'

'Who doesn't know where one of the most successful whaling captains lives? We've to go across the river.'

Whitby was alive with morning work and gossip, but Marietta, with her mind so focused on the possible encounter ahead, had little time to consider what was going on around her.

Sweep stopped at the bottom of the steps leading up to Prospect Place. 'That's the house, miss.' He indicated the one he meant. 'I'll wait for you here.'

Marietta hesitated, looking the building over without really seeing it. Then she sharpened her perception, resolved to make her approach head on and stepped past Sweep. He sat down on the bottom step to watch the movement of boats along the river.

Marietta, the tightness of apprehension in her chest, rapped the knocker. A few moments later the door was opened by a young woman of about her own age.

'Hello,' Sarah said as she cocked her head enquiringly on one side.

'Good day,' replied Marietta. As soon as the words were out she wished she hadn't made her greeting so formal. She lightened her voice as she asked, 'Would I find Richard Parker here?'

'You are at the right house, but I'm afraid he's not at home.'

'Oh.' The tone of her disappointment and the downcast look on her face made Sarah curious.

This was the second young lady in only a few weeks to be looking for her youngest brother. What had he been up to? How many hearts had he conquered? Her mother had dealt with the first one then, without giving a reason, had admonished her and Maggie for revealing that Richard was with the whalers. Better if she dealt with this one as well.

'I think you should have a word with my mother. You had better come in.' She held the door while Marietta stepped inside, and then showed her into the living room. 'I'll call her, she's upstairs with my sister, Maggie, changing the beds.'

A few moments later Marietta heard footsteps coming quickly down the stairs. An older voice said, 'You go and help Maggie finish off.' Then the door opened and the woman came in. She was smoothing her dress from which she had removed an apron as she came downstairs. 'Good morning, miss.' Her voice was friendly, her smile warm, though her eyes probed with curiosity. Marietta felt immediately at ease with her.

'Mrs Parker, I presume?' said Marietta.

Martha nodded and said, 'Please sit down. I understand you are looking for my son?'

'Yes,' replied Marietta. They both sat down facing each other from armchairs neatly positioned on each side of the fireplace. 'First I must introduce myself. I am Marietta Kemp and I met him in London.'

'Sarah told you he was not here. Well, when he came home at the end of February he signed on to sail with his father, a whaling voyage to the Arctic.' Martha saw no reason to withhold that information now that her daughters had revealed the truth to Mrs Campion who was still in Whitby passing herself off as Miss Mann.

'Oh, dear,' remarked Marietta, her thoughts thrown into

211

confusion. Richard must have left before Charlotte reached Whitby. So where was she? She must, after all, have gone to Reed Hall from here. Marietta felt relieved that the situation might have given her time to reconsider her actions.

'May I ask why you want to contact my son?' Martha asked. She had been scrutinising Marietta in her own way. She liked her outward appearance. She was well dressed, held herself neatly and had an attractive open face, pretty, in a slightly different way to Mrs Campion. There was a gentleness about her which Martha liked, but her best feature was her dark eyes expressing a warmth which she could feel. She marvelled that Richard had met two such attractive young women, who should come seeking him. She had noticed that this one did not wear a wedding ring, but then neither did Mrs Campion, whom she suspected had removed it before approaching her; there had been the telltale mark on her finger. There was none on this young lady's. If Richard liked this one why had he got entangled with the other?

Marietta hesitated, wondering what reason she should give. Was there any reason to disguise the fact that she had really come looking for Charlotte? Maybe Mrs Parker knew nothing of Richard's involvement with Charlotte. Would she be betraying him if she said anything? Maybe it was better to take that risk. If Charlotte had been here would Mrs Parker tell her? But she had to know, otherwise she would have to take the chance that Charlotte had gone to Lincolnshire.

'Well, Mrs Parker, it is not strictly true that I was looking for your son. I was really looking for someone else and I hoped he might be able to help me locate this person.' She held Martha's intent gaze to prove the honesty of her statement.

'Are you looking for a lady?'

Marietta looked at Martha with disquiet. What did Mrs Parker know? 'Er, yes.' She drew the words out.

'A married lady?'

'Yes.'

'Mrs Campion?'

'Yes. You know her? She's been here?' Marietta's eyes had brightened with hope. Her questions were incisive.

Martha nodded. 'Yes, she's been here.'

212

'Where is she now? Do you know?' Marietta persisted.

'Before I answer that, what is she to you?'

'A friend. A very dear friend. I don't want to see her marriage ruined through scandal.'

Martha's hackles came up. Her eyes narrowed, never leaving Marietta's. 'Are you blaming Richard for this?'

Marietta recognised a mother's protective arm shielding her son even in his absence. She hastened to give her reassurance. 'No, Mrs Parker, I'm not. I got to know Richard in London, through Mrs Campion. I admire him and his work. Maybe he could have done something to prevent feelings developing between them but I know Charlotte – Mrs Campion, and I am sure she should shoulder most of the blame for what has happened. If that was not so then Richard would not have left London and she would not have come looking for him. I am here to try to persuade Charlotte to return to London with me and allow Richard to continue his career as an artist, for I think it would be a great loss, not only to the art world, but to himself. He has talked to me about his ambition and how you encouraged him. I want to see that fulfilled. I hope I can make Charlotte see what she might ruin apart from herself.'

Martha had let the words pour from Marietta without interruption. She had been shrewdly weighing up her information and her attitude. There was a determination about her which encouraged Martha's hope that this explosive situation could be solved before Richard's return. She admired Marietta's faith in Richard's work, and she just wondered if this young woman had feelings for her son which might be reciprocated if Mrs Campion was to resume her married life as she should.

Martha nodded. 'I see. You seem to be very understanding. Well, Mrs Campion is still in Whitby, but she is not going by that name. She is using the name she gave me – Miss Grace Mann.' Marietta raised her eyebrows in surprise. 'But I was not fooled. though she does not know I recognised her.'

'Recognised?'

'Yes, from one of Richard's sketches. He was showing me some when he came home for Christmas. One slipped from the back of his pad. I don't think I was meant to see it. He admitted it was the young lady whose portrait he was painting and later, when I tackled him, he said he was in love with her. I advised him that only trouble would come of it. But he had to return to finish the portrait. I warned him to be very careful about their feelings for each other. When he came home after finishing the portrait he told me he was back in Whitby for good and that he would be contented to pursue his art work around here. That hurt me for I realised the opportunities he was throwing away, chances he deserved for being so devoted to his work.' Her voice faltered. Tears were damping her eyes.

'Mrs Parker, we both want the same thing. Maybe we can achieve it together.' Marietta spoke softly but with a firmness which offered hope. At the same time it lifted any barrier there might have been between them. She was offering trust and good will, things they must share if they were to save what could so easily be lost. 'May I ask you why he sailed with the whalers? He told me he hated the life.'

'He does. I believe he went hoping it would purge any feelings he had for Mrs Campion.'

'And we won't know that until the whalers return.'

'Any time in July and August, depending on how good the whaling is.'

'So if I can persuade Mrs Campion to return with me to London she would not be here to confuse Richard's feelings when he returns.'

'Any influence she had would be gone.'

'I'll go to see Charlotte immediately. Where does she live?'

'In Cliff Lane. She is running a school there.'

'A school?' Marietta did not disguise her surprise. 'So it looks as if she intends to stay until your son returns. It will be hard to try to make her see sense.'

'What about her husband?' asked Martha, now curious that he had never been mentioned.

'Charles. A fine man who dotes on his wife. Twenty years older than Charlotte – and that may be the trouble after she met someone of her own age.'

'But surely she had met younger men before.'

'Oh, yes. Being friends we moved in the same circles but I can tell you there wasn't one who could match your son.'

Martha felt a little flicker of pride at this praise and she also detected there might be more than admiration in Marietta's voice.

'Charles is a rich man. Charlotte wants for nothing. He is a successful merchant, a shipowner and has an interest in other businesses as well as extensive estates in Lincolnshire.'

'Does he know what has been going on?'

'Oh, no. He doesn't even suspect.'

'Then how has Mrs Campion managed to come to Whitby?' Martha was mystified.

'He's on the Continent on business. Charlotte told her father and mother that she was going to Lincolnshire, but she confided in me as to her true destination. I tried to dissuade her but it was no use. Word reached London that Charles had been taken ill and his homecoming would be delayed. I said I would bring the news to Charlotte and hoped it would help me persuade her to return.'

'Are you going to see her now?'

'Yes. There is no point in waiting.'

'Should I come with you?'

Marietta looked thoughtful for a moment. 'Let me try first. If not then a mother's plea may help.'

Martha nodded. 'I think you are right. Would you like one of my daughters to show you the way?'

'No need, thank you. I have my own guide outside, a boy called Sweep.'

Martha smiled. 'You'll be all right with him.' She stood up. 'Let me get you a cup of chocolate before you leave.'

Though anxious to confront Charlotte as soon as possible, Marietta knew that by partaking of this offering she would be cementing not only an alliance but a friendship.

When she came outside to see Marietta on her way, Sweep politely thanked Martha for the drink. 'You could have come inside, Sweep.'

'I know ma'am, your daughter said so, but I enjoyed it while watching over my Whitby.'

Martha smiled. 'Your Whitby?'

'No place like it, ma'am,' replied Sweep brightly.

'I suppose not,' she replied, for she too was happy where she lived. 'Now, Sweep, I want you to take Miss Kemp to Cliff Lane to the new school there.'

'Miss Mann's Academy.'

'That's right. There's not much you miss around here.'

'Not a thing, ma'am,' he grinned proudly.

When they arrived outside the house in Cliff Lane where a plaque by the side of the door announced its purpose, Sweep jerked the bell pull hard and then moved away to sit on the ground to await Marietta's return.

Liza opened the door and gave the well-dressed stranger a smile. 'Can I help you?' she enquired pleasantly.

'I would like to see Miss Mann, please.'

'Very well. Please step inside.' Marietta did so with some trepidation and stood to one side while Liza closed the door. 'Come this way.' Liza opened the second door on the left and let Marietta into a room which she quickly surmised could be used as an office or a classroom. 'Your name please?' asked Liza.

'Just say an old friend would like to see her. I want to give her a surprise.'

'Very well,' said Liza, drawn into the conspiracy by Marietta's disarming smile.

Left alone she cast a critical and assessing eye around the room. It certainly looked as though Charlotte meant to stay. She had little time for detail when the door opened and Charlotte came in.

Her thoughtful look, as to who the old friend could be, changed to one of shocked but delighted surprise. 'Marietta!' Charlotte flung her arms wide and came quickly to her friend, who received her with equal joy. They embraced in the loving affection they brought each other. 'What are you doing here? How did you find me?' She led Marietta by the hand to the sofa.

'Miss Mann?' Marietta gave a grin.

'The first name I thought of,' laughed Charlotte. 'I didn't want anyone to know who I really was – you never know, though Whitby is remote enough. But how did—?'

'Mrs Parker,' she cut in.

'But she only knows me as Miss Mann.' Charlotte was mystified by Mrs Parker's knowledge.

'She recognised you from one of Richard's sketches.'

Charlotte nodded. 'Ah, now I understand. But I wonder why she kept it to herself until you came along?' She saw the

216

answer as of no consequence and turned away from it by asking, 'How are Mother and Father?'

'They are very well.'

'And they don't know I'm in Whitby? You've kept my secret?'

'They think you are at Reed Hall.'

'Any word from Charles?'

So he's not completely obliterated from your mind, thought Marietta, even though it looks as if you mean to stay in Whitby, banking that Richard's love for you is still there when he returns. Instead she said, 'I have a letter from him for you. Your father got one at the same time. I'm afraid it's not good news.'

Charlotte had a look of serious concern as she took the envelope and slit it open. She withdrew the sheet of paper and read it quickly. Looking up she said, 'I suppose this carries the same news as the one to Father. Charles is ill and says it might delay his return to England.'

'Yes, but your father's letter also contained some work Charles wanted your father to see to. That saved you, for it meant he had to stay in London. Otherwise he would have gone to Reed Hall. I said you had invited me to visit you, so I would bring the letter.'

Charlotte looked relieved. 'You are a dear friend indeed.'

'But what are you going to do? Don't you want to go to Charles?' Marietta had been surprised that this had not been Charlotte's immediate consideration.

'On the Continent?'

'That's where he is.'

'What's the point?'

'Charlotte!' Marietta looked shocked.

'Well, what is? All the trouble of getting to . . .' she glanced down at the letter, '. . . Rüdesheim, in Germany and when I get there he might have recovered and moved on.' She shook her head. 'He says not to worry, he's being well looked after.'

Knowing Charlotte, and recognising the resoluteness in her voice, she knew it was no use insisting that she should go to her husband. 'What about when he comes home?'

'I'll deal with that when it arises.'

'So I take it that you made up your mind to await the return of the whaleships when you learned Richard had gone with them?'

'Yes.'

Marietta looked distressed at this admission even though it was what she expected. 'That was foolish.' Her temper had risen a little. 'You must have known that Charles would be back before then and wonder where you were. He was bound to find out and then you couldn't have avoided the scandal.'

'I am willing to face that. Here in Whitby Richard and I will be all right, so I decided to start this school to bring in a living. Besides, who here is going to be bothered about scandal?'

'Don't be so naïve, Charlotte,' Marietta snapped, impatient at her friend's casual attitude. 'Scandal hits all communities. And what about Richard's art? I thought you were going to persuade him to return to London so he could continue with it there.'

'I began to see that it might lead to an impossible situation trying to keep our love a secret, and goodness knows I wanted it to be that way so Charles wasn't hurt.'

'What you are planning now will devastate him.'

'It will be better to get it over and done with.'

Exasperated by this attitude, Marietta tried another tack. 'But you can't be certain that Richard will still feel the same for you when he returns. I suspect he went with the whalers to try to forget you.'

'Is that his mother speaking?'

'She knows her son.'

Charlotte gave a contemptuous laugh. 'Even if he did go for that purpose, I'll wager it didn't work.'

'So you think your influence is that strong?' There was a touch of disdain in Marietta's voice. 'You might get a shock. Wouldn't it be better to come back to London with me until after he returns? If he thinks anything about you he'll come to you. If he doesn't, then neither Charles, nor anyone else, need know what has gone on.'

Charlotte shook her head. 'No. I feel near him, here in Whitby.'

'That's imagination. Stupid talk,' spat Marietta with even more indignation. 'Don't be a fool. Return home. Forget your feelings, think of Richard's desire and ambition to be a great artist. Would you destroy that? You will if you carry on with this foolish scheme.'

Charlotte's eyes darkened. Her face took on a grim expression. 'I thought we were friends, but now you are preaching at me, telling me what I should do with my life, accusing me of wrecking Richard's career. Well, let me tell you, he was willing to sacrifice it for love of me. He wanted to spare me scandal so decided it would be avoided if he left London and returned to Whitby. I had no idea he would go with the whaleships. I only found that out when I came here. So I decided that if he was willing to make his sacrifices for love then I should be willing to sacrifice my marriage for love. So here I am and here I stay.'

'And you both will suffer, and from that, resentment can grow and that will be compounded by the thoughts of what you both have missed. You're heading for a very uneasy relationship and one which will only lead to upheaval for many others besides yourselves.'

'They'll get over it!' snapped Charlotte, beginning to feel bitter towards her friend.

Marietta gave a small laugh of derision. 'You'll break Charles's heart, as well as your mother's and father's – you an only daughter going down the road to oblivion after what they have done for you. And Richard's family, how do you think they'll feel, especially his mother? What about your friends and neighbours in London? What about Charles's friends in Lincolnshire? Don't you see what you are proposing will affect more than you and Richard?'

'And what about you? How will it affect you, Marietta?' Her tone had become laced with scorn. Her eyes blazed. 'Aren't you trying to get me back to Charles so you can get Richard for yourself? Don't think I didn't notice how you forced yourself on him when he went sketching in Lincolnshire, and how you enjoyed teaching him to dance and skate when you knew I couldn't make a move when Charles was there. Didn't I see a fawning look in your eye when you were watching him paint my portrait?' She snorted. 'I think bringing the letter was a ruse to see what was happening here and to try to get me out of the way, back to London and Charles.'

219

Marietta jumped to her feet. 'You've said enough, Charlotte. Don't you accuse me.'

Charlotte too had risen from the sofa. They faced each other, friends, who a few minutes ago had hugged each other with deep affection, now at loggerheads.

'You think calmly on what I have said.' Marietta's voice was scarcely above a whisper but it was penetrating, filled with hope that Charlotte would see sense and not destroy Richard's life. She turned to the door and without a word of goodbye left the house.

Charlotte, shaken by what had taken place, did not move. Was this the beginning of what could happen? Had she lost someone who had been a friend since childhood? Could Marietta be right about Richard's attitude when he returned from the Arctic? Might his experiences have had a profound effect on his feelings for her? She stiffened her spine and tightened the grip on her thoughts so strongly that she dismissed all doubt Marietta had raised. She was sure Richard would be pleased to see her and be delighted that she planned to stay in Whitby.

Marietta was numb, hurt by the rift in a deep friendship which she had expected to last forever. Even Sweep's bright chatter died as they walked along Cliff Lane and he realised that, in such a sombre mood, she did not want to talk.

'Where to, miss?' he ventured when they reached the end of Cliff Lane.

She sighed. 'Mrs Parker's, I suppose.' She knew Richard's mother would be anxious to know if she had been successful in persuading Charlotte to return to London.

Martha was full of hope when she opened the door but, on seeing Marietta's glum expression, her expectations were shattered. 'I take it your visit did not go well?' she said as they sat down.

'You might say it was a disaster. No matter what I said, no matter that I emphasised the folly of her actions, she was adamant that she was staying here.'

'Then I must go to her, see if I can talk sense into her,' said Martha, with a steely determination which left Marietta with no doubt about the scene which would take place.

'I think it best if you wait, Mrs Parker. The mood she was in when I left won't let her see reason.'

'But I must do something for my son. I can't stand by and see his life and career ruined.'

'Wait until after I've gone. I'll take the next ship for London.'

'Thee days' time, Thursday afternoon. Can I afford to wait that long?'

'It will give Charlotte time to calm down and think about what I said to her and maybe she'll see reason. I'll make another effort the day before I leave. I hope I might have her with me on the ship to London. If I haven't then you can try.'

'Very well.' Mrs Parker made the concession reluctantly. 'You'll let me know what happens before you leave?'

'Of course I will. I don't want to see what promises to be a wonderful career ruined. I'll do all I can to prevent that.'

Those words came back to her after Marietta had left and she realised that this young woman was as much concerned for Richard as she was for her lifelong friend, maybe even more so. Had she feelings for Richard that she had not displayed or told him about? She was a nice person, attractive, unmarried and obviously thought a lot about him. Oh why hadn't he taken up with her rather than a married woman?

When she stepped outside, Marietta, who had given Sweep sixpence when they had reached Mrs Parker's, was surprised to find him still waiting.

'I thought you had gone, Sweep.'

'Waited, miss. You looked a bit down in the dumps, thought I might cheer you up.'

Marietta gave a wry smile, touched by the boy's thoughtfulness. She could not throw kindness in his face so she said, 'Right, Sweep, for the rest of today and tomorrow you can show me something of Whitby. I go back to London on Thursday.'

'What about Wednesday, miss?'

'I have to see my friend in Cliff Lane that day.'

She enjoyed his company. His chatter, as they walked around Whitby, helped to dispel some of her gloom. The result was that she approached Miss Mann's Academy the following Wednesday in a more hopeful mood than she might have done.

Once again it was Liza who showed her to the same room as before. Marietta steeled her determination to do all she could to save her friend's marriage and in doing so make sure that Richard's career forged ahead undisturbed.

'Well, have you come again to try to persuade me to return to London?' Charlotte's voice was icy. There was no friendly greeting and Marietta realised damage had been done on her last visit. Already she felt that what she was about to attempt would be to no avail.

She nodded. 'Yes. I hope you've thought the situation over and that you've seen reason. I hope you've realised what you will be doing to yourself if you stay. If you can't see that, or won't, then think of what you'll be doing to Richard.'

'I'll be making him happy.'

Marietta snorted with disgust. 'Happy? Do you think you'll be happy the way you will have to live? At least Richard must have seen that when he left London without you. Can't you think of him?'

'I am. I know he loves me and I love him.'

'Then show him. Persuade him to go back to London promising him that what there has been between you will never be mentioned again, that the whole thing is finished. If you come back with me now, nobody need ever know you have been to Whitby. Your mother and father believe you are at Reed Hall. Charles is not home yet. Only you and I know the truth.'

'I thought you wanted me to persuade Richard to return to London. I cannot do that if I am not here,' mocked Charlotte.

'We can do it through his mother.'

'Ah, you have thought of everything,' sneered Charlotte. 'Well it won't work. Here I am and here I'm staying.'

'Don't think Charles is going to let you go without a fight. He won't agree to a divorce, and if he did it would be long and messy. Scandal will break around your heads if you desert him. You'll find parents paying for their children's education are very particular about who teaches them.'

'If you have finished preaching you had better leave.'

The coldness of the dismissal hurt Marietta.

'Charlotte, come with me. Don't pursue this foolhardy course. It can only lead to tragedy. How can you be happy knowing what you have done not only to yourself but to others?'

'Out!' Charlotte's temper broke. 'I want to hear no more of this. You have no right to come here passing judgement on me.'

'I have every right to try to save someone who was once a dear friend,' snapped Marietta. 'I have every right to try to save people I admire and respect from getting hurt.' Her voice was cold as penetrating steel. 'I have every right to save the career of a man who one day could be a great artist. You will be destroying a God-given talent. You have no right to do that.'

'Love.'

'Yes, I have every right to try to save the man I love.' Marietta had misunderstood Charlotte's meaning and, before she realised what that really was, she could not withdraw her words.

'Ah! So now the truth is out!' Charlotte seized on Marietta's statement. 'You aren't thinking of me, you aren't thinking of Charles, or of all the others. You aren't thinking of Richard and his career. No! You're only thinking of you, wanting him for yourself.'

Marietta gasped at what she had let slip and the venomous reaction it had brought from Charlotte in whose eyes she saw a deep and shocking hatred. 'You can't have him. He's mine. Now get out and get out of Whitby and don't ever come back!' She jerked the door open wide and stared at Marietta, defying her not to leave.

She was beaten by the verbal pounding and the malevolence which, because she had never seen it in Charlotte before, made it all the more frightening. Her knees felt weak. She faltered to the door, paused and looked at Charlotte but before she could utter a word, Charlotte's voice expressed her loathing of the girl with whom she had only known happy times. 'Get out!'

Chapter Fifteen

Marietta was dazed by Charlotte's attack. She had never intended to reveal her love for Richard, but she had and there was nothing she could do about it now.

With the revelation, hurt had heightened for it had made her realise how deeply in love she was with him, and that she loved a man whom she knew liked, admired and respected her but was not in love with her.

Tears ran down her cheeks. Her progress was automatic along Cliff Lane to the bridge spanning the Esk and then on to Church Street. People hurrying about their business, chatting in groups, exchanging greetings across the thoroughfares, bustling on the quays, meant nothing to her. She was hardly aware of what was going on.

Her legs were heavy as she climbed the steps to Prospect Place. The knocker seemed to resist her attempt to use it, but the feeble rap on the woodwork had been heard.

Mrs Parker's eyes widened when she saw Marietta's distressed state. The tears had not stopped. Her hands were clenched tightly and though her lips were set in a grim line they quivered as she attempted to hold back her sobs.

'Oh, my dear, come in, come in.' Mrs Parker hastened to usher her inside. As she showed her into the living room, she shouted, 'Sarah, tea!' Marietta sank on to a chair. 'What happened?' asked Martha, her eyes filled with concern.

'It was no use,' replied Marietta, fighting to control her bruised emotions. She went on, between gradually subsiding sobs, to tell Martha what had happened. 'She was so nasty, especially when I told her I love Richard. Oh, Mrs Parker

224

what are we to do? I cannot stay in the same place as her any longer. I'd dearly love to await Richard's return but that would only aggravate the situation and place him in an impossible position. I must return to London.'

The admission by Marietta of her love for her son did not come as entirely unexpected to Martha. A woman's intuition had made her suspect that there was more to Marietta's feelings towards him than she had first expressed.

'You love Richard? I thought as much. Does he know?'

Marietta shook her head sadly. 'No.'

'Then he should be told.'

Marietta started. 'Oh, no, please, you can't do that. It would place him in an awkward position and I don't want that. If he wants to be with Charlotte then so be it.'

'You won't stay?'

'No.'

'You should fight for him.'

'There would be too much hurt.' She sought reassurance from Martha. 'Mrs Parker, please promise me that you won't mention my love for Richard to either of them. It won't solve anything.'

Martha hesitated to make a full commitment to Marietta's wishes. Instead she said, 'Only if the situation demands it.'

The ship left Whitby under a dull-grey, lifeless sky. It fitted Marietta's mood of failure. The only easing of her depression had come when Mrs Parker and Sweep appeared on the quay.

Mrs Parker's words of attempted consolation did a little to alleviate the regret at the rift which had come between her and Charlotte. 'Try not to worry, my dear, I'm sure everything will turn out right in the end. I'll pray for that and for you.'

'You have been so kind and understanding, thank you.' She embraced Mrs Parker and kissed her on the cheek.

Though he sensed unease, Sweep put on a bright smile and expressed a hope he would see 'Miss' again. 'I enjoyed guiding you round Whitby.'

'And I enjoyed it too.' Marietta mustered a smile. 'I won't forget you. Maybe I'll be back one day.' She shrugged her shoulders. 'I don't know.'

By the time the ship reached London, Marietta had decided that for the present she would keep the whereabouts of Charlotte secret. If Mrs Parker was not successful in persuading Charlotte to return to London then she reckoned the first person who had a right to know was Charles.

On arrival in Russell Square she went straight to the Wakefields.

'Has Charlotte not come with you?' Gertrude showed a motherly concern that the expected arrival of her daughter had not materialised.

'No, Mrs Wakefield. She decided there was no point.'

'But Charles? Was she not concerned about him?'

'Oh, yes, but as his letter did not express any serious doubts about his condition she thought that by the time she went to him he would have recovered and be about his business again. She thought it better to stay at Reed Hall and have everything ready for him to have a quiet rest there as soon as he returned.'

Gertrude nodded. 'I suppose there's some sense in what she decided. How was she?'

'She was in good health and enjoying Lincolnshire.' Marietta had her fingers crossed behind her back as she garnished the untruths.

She had kept Charlotte's secret, but for how long? She hoped she would never have to go deeper into the deceit but in the mood she had left Charlotte she doubted if she would escape.

As she came to grips with the consequences of her final confrontation with Marietta, Charlotte experienced a mixture of regret at falling out with a friend of long standing, and an unblinkered view that she had done the right thing. Surely her love for Richard transcended all other feelings and was more powerful than her obligations to other people? Oh, she was sorry about what Charles would feel, regretted hurting her father and mother, but she told herself being in love with Richard was to enter a magical world that meant more to her than anything else.

They could be happy together here in Whitby. Her school

was well established and she felt sure it would grow. He would have no need to go with the whalers again. He could do his painting here. He might not achieve the fame everyone predicted for him but could they be sure? Was he really as good as they said? She had to admit that her portrait was good and had brought praise from everyone but could he achieve it again? And did it matter if they were happy in this Yorkshire coastal town?

And that madam, Marietta, how dare she profess a love for Richard? She has no chance. Does she think he is in love with her? If only she knew what he feels for me. Does she think she can wheedle him away? She gave a little laugh of derision at such a possibility. Never! Besides, we'll be here in Whitby and I doubt if she'll ever come back after what I said.

Her antagonistic thoughts calmed with the passing of time and three days later she was wishing that she had not been so harsh with Marietta. They had shared so much of life together, had so many happy times. She would miss her but she was so in love with Richard and that overruled any reconciliation. She determined to throw herself vigorously into promoting her school and into her teaching, for she realised it would only be a success if it produced good results. The two Billys were setting a standard in brightness and with several other capable children she felt sure her reputation would grow.

But she was reminded that life's problems were not to be solved easily when Liza announced that Mrs Parker was at the door. For a brief moment Charlotte had thought of refusing to see her but this was Richard's mother and if she could get her as an ally then the future may be made a lot easier.

'Mrs Parker,' she greeted her amiably. 'Do sit down.'

'I am sorry to interrupt your work, Miss Mann, though I think I should say Mrs Campion.'

Charlotte gave a wry smile. 'So you recognised me on my first visit – Miss Kemp said you had seen a sketch. Why did you not reveal your knowledge then?'

'You weren't straight with me and I wondered what you were really up to,' replied Martha coldly.

'And now you know. I suppose you learned that from Miss Kemp?'

'Yes.'

'I am in love with your son.' Charlotte was blunt but she saw no reason not to come straight to the point.

'Mrs Campion, what future is there in that? You are a married woman.'

'A life of happiness together.'

'Do you really believe that? Do you think it will survive all the scandal and all the fingers pointing afterwards? You'll both be outcasts. There'll be no future for either of you. Parents will not want their children taught by someone whom they will term a scarlet woman, an unfaithful hussy.' The words poured out until they were terminated by Charlotte's forceful interruption.

'Stop, Mrs Parker! I'll not be spoken to like this. And you overlook one important fact. Richard is in love with me.'

'I know that, he told me.' Martha could tell from Charlotte's reaction that she was surprised that Richard had spoken of their relationship. Her eyes narrowed. 'And he has had the decency to see the folly of it. He left London so that you would not suffer any scandal. He signed on his father's whaleship, to a life he hates, to get away and try to purge his feelings for you.'

'And do you think he will succeed?' There was a touch of mockery in Charlotte's voice.

'He might. The chances would be better if you weren't here.'

Charlotte smiled. She shook her head. 'Mrs Parker, you will not persuade me to leave.'

'Not even if I appealed to you to have a thought for his career as a painter, his ambition to become a great one? From what Miss Kemp told me he has every chance of that.'

'The only way he can do that is if he returns to London.' Charlotte looked thoughtful and nodded. 'Yes, that is a possibility. Our love could continue in secret.'

Martha looked shocked at this suggestion. 'But you'd be found out eventually. Scandal would follow and Richard's career would be in ruins. Does your love for him overrule these possibilities?'

'It does. And I'd rather face scandal in Whitby than in London.'

'And what do you think Richard will say to this? He will not expect you to be here.'

'We shall see when he returns.' Martha started to open her mouth but Charlotte stopped her. 'You are wasting your time trying to persuade me to go, so please, if you will, leave now so that I can get back to my pupils.'

Martha hesitated then, meeting the cold stare from Charlotte, stood up. She looked hard at her. 'I love my son, I don't want him to get hurt. I don't want his career ruined. I will do all I can to prevent those things happening. I will say one last thing, Mrs Campion. You are a pretty young woman and I must admire your profound expression of love for Richard, it must be strong for you to come here looking for him and be prepared to meet the scandal which surely you know will follow. But please try to see there is no future in it and remember it will be a trial for any future happiness if Richard is ever able to say, "I wonder if I would have made a great painter."'

Charlotte did not reply. She opened the door and not another word passed between them as Mrs Parker left the house on Cliff Lane.

Two months in the Arctic saw the whaleship *Phoenix* half full. The whaling had been good and if it continued so it would mean an early return to Whitby, in July rather than August.

The voyage north had been good. The weather had held fair and threatening storms had disappeared over the horizon.

The spirits of the crew were high. Most had sailed with Captain Parker before and those few who hadn't, had sailed on other whaleships so they were all used to the cramped conditions, the damp, the cold, the monotonous food along with the risks when hunting huge whales from open boats. And danger followed from the razor-like flensing knives. They were wielded with expertise but a slip of concentration could mean disaster and horrific injuries.

Richard had settled well. Being at sea lifted his spirits and, once the crew realised he expected no pampering from his father nor from his brothers, and that he worked as well as any of them, they accepted him and stopped taunting him. There were raised eyebrows, a few snide remarks when he isolated himself from other off-duty activities to sketch. But gradually the men became interested in what he was doing and, when they realised they were seeing an exceptional skill, were always eager to see more of his work.

Though he still yearned for Charlotte and recalled every detail of her features, he was satisfied that he had made the right decision in leaving London. But as the weeks passed and he recognised improvement in his drawing he began to speculate if he would have become a great artist. The chance had been there but he had sacrified it. He wondered if Jacob Craig had returned to London and what he thought of the portrait of Charlotte. He was sorry he would never meet him and he regretted letting down Mr Wakefield who had been so kind to him.

When the men had been mustered to make the selection of crews for the boats, Richard was chosen by his brother Jim to be one of his oarsmen. Jim was the harpooner in command of the boat during the hunt. Richard was pleased that his friend Jeremy had also been chosen by Jim. Brother Will, an harpooner in his own right, chose his crew with the proviso that the boatsteerer stood down whenever his father decided to take over as harpooner.

The choice of men for the six boats had proved to be good working units and the hunt had gone well with Captain Parker seeming to be able to detect the presence of whales before they were seen.

Richard had been nauseated by the first kill and the subsequent flensing, when the sea and the deck ran with blood and grease, but he forced himself to come to terms with it. By the second week in June he was even including the hunt and the kill in his sketches, seeing them as marvellous action pictures for future paintings connected with the sea.

'Francis, I must see the young man who painted that portrait.' Jacob Craig made the pronouncement just as he did every time he visited the Wakefield home in Russell Square and stood, in silent rapture, staring at the work of art, appreciating the skill and the talent.

'I know, Jacob. He will be back, of that I am sure, though I must admit I am mystified as to why he has stayed away so long. I am sure there will be a perfectly good reason. He's a good man and I know he was looking forward to meeting you.'

Ten minutes later their conversation was interrupted when the maid, who had answered the front door bell, came in to announce that Mr Campion was back.

Francis jumped from his seat to meet the man who hurried into the room. 'My dear, fellow, how nice to see you and have you home.' He took his hand and wrung it firmly, expressing his deepest welcome. 'How are you? Thoroughly over your illness, I hope?' He was searching his son-in-law's face. He had expected him to look drawn and listless but Charles seemed lively. His eyes were bright and though he was a little pale that could be the exhaustion of travel.

'I'm very well,' replied Charles with a smile. He held out his hand to Jacob. 'Nice to see you, Mr Craig. Do you like the portrait?'

'Splendid. That young man has a wonderful career ahead of him. But now I must go and not intrude on your homecoming. Don't come, Francis, I'll just ring.' He had moved to the bell sash by the fireplace as he was speaking. 'Your maid will get my coat and see me out.' He hurried from the room, leaving the two men to themselves.

'Did you have a bad time?' asked Francis with concern.

'I did but I was well looked after and when I had recovered sufficiently I had a spell recuperating in Switzerland. It did me good. I must take Charlotte there. Is she here?'

'I'm sorry to say she isn't,' replied Francis. 'She's at Reed Hall. She went there shortly after you had gone. We were alarmed when your letters came. As the business interests were going to keep me in London, Marietta offered to take the letter to her. We expected Charlotte to return with her but she thought it better to stay in Lincolnshire and have the Hall ready for you to go there and recuperate.'

Charles nodded. 'A good idea. Very thoughtful of her.'

'Marietta will be able to tell you more. Why not go and see her?' Francis threw up his hands in disgust with himself. 'I'm a fine one to welcome my son-in-law home – not even offering you refreshment after your journey.'

'No, sir, think nothing of it. I really don't want anything. My appetite is not fully restored but it won't be long before I'm matching yours.'

'Well, we'll try you out in an hour, the evening meal should

231

be ready then. Gertrude will be back, no doubt wanting to know all about your illness.'

Charles crossed Russell Square quickly, was admitted to the Kemp residence and announced to Marietta who was sitting in the drawing room reading *The Monastery* by Walter Scott.

The mention of his name sent a flutter through her. The moment of meeting with Charles and its consequences had slipped from her mind. Now it was suddenly thrust upon her and it seemed as if the peaceful world of a moment ago had been turned topsy-turvy.

'Charles.' She kept her voice calm as she put down her book and rose to extend a hand to him.

'My dear Marietta, a pleasant vision for an Englishman so long abroad.' He took her hand, bowed and kissed her fingers lightly.

'Welcome home.' The words sounded ironic to her. 'I trust you are fully recovered.'

'Yes, thank you, though, as I just said to Mr Wakefield, my appetite needs a little encouragement, but some good English dishes will soon put that right. He tells me Charlotte is at Reed Hall and that you paid her a visit. How was she?'

'In splendid health. There is no fear on that score.' Her tone had no ring about it and threw doubt into Charles's mind.

'Is something else the matter?' he asked, his face taking on an expression of disquiet. She hesitated. 'Your wording, your eyes, touched by trouble, lead me to think that there is something wrong with my wife.'

'I think you had better sit down, Charles.'

'Now I know there is something.' He frowned in that moment of anxiety which seems to stretch interminably between the unknown and the known, when fearing the worst is countered by the hope that the revelation will not be as bad as expected. He sat down, his eyes never leaving Marietta's face.

When she was seated, she looked down at her hands where her fingers worked nervously at each other. How could she break the news without hurting this nice man whom everyone respected?

She looked up. 'Charles, this is difficult.' She paused

232

slightly as if searching for the right words to ease the pain, but there weren't any. 'Charlotte isn't at Reed Hall.'

He looked puzzled. 'Not at Reed Hall, but her father said ...'

'He believes she is there, because she said that was where she was going.'

'And she isn't?' He gave a little shake of his head. 'I don't understand.'

'I am the only one who knows where she really is.'

Charles looked as if he just couldn't comprehend that his wife was not where she said she would be, and where everyone but Marietta thought she was. 'But Mr Wakefield said you took my letter to Reed Hall.'

'Yes, that's what I said I would do.'

'But you didn't go there either?'

'No. I knew Charlotte wouldn't be there. She had confided in me that she was going to Whitby.'

'Whitby?' This was even more puzzling to Charles. 'And that is where she is now? That is where you saw her?'

'Yes.'

'Marietta, what is going on? Her parents don't know where she is, only you do?'

'When she left London, she swore me to secrecy.'

'Even from me?'

'Yes.'

'Then why are you telling me? What is the mystery?'

'I'm telling you because when I saw Charlotte I realised the situation could be retrieved, possibly by you. I tried but failed.'

'Then I must know everything.'

Charles's frown deepened as Marietta told of Charlotte's love for Richard.

He shook his head slowly when she finished. 'I had no idea this was going on.'

'Nor had anyone else. As close as I am to Charlotte I would never have known if she hadn't felt she needed to tell at least one person where she was going?'

Charles's lips tightened. As the impact of what had happened began to dominate, his anger rose. 'Damn the man, damn him for luring Charlotte away. I'll have him horse-whipped. I'll see he never gets another commission in his life. His name will be besmirched throughout the art world and throughout the society who would have employed him.'

'Charles, hear me out. I have told you the facts of what happened. Let me clarify a few things for you.' Her voice was quietly forceful, quietly persuasive. Charles calmed a little. If there was more to tell then he must hear it. 'These two people fell in love.'

'But they could have stifled their love, seen the folly of it before it took hold.'

'I believe they knew that. Mr Parker left for Whitby on the excuse that he wanted to be there for his mother's sake when his father and two brothers left to go whaling. He did not return at the expected time and it is my firm belief that he never intended to return, that he was making the break from Charlotte and from London to save her marriage and to save her from any scandal which would ruin her life. He was prepared to forsake his own promising career for that.'

'Then why did Charlotte go to Whitby?'

'She had expected him to return and when he didn't she began to suspect that he was never coming back. She went to Whitby hoping to persuade Richard to return to London, continue with his art, when they would go on seeing each other secretly.'

'So why is she still there? Didn't he agree? Did he persuade her to stay?' His anger at Richard was rising again.

'No, when she got there he had sailed with the whalers. I spoke with his mother and she believes he went on a voyage he hated in order to get away to try and forget Charlotte. When I learned he was not in Whitby I realised that there was a chance of retrieving the situation. I tried to persuade her to come back with me. I hoped that if she did she might see things in a different light. But she would have none of it. She hated me for trying to interfere in her life and said such harsh things to me that our friendship is irreparably damaged.' Her words stabbed at his heart. Charlotte's attitude to her life-long friend made him realise how seriously his wife viewed her relationship with Parker, but he took heart when Marietta added, 'The whaleships don't return until July or August. Maybe a visit from you ...'

234

By the time Marietta left the suggestion unspoken, Charles's clear logical mind had taken full grasp of the situation and what must be done. Though he realised that some blame must be attached to his wife, most of his anger was naturally directed at Richard whom he judged must have forced his attentions on her, even though there was some mitigation in the fact that he had intentionally left London for good, not expecting Charlotte to follow him. Going to Whitby and electing to stay must have been her own calculated decision. That was hard for him to bear. It left him numb and seething but determined to try to save his marriage from the consequences of his wife's actions.

Charles left Marietta's with a resolve to go to Whitby, but first he must inform Francis of what his daughter had done. Her actions could no longer be kept a secret from her parents. Oh, why had Francis brought this young man from Whitby? Why had he to satisfy his desire to discover a great painter? If only Francis had not taken a holiday in Whitby, none of this would have happened. The happiness he had found in marriage, and his love for Charlotte, would still be secure.

'You saw Marietta?' queried Francis brightly when Charles returned to the Wakefield residence.

'I did and I've come away with bad news.' Charles did not believe in holding back. 'Charlotte is not at Reed Hall, and never has been. She is in Whitby.'

'What?' Francis gasped unbelievingly. 'She can't be. Marietta saw her at Reed Hall.'

Charles shook his head and went on to tell him all he knew.

The weight of the news pressed down on Francis like a black, threatening storm. His ears had heard the truth but did not take it in. He knew it was there, menacing the whole future. Before Charles had finished Francis sat, his elbows on his knees, his hands holding his head like a protective shield, wanting to hold back any more shattering news.

Charles's voice stopped, his information exhausted. The room was filled with a charged silence. Then came a low moan. Francis dropped his hands. His face was drained of its colour, the eyes, which always sparkled with an enjoyment of life, were now dull, lifeless. 'What has she done? Why, after

235

all you have to offer?' His lips tightened. 'If only I hadn't brought him here! If only I could have seen what might happen! Oh, Charles, I am so sorry for what I have done.'

'You have done nothing. You weren't to know.'

Instead of the expected despondency, he saw in Charles's eyes the gleam of determination to stave off what could wreck his life. In that moment Francis knew that Charles needed his support. He could not afford to succumb to the shattering news no matter how much it hurt at this moment.

'What do you intend to do?'

'I'm going to Whitby. I'm going to bring her back.' There was crispness of resolve and surety of purpose in his voice. 'I'll see her before the whaleships return, so, with Parker not knowing she's in Whitby, I may be able to save the situation without any confrontation with him.'

'I'll come with you. A father's voice may help.'

'I would appreciate your company and support, but I must ask you to let me see Charlotte alone first.'

'Of course,' Francis responded. 'I would not dream of interfering in something which concerns husband and wife unless it was absolutely necessary.'

Chapter Sixteen

Francis had an uneasy voyage. He found conversation with Charles difficult, for his mind was occupied with the distraught wife he had left behind and with the worst possibility which might face them.

When he had disclosed the troubling news to Gertrude she had broken down into a wailing scene in which little consolation could be found. She bemoaned the fact that her daughter had taken this terrible course which would bring scandal on them all. 'Had she no thought but for herself?' 'How can she expect to find happiness with an artist?' 'Why did you have to find him and bring him here?' 'Can't she see what she's giving up, a fine man like Charles, riches, land, a house in London, an estate in Lincolnshire? The girl's a fool.' Francis had had great difficulty in stopping her flow, which subsided only to be taken up again and again.

She beseeched him to bring Charlotte back. 'Make her see sense.' 'Avoid the scandal.' 'I'll never be able to face my friends again.' 'There'll be sniggering and scorn behind our backs.' The last tirade had been as he and Charles were getting into the carriage to take them to the ship. It had been a relief when the carriage started to leave Russell Square.

Charles appeared to be taking the upheaval calmly. He enjoyed the sea air and his walks around the deck, engaged in conversations with other passengers. 'It takes my mind off what lies ahead,' Charles informed Francis when tackled about his outward demeanour. 'But you can't see what I feel inside. I'm determined that it won't get the better of me for I must be calm when I see Charlotte.'

237

As they had planned, they went straight to the Angel Inn and took two rooms for an indefinite period. 'Maybe one night, maybe several, it depends on how our business progresses,' they told the landlord.

The ship had docked in the early afternoon and they wasted not one moment after they had taken their rooms and disposed of their small amount of luggage. As arranged Charles set out immediately after he had washed and changed, leaving Francis at the inn. He followed the landlord's directions to Cliff Lane and soon found the plaque announcing Miss Mann's Academy.

When the door was opened by Liza he said, 'May I see ... er ...' he pulled himself up quickly, shot a glance at the plaque, 'Miss Mann.'

Liza had summed up the stranger quickly. His clothes were impeccable, well cut, he held himself erect, he was handsome, with a pleasant face and steel-blue eyes which would capture anyone's attention. 'Certainly, sir, do step inside.' She held the door wide and closed it after him.

Childish laughter came from one of the rooms. 'Schoolroom?' he asked, indicating the door.

'Yes,' replied Liza. 'Miss Mann is teaching at the moment. Come this way, sir.' She led the way to the next door. 'Please make yourself comfortable. I'll tell Miss Mann you are here. Whom shall I say, sir?'

'Mr Campion.'

When Liza had closed the door. Charles looked around the room. A far cry from their house in Chelsea and hardly a match for Reed Hall, but he saw that Charlotte had furnished and decorated it well. She had made it a room where she could interview or entertain parents and, from the small table and three shelves containing some school books in the corner, he judged it was also used for individual tuition if necessary.

'A gentleman to see you,' Liza interrupted the lesson.

'Very well,' returned Charlotte. She looked back at the class. 'Look at the pictures on page six of your books. I will ask you questions about them when I return.'

'I'll look in on them in a few moments,' said Liza when they had moved into the hall. 'Looks like a prospective parent,' said Liza conspiratorially with a knowing smile. 'And, oh my, how handsome. A Mr Campion.' She hurried on to the kitchen.

Charlotte stopped in her tracks. She felt the colour drain from her face. Charles, here! How had he found her? Only Marietta knew where she was. The deceiver! She's broken her promise. What a friend she had turned out to be. Had she made the disclosure out of revenge for the way she had treated her, or was she hoping Charles would be able to persuade her to return to London and leave the way clear for her to ensnare Richard? Well, that young lady would need to think again. Even as these thoughts and resolve flashed through her mind, she found herself shaking, almost fearing facing her husband. She must pull herself together. She pinched her cheeks, trying to bring colour back into them. She stiffened her spine, pulled back her shoulders, opened the door and stepped into the room.

Charles had his back to the door but on hearing it open he swung round. The resentment at what she had done, which had been building while he was waiting, vanished at the sight of her. His heart lurched. She was as beautiful as ever. Though her dress was plainer than he had been used to, it was, nevertheless, of good quality and fitted to perfection. Its plainness enhanced the delicate white lace collar and the rose brooch pinned just below the shoulder on the left-hand side. He could not lose this lovely young woman whose presence filled any room and enhanced any company, who had changed his life for the better and had given him insights into worlds where he would never have ventured.

'Hello, Charlotte,' he said quietly.

'Charles.' Yes, Liza was right, he is handsome. She could do nothing else but admire him. He exuded an aura of reassurance and dependability. She sensed his love for her and at the moment realised what she would be losing; he would spoil her without marring her independence, she would want for nothing for the rest of her life and she would have his undying love. Her thoughts began to run away with her. She had to pull them up sharply before they overpowered her. She reminded herself forcibly where she was and why she was here. It was Richard she was in love with, Richard she wanted home, safe from the rigours of the Arctic, untouched by the purging he had expected to find there.

'I've come to take you home, my dear.' Charles's quiet

statement broke into her thoughts.

She ignored it. 'I expect Marietta told you where I was.'

'She felt obliged to.'

'Did she tell you everything?'

'As far as I know. I am sorry this has happened. Come back with me now and we can forget the whole thing. It need never be mentioned again.'

A shiver of discomfort ran along her spine. He was kind, forgiving and it made what she was doing to him all the more hurtful for it was hard to throw his peace offering back at him. She could have coped better if he had stormed in, shouted and cursed her but he hadn't, he had simply put a proposition to her which would solve and settle the future, and now he waited patiently for an answer.

She avoided it even though she knew she could not do so forever. 'Do my parents know?'

'I thought they ought to, especially as I decided to leave for Whitby immediately Marietta told me where you were. Your father would have thought it strange if I had left without telling him, especially as we had some business to attend to. He is with me.'

'But not outside?' There was a touch of alarm in her voice. She knew an interview with her father would be more unforgiving than that with Charles.

'No. I insisted that I see you first. He is at the Angel.' He looked hard at his wife. 'Come back with me.' He repeated his plea. He strengthened it by adding, 'Quell any guilt you are feeling, and I know my dear, dear Charlotte will be feeling that. Her nature is too sensitive not to, but cast it from your mind.'

His softly spoken words touched her, 'Charles, please, don't make it hard for me. You are too nice a man to hurt. I don't want to do that. I love you too much to make you suffer but I'm—'

'If you love me then why . . . ?' he broke in with a touch of impatience. 'Was it because I am older? Did the age difference influence you? Were you mesmerised by younger attitudes than mine? This is something I have pondered. Believe me if there is anything I can do to close that gap I will do it. Only tell me, please.'

'Age had nothing to with it,' she replied firmly.

'What then?' A snap came to his voice, a darkening to his eyes.

'I love you, Charles, but I'm not in love with you.'

He frowned, puzzled.

'Look, I love my father, I love my mother, I love Mr and Mrs Kemp, but I'm not in love with them.'

'And you are with Richard?'

'Exactly.'

'Is he in love with you?'

'Yes.'

'But he left London.'

'I expected him to return.'

'But he didn't. It looks as though he never intended to. Do you think he's still in love with you?'

'I think it's because he's still in love with me that he decided not to return to London.'

'So you, a married woman, came here prepared to wait for him on the off chance that he still loves you.' There was contempt for her action in his tone. His voice rose. 'Did you not consider the scandal which can blight your lives for ever and wreck the lives of those who love you, me, your parents, his family? Do you think this school will continue once your pupils' parents know about you? They won't want their children educated by a woman living in sin.' His eyes flashed angrily, his whole demeanour was tense. 'That's what you would be, because, Charlotte, you can be sure of one thing, I will not divorce you. You are mine by the law and mine you will remain.'

Charlotte flinched. She had never seen him as forceful as this. 'So be it, Charles. Richard and I will survive.'

Charles gave a loud laugh of derision. 'You'll find that you are wrong if you persist in this stupidity.' His voice went quiet. He met her eyes with the steel of determination to make one more appeal to reason. 'Come back with me now and nothing of what has happened need ever be known. Think of your own happiness, you won't find it here.'

'And could I with you?' she queried coolly.

'Yes. Our lives will be the same. You will have the blessing of your parents. You will be able to move among your friends and make new ones in the way you have always done. You won't find any of that here. And provided you never see Parker again, he could return to London and take up the offer I know Jacob Craig is waiting to make him. Think of what you and he will lose.'

'Yes. Each other.' There was a finality about her statement which sent a chill through his heart. They sounded like words of dismissal, a barrier thrown up between them which she did not want tearing down.

His lips set in a tight line of anger, which flared furiously across his face. It took all her will to stand against the blast she felt coming.

'You're a fool if you think everything will be straight sailing for you. You are driving into turbulent waters which will sink you and cast you both to obliviion.'

'And will you make sure that happens?' she asked with a toss of her head.

'It will be your own doing. No one else's. You will condemn yourselves. And there'll be no road to recovery, for no one will want to know you no matter how low you sink. You'll have no friends. Do you really want to fall into the underworld?'

Charlotte gave a scornful laugh. 'You make it sound so dramatic.'

'So it will be,' he rapped harshly. 'This school will be doomed. What will you live on?'

'Richard's paintings.'

'No decent people, those with the money his paintings deserve, will buy from him. Where will you live?'

'His mother won't see us homeless.'

'Her son, maybe, but do you think she'd welcome you, a married woman who's left her husband?' He shook his head. 'She's the wife of a whaling captain, a respectable woman. She won't want scandal under her roof, which could ostracise her from her friends and the whole of the Whitby community in which she moves. She'll not risk that.'

The points he was making were becoming a jumble of confused thoughts in her mind. She fought hard to keep her view and to do so reminded herself she was in love with Richard.

'You think hard on what I have said, Charlotte.' His voice was going insidiously on, penetrating those thoughts with which she was trying to steady herself. 'You face ruin, I can save you from that. You're my wife, I'll take you back and the past few months of your indiscretions will be forgotten. Our life together will go on as before. There is nothing here in Whitby for you, nothing.' Charlotte's resistance broke. She clamped her hands over her ears, trying to muffle Charles's voice. 'He won't want to face a life of poverty and disgrace. He'll cast you aside if you are here when he returns. You can save yourself that humiliation. Come back with me now.'

'Stop! Stop! I don't want to hear any more.' She looked up sharply, her eyes now ablaze with fight. 'You are wrong. Wrong! It won't happen like you say. People are kind and understanding. They will help us when they see how in love we are.'

Charles let out a great laugh of scorn. 'You believe what you want to believe. But you will find out who is right. Only you have the saving of yourself and of others. Do it before it is too late.'

The assurance in his look, the certainty that he was right bit hard at Charlotte. Her anger rose like a boiling volcano and exploded with a violence which shook Charles. 'Get out! Get out!' The words hissed like a striking snake. Her fists clenched in the desire to drive him away. Her eyes smouldered with a determination to end this matter here and now. 'I'm here to stay. I'll not come back. Never! Get out!'

Their eyes locked, hers blazing defiance, his sympathy and sorrow with a mixture of anger at her and at himself for not succeeding.

He strode past her to the door. He paused, his hand on the knob. He turned and looked at her. 'I still love you, Charlotte. You have time to change your mind.' He opened the door and left the house.

As she heard the front door close she sank on to a chair and wept.

Charles's steps were heavy as he walked along Cliff Lane. He was weighed down by the confrontation which had drained him of all energy. He seemed to be fighting a fog of sloth. A

243

hammer pounded in his head, and his eyes were unseeing.

Where had he gone wrong? He had expected to persuade Charlotte that what she was doing was wrong, that there was no future in it and the only happiness she could find was with him, and yet things had turned sour. She said she loved him but that did not appear to be enough for her. If only he had been younger! But there was nothing he could do about that. It seemed his only hope was that when her antagonism had died down and her thoughts were on a more even keel she would be able to see reason, see that there was no future in what she was doing. Should he visit her again before he left Whitby? He had opened the door for her return, maybe one more attempt would fling it wide for her to walk through unscathed and back into his arms. But first, maybe her father could take his love and persuasive power into that misnamed school and tear down the impediment Charlotte was throwing up against all that she once held dear, as if she was frightened to remove it herself.

Charlotte heard laughter coming from the next room. She heard Liza's friendly voice raised in enjoyment of being with the children. She straightened her back, took a handkerchief from her sleeve and wiped her eyes. She bit her lip in regret. Why had she stormed at Charles? Had she expected to walk away from a marriage, which everyone thought ideal, without a feeling of guilt? And that was exactly what he had raised in her. That was why she had lost her temper and viciously ordered him to leave – annoyance with herself for giving way to guilt, something she had determined to steel herself against. But now what was done was done. She shook her head sadly. What did the future hold?

Francis had spent an uneasy time since Charles had left the Angel. He tried the solitude of his own room but found his mind playing all sorts of mischievous tricks with him. Company might be the answer, so he had recourse to the warmth of the main parlour where the landlord brought him a tankard of strong locally brewed ale.

'If I don't see Mr Campion when he returns please tell him I'm in here.'

'Very good, sir.'

Francis sipped at his ale, eyed the other people in the room and tried to keep his mind occupied by wondering who they were and why they were here. Mother and daughter partaking of hot chocolate, were they here to meet husband and father off the coach? Two men, glasses of whisky on the table, heads together, were they attorneys conducting business in an atmosphere less staid than that of their offices? A clergyman sat quietly in a corner: awaiting an onward journey? A man exchanged an amusing story with a companion, well dressed, an air of affluence, merchants awaiting an associate from Scarborough? Everyday life was flowing around him and made him wish that his life was back to normal. In fact he wished it had never been upset. How a simple desire to see the place of his childhood had brought consequences he could never have expected! He gave a long deep sigh of regret. But maybe Charles had halted the upheaval, maybe soon all the players would be back in their rightful places and life could resume its ordinary routine.

With each passing moment he wished Charles would return. Every time the door opened he looked up hoping to see not only his son-in-law but Charlotte also.

When Charles did return, he was alone. Disappointment welled inside Francis, sending a cold chill to his heart.

Charles walked across the room and slumped into a chair opposite his father-in-law. He leaned forward on the table and in a low voice, scarcely audible above the joviality of the other occupants of the room, told Francis of his interview with Charlotte.

As the story proceeded, Francis's sorrow at his daughter's non-appearance turned to anger. His face darkened when he was told of Charlotte's hostility and her ordering her husband to leave.

'How could she be so stupid? Can't she see your generosity, that you have opened the way for her return with no recriminations? She need never see that damned man again. I'll go and talk sense into her.' He sprang to his feet.

'In the mood she was in when I left I doubt if she will,' said Charles.

'Well, we'll see!'

*

When Charlotte heard the front door bell tinkle she guessed who would be there. She left the schoolroom to meet Liza hurrying along the passage.

'I'll get it, Liza. Just keep an eye on the children. On second thoughts it might be better to send them home.' She turned towards the front door without further explanation.

Liza glanced after her. It was unusual for Miss Mann to answer the door. She must have known who was coming. When the last gentleman was here she had heard raised voices on one occasion. Hardly an interview with a prospective parent. As she went into the schoolroom and was calling to the children to put their books away, she heard a man's voice, and the name Charlotte spoken as if it was addressed to someone rather than uttered about somebody. Grace being called Charlotte? Liza was puzzled. Footsteps entered the other room and the door closed. She hoped Miss Mann wasn't in trouble, but hers not to query.

'Father, before you say anything, I am not coming home.'

The statement stunned him, the finality in the way she spoke was like a spear thrust into his hope. But he had to fight.

'Hear me out, Charlotte.' He was trying hard to hold back the anger which threatened to erupt. He knew, if it surfaced at this moment, it would only make her more defiant and would destroy any attempt he might make to bring reconciliation.

She indicated a chair with a gesture of 'very well, if I must.'

He nodded his thanks and sat down, placing his hat and cane beside him.

She sat facing him, her back straight, her hands resting together on her lap. Her eyes, those blue eyes which he knew could sparkle with charm when she wanted to wheedle her way round him, now fixed him with a steely coldness.

'There is no need for me to tell you how devastated Charles is. You've seen him. Your mother is distraught, she'll be ill if you persist in this foolishness. And as for myself,' he sighed and shrugged his shoulders, 'my world will be shattered if I lose you.'

For a moment Charlotte weakened. To see the doleful look on the face of a man she adored, a man who had given her so

246

much happiness, tore at her. His effervescence had gone, the light in his eyes was dim. She had done this to him.

'Come back with us. Charles has assured me that what has happened will make no difference. Life can go on as it was.' A pleading look came into his eyes. 'Don't destroy yourself, nor us.'

'Life would not be the same,' she replied quietly. 'Oh yes, outwardly it would be, and Charles is so generous in his forgiveness. I don't want to hurt him, nor you, nor Mother, but I can't ignore the fact that I am in love with Richard.'

'If you are, would you destroy his career?'

'He will still paint.'

'But he won't have Jacob Craig to guide and promote him, he won't have the patronage.' Francis's voice heightened a little. 'You would destroy a great painter, one I found.'

'So that's what you are thinking about, a reputation you've always wanted as a discoverer of a wonderful talent.' There was a touch of contempt in her voice that he should adopt this selfish attitude.

Francis's lips tightened, annoyed with himself for putting a point which really had nothing to do with his real feelings. He sat upright. 'That doesn't matter. I wish I'd never set eyes on him, wish we'd never come to Whitby, but we did.' His voice hardened. 'He has betrayed me, betrayed my trust, thrown my generosity back at me, had no thought for the opportunities I was giving him, or for me.'

'That's not true, Father. He was grateful to you,' snapped Charlotte.

Francis snorted. 'A fine way he had of showing it, seducing my daughter!'

Charlotte bristled. 'That is not what happened. We fell in love, and that's all that happened, but that was something tremendous. If it had been merely that he had seduced me than I could have thrown that off as meaning little more than a temptation into which I had fallen. I could have ignored the feelings of the moment, but what I am experiencing by being in love is something I cannot dismiss lightly.'

'So you are determined to stay in Whitby until Parker returns?'

'Yes.'

'There is no need for me to point out the consequences of scandal, Charles tells me he did so. And you think you can survive that?' He shook his head sadly. 'You are very much mistaken.'

'I don't think I am.'

'What if Richard no longer feels the same way about you when he returns?'

'He will. If he was sufficiently in love with me to leave London and turn his back on his career, then I think his love will have survived a whaling voyage.'

'And do you think it will survive the ostracism and poverty which will follow?' Francis's voice rose in disgust. 'You're a fool if you do. The only course for you to rescue anything out of this stupid escapade is to come home with Charles and me.'

'I am not coming. And I don't like being called a fool.' Charlotte's voice was cold.

His eyes widened and darkened with anger. 'That's exactly what you are, and, more than that, you are a destroyer of lives and you are blighting a talent which could have shone like a beacon in the British art world.' He stood up, glaring down at his daughter. 'You are a selfish fool.'

Charlotte sprang to her feet. She matched his glare. 'I told you I don't like being called a fool. Now, I'll say what I said to Charles, get out!'

The fierce passion in her eyes, which had been gently beguiling when she had sat on his knee as a child, shattered his hope that she might relent. The frenzy in her final two words hit him hard. He had never dreamed that there would be a day when his beloved daughter would use them at him.

He grabbed his hat and cane and strode to the door. There he swung round. His jaw was tight, his muscles knotted, his colour high. He drew himself up, seeming to fill the room with an authority which had been challenged in this confrontation he had never wanted. His eyes added a cold threat to his words which came spear-like from his trembling lips. 'I despair of you. Your actions are unforgivable. You aren't the daughter I once knew. You have thrown contempt on all that we once meant to each other. My work, my life was for you. You are destroying a lifetime's endeavour. You will regret this folly and your final words to me will haunt you to your dying day.' He flung open the door and was gone.

Charlotte was transfixed and it was only the slamming of the outside door which brought her back to reality. Her whole body was taut, her fists were clenched tight, her eyes closed tightly and her face screwed up with passionate anger directed at herself for causing what, at this moment, seemed an unspannable rift in a relationship she had held dear. Remorse filled her but tears did not come for the numbing hurt of her father's condemnation held her heart in an icy grip.

Automatically she crossed the room and closed the door. She sank on to a chair, her eyes unseeing, her mind unable to concentrate. How long she sat there she did not know. It was only when a knock on the door sounded that she started. She quickly composed herself and called, 'Come in.'

'I didn't hear you moving. I was worried.' Liza frowned, her eyes searching for some tell-tale sign that her employer was not well.

'I'm sorry, Liza. I had a lot to think about.' She offered no more explanation and Liza knew better than to pry. She reckoned it had something to do with the two gentlemen who had visited the school, and the slamming of the outside door by the last one was not a good sign.

'You look a little pale, Grace. May I fetch you a cup of tea?'

Charlotte nodded and gave a wan smile. 'That would be nice.' As the door closed she thought, 'If only my troubles could be solved with a cup of tea.'

Charlotte recognised Charles's handwriting on the envelope which had just been delivered by one of the servants from the Angel Inn. He had been told there would be no reply and had left immediately he had handed the envelope to Liza who had answered the door. Charlotte sliced the envelope open with her paper-knife and withdrew a sheet of paper. She read:

My dearest wife,

Your father and I sail in one hour. We hoped that you would come to the inn, but you have not. We still hope that you will be on the ship to sail home with us.

Let me repeat what I told you, come and nothing will be

held against you. I will give you my love and devotion unmarred. The past indiscretions will be forgotten, never mentioned, there will be no recriminations. No one other than the six people involved need know what has happened and I am sure none of them will say a word.

I love you, Charlotte. I always will. I cannot imagine my life without you. The door is still open for you. You can walk across the threshold as if nothing had happened. It will remain open unless you decide to shut it and lock it forever. I can only see that happening after you have seen Parker, for who knows, his whaling voyage may have changed his whole outlook on life and the feelings he has expressed for you may have vanished in the freezing cold of the north and in the harsh life of a whaleman.

Come home, Charlotte. I need you.

Your ever loving and devoted husband,

Charles

A tear trickled down her cheek. She brushed it aside, and grasping the letter tightly went upstairs to her bedroom.

The voyage to London without Charlotte was a heavy burden for the two men.

Charles's gloom was lightened a little by the expectation that his letter might still strike at his wife's conscience and she would seek a reconciliation with him before the whalers returned. But his daughter's vicious attack left Francis in the depths of despondency. He felt certain that Charlotte had made the final break and nothing would bring her home. He felt angry at her for her rejection and at himself for not succeeding.

Having said a morose goodbye to Charles, who had decided to go to his Chelsea home, Francis's anger became a white heat as he approached the front door of his home. He stormed past the maid who opened the door, startling her with the thunderous expression on his face. On hearing his arrival Gertrude came rushing into the hall expecting to see her daughter, but the smile of welcome was wiped away and in its place came a look of horror at the malevolence in her husband's eyes.

'Jackson! Jackson!' The explosive shout echoed through the house, alarmed the maid who awaited her employer's hat and coat, and brought the butler rushing into the hall.

'What is it, Francis?' cried Gertrude, all aflutter at her husband's storming arrival.

He strode past her into the drawing room, throwing off his coat and hat as he did so, leaving them lying on the floor for the maid to retrieve.

Gertrude followed at a flustered run, with the butler, who had never seen his employer in such a furious rage before, only a step behind.

Francis stopped in the middle of the room. 'Get that portrait down, Jackson, and throw it out!'

'Sir?' the butler, astonished at the order, hesitated.

'Do it! Get rid of it. I never want to see it again!'

Adam knew better than to question further. He hurried away to get some steps.

'Why, Francis? You can't mean it?' queried Gertrude, confused by her husband's sudden hatred of the portrait about which he had enthused so strongly.

'I do,' he thundered. 'After what that girl said to me. I tell you, Gertrude, you'd have been shocked at how she treated her father.'

The butler returned with the steps and Francis signalled his wife to ask no more until Adam had gone.

The portrait was soon down and as the butler took it away Francis said, 'You can put that landscape out of the dining room in its place later on.'

'Very good, sir.'

Once the door was closed, Gertrude looked anxiously at Francis. 'Now, what happened to bring all this on? I presume Charlotte isn't even with Charles.'

'You presume correctly. And I don't think she'll be coming back from Whitby.'

'Oh, no.' Gertrude let out a sigh of despair and shock as she sank on to a chair.

Francis went on to tell her what had happened and concluded, 'Charles has left the door open for her. If she returns to him before the whaleships reach Whitby he will take her back as if nothing has happened. But from her attitude,

251

when I saw her, I don't expect she will. She seems obsessed with Richard Parker. I wish I'd never set eyes on him. And I don't want reminding of either of them by that damned portrait.'

Four days later Jacob Craig called on Francis.

'Now, where's this young painter? I thought he should have been back from Whitby long before now? I thought he was only going to be away three weeks?' he asked after they had exchanged greetings.

'That's what I expected,' replied Francis. 'I've been to Whitby to try to find out why he hadn't returned only to learn that he had signed on his father's ship the *Phoenix* and is in the Arctic whaling.'

They had reached the door of the drawing room. Jacob stopped in his tracks. 'What? He can't. He must come back.'

'It doesn't look as though he will.'

'Why? What on earth happened to change his mind?'

Francis shrugged his shoulders. 'Impossible to say.' He did not want to reveal the traumas and shame of the past weeks to Jacob. He opened the door to the room.

Jacob's eyes fell immediately on the landscape over the fireplace. 'The portrait? Where is it?'

Francis quickly controlled his fluster. He had forgotten that Jacob would notice its absence. 'Oh, I'm trying it in our bedroom.'

'But people won't see it there. It would do Mr Parker more good if it was back here,' protested Jacob.

'It doesn't matter. I told you I don't think he will be returning. It would seem his interest in an art career in London has paled.'

'No. I won't have a talent, such as I could see in that portrait, wasted. He must come back. I must have him at my studio.' Jacob's attitude was imperious. 'I shall go to Whitby and see him for myself. He cannot throw away his talent. I won't have it. When do the whaleships return?'

'That depends on how successful the whaling has been. I'm told it can be any time in July or August.'

'A month or so.' Jacob looked thoughtfully. He nodded. 'Yes, I can manage it. I'll go in good time. He must get this foolish idea of giving up his career out of his head.'

Francis made no comment, nor did he reveal anything else to his friend. Jacob would in all probability see Charlotte and there was nothing he could do about it if he did. The scandal would emerge sometime. But maybe Jacob's visit to Whitby would solve the dilemma of the relationship between Charlotte and Richard. And if it brought them both back to London he would make sure that they came on the understanding that they never saw each other again. And with the portrait gone there would be nothing at Russell Square to remind Charlotte of Richard.

Chapter Seventeen

'There she blows! There she blows!' The cry rang clear on the crisp air from the lookout at the masthead.

Exictement coursed through the ship. Men not on duty, lazing on the deck or below in their bunks, jumped to their feet, hoping the sighting would mean a kill. Four more and they would have a full ship and be away from the Arctic early, home to loved ones and money in their pocket.

'Where away?' yelled Captain Parker.

'Starboard bow!'

Men rushed to the rail eager to make a sighting.

'There!' 'There!' 'There!' Cries went up as spout after spout rose on the cold air. Surely they couldn't fail to make their killings, unless the whales swam for the cover of the ice.

'Away all boats!' Captain Parker's order sent men racing to the boats to which they had been allocated on the voyage north.

Five boats hit the water almost simultaneously. Oars were out and in a matter of moments the crews were rowing hard. The captain's boat, with his son Will as his boatsteerer, was in the lead, with Jim's, which he, as harpooner, commanded was close behind.

There would be no letting up until they neared the whales, and Jim, always eager to make a kill, was a hard taskmaster.

'Bend y'backs, lads.' The quietly firm voice would brook no slacking. 'Bend it, Richard.'

He strained harder on the oar, his muscles bulging. In spite of the cold he was soon sweating. In unison the oars swept through the water, sending the boat skimming across the

254

waves. They must be nearing the whales by now. The temptation to look round, to see how much further they had to row, and how far they were behind his father, was strong but he knew that could prove fatal. It could divert his concentration from the rowing, he could miss his stroke and that could lead to accidents. He glanced at the following boats and then watched the boatsteerer, longing for him to call a halt to the rowing.

The man in the stern leaned against the long steering oar, manoeuvring the boat on the shortest possible course to the spouts on which he kept his gaze.

On they rowed, coming closer and closer to the unsuspecting whales. Then came the signal from the boatsteerer. Rowing ceased. Physical relief swept through the crew as the boat still glided forward under its own momentum, but the tension was still there. Chests heaved, drawing air into their aching lungs, each man careful not to make any noise which might warn and frighten off their prey.

Jim shipped his oar, stood up and braced himself against the bobbing of the boat. Jim picked up a harpoon. He saw his father was in a similar position about twenty yards to port, closing in on a huge whale on the edge of the six they had sighted. Other boats were stringing out across the water preparing for an attack but waiting for the captain to throw first. Immediately the harpoons struck their targets the sea would turn into a maelstrom of heaving bodies weighing anything up to sixty tons each.

The boatsteerers sculled their boats gently forward, slowly closing the gaps between themselves and their quarry. Harpooners, tense with anticipation, forced themselves to relax so that they made sure of a throw unmarred by an impediment. They checked their hold on their harpoons. Satisfied, they waited.

The boats moved forward. Nearer and nearer. The oarsman could do nothing but wait. Their fate was in the hands of two men, one in the stern, the other standing in the bow, poised ready to make a throw. Fifteen yards. Twelve yards. Ten. Five! Captain Parker's body arched backwards, then, with all the power he could muster, it sprang forward, his arm moving in an arched trajectory. At the precise moment to make the strike he wanted he released his hold on the harpoon. It curved through the air, soaring over the waves towards the bulk which towered above the boat. Captain Parker watched anxiously. The harpoon dipped, plunged, struck, pierced and buried itself in the blubber where the barbs took their relentless hold.

As soon as the other harpooners saw their captain's movement at the start of his throw they too hurled their harpoons.

All hell was let loose as the frightened whales churned the sea. Flukes came out of the water and crashed down, sending foaming water high into the air.

The cries of 'Stern all' rang out from each harpooner who had made a strike. Immediately backs were bent to drive their boats away from the whales as quickly as possible. Boat six had made a hit and the crew's ability was concentrated on running with the whale. The harpooners in boats four and five were a fraction late with their throws. The alarmed whales were already sounding and the harpoons fell harmlessly into the sea.

Jim's order of 'Stern all!' was not quite soon enough and, before the boat was clear, the huge flukes crashed down across the bow. The boat shattered, the bow completely disintegrated and the stern shot into the air sending the crew hurtling into the sea.

Richard was unable to grasp what was happening, for he had seen nothing except the look of horror on the boatsteerer's face. He hit the sea with all breath driven from his body and went under. He kicked upwards. Cold clamped his body. He broke the surface gasping for breath. He could hardly take in the scene of chaos around him. Their whale had gone, taking the harpoon and line with it. A boat was alongside him, hands reaching out to him. Automatically his mind told him to help. He grasped at the boat and pulled. Strong arms heaved him over the side. He was left floundering in the bottom while they went on with the rescue. Other bodies flopped beside him choking for air. In what was only a few minutes, but seemed an eternity, the boat was heading back for the *Phoenix*.

Richard struggled to sit up more. His mind sharpened. Jim? Where was Jim? He must have taken the full force of those enormous flukes. He pushed himself straighter in the boat,

256

looking round anxiously. The nearest oarsman saw the concern on his face.

'Lost two men,' he gasped as he heaved on his oar. 'Your Jim's up yonder,' he nodded towards the bow. 'He jumped just in time but he did take an unholy whack. Reckon he'll have a few broken bones.'

Richard sank back. He hoped his brother wasn't too badly hurt but at least he was safe.

He knew he was in boat three. 'Lose your whale?' he asked.

'Cut the line and let it go when we saw what happened to you.'

Richard nodded and glanced across the sea. Two boats were going to the assistance of another which was starting to tow its catch to the ship. Of his father's boat there was no sign. He must be running with the whale.

Once they reached the *Phoenix* eager hands helped the shocked and wounded men on board. Greater care was taken with Jim for he was unconscious and he had several bones broken. The mate ordered four men to take him to the captain's cabin, for he knew that was where Captain Parker would want him.

Those who had suffered a soaking in the bitterly cold sea were helped to shed their clothes before they froze. A rough vigorous rub-down sent blood circulating. A hot drink drove heat into them and dry clothes brought comforting warmth. All had bruising, some more so than others, and one had lacerations from splintered timbers. Richard regarded himself as extremely fortunate that he had escaped with little more than a drenching. Once the warmth was circulating through his body he hurried to his father's cabin where he found the mate concerned about Jim.

'He has a broken left leg, some broken ribs on the same side and his left arm is in a hell of a mess, broken in several places.'

Richard was scared by the gravity of the mate's delivery. 'Can we do anything for him?' he asked anxiously.

'We'll do the best we can. Cook's dealt with broken bones before, but that arm might just be more than he can cope with. I reckon it's set sail for home as soon as the captain returns.'

'Is he not back yet?' He put the question automatically but

at once he realised the stupidity of it. If his father had been on board he would have been beside his son now.

'Last seen fast to a whale and running with it close to the edge of the ice,' replied the mate.

Richard left the cabin and hurried on deck hoping to see his father alongside the ship but there was no sign. Panic gripped him. Some of the crew were securing the whale captured by boat six alongside the larboard side. Life was going on as if his father was on board. But he wasn't! He scanned the sea. Nothing. The ever-moving undulations mocked him. He stepped on to the rail and swung on to the ratlines, climbing higher to widen his view. He looked towards the edge of the ice; there was no sign of a boat.

A sick feeling hit the pit of his stomach. 'Pa! Where are you?' He wasn't aware that he had shouted aloud.

The mate, having left the cook in charge of Jim, had just come on deck and heard the shout.

'Parker, see anything?'

'Nothing, Mr Mate.'

The mate turned his eyes further upwards. He cupped his hands around his mouth. 'Lookout!'

'Aye, aye, sir.'

'See anything of the captain's boat?'

'No, sir. Last seen fast on, running with the whale close to the edge of the ice.'

The information brought a dread which hung heavy on the ship.

'Whither away?'

'Running west.'

The mate took charge. Orders came fast. The dead whale was cast off and the *Phoenix* got under way, moving westwards and closing in on the ice. The mate ordered more lookouts on to the ratlines and yards.

With every passing minute Richard became more and more anxious. His uneasiness was filled with the fear of the worst and that was heightened when someone yelled, 'Timber!'

All looked to see who called and saw one of the crew high on the yards pointing towards the ice a little ahead of the ship.

The mate's orders were obeyed instantly by a crew concerned about their captain. The ship was brought about and a boat lowered. Six men rowed just as vigorously as if they were hunting a whale. Soon they were scooping timber from the sea and from the edge of the ice. A disquiet settled over the boat and even before it reached the ship the crew, lining the rail, anxious for news, felt the blow of doom.

'Captain's boat,' called one of the men to those on deck as the boat came alongside.

When they came on deck the mate confirmed the boat crew's identification. He turned to Richard who, standing beside him, was staring unbelievingly at the evidence. 'Sorry, son,' said the mate with quiet sympathy.

'What's this mean?' asked Richard, his mind in a daze.

'It looks as though the whale, in trying to escape, dived under the ice. The action must have been sudden and unexpected, otherwise the captain would have cut the rope. But he didn't and probably before he knew what was happening the boat was being dragged under the ice. Some of it has caught the edge, broken, leaving us this evidence.'

'What can we do?' cried Richard, his face twisted with distress.

'Nothing.' The mate shook his head sadly.

'But we can't just leave them,' cried Richard. 'It's my father!'

'I know son, I know. But you can see for yourself, there's little hope of even finding one of them. If anybody got out of the boat or was thrown out there would be little chance of survival, trapped under that ice.'

Richard bit his lips trying to hold back the tears which welled in his eyes. He knew the mate was right. His father and brother gone and Jim badly injured. Had he cast an hoodoo on the voyage? He looked towards the ice. It looked so calm and peaceful, shimmering in the sharp Arctic light, with the sea washing it gently. It bore no resemblance to a place of tragedy, a place of death. He felt numb, unable to realise that he would never see his father or Will again.

The mate's voice roared across the deck and the crew jumped into instance obedience. The boats still on the water were hauled on board.

'Hoist topsails!'

The crew were eager in their actions. They knew what the next order would be.

259

'Steer south!'

'South it is, sir!'

Richard started. It was this last shout which brought him back to reality. He swung on the mate and grabbed his arm. 'You can't leave them! You can't!' Fury blazed in his eyes, condemning the mate's orders.

'Belay there, Parker!' He glanced down at the hand which gripped his arm and then upwards to meet Richard's wrath. 'There is nothing we can do and for your brother Jim's sake the sooner we are home the better.'

Richard let his hand slip from the man's arm. As the mate moved away to supervise the sailing, Richard looked back to the ice, which marked his father's and brother's grave. He wept.

'Whaleship! Whaleship!' The cry first made by two boys as they ran from the cliff top where they had been playing, was taken up time and time again, and swept through Whitby like a sudden gale.

People left their homes, left their offices, downed their tools, threw the nets they were repairing to one side and ran, swelling the stream of folk hurrying to the staithes, the piers and the cliff tops. The cry had come earlier than expected. Did it mean a full ship, and therefore more money for the port and more in people's pockets? Or was there some other reason for the ship's early return? There was a buzz of excitement and expectation with the eagerness to identify the vessel.

The cry reached the school in Cliff Lane where Charlotte had already dismissed the pupils for the afternoon. Liza and the two Billys were just leaving for home when the news swept along the lane.

'Do you hear it, Grace?' Liza had stepped back into the house, the two boys having raced away, hoping to see the whaleship on which their father served.

'Yes, I hear it,' replied Charlotte. The cry had brought a strange feeling to her. This was the news she had been longing to hear and now it had come she wondered what it would be like to face Richard again after these months of separation. Her mind had been filled with apprehension about a reunion after what had passed between her and Charles, her father, and Marietta. All had sown facts in her mind which she could not deny, all had pointed out her folly and had tarred it with selfishness saying she was denying Richard's ambitions for her own feelings. She had forced these thoughts into the background, concentrating on her own singleminded view of a future with Richard. But now with his homecoming they had returned.

'Are you coming to the cliff?' Liza asked.

Charlotte started. 'Yes, of course. I cannot miss the joy of a returning whaleship?'

'It's not always pleasant,' warned Liza.

Charlotte ignored the caution and grabbed a coat and shawl. The two women hurried from the house. Crowds were swelling on the west cliff. People were streaming along the river bank, crowding the staithes and the piers, and gathering on the east cliff. It seemed as if all Whitby had turned out to welcome the whalemen home.

'Which ship?' Liza asked as they joined the crowd.

'Too far off to be sure,' came the reply.

Anticipatory excitement gripped the crowd until one old sailor trained his telescope on the distant vessel. 'The *Phoenix*!' he announced with surety.

Charlotte's heart fluttered. Richard was home.

The name spread quickly through the mass of people. Captain Parker's skill must have given them a full ship early.

But then the old man added, 'There's no bone at the masthead.'

The excitement subsided. The traditional way of letting the Whitby folk know that the voyage had been successful was missing.

People now speculated as to why the *Phoenix* was home early and not full. Trouble on board? Ship damaged in the ice? There could be any number of reasons for an early return.

Charlotte watched the distant speck grow larger. The ship was slipping easily through the undulating sea, its sails catching the helping wind.

'Liza, do you know where she'll tie up?' she asked.

'East bank above the bridge.'

'Can we go?'

'Aye, if you want to.'

Charlotte nodded and Liza led the way through the crowd, descended quickly along the streets to the bridge, and crossed to the east side before the *Phoenix* had reached the piers and the river.

They mingled with the crowd already gathering on the quay where the vessel would dock. Here there were wives with children at their sides or held in arms, mothers and fathers eager to welcome a returning son, sweethearts yearning to feel the arms of their betrothed around them, friends and sight-seers, and on the periphery, ignored by most, prostitutes willing to relieve sailors of their pay after long lonely times on distant seas.

Across the throng Charlotte glimpsed Mrs Parker with Sarah and Maggie talking to a group of people.

There was no cheering from the piers or the cliffs. The silence was uncanny and when it seeped from there to the quay the hum of conversation gradually faded. Something was wrong. An uneasy quiet hung over the people awaiting the ship. She came in sight. People strained trying to get an early indication of what was wrong. 'Captain Parker's not at the helm, the mate's bringing her in.' The whisper swept across them like a wind rustling the grass. The crew were sombre. The gaiety which marked a crew's return was missing and it had transferred a message of tragedy to those on shore. The pall of doom hung heavy.

Charlotte looked across at Mrs Parker for whom the crowd had parted so she could be nearer the gangway when it was run out. She saw that her face bore all the worry of a wife whose husband sails in dangerous waters and who, though never prepared for the worst, always fears it may happen and then knows it has.

Anxiety gripped coldly at Charlotte's heart. Was Richard all right or had the Arctic played a role in shaping their destinies? She could only wait and watch with deepening dread as the ship came slowly towards the bridge which had been opened to allow her to pass upstream. As the ship was manoeuvred carefully to the quayside she searched the deck for a sight of Richard.

Relief swept over her. He was there. Her legs felt weak as the anxiety drained from her. But she was alert to the fact that

262

Richard's face bore the signs of unwanted catastrophe. His eyes were searching the people on the quay with a sadness he wished he was not expressing. Then she saw them fix on his family and she saw the deep love of a son for his mother, a son who wished he could dispel the tragic news he was bringing.

The ropes were out, the ship tied up, the gangplank fixed in place. The crowd were silent. The mate signalled to Richard to go ashore first, allowing him the privilege which would have been the captain's on seeing his family on the quay.

As he came ashore tears filled his eyes. He took his mother in his arms and held her tight, then he opened his arms, brought his sisters into them and hugged all three.

'A whale took his boat and crew under the ice. Will was with him.' The words were barely above a croak.

'Oh, no, no.' Mrs Parker gave a low moan.

The two girls could not speak but the shock of their loss brought tears streaming down their cheeks.

They stood for a few minutes unaware that sailors were coming ashore, welcomed into the arms of their loved ones. News of the missing men and the injured was transferred with sympathy and regret to those on the quay who sought in vain.

'Where's Jim?' Martha asked anxiously.

Richard eased his mother and sisters from his arms. 'I've more bad news.' His face was solemn.

'Not him as well?'

Richard shook his head. 'No, but he suffered injury when our boat, for I was with him, was struck by a whale. He's likely to lose his left arm.'

Martha's eyes were wide as she looked to the ship. She knew Dr Berry always was at hand when a whaleship docked, ready to administer whatever aid was necessary to men returning from the icy wastes of the north. She saw activity on board and saw someone being brought across the deck on a ladder carried by two men and with the doctor beside it.

Seeing her, the doctor came on to the quay first. 'Mrs Parker, I'm sorry,' he said with deep sympathy in his eyes. 'Jim is in a bad way. I'm taking him straight to my house. I can deal with him there and my wife will help.'

'I'll come,' she said, a mother anxious for a troubled son.

'No, please don't. There is nothing you can do. I would rather you were at home. As soon as I have attended to him I will come and let you know how he is.'

'But ...' Martha started to protest.

Richard put his arm around her shoulder. 'Dr Berry knows best.' He looked at him. 'Take good care of him.'

'I will, son, I will.' He patted Richard on the shoulder. 'Take your mother home and get her some hot sweet tea. I'll be with you as soon as possible.' He looked at the two girls. 'Take care of her.'

The two men with the ladder had reached the quay. Mrs Parker stepped forward to bend over the prone figure of her son. 'Jim.' With tears in her eyes she kissed him on the forehead.

He smiled weakly. 'Ma.' His eyes expressed sorrow for her at what had happened. He glanced at his sisters and winked at them, hoping to stem their renewed tears.

Richard held his mother's hand. They watched the people clear a path as Jim was carried away. With the crowd closing in again he was lost to sight.

'Richard, I must see those families who have lost someone,' said Martha, drawing herself up straight and strengthening her determination to throw up a barrier against her true feelings. Those could be released in the privacy of her room.

'Won't that be too harrowing for you?' he countered.

'Your father would have done so. I must do it for him.'

Richard understood. He guided his mother among the people who were beginning to disperse slowly. Brief words of sympathy were uttered in the hope that they brought some consolation.

Charlotte deemed it wise to withdraw. Richard had not seen her, and, as much as she wanted to be with him to try to ease his suffering, she would not intrude on family grief. Richard had enough to worry about at this moment without knowing that she was in Whitby.

'I think we'll go,' she said to Liza in a subdued voice.

'Do you want me to come back with you?' Sensing that Charlotte was upset by the first tragic homecoming of a whale-ship she had witnessed, Liza made the offer.

264

'No. Thank you all the same. You had finished and no doubt the boys will be waiting for you.'

They walked to the end of Tin Ghaut together, made their goodbyes, and Charlotte turned towards the bridge. As she crossed the river, her steps were slow, seemingly with little purpose. She sensed, in the breeze from the sea, the wild and tempestuous waters of the distant north, where a tragedy which affected so many lives, in a variety of ways, had unfolded. She shivered and quickened her step to Cliff Lane.

The door closed behind her. She suddenly felt utterly alone. She threw off her coat and hat, thoughtfully poured herself a glass of Madeira and sat down with a deep sigh. Had events overtaken her? Richard was safe, she was thankful for that, but how had the tragedy affected him? The question now was what should she do? Call on him? Wait for him to come to her? She sipped at her wine, her thoughts a tumult of confusion and emotion. How long she sat she did not know and she only stirred herself when a decision forced itself into her mind. She would write him a note. She went to her desk, drew a sheet of paper from a drawer, picked up a pen, dipped it into an inkwell, paused for a moment, then started to write.

By the time they reached Prospect Place Martha had composed herself. Though her heart was breaking at the loss of her husband and son she knew she had to be strong for those who were left, a son whose life might at this moment be in the hands of the doctor, another who must seek answers about his future and two daughters who would have to come to terms with the tragedy which had beset them.

She took charge immediately they stepped through the door. 'Maggie, kettle on. And don't forget Richard's favourite fruit cake especially made for his homecoming.'

'It was Father's favourite too,' said Maggie, a catch in her voice, as if it was sacrilege to touch it without him being there.

'And he would want us to have it,' said Martha firmly. 'Sarah, lay out a change of clothes for Richard. I'm sure he would like to get out of his sea things.'

'Aye, I would,' he agreed, as if he wanted to cast off something tainted.

The two girls hurried away.

'Sit down, Richard. Tell me what happened.'

Richard frowned. 'Do you really want to know?' There was a touching plea to release him from causing her pain.

'Everything,' she said with emphasis, settling herself straight in her chair, her hands resting in her lap, her eyes fixed on her son. 'It will help to know how they died and what happened to Jim.'

'Should the girls hear it too?' he asked.

It took only a moment's consideration for Martha to decide they should.

When Sarah returned Richard slipped away to change. By the time he came back Maggie had tea and fruit cake ready. He told his story, sparing nothing.

There was a moment's silence when he had finished. He felt drained of energy having relived the tragedy of the Arctic wastes. But everyone felt a certain sense of relief that the lamentable loss would never be a mystery.

There was a knock at the door which Maggie went to answer. A moment later she was showing a grave-faced doctor into the room. Richard sprang to his feet to get the doctor a chair. From the serious expression on his face Martha knew that he was not the bearer of good news.

'Spare us nothing, doctor. It cannot be worse than losing a husband and son.'

He licked his lips. 'Well, Jim's taken a beating from that whale. His left leg was broken but that was a straightforward break. The cook of the *Phoenix* did a good job on that, and thankfully he did nothing to the injured ribs and they have healed themselves without any internal injury. They'll be sore for quite a while yet. But his left arm,' he shook his head sadly, 'that I'm afraid is beyond repair. He will lose it.'

There was a gasp from the two girls. Their brother with only one arm, he'd be devastated. Richard had expected this and so showed no reaction. Martha was shocked, her thoughts were the same as the girls', but she kept her emotions under control. She nodded.

'I'll keep him until he is well enough to return home. My wife will care for him and you can visit,' the doctor concluded.

266

'Thank you,' replied Martha.

'Jim will need all the help he can get when he comes home. I don't mean physically, though he will need assistance; I was thinking more of the mental scars, of having a feeling of being useless.'

'All of us will do what we can,' said Martha. 'Thank goodness it wasn't his right arm. He's naturally right-handed and there'll be lots of things he can do.'

'It's good to hear you talk so strongly after what you have been through. If you need me send for me any time. Now I must get back to Jim.'

Maggie saw the doctor out and when she returned Martha cleared her throat and looked round her children. 'There is no need for me to tell you that life will be different from now on but, if we've a mind to it, we will cope.'

Chapter Eighteen

The following morning Sarah and Maggie persuaded their mother to accompany them on their usual shopping expedition. Knowing it would occupy his mother's mind, Richard gave weight to their suggestion, adding that the fresh air on such a fine morning would do her good.

Although he had been excused duty by the mate of the *Phoenix*, Richard, feeling that if he was on board he would be fulfilling the wishes of his father and brother, decided to visit the ship. He was nearing the bottom of the steps from Prospect Place when two boys raced on to them from Church Street.

'Now Billys, you seem to be in a rush,' he said, mustering a grin as they stumbled to a sharp stop in front of him.

Gasping for breath, one of them held out an envelope to him. 'For you, Mr Parker,' one spluttered, holding up one finger.

'For me?'

'Yes, from Miss Mann. She said not to wait for an answer.'

'Miss Mann?'

'That's right.' Billy Two held up his fingers. 'Come on, One.' He jabbed his brother in the side and raced away. With a shout One tore after him.

Richard smiled at their exuberance and then, in puzzlement, looked down at the envelope. His heart missed a beat. The neat copperplate writing which spelt out 'Mr Richard Parker' was just like Charlotte's. But it couldn't be. The Billys had said it was from a Miss Mann, yet her writing ... He ripped the envelope open and pulled out a sheet of paper. As he unfolded it he glanced first at the signature. The final words seared into his mind. 'Your ever-loving Charlotte.'

His mind whirled. This just wasn't true. Charlotte couldn't have written this. She couldn't be in Whitby. Where had the boys got it? He looked up but they had vanished from sight. Miss Mann? They said she had given it to them. Who was she? A friend of Charlotte whom he didn't know? Was she visiting Whitby and had brought it from London? He looked down at the paper and read:

My dearest Richard,
This will no doubt come as a surprise to you. I am here in Whitby.
I have left Charles for you, but will explain all when I see you. You will find me at Miss Mann's Academy on Cliff Lane.
I was on the quay when the *Phoenix* docked but I could not intrude on family grief. I am so sorry about your father and brothers. Please give my deepest sympathy to your mother and sisters.
Your ever loving,
Charlotte

Richard stared at the paper, hardly believing what he had read. Charlotte here in Whitby? She couldn't be. He read the words again, more slowly. Convinced of their truth, he stuffed the letter in his pocket and strode with purpose along Church Street towards Bridge Street. The *Phoenix* was forgotten. It received only a casual glance as he passed her, for his thoughts were on Cliff Lane. Miss Mann's Academy? He had never heard of it.

He was soon knocking on the door next to the plaque which told him that he had found the right establishment.

Liza opened the door. 'Ah, I see the two Billys found you, Mr Parker.' She stood to one side to allow him to enter. 'I was ever so sorry about your father and brothers.'

'Thank you, Mrs Brodrick.'

'How is your mother?'

'She's bearing up very well, thanks.'

'Miss Mann is teaching, but I'll get her.'

'No. I've come to see Mrs Campion, I understand she is here.'

Liza looked mystified. She shook her head. 'There's no one of that name here.'

'But your two boys brought me the note.' Richard was puzzled.

'Yes. Miss Mann sent it.'

'She may have told your sons to deliver it but it was from Mrs Campion.'

'I think I'd better fetch Miss Mann.' As she entered the schoolroom the noise of laughter spilled out into the hall.

A moment later Charlotte appeared, leaving Liza in charge of the class. 'Hello, Richard,' she said quietly.

'Charlotte!' His puzzled frown vanished almost as soon as it came, for the reality of the situation dawned on him. 'Miss Mann? You're Miss Mann?' She nodded. 'Now I know why Mrs Brodrick sounded confused just now.'

'She doesn't know my real identity. Come, we can talk in here.' There was urgency in her voice as if she wanted privacy.

As soon as the door closed her face expressed joy as she turned to him. 'Oh, Richard, I'm so pleased to see you. I've missed you so much.' She came to him, eager to eliminate any possibility that the Arctic had changed his attitude to her.

His hands came to her shoulders and gently held her at arm's length. She felt disquiet because he had not embraced her.

He looked seriously at her. 'What is this all about? You in Whitby running a school?'

'You did not return when you said you would and after a while I realised what you had done and why you had done it. So I came to find you, only to learn you had gone with the whalers. I decided to await your return and started this school.'

'That looks as if you mean to stay.'

'I do.'

'But what about Charles?'

'He and father have been here.' They sat down on the sofa and she went on to tell him all that had happened since her decision to come to Whitby. 'So you see,' she concluded in a tone as if the matter was all settled, 'I'm here for you.'

He did not speak for a moment. Then he fixed a solemn look on her. 'Charlotte, things have altered since I went whaling with my father.'

Her heart slipped towards despair. The voyage to the Arctic had changed him. She felt cold, as if life was draining away.

'The loss of my father and brother and Jim's maiming mean that I am now the breadwinner. I must concentrate on that. I cannot take on any other responsibilities. I owe it to my mother, to Jim and my sisters.'

Charlotte brightened at hearing these words. His feelings for her had not been changed, it was only his attitude to the tragic turn in his life. 'I'm so sorry about what happened. It must have been a terrible ordeal for you.' She leaned towards him and touched his cheek with a compassionate kiss. His arms swept round her drawing her close as he sought sympathy and understanding, then those feelings were overpowered by the love they still shared. 'I can help.' She emphasised her enthusiasm. 'This school is going well and I can see it growing. I've had a number of enquiries from parents who have heard of my capabilities.'

'But I couldn't expect you to help to support my family.'

'Of course you can. What does it matter if we are together? That's the most important thing.'

'But won't Charles and your father make trouble? And that could have an adverse effect on your school.'

'I think they know I am determined to stay. And, even if it becomes known who I really am, I don't think it will harm the school. Surely parents are more concerned about the quality of the education I am giving.' She saw doubt in his eyes. 'Oh, Richard, don't you see that this is our chance to be together? I'm sorry your art career in London won't materialise but does that matter when our love is strong?'

He made no comment. 'There's so much to think about, Charlotte, you'll have to give me time to get used to everything.'

She came to him and held his arms. 'You poor dear, this has been a shock to you finding me here and, coming on top of your loss, it is too much to cope with at once. When things are settled and sorted out we will be able to look at life with a more reasonable perspective'. She kissed him on the cheek. 'Come and see me again soon.'

Liza's mind was only partly on keeping the children occupied, for she was puzzling over Mr Parker's request to see Mrs Campion and not Miss Mann, who had sent him the note. Mrs Campion? She had heard the name before – the handsome man who came to see Grace had announced himself as Mr Campion! Her father? No, he was too young to be that, the second gentleman had been more of that age. Then who ...? Husband? Surely not! But who else? She had heard raised voices and she had sensed a taut atmosphere after he had gone. And it was the same after the older man's visit. Was Grace Mrs Campion? She said she was from London and Richard Parker had gone to London to pursue an art career. Had they met there? Had there been an illicit affair?

Liza was worried. She liked Miss Mann, whoever she was, and she ran a good school, but she could see trouble ahead if what she thought was true. Should she warn her? Had she the right? She pondered the idea for the rest of the day and was so worked up by the time she was leaving that she sent her sons home ahead of her.

'Grace, I don't want you to think I'm interfering or that I'm talking out of curiosity, but I have been troubled all day.' She paused as if she was seeking the right thing to say. 'I'm speaking as a friend who admires you so much. I have drawn some conclusions from your recent visitors—'

Charlotte held up her hand. 'I'm sorry, Liza it really has nothing to do with you.' Her voice was cold and Liza flinched as if she had been struck on the face. 'But,' she went on, her tone a little more amiable when she saw Liza had been hurt. 'I know what you are going to say and I know you speak with every good intention, so I'll be straight with you. I am really Charlotte Campion and Richard Parker painted my portrait in London—'

It was Liza's turn to interrupt. 'Say no more, please. I can read the situation, but may I offer a word of advice. I know Whitby people and I know how they would react if they learn, and I'm sure they will, that their children are being taught by someone who has left her husband and will be living in sin. Your school would soon lose its pupils.'

272

Charlotte frowned, troubled by this warning coming again and this time from someone more familiar with the people of the town. 'Surely not?' she queried doubtfully, but there was an inkling in her mind that Liza might be right. If not why should she issue what amounted to a warning?

Concern lined Liza's face. 'I'm afraid it will be so. I'm sorry.' She left Charlotte to ponder her words.

The answer was to leave Whitby, go to somewhere where they were not known. But would Richard agree now that he had a greater responsibility to his family? If he did, and his art work blossomed, their whereabouts would be known, scandal would ensue and his career ruined. Charlotte was perturbed by the prospect.

By the time Richard reached home his mother and sisters had returned. Martha, trying to occupy her mind, was busy baking with the help of Maggie while Sarah was upstairs tidying the bedrooms.

'Mother, can I have a word with you?' he asked.

She nodded, made no comment but washed her hands and followed him into the drawing room.

'Why did you not tell me that two friends had come looking for me?'

'Richard.' There was a touch of admonishment in her tone that he had not considered a reason. 'Our loss drove everything else from my mind.'

Realising he had upset her, he was repentant. 'Of course. I'm sorry.'

She gave a little dismissive wave of her hand. 'No, I should have told you. How did you find out?'

'Mrs Brodrick's two Billys brought a note just as I was leaving to go to the *Phoenix*.'

Martha nodded. 'And?' she prompted.

'I went to see Charlotte.'

'So you know everything?'

'Yes. As you know I left London so she would face no scandal. I did not expect her to follow. You may not know that she has had a visit from her husband and her father.'

Martha looked startled. 'I didn't. She's still here so she must have rebuffed them.'

'She intends to stay.'

A look of deep consideration came to Martha's eyes. 'She must love you very much.'

'She does.'

'And you? You must love her to have given up the goal on which you had set your heart.' Martha shook her head sadly. 'But the situation is impossible unless her husband—'

'He won't entertain releasing her.' He went on to tell his mother what had transpired when Charlotte was visited by Charles and Francis.

She listened carefully, weighing every word. When he had finished she looked hard at her son. 'And you? What have you decided?'

He showed no hesitation. 'I must remain in Whitby for you, for Jim and my sisters. I am the breadwinner.'

'And if Mrs Campion stays, as she seems determined to do?'

'She wants to help as well. Her school is flourishing.'

'No, Richard. I cannot and will not accept charity.' Martha drew herself up, indignation clouding her face which also showed surprise that her son should ever have considered such help. 'Besides, once it is known who the schoolteacher really is, the school will collapse.'

'But—'

'Don't try to fool yourself, and you should not encourage Mrs Campion to do so. You know I'm right. Richard, consider the situation very carefully. I am grateful for the way you are taking into account our position, it is what I would have expected of you. I know you will want to try to support us financially, so consider this: I think ...' She paused. 'No, I know you could do that best by going to London and following your art career. From what you have told me about the chances there, about the commissions you received both there and in Lincolnshire, you will make more money than staying here and will be doing something you love.'

'I must be here to help.'

'We'll manage. But if you are to help in the way I think is best for you and for us, you are going to have to be firm about your relationship with Mrs Campion. As I understand from what you have told me her husband has left the way clear for her to return to him. See that she takes it.'

Martha, wanting these words to make an impact, precluded any more discussion by rising from her chair and leaving the room quickly.

Richard leaned forward and buried his face in his hands. If only he could shut out all problems like this.

He spent an uneasy day and night and when he awoke the next morning he was no nearer making a decision. His mother read his troubled mind and wished she could help but she had said what she wanted to say and now did not add to it. Richard had to make up his own mind about his future.

He left the house without saying where he was going, wandering through familiar parts of Whitby without being fully aware of where he walked. He acknowledged expressions of sympathy from folk without recalling the moment or their names. It was only when his legs became leaden that he realised he had started up the Church Stairs. He reached the top, walked past the old parish church and, with the gaunt ruins of the abbey to his right, ambled along the cliff edge.

The day was bright, the blue sky marked only by small white clouds, scattered as if they had been torn from a mass of cotton wool. They played shadows with the sun, dappling the smooth sea with dark patches which raced before a fresh wind.

Richard loved this weather. He breathed deep lungfuls of the fresh, tangy air. He gazed across Whitby's red roofs, touched with a warm glow by the sun. Fishing boats, tied up against the west bank of the river, were making ready to sail. Beyond, the sea sent gentle waves running along the sand which curved away towards the tiny village of Sandsend, dominated by the high cliffs of Sandsend Ness. This was his country.

Why had he ever thought of leaving? He screwed up his face with annoyance. Oh, why had Mr Wakefield come to Whitby? If only he had stayed away! But if he had he would never have met Charlotte, would never have known what it was like to be in love with the most beautiful girl he had ever seen. Heady thoughts came to him. He could not lose her. Even if he could never marry her they could be together. They would survive, they could, here in Whitby. He must not give way to criticism. He must not succumb to well-meant advice even if it was from his mother.

His mind was made up and he felt a surge of satisfaction. His destiny was shaped. He retraced his steps along the cliff top, hurried across the churchyard, down the Church Stairs, through the crowds thronging Church Street, over the bridge and into Cliff Lane. His pull on the bellstop had an urgency about it and brought Liza hurrying to the door.

'You want to see Mrs Campion?' she asked, knowing full well that that could be the only reason he was here. She was turning to the schoolroom door when he answered, 'Yes, please.' She nodded and indicated to him to go into the next room.

A few moments later Charlotte came in. She had only just closed the door when he was beside her. He swept her into his arms. 'My love, my love, our future is here in Whitby.' There was the joyous knowledge of a decision, which would brook no questioning, having been made.

Charlotte, momentarily taken aback by the ardour of his greeting, relaxed in his arms, delighted at hearing the words she had hoped he would bring her.

'Oh Richard, I love you so. You'll never regret it. We'll be so happy.'

Their lips met, binding a love which in this moment of ecstasy they thought unassailable.

When their lips parted she held his hand and led him to a sofa. As they sat down she said, 'I thought your mother might persuade you otherwise.'

'She did.' When Charlotte pressed him for details, because she wanted to know exactly how she would stand with her, he told her everything his mother had said.

'I thought she might refuse my help,' she commented. 'She's a proud woman, and to be admired for it. But we'll see your family does not suffer because of the tragedy.'

When Richard left, promising to return after the children had gone home, Charlotte found her thoughts turning to the other points and suggestions his mother had made, particularly about the way she thought her son could best help his family. She tried to dismiss them from her mind. There was no point in giving them credence. But they kept dogging her.

*

Richard did not feel like facing his mother with his decision until he had talked further with Charlotte. The more definite their plans the better. He had a pad of paper and pencils which he always carried in his pocket and, after visiting Jim, and giving him words of encouragement, he spent the rest of the day until mid-afternoon wandering around Whitby. He stopped occasionally to sketch, hoping it would take his mind off the decision he had made. Instead he found it only exacerbated it all the more, for it highlighted what he was giving up. Annoyed with himself for doubting life with Charlotte, he strode along the pier where the sharp sea air cleansed his doubt.

As he made his way to Cliff Lane he took little notice of the London packet which was manoeuvring to its berth.

'Good day, Captain, my thanks for a safe and enjoyable voyage.' Jacob Craig shook the officer's hand.

'Good day to you, sir,' replied the captain. 'I hope I shall see you on your return voyage.'

'I hope so too, though I am not certain when that will be. I believe you are a native of Whitby, so will you tell me where I can find the Parker residence?'

'Captain Parker?'

'Yes. A whaler.'

'If it's the captain himself you be wanting then you can't have heard of the tragedy.'

'Tragedy?'

'His ship, the *Phoenix*, yonder.' He nodded in the direction of the whaleship lying sombre in its berth. 'Home early. Captain Parker and one of his sons lost in the Arctic, another badly maimed.'

'My God!' Alarm shot through Jacob. 'It's Richard Parker I really came to see. He wasn't ...'

'No.' The captain hastened to reassure him. 'He's safe, unharmed.'

Jacob heaved a sigh of relief. 'Thank goodness. My journey won't be wasted. But I am sorry to hear about his loss.'

Solemn-faced, the captain nodded. 'A disaster for us all. John Parker will be greatly missed. A likeable man, a good and fair captain and an expert whaler. He had a nose for them, rarely came back without a full ship. But that's life and it's got to go on. Now, you want to be at Prospect Place. Go in that direction,' he pointed to his right. 'You'll see some steps leading up to it.'

He thanked the captain and, picking up his bag, left the ship.

He merely smiled and shook his head at the boys who vied to carry his bag, a small one, for he had anticipated only a brief stay and had brought little with him.

He followed the captain's direction with barely an interest in the pulsating activity around him, for his attention was fixed on meeting the young man whose portrait of Charlotte Campion he so much admired and in which he detected a great talent. He was determined that he should provide the opportunity for its development and that this young man should grace his establishment in London.

His knock on the door in Prospect Place was answered by Martha.

'Good day, ma'am.' He raised his hat. 'Have I the pleasure of addressing Mrs Parker?'

'You have.' Martha had been taken aback by being confronted by this elegantly dressed stranger, but his bright face was disarming, and though it held a touch of solemnity, it could only draw a friendly response from her.

He bowed. 'May I present myself. Jacob Craig. Before I explain the reason for my visit, may I extend my deepest sympathy for your recent loss. I only just heard when I left the London packet.'

There was a sincerity about the stranger's words and manner that gave Martha an instant respect for him. She thanked him.

'I have come straight from the ship to see your son, Richard, even before I have found accommodation.'

'Then it must be of some importance.'

'Indeed it is. It concerns his future.'

She raised her eyebrows. 'Then I think you had better step inside and explain yourself more fully.'

Jacob thanked her and followed her into the drawing room. She indicated a chair but he waited for her to sit down before he did so. She sat straight-backed, her hands folded neatly on her lap, as if steeling herself against unwanted news. Was his visit likely to be in connection with Richard's relationship with Mrs Campion? Martha was troubled and yet she felt sure that she had heard this man's name before.

In contrast to her, Jacob leaned back in his chair in an attitude of relaxation, but there was a certain tension about him as if he was about to reveal something of importance.

'Mrs Parker, I take it your son is not at home at this moment, otherwise you would have called him.'

'You think correctly.' Martha was guarded.

'Then let me tell you, he has a God-given talent as an artist which I deem it my duty and privilege to see developed to the full.' He paused as if gathering his words.

Martha's thoughts were swept by relief. Jacob Craig – of course, this was the man whom Richard had mentioned. She waited for him to go on.

'I have never met your son. I was absent on the Continent when he was in London. When I returned I visited my good friend, Mr Wakefield, and saw your son's portrait of Charlotte Campion, Mr Wakefield's daughter.' He went on to explain his role in encouraging and developing artistic talent. 'When I saw that portrait I knew I had to take Mr Parker under my wing. Mr Wakefield told me that Mr Parker had come north to see his father sail and would soon be back in London. When he did not return we learned that he too had gone to the Arctic, so I decided to come north and await his return. Here I am, hoping I can persuade him to come back to London, take up his art career and overcome whatever it was that brought him back to Whitby and took him on that disastrous voyage.'

Martha had listened most carefully to his story. There was no implication that he knew of Richard's real reason for not returning to London five months ago, nor did he appear to know of Charlotte's presence in Whitby. Should she tell him or not? That question was turning over in her mind when she asked cautiously, 'You don't question Richard's talent?'

Jacob threw up his hands as if he had not expected his judgement to be questioned. 'My dear lady, I have no doubt whatsoever. That young man has a tremendous gift. It is so evident in that portrait. Oh, I'll not say there are some aspects

279

where guidance would not be useful. I can do that. This is what I do with the other young men I have at my studio, but I do not stifle their natural talent. Your son will benefit. Also, with my connections I can guide him to a great and profitable future. Mrs Parker, I think I am right in saying that he can become one of England's greatest painters. Can? No! Will! I am certain of it!'

'Mr Craig, it gives me great heart to hear you say this, for only yesterday I was encouraging him to return to London and resume his art work again. He has always had a deep love for it and dreamed of becoming a great painter. I would like to see those dreams fulfilled.'

'But now he is concerned for you in these trying times? He wants to help you?'

'Yes.'

'Well apart from being with you, giving you the support of his presence in this house, I believe he can help you just as much, if not more, by his art in London. His work will sell, and will do so for good money. Maybe I can persuade him to consider that. But I will only do so, ma'am, with your permission. If you think it will upset family relationships then I will return to London without seeing Mr Parker.'

'Mr Craig, you are a kind and considerate man. I appreciate your thought.' Jacob dismissed her thanks with a slight shake of his hands. 'You have my blessing to try and I hope you succeed.' Thinking that the surprise of being confronted by Mr Craig might have more impact on Mrs Campion if he did not know that she was in Whitby Martha kept that knowledge to herself. 'As you so rightly observed, Richard is not here but, if you want to contact him immediately, I can tell you where he is.'

'Excellent. There is no point in wasting time.'

'You'll have to go to Miss Mann's Academy in Cliff Lane. You'll find him there, I'm sure.'

Jacob thanked her, obtained directions to Cliff Lane and received a recommendation to find accommodation at the Angel Inn.

Chapter Nineteen

The sound of the doorbell interrupted the discussion about their future in Whitby. The children had departed to their homes at the close of the school day. Liza and the two Billys had made their farewells ten minutes ago and Charlotte and Richard, with much to plan, had settled down to do so.

Tightening her lips with annoyance, Charlotte hurried to the front door, eager to get rid of the caller and resume more important things.

'Good day ...' Jacob's voice trailed away, his arm stiffened in the act of raising his hat to the lady. 'Mrs Campion!' He looked bewildered. The unexpected had stunned him.

Charlotte was equally taken aback. Her eyes widened in a mixture of surprise, horror and guilt as if she had been caught in a compromising situation. Her face paled. 'Mr Craig!'

Jacob, his mind seeking answers to the questions which were whirling in his mind, made a stumbling attempt to recover his composure. 'I didn't expect ...'

Charlotte was quicker to control herself. 'To find me here,' she finished for him. 'If you are surprised to see me here then I know my father did not send you.'

'No, he did not.' Jacob gave an emphatic shake of his head. 'I came to Whitby to find Richard Parker. His mother said I would find him at Miss Mann's Academy.'

'I think you had better come in.' She made way for him and closed the door. Without a word she led him to the room she had just left. As she entered she said, 'Richard, here is someone to see you.' Then, remembering that he had never met the art connoisseur, she added, 'Mr Jacob Craig.'

Astounded, Richard jumped to his feet. In his present situation he had dismissed Jacob Craig from his mind. Now here he was face to face with the man who Charlotte's father had indicated could make him a great artist. All sorts of visions flashed through his mind. The studio in London, demonstrations by masters of their craft, advice, pencil drawings, watercolours, oils, landscapes, portraits, buyers, collectors praising work; and himself drinking in the adulation but keeping a firm hold on his feelings to ensure that his talent was never prostituted to the whims and fancies of others. His art was his own.

'At last I meet the young man who painted that wonderful portrait.' Jacob had gathered his wits. As he had followed Charlotte, his mind had been full of possible answers to the question; what was she doing here? There could only be one answer, an answer he dreaded. These two young people, thrown together through Francis's desire for a portrait of his daughter, had fallen in love. Why else would she be here under the name of Miss Mann? He had no doubt that was who she had declared herself to be on arriving in Whitby. To establish a school seemed to indicate that this was where she intended to stay. And that meant deserting her husband, which could only lead to scandal. The horror of that alarmed him. It would mean he could never sell this young man's work to the clientele it deserved. He must try and salvage the situation. Was that why Francis had never told him that Charlotte was in Whitby? Was he hoping that his meeting with Richard, when he would expand on the possibilities for his talent, would make this couple see sense before the scandal broke?

'Sir, you are generous in your praise,' said Richard, taking Jacob's proffered hand.

'Not at all. Your talent is obvious and I hear that when you were in Lincolnshire you sold some paintings. I hope I shall be able to see more of your work.' He glanced round. 'May I sit down?'

'Of course,' replied Charlotte tightly. 'I forget my manners.'

'Not at all, Mrs Campion. Seeing me must have been a shock to you.' He sensed she was wary of his visit. He must be careful not to offend. Her presence here, although it

282

touched upon his ambition to develop this young man's talent, was really something private. He could make no direct reference to their relationship no matter how much it could affect their future. 'But I came because I was expecting Mr Parker ... to be returning to London, in fact I gather that your father had thought he would be back before I came home from the Continent.' He glanced at Richard. 'Your prolonged absence brought me north to see when I could expect you to take up residence in my studio, for I did not want to lose such a talented artist.'

'You must think highly of my ability?' queried Richard.

'Indeed I do,' replied Jacob enthusiastically. 'My dear fellow, I do not offer places in my studio, which I believe you have seen, lightly.'

'And you think I have the necessary qualifications?'

Charlotte noted the interest in Richard's voice. The sparkle in his eyes at Jacob's praise came from deep feelings for his art. Would she be thwarting him from fulfilling his ambitions? Were others right in saying that scandal would ruin his chances? But she was in love and she knew he was. Wouldn't that love surmount anything which threatened their life together? Her thoughts were interrupted by Jacob, who was continuing with a keen fervour.

'Think? I know you have. I can tell you have done a lot of drawing and that says something for an artist. Drawing is the basis of all art work. It influences your thinking, painting, composition, in fact every aspect of art.'

'If Richard is as good as you say is there any need for him to come to your studio?' put in Charlotte.

'My dear Mrs Campion.' Jacob looked shocked at the suggestion. 'Mr Parker is good, better than most who have come to me, and he may be able to earn something of a living here in Whitby but there are some aspects which need honing. In this I can guide him without destroying his natural talent. Not only that but through me he will sell to the rich and the famous and that in turn will reflect on him.' He paused momentarily, glancing quickly from one to the other. 'In fact I will predict that he could become one of the most famous painters in the country.'

As this prediction was made Charlotte shot a look at

283

Richard and saw an unmistakable delight at the statement and a desire to reach that goal. Almost as it came it was gone and serious concern came to his face.

'Mr Craig, I don't think I could ever live up to your expectations so I think it best—'

'Nonsense,' Jacob broke in sharply. 'Do not question my judgement. It is second to none.'

Richard felt rebuked and an apologetic look replaced his misgiving. 'Sir, I did not distrust ...'

Jacob waved his hand dismissively. 'I know you weren't doubting me, my boy.' The tension had gone from his voice. 'I know from what I have seen that I am right. I am not given to making irrational statements. Now, my boy, when can I expect you in London? I will delay my sailing and we can return together.'

Worry was beginning to nag at Charlotte. Was Jacob becoming too persuasive? Would the temptations he was placing before Richard weaken his resolve? Was his love not strong enough to resist the call of fame?

'Mr Craig, I appreciate all you have said, but the fact is that I must remain in Whitby. Your visit to my mother must have revealed the tragedy which has beset my family.'

'Indeed it has,' Jacob broke in. 'And I must apologise for not extending my sympathy and commiserations to you as soon as I arrived. Let me assure you that they are no less sincere when offered now.'

In Richard's thanks there was also his understanding. 'Well,' he went on, 'you must see that I have to remain in Whitby. There is my family to consider, they will need my support and my financial contribution. I have got to turn down your generous offer, Mr Craig. I'm sorry.'

'I understand the situation,' replied Jacob quietly. 'But have you never thought that you will be able to provide more for your family through your art, even though you are in London?'

Richard gave a wan smile. 'There is no certainty that my work will sell.'

Jacob threw up his arms in horror. 'My goodness. You'll sell. I'll guarantee that. I'd stake my life on it.'

'But my family would like me to be here.'

284

Jacob wondered whether to mention that he knew Mrs Parker's view, that she desired her son to pursue his art career in London. But he deemed it wiser to leave that unsaid. Richard knew what his mother thought.

'Maybe there is something in what Mr Craig says,' put in Charlotte tentatively.

'Think about it,' put in Jacob quickly, seizing on the fact that she appeared to support him. He stood up. 'I am staying at the Angel, you can get in touch with me there. I will not leave until I hear from you.'

'Thank you,' returned Richard and the two men shook hands.

'I'll see you out,' offered Charlotte. Jacob followed her, closing the door behind him.

When they reached the front door, Charlotte paused and looked seriously at Jacob. 'Mr Craig, you are no fool. You asked no questions but I have no doubt that you have guessed what lies behind my being here.'

'Ma'am, that is something private between you. I have no wish to interfere.'

'You are understanding. Can I ask you, do you honestly think that Richard will have a wonderful career if he takes his chance with you?'

'Undoubtedly.' He emphasised the word, then added soberly. 'But there would have to be no scandal attached to him. That would completely ruin his prospects and career. No one would buy his work, they would not want to be seen supporting someone who had wrecked the marriage of a very respected man. They would seem to be condoning his behaviour. I will say no more, Mrs Campion. Decisions are out of my hands, but I would hate to see such a talent lost. Goodbye, and thank you for listening to me. I will be in Whitby for a week should you want to talk to me again.'

She closed the door when he left and with a sigh leaned back against it. She knew she was not mistaken – he had put a slight stress on the word Mrs as if he was reminding her of her true obligations.

She opened the door into the room quietly and found Richard, his head in his hands, deep in thought. Suddenly aware of her presence he looked up sharply. He gave a forced smile. 'Well, that was an unexpected visit.'

She nodded and sat down. 'You would have liked to say yes to him.'

'Of course I would, but that's of no consequence. It is you and I who matter.'

'You are right, that is the important thing,' she said wistfully.

He caught her mood. He came quickly from his chair and knelt at her feet, taking her hands in his. 'You are not having regrets?' He looked anxiously into her eyes.

'About our love? Never. But I am ruining your chance of a great career.'

'Oh, my love, you must never think that.'

'But one day you will wonder what might have been.'

'No.'

She smiled wanly. 'You will.'

He shook his head. 'Never.' He kissed her on the lips, and when he would have drawn away she held him until their passion almost overwhelmed them.

'I love you, Charlotte. I always will, without any regrets.'

'And I will always be in love with you,' she whispered.

In the silence of the night, when sleep would not come, Jacob's words haunted Charlotte. Slowly and insidiously they were intertwined with those of Richard's mother. She twisted on her pillow, gasping for breath. Was this what the future held? Would the torment of scandal dictate their lives? Would Richard regret forfeiting his chance to become a great artist, as his mother said he would? Would he, in his heart, blame her for the lost opportunity even if he never voiced it? The questions pounded in her mind until she was forced to cry out loud to try to drive them away. But they persisted.

In the morning light her horrors of the night seemed less menacing but two days later they became more than just upsetting thoughts.

Charlotte was at the door greeting her pupils for morning school when she was approached by two late-middle-aged ladies. Their faces were set with determination, their eyes were cold, and their walk had a no-nonsense step to it. They held themselves erect, their hands clasped in front of them, their bonnets set straight. Their well-fitting coats open at the collar revealed high-necked blouses tight at the throat. They bore an air of support for each other and Charlotte sensed they would be formidable opponents.

'Miss Mann?'

Charlotte nodded. 'Yes.'

'I am Mrs Scales and this is Mrs Featherstone.'

'It is a pleasure to meet you both.' She tried to sound sincere and offered a smile but received only blank stares in return.

'We would like a word with you if we are not intruding on your time.'

'Come this way. Lessons don't begin for another ten minutes.'

'Time enough for what we have to say.' Mrs Scales's voice held no warmth.

They followed Charlotte into her study. 'Please sit down,' she offered pleasantly, trying to lighten the dour atmosphere which had come to the room with these two women.

'No, thank you.' Mrs Featherstone's marked hostility made it obvious that she was not going to accede to Charlotte's wishes.

'We can say what we came to say standing up.' rasped Mrs Scales, making it plain that she had no wish to linger.

Charlotte's eyes turned hard. 'Well?' she said curtly.

'I am Veronica Long's grandmother,' said Mrs Scales.

'Camilla Clark is my granddaughter,' added Mrs Featherstone.

'Two of my brightest pupils,' said Charlotte hoping this information would please.

'No longer,' said Mrs Scales, a rapier thrust in her voice. Mrs Featherstone nodded in agreement.

Charlotte, her worst fears rising, looked sharply from one to the other. 'You mean ...?'

'They will not be attending this school again.' Mrs Scales finished the sentence for her.

'Never, ever,' chorused Mrs Featherstone.

'Why, may I ask?' said Charlotte, her quiet tone demanding an explanation.

'Why?' Mrs Featherstone's eyebrows shot up with the rise in her tone. 'I don't think you need ask.' She gave a small contemptuous grunt.

'But I do,' Charlotte insisted.

'Then you shall have the answer,' snapped Mrs Scales. 'We don't want our grandchildren coming under the influence of a married woman who has left her husband for another man.'

Though she had half expected a statement like this, nevertheless it hit her hard when it came. The truth was out. Where would it end? Rumours would grow. She would be regarded as an outcast. Mrs Parker and Liza had warned her.

'It seems I have struck home!' The triumph in Mrs Scales's voice was accompanied by a flicker of satisfaction on her lips.

Charlotte fought to keep her temper under control. She wanted to call them interfering old busybodies but she knew that would get her nowhere. 'Mrs Scales, Mrs Featherstone,' she said, her voice distinctly chilly. 'My private life is my business, not yours. I am a good teacher, I run a good school. If you want your granddaughters to miss the education I have to offer then ask me to take them off the register. But do their parents want me to do that? It was they who enrolled them in the first place, not you.'

Mrs Scales drew herself up, casting Charlotte a withering look for doubting her authority. 'They certainly do. I told them they should not have their daughter taught by a woman of low morals.'

'Camilla's parents feel the same,' verified Mrs Featherstone forcefully.

Charlotte's hackles rose. Her hands clenched until the knuckles were white as she compelled herself to keep her dignity. 'Very well, I will not expect to see Veronica and Camilla again.'

'You certainly won't!' said Mrs Featherstone. 'And what's more, there will be many more of your pupils leaving.' She looked at Charlotte with contempt, brushed past her and opened the door. Mrs Scales looked her up and down, disgust in her eyes, and followed her companion, leaving Charlotte to contemplate the encounter.

She stood for a few moments, tense with animosity towards the two strangers who had dared to voice their opinions of her.

Then the impact of what they had implied startled her. Were they right? Was this encounter confirmation of what Mrs Parker and Liza had said would happen? Her charged emotions drained from her, leaving her weak and shaking. She sank on to a chair, her hands clasped tight as if trying to find support for herself.

These were people she would have expected to mix with – parents and grandparents of her pupils – people whom she saw as potential buyers of Richard's paintings. For love of him she had been willing to accept changes to her life which meant she would no longer have the protection and understanding of her family to fall back on whenever anything troubled her. But now? A question mark hung over their future like the Sword of Damocles.

She had no doubt that the two women would take delight in recounting their confrontation with the new school teacher, painting her as a hussy who was not worthy of attention. Their condemnation of her would spread and she and Richard would suffer. The future, in which they would be outcasts, looked bleak.

The attitude of her morning's visitors nagged at her all day. How had they learned her true identity? Richard's mother? Liza? Maybe his sisters? Charles? Her father? A dropped word, a conversation overheard in the Angel? Jacob Craig? She could not condemn them all so she condemned none, taking the situation as a *fait accompli*.

She got through the day with some effort and was glad when it was time for the children to leave for it meant that Richard would soon be with her.

He sensed something was wrong as soon as she opened the door to him and this was confirmed in her anguished greeting and the way she clasped him to her as if she was seeking reassuring protection.

'What's wrong?' he asked, gently easing her away so that he could look into her eyes. They were clouded with anxiety and dampness on the verge of tears.

'I've had visitors this morning and what they said does not augur well for our future.' She looked at him with a mute cry for help.

'Take it calmly and tell me all about it. Nothing can be that bad.'

'Oh, but it is.'

'Let's sit down.' He led her into the room and sat down beside her on the sofa, taking her hand in his, offering comfort. He listened without interrupting as she recounted the visit of Mrs Scales and Mrs Featherstone.

'Oh, those two old battle-axes,' he said contemputuously. 'Take no notice of them.'

'They can do us a lot of harm. Life could become unbearable.'

Richard's lips tightened. He knew she was right but he did not want to admit it. He knew he would have to be strong for both of them. For now, he tried to make light of it. 'Don't worry, my love, people may adopt a shocked attitude at first but that will die down. We'll be all right.'

But Charlotte was not so sure and she spent much of the night agonising over the situation. Her love for Richard was powerful, but Jacob's words came strongly to her and she realised she had Richard's future and destiny in her hands. She felt an overpowering and ominous responsibility. Could she, for the sake of satisfying her own desires, wreck the ambitions of the man she loved? She knew he was willing to sacrifice them for her, to banish them in his love for her, but had she the right to impose this on him and subject him to ostracism which would stifle his talents? She reasoned and counter-reasoned far into the night and wondered if the dawn of a new day would change the decision she had come to.

It did not, and there was a new determination about her when Liza arrived at the school.

Pupils who had already arrived were being sent home. Puzzled, Liza asked, 'What's happening?'

'I am returning to London for good,' explained Charlotte and told her something of Jacob Craig's visit.

When she had finished there were tears in Liza's eyes. 'I think what you are doing is right, and I hope that it will bring you happiness and fulfilment.'

'Liza, this house is yours, everything in it is yours. Do with them what you will. I am grateful for your friendship and I hope you will always remember me with good thoughts?'

Bewildered, Liza gasped. 'But I couldn't ...'

'It will please me if you will accept it. You were a dear friend when I needed one. I have contacted Mr Craig this morning and we leave on today's sailing. I have written a letter for Richard. Please see that the Billys deliver it at sailing time, and not before.'

'I will.'

'Now, send the other pupils home, and will you please inform all parents that it is with regret that I have had to close the school and return to London. They need know nothing more.'

'I'll see to everything.'

'Thank you. You are a good friend. I'll see that the house and furnishings are handed over to you legally.'

Liza brushed away a tear. 'You are too kind. I will miss you.'

'I have only a few things to take with me. Will you help me pack?

Liza nodded.

When all was ready they hugged each other, their friendship short but deep-rooted. It was one neither of them would forget.

Charlotte left for the Angel Inn and Jacob Craig.

Richard regretted the upset experienced by Charlotte and he hoped that he had made her see that nothing mattered but their love. Though he knew the situation would become unpleasant when their relationship became public knowledge, he was prepared to face whatever happened and was determined to shield Charlotte from the worst consequences. He hoped they could find happiness without regrets for what might have been.

His mind moved wistfully. He saw himself absorbed in bringing a canvas to life in Jacob Craig's studio. He pulled himself up sharply, dismissed his thoughts and swore, for Charlotte's sake, never again to contemplate what he might have achieved.

'A letter for you,' said Maggie, who had answered the knock on the door. 'The two Billys. They said there was no reply needed.' She held out the envelope to her brother.

291

He took it with a feeling of misgiving. If the two Billys had brought it it must be from Charlotte. But why had she written? He would be seeing her after the school had closed. He slit the envelope open and drew out a sheet of paper.

My darling one,
    When you read this I shall be on board the London packet ...

He read no more. He stared disbelievingly at the words for one brief second and then with the letter still in his hand he tore from the house.

He took the steps from Prospect Place two at a time and raced along Church Street. Eyebrows were raised, scowls were cast at him as he bustled his way through the flow of people, ignoring their protests. The quay where the London packet should be tied up was deserted. He ran on as if he could catch the ship and stop her. The bridge was closed again. The ship was downstream nearing the gap between the piers.

Anguish gripped him. His heart was torn in two. Charlotte gone! His face creased with grief and silent tears began to stream down his face. He raced to the cliff top near the abbey, compelled by a force within him to watch the ship taking his beloved away from him.

He stood close to the edge of the cliff, a silent figure, the light breeze ruffling his hair. He felt numb, as if his whole world had caved in. He knew when he read the rest of the words in the letter there would be a finality about them.

He watched the ship clear the piers and take to the sea. He saw sails unfurl, catch the wind and speed the ship onwards carrying his love away. He brushed the dampness from his eyes to see better. Was she one of the few passengers on the deck? His gaze cut through the distance, searching, searching. Jacob Craig! Charlotte? Had she changed her mind? Had she stayed behind? A figure came from below deck. Charlotte! His one moment of hope was dashed. She came to the rail and stood beside Jacob. Despondency swept him. He felt drained, unable to raise his arm in one last gesture of love and farewell.

*

292

'The person on the cliff?' Jacob put the question, drawing Charlotte's gaze upwards.

She swallowed hard and bit her lip, trying to hold back the tears. She nodded. 'Richard.' The word came as a whisper but Jacob sensed it was not a confirmation for him but a word full of love for the man watching from dry land.

Charlotte's heart ached. She had no doubt that Richard's was breaking too. What had she done? Regret threatened to swamp her but what was done was done. There was no turning back. She gripped her hands tightly making certain she did not break down.

'My love,' she mouthed the words silently. 'I will always be in love with you. Be happy.'

The ship had been taken by the horizon. Richard felt weak, hardly able to raise the letter. He read:

My darling one,

When you read this I shall be on board the London packet. You will be unable to prevent me leaving and that will be for the best.

It breaks my heart to leave you but I cannot stand in the way of the career you wanted so much. If only I had been free we could have shared it together. As it is I will only be able to watch it from a distance, but I will do so with the same interest as if you were my own darling husband. People have made me see the tragedy which could occur if our illicit relationship continued. Your career would be destroyed and our lives marred by gossip and pointing fingers. I don't want that for you. I want your art to blossom without hindrance. So come back to London, take up Mr Craig's offer and go from success to success. To attain this our paths must not cross. We must never see each other. Promise me this, Richard, for it is the only way to save heartache and maybe catastrophe.

I have no regrets for our love. I will always bless the day my father brought me to Whitby and discovered you.

Remember me.

I will always be in love with you.

Charlotte

*

Richard's arms sank to his sides. His eyes were on the far horizon where he had last seen the ship. 'I will never forget you, for I know there is love in the sacrifice you have made. Goodbye, my darling.'

Chapter Twenty

The London packet proceeded slowly up the Thames. Even here the pulsating life of the city enveloped all and it focused Charlotte's thoughts on the future and what it might hold.

The heartache at the start of the voyage had been accompanied by a numbness which dulled all physical feeling, but as the Yorkshire coast fell from sight she was transferred into a limbo where nothing mattered. She had given up the man she loved and life stretched endlessly ahead without feeling.

Now, as she came from her cabin, she was brought back to reality by the sounds of the river, the shouts of sailors, the cry of gulls, the swish of water, the crack of sails, the creak of ropes, and the movement of vessels. Life went on. Soon she would face Charles. She hoped his forgiveness and his promise for a future unhampered by the past would still hold good. She strengthened her determination to do her best to make him happy. In doing so she hoped she would reap some happiness in return even though Richard would still have a place in her heart.

'Good morning, Mr Craig,' she said when she joined him at the rail.

'Good morning to you, Mrs Campion,' he replied, raising his hat. 'Splendid weather.'

'Indeed it is,' she agreed, trying to match his effervescent mood. 'I trust you had a settled night?'

He nodded. 'As much as I generally do when I am at sea.'

'It does not agree with you?'

'Below deck, no. On deck, yes. Would you care to take a stroll?' He held out his arm. She took it and they exchanged pleasantries as the ship moved upstream. Eventually they stood at the rail, watching all the activity and admiring the skill with which the ship was brought alongside the quay.

'And so, Mrs Campion, London at last. I must escort you home. Where shall it be? Chelsea or Russell Square?'

'That is most kind of you, but there is no need.'

Jacob gave a little shake of his head. 'No, ma'am, I insist. I must see you safely home.'

Charlotte realised he would not take her refusal. Really she was glad, for his presence would give her no time to speculate on the reception she would receive from Charles.

Jacob quickly had everything organised. A carriage was hired, their bags loaded, and, ensconced as comfortably as possible inside, they were soon on their way.

Reaching Charlotte's Chelsea home, Jacob stepped out of the carriage to say goodbye. He refused the invitation to meet Charles. This had to be a private homecoming. He bowed as he took her hand. 'Mrs Campion, you are a remarkable and brave woman. May I, in expressing my admiration, wish you every happiness for the future.' He paused, then the romantic in him added softly, 'I am sure you will find it even though a little piece of your heart may be elsewhere.'

She made no reply. He did not expect one. He climbed into the coach. It drove away. She watched it for a moment, sensing in its departure a removal of the past. She turned to the house. A maid opened the door. She walked into another life.

'The master?' she queried as the maid took her bag.

'In his study, ma'am.'

She walked across the marble floor. She slowed. Hesitated. Gone was the boldness she had thought of adopting, gone the casual attitude she had thought of displaying. In their place was nervousness. Maybe contrition would be best. She pushed the door open, stepped into the room and allowed the door to swing shut behind her.

Charles, who was sitting at his desk, looked up from the papers he was studying. For one moment tension sparked across the room but it was banished the instant Charles said, 'Charlotte' for his voice held an enveloping warmth which dismissed any antagonism. With a smile of pleasure he rose from his chair and came to meet her with outstretched arms.

She stepped into them, bent her head against his chest and felt reassurance in their strength.

'You've come home,' he said softly. 'Thank you.'

Those two words tore at her heart. She didn't deserve thanks. She was the sinner. She should be thanking him for being understanding and taking her back. She looked up at him, 'Forgive me?' she pleaded.

He looked deep into her eyes. He gave a small smile. 'Whatever there is to forgive I do so. I promised you that life would continue as before and that the past would not be mentioned.' She nodded. 'But there is only one thing I would remind you of now, and then it will never be mentioned again. I presume Mr Parker will be taking up Mr Craig's offer and coming to London?'

Again she nodded and said, 'I expect so.'

'Remember I said if you returned you must never see him again.'

'Yes.'

'And the promise will be upheld?'

'I will never see Richard Parker again.' The words were hard to utter but she knew for Richard's sake, for his career and chance to become a great artist, they must be adhered to.

He kissed her gently. She responded as she knew she must and in doing so sealed a future in which she realised she could find a great deal of happiness with Charles.

He took her hand. 'Come, let me show you something.' He led her round the desk and she saw the papers he had been studying were in fact maps of France. 'Next week I have to go to France on business. I will be travelling around.' He pointed out the places he had to visit. 'I was just trying to work out the best itinerary. Come with me and we will turn it into a holiday.'

'Very well, Charles. It will be exciting to explore France with you. How long will we be away?'

He smiled and shrugged his shoulders. 'A month, two months. Who knows after my business is finished?'

'And can I help in that?'

'Of course. You can charm the men I deal with, entertain their wives, learn something of the business.' He hugged her.

'It will be a delight to work together. Get yourself a whole new outfit of clothes for every occasion.'

'Can I, Charles?' she asked in surprise.

'Of course. Spare nothing.'

'You're so generous.' There was laughter on her lips. She was back in the life she had once known. The life that might have been was drifting into the mists of time.

'Now, my dear. I think we had better go and let your mother and father know you are home.'

As they approached the house in Russell Square, Charlotte was more nervous than when she was about to face her husband.

When they entered the drawing room, Francis, who had been reading *The Times*, sprang to his feet, dropping the paper beside his chair. Gertrude, who had been working on a tapestry, gasped at the sight of her daughter. Her hands trembled and her sewing kit fell to the floor.

'Charlotte, you're back,' cried Francis, expecting to find an expression of remorse and humility on his daughter's face. Finding none he scowled. 'I hope all that nonsense is out of your head.'

The sharp words banished her nervousness and brought defiance but before she could utter a word Charles intervened. 'Everything is in order.' He gave his father-in-law a look which said, 'Say no more. Remember we agreed that if Charlotte returned we would forget the past.'

Catching the recrimination, Francis blustered. 'Welcome home, daughter.' He came forward and offered his cheek for a kiss. He was embarrassed when she whispered close to his ear. 'I still love you.'

'Yes, yes,' he spluttered and patted her on the shoulder. 'Go and stop your mother's tears.'

She sank on her knees beside her mother, kissed her and held her in her arms.

'I'm so glad you saw sense and returned to us. If you hadn't my heart would have broken.'

'I'm home, Mother,' said Charlotte with conviction, then added brightly as she stood up, 'but not for long. Charles is taking me to France.'

'Splendid, my boy,' cried Francis, slapping Charles on the back. 'A splendid idea. Get her involved in other things.'

Gertrude rang for some tea and while they were waiting for it, Francis saw Charlotte glance at the landscape hanging over the fireplace where her portrait had once hung.

Charles was in conversation with Gertrude about the forthcoming trip to France so Francis drew Charlotte to one side to offer her an explanation for he had seen the questioning look in her eyes.

'I got rid of it,' he told her. 'If you returned I did not want it there to remind you of him. And I didn't want it to remind me of how he let me down. It's gone and won't be seen again.'

A week later Richard left the ship from Whitby and made his way to Jacob Craig's house.

His mother and sisters had helped him to throw off the despondency which had filled him at Charlotte's departure. Eventually they persuaded him to return to London to take up the life of an artist which Jacob Craig had offered. His mother made him see that he owed it not only to the people who had faith in his ability but also to Charlotte who had made a sacrifice so that he could achieve his ambition.

Jacob Craig welcomed him with an overwhelming enthusiasm. 'I knew the true artist in you would prevail. Once you have achieved the joy of depicting life on a canvas or through a sketch you can never resist the temptation to do it over and over again, ever straining for perfection though you know it will never come.'

Richard settled in quickly, though three days later he felt the urge to contact Charlotte. He resisted the temptation, knowing that no good would come of it. By the end of that day Jacob had sensed the unease in Richard and had made a shrewd guess at what troubled him. After the convivial evening meal with all his pupils he took Richard to one side and sat down to enjoy a glass of wine.

'Have you decided what you will work on?' he asked.

'I can't really settle on anything particular,' Richard admitted. 'Oh, I have several ideas but none seems to be urging me to get on with it.'

'I have several suggestions I could make,' replied Jacob,

'but if you will allow me to do so there is one in particular I would like to put to you.'

'Please do so,' said Richard. 'I need something on which to focus.'

'Very well.' Jacob hesitated a moment while he took a sip of his wine and then, with his eyes fixed on Richard, said, 'Before . . .' The slight pause he gave was full of meaning and he saw that Richard had understood. 'You were commissioned to do a portrait of Miss Kemp. I believe you got no further than the preliminary stages. I would suggest that you take up where you left off.'

'But . . .'

Jacob scotched the doubt in Richard's voice. 'It will get you back into drawing and painting. It will test your desire to produce a portrait better than any you have done before.'

Richard looked thoughtful. It might be a good idea. He would be fulfilling Mr Kemp's commission and would be redressing a wrong in having appeared to let him down. And it would be nice to renew Marietta's acquaintance and let her see that the faith she had in his ability would not be lost. He nodded. 'Very well.'

'Excellent. I am sure you will never regret restarting in this way.' Jacob raised his glass. 'Here's to success.'

As he walked into Russell Square the next morning memories came flooding back. It was hard to dismiss them. He glanced across at the Wakefield residence and thoughts of Charlotte and her portrait dominated his mind. He wondered what he would do if she came out of the house now. And what would she do? But there was no sign of movement. Of course, Charlotte would more likely be at her home in Chelsea. That thought helped to turn his mind back to the quest in hand.

The maid's announcement that Mr Richard Parker was here to see her brought Marietta hastily to her feet, dropping the book she had been reading.

'Richard!' she came to meet him with both hands held out in greeting.

He took them in his and was drawn by the warm excited smile on her face. 'Marietta.' There was genuine pleasure in his voice, for suddenly he no longer felt alone. He had Jacob

300

as a mentor and the other students were friendly but that was not the same as someone with whom not so long ago he had an empathy which had gone a little beyond friendliness.

'I'm so glad you have come back to London. I presume you are taking up your career with Mr Craig?' She had led him to a sofa where they had sat down.

'Yes.'

'And everything else?'

'Finished,' he replied. 'Marietta, you were a good friend to me when I was in London before. I know you went to Whitby to see Charlotte. My mother told me. And I believe that your reception by Charlotte was greeted with hostility.'

'I am afraid the damage is irreparable.'

'For that I am truly sorry; you were such good friends.'

Marietta gave a shrug of her shoulders. 'If that is the way she wants it then so be it. I knew she had returned to London but she has made no attempt to contact me and I heard yesterday that she has gone to France with Charles.'

That information gave Richard mixed feelings. Charlotte and Charles must be together without recriminations. For that he was glad. But he also felt a pang of jealousy. He threw it off. He had Marietta's friendship.

'Marietta, I feel I owe you something, some explanation of what happened.'

'You owe me nothing, Richard.'

'You know most of it but not what happened after I returned from the whaling.'

'If it hurts to talk about it then say nothing. If you feel it would be a catharsis which would help the future then I am a willing listener.'

'I would like to tell you.'

She listened intently, sympathising with the family loss and sharing with him the horrors of that voyage. She understood about the developing situation in Whitby, about Jacob Craig's visit and the resultant departure of Charlotte. 'I would like you to read the letter she wrote me.'

'But that is too personal,' protested Marietta.

'I would like you to,' said Richard, taking the letter from his pocket. 'It will let you see what Charlotte did.' He held out the paper to her.

She hesitated. 'Are you sure?'

Their eyes were locked on each other in confidential friendship. He nodded.

She took the letter and read it. She was silent as she folded it and held it out to him. As he returned it to his pocket, she said, 'Thank you for showing it to me.' She gave no expression to her thoughts. He did not want any.

Richard broke the silence which stretched between them, a silence in which they seemed to be watching part of a past life fade away. The reading of that letter had brought an episode to its close. That was confirmed when she asked, 'And you?'

'The past is the past; a little of it will remain with me but there is a future to get on with, and, Marietta, you I hope will provide a start to that future.'

'I?' She wondered what was coming, but she knew in her heart that she would comply with whatever was asked by Richard.

'I would like to finish your portrait and fulfil your father's commission.'

'A simple request. You can start whenever you like.' Joy sang in her heart for now she would see a lot more of him.

So it proved. Jacob was delighted at the progress Richard made, and when the portrait was finished it was praised by everyone. Richard's flair was evident. What no one guessed, at the time, was the developing relationship between painter and sitter. They had both found pleasure in their meetings which began to take place in society as well as in the studio.

Marietta took delight in the invitations to view Richard's work at Jacob Craig's studio and also his requests to accompany him to the theatre. They became constant companions at parties and balls, something which Jacob encouraged for it was getting his pupil known in society and thus bringing more people to view his work.

Richard was ever grateful to Marietta for the interest she showed in his art and the encouragement she gave him. He found her pleasant to be with and whenever they parted he looked forward to their next meeting, which he made sure became more and more frequent.

302

Chapter Twenty-One

Two years later (1823)

Jacob Craig hunched himself against the rain. It dripped from his hat, ran down his coat and spattered his leather shoes. The heavy downpour had persisted for most of the afternoon and drenched everything and everyone in a few minutes. He hated days like this when with no wind the pall of smoke, rising from the forest of chimneys across the city, seemed to be held down in an unforgiving cloak by the rain. Thank goodness he would soon be home in the more elegant, spacious part of London where he could breathe more easily.

He turned into a side street. A short cut would save him a few minutes, but the dingy street, with buildings crowding on each side, and the rain sending streams of water flowing over the irregular cobbles, did nothing to improve his temper.

He had just come from an art exhibition, at which in previous years his students had sold some of their work, but this year they had sold none. Something would have to be done about it. A good talking to, a sharp and to the point reminder of their talents and the world which could be theirs was needed to resurrect the enthusiasm they had let slip. And none needed it more than Richard Parker.

In his first year his talent had blossomed. His heart and soul were in his work but these past twelve months, when he could have expected a great stride forward, when the demand for his work should have increased, when patrons should have been lauding his talent more than they had the previous year, the spark had gone. His work was still good, better than anyone else's in the school, but it had stood still. It had become mundane, lacking ideas, void of experiment. It seemed Richard was merely content to paint. Jacob was disturbed. He knew if he didn't do something, interest in Richard Parker would wane and England would lose a great painter. But what could he do but talk, cajole and threaten and Richard wasn't the type to react to those tactics. He might only succeed in driving him further into the shell he had built up around himself these last few months.

Head down, Jacob took little notice of the buildings and shops as he passed from dingy street to dingy street. He almost collided with someone. He muttered his apologies, but received only a curse in return from a hunched figure in a tattered coat and battered hat. Jacob ignored him and strode on. Then he halted suddenly. For one brief moment, as he had avoided bumping into the man, his attention unconsciously took in the contents of a shop window among which something had stood out. He had caught only a glimpse but ... It couldn't be, could it? Impossible. He started to walk on. Then he paused again, half turned and looked back. Yes, there was a shop. He moved tentatively to the window. It was dusty, grimy and rain streaked the windows. He peered more closely. Junk. But it was there, propped at a precarious angle against a rickety chair, among pots and pans, old boots and coats, a hobby horse and broken dolls' house. He stared unbelievingly.

Eyes still on it, as if it would disappear if he diverted them, he moved to the shop door which pushed open. A bell jangled. He found himself faced with a clutter of motley items, chairs, a sofa, a cupboard, several ewers and chipped basins, a stuffed hare, rusting tin baths, a miscellany of rubbish, with everything covered in a layer of dust. From the back of the shop there emerged a small man. He shuffled forward, peering from narrowed eyes to try to identify his customer. His black coat and trousers were stained and dusty, and a grimy shirt, with a wing collar and tatty cravat, was no cleaner. He was rubbing his bony hands in anticipation of making a sale. Sunken eyes gleamed with that hope and glinted hawk-like at the potential customer.

'Good day, sir.' His voice croaked. He coughed, cleared his throat and added, 'What interests you?'

'That picture in the window.'

'Ah, sir, a handsome portrait.' His shabby shoes scraped the floor as he moved several items to get to the window. He manoeuvred the canvas, fortunately still in its frame, on to the shop floor and propped it against an old chair.

Jacob came forward and bent down to examine it. 'Where did you get it?' he asked over his shoulder.

The man grunted. 'Brought in by a tramp last year. Said he'd found it on a rubbish dump. I had no reason to doubt him. He was desperate for his daily grog.' The man was beginning to have qualms. From the way this well-dressed gentleman was examining the portrait it appeared that he knew something about it. Was it stolen? Could he be in trouble for receiving?

Jacob made no comment but went on with his careful surveillance. The canvas was well preserved. Fortunately there were no tears. Remarkable, considering the treatment it could have had since Francis threw it out. There were several dirt marks, but they could be cleaned. Professionally handled, Jacob reckoned, it would be as good as the day it was painted.

He straightened, still looking at the picture. He pursed his lips thoughtfully.

'Are you interested, sir?' squeaked the man hopefully.

'I might be.'

'Do you know the young lady?'

Jacob did not want to betray his knowledge. It would only set this miserable man seeking an exorbitant price. He shook his head. 'The picture is a pleasant one, that is all, and I have a place where it would hang, but I'm not prepared to pay very much.'

The shopkeeper's hopes dropped. If the young lady had been known, he would have got more for the picture, for this man would have been desperate to have it.

'Five pounds, sir.' He made his price known like a ferret pouncing on its prey.

'Ah, no.' Jacob straightened to his full height. Though he was not tall he towered over the shopkeeper who was hunched in a pose seeking sympathy.

'No? Sir, the painting is worth that, if not more,' he protested.

'Nonsense,' returned Jacob.

'The frame—' started the shopkeeper only to be cut off by Jacob's sharp interjection.

'—is broken. It's worth nothing. The picture, two pounds.'

The man threw up his arms in disgust. 'Sir, I have to make a living.'

'You'll make a handsome profit at that. No doubt you gave the tramp coppers.'

The man tightened his lips, annoyed with himself at disclosing how he had come by the picture. 'Three pounds, sir?'

'Two pounds ten shillings.'

The shopkeeper looked away in disgust.

Jacob shrugged his shoulders. 'You keep the picture.' He started for the door.

'Wait, sir.' The picture had been taking up window space for too long. He wanted rid of it. 'Very well, sir. Two pounds ten shillings.' Then he added in a grumbling tone, 'But you are robbing me.'

Jacob gave a little smile. 'I think not.' He fished in his pocket, brought out the coins and dropped them into the claw-like hand eager to close over them.

A week later Jacob, in a buoyant mood, took delivery of the painting, cleaned and newly framed. He unpacked it carefully and stood back to admire it. It was as he first saw it and its magic still moved him.

But the talent which had resulted in this painting had not been exploited to the full. It lay dormant at the moment, and his efforts to stir it into fire since the exhibition had come to nothing. He was in despair but he would try one more time.

He picked up the portrait and went upstairs where he knew Richard was working in his own studio.

Richard, behind a large canvas, could not see who had come in but he recognised the voice. 'Hello, Mr Craig, I'll be with you in a moment.'

Jacob took the opportunity to place the picture strategically so that the light from the window brought Charlotte's face alive.

Richard came from behind his easel, brush still in hand, then stopped. His smile faded. His cheeks drained white as he

306

stared incredulously at the face which looked at him from the canvas. He could not speak but stood taking in the love for him which poured from the eyes of the image. Image? No, this portrait was alive, saying all manner of things to him. He almost reached out with gentle fingers to touch the corners of her lips. Memories crowded in on him, memories of her in his arms, of moments shared, of what she had meant to him, and recollections of his loneliness on a Whitby cliff watching a ship taking her away from him for ever.

'Where did you find her?' he whispered slowly.

Jacob hadn't the heart to break into Richard's thoughts but, having watched his reactions carefully, he now knew what he would do.

'In a junk shop a week ago. I had it cleaned and reframed. It arrived here a few minutes ago.'

'And what are—'

Jacob did not let him finish the question. He knew what it was. 'It is yours. Hang it above the fireplace where you can see it when you are painting. You are good, but you are drifting into mediocrity. Your work needs more feeling – put passion into it like you used to.' He pointed at the picture. 'Remember her.'

He did not expect a reply. He had seen a new gleam come to Richard's eyes on hearing those last two words and he knew he had revived the spark of genius which had lain dormant for a year.

Chapter Twenty-Two

Three years later (1826)

The murmurings among the small congregation in the church of St James were drowned then silenced by the triumphant notes of the organ heralding the arrival of the bride.

Everyone stood up and half turned in greeting to Marietta who entered the church on the arm of her father. Whistles of admiration swept from the guests, not only acknowledging the beauty of her dress but also her radiant happiness, which drew them all into sharing it with her.

Her smile, warm with greetings and thanks, flitted quickly from side to side before focusing directly ahead on the man she was to marry.

She could sense his love, combined with respect, admiration, devotion and friendship, which she expressed in return. She looked forward to their life together, a life in which she was determined to continue dedicating herself to helping him achieve his ambitions as a painter. His work had blossomed in the last three years and now, to go forward, he deserved every support she could give him.

With his brother beside him he watched Marietta come slowly to him. She was exquisite. The white net of her gown was embroidered with motifs of leaves and clusters of roses, its trimmed edge just trailing the floor. It came tight to the waist then flared out, and had a high square neck with small lace collar. The sleeves, puffed from the shoulders to the elbows, came tight to the wrists. The gleam of the white satin underdress made the net sparkle as if it was alive. A pink shawl matched the wide-brimmed bonnet worn tipped back from her face and tied with a white ribbon below the chin.

Richard glanced at his mother, who seemed to have anticipated his look. In her smile and nod he read approval of the choice he had made.

Marietta was beside him. They smiled at each other and their eyes, even before the official words of the service had been spoken, vowed a life of love and devotion to each other.

'Wilt thou, Richard Parker take Marietta Kemp to be thy lawful wedded wife ...'

'I will.'

'Wilt thou, Marietta Kemp take Richard Parker to be thy lawful wedded husband ...'

'I will.'

Chapter Twenty-Three

Thirty years later (1856)

Charlotte picked up the newspaper. Copies of *The Times* covering the last week had just arrived from Boston, having been brought north by one of the Campion ships which sailed weekly between there and the capital.

She was seated comfortably in front of the large window which gave broad views across the estate. She often sat here and counted her blessings, though they did not include children. The inability had worried her until, helped by the consideration of her loving husband, she had thrown off her depression. He had encouraged her to increase her interest in his businesses and the estate. If they had had a son it might have been different, for there would have been someone to follow Charles in running his enterprises. As it was, Charlotte had been able to do that when he died. She had even expanded and had always been well off, with servants to tend to her every need. She in turn was generous to them and was well liked in the Lincolnshire countryside as well as in the business world where she was regarded as something of a phenomenon – a woman competing in a man's world and often outsmarting her male counterparts.

She looked at the date on the page. Four days ago. As she turned the pages, she suddenly stiffened. Her eyes froze on three heavily printed words:

Disbelief held her transfixed. Then she forced herself to read on:

Severe Loss to British Art

Richard Parker, who it was thought would be knighted within the year, died suddenly at his London home aged fifty-six. Born in Whitby, on the Yorkshire coast, he was brought to London in 1820 by Mr Francis Wakefield, a London merchant, who while on holiday in Whitby saw the young man sketching on one of the piers.

Charlotte's eyes, glazed with tears, read the rest of the report through a mist. It told her no more than she already knew, for she had followed Richard's career ever since their parting. She had visited galleries where she knew his work was on display, had attended exhibitions, but had always been careful that their paths should never cross. She owed that to her devoted Charles and of course to Richard. Her parents had lessened the possibility of a meeting by moving away from Russell Square when it became known that Richard and Marietta were seeing a great deal of each other.

The sheer genius of Mr Parker's painting will always stand as a beacon in British Art. He leaves a wife and four children.

Tears flowed and envy burned in her heart as she reread those last two words.

Chapter Twenty-Four

Two weeks later

Charlotte was sitting in the same chair at the same window when her attention was drawn to a one-horse carriage coming up the long drive towards the house. She was curious. She was not expecting any visitors. Elsa Bonner was expected to tea tomorrow, a friendly engagement before Charlotte departed on a business visit to London the day after. So who could this be?

She leaned forward to get a better look at the carriage when it stopped at the front door.

The coachman jumped down and opened the carriage door. A lady alighted and waited while the coachman reached into the carriage. He handed the lady a small bag, the sort that Charlotte would have used for an overnight stay. But she had made no arrangements for anyone to come to Reed Hall. Puzzled and curious, she frowned. Who was the person still standing by the coach? Her bonnet was shielding her face. If only she would raise her head. The coachman removed a large and well-protected object from the coach and accompanied the stranger towards the front door. The lady turned her head. Stranger? No, Charlotte could hardly believe her eyes. She rose to her feet and hurried from the room. As she came lightly down the wide staircase her heart was aflutter. Marietta! After all these years!

She was halfway to the hall when the butler, having heard the doorbell, opened the door. There was a brief exchange of words and the butler stood aside to allow Marietta to enter the house. She was followed by the coachman who placed the package against the wall near the door and made his exit.

'Marietta!' Charlotte hastened down the last few stairs and flung her arms wide in welcome.

Marietta, who had been wondering what sort of reception she would get, smiled at Charlotte's enthusiastic greeting as they hugged each other. The years fell away. They were young again.

'Thomas, take Mrs Parker's things.' She eyed the bag and looked back at Marietta. 'You're staying?'

'I hoped you might invite me at least for tonight.'

'Two nights. I go to London the day after tomorrow, we can travel together.' She turned to the butler who was taking Marietta's coat, bonnet and bag. 'Ask Alice to bring some tea into the drawing room.'

'Certainly ma'am.' He looked at Marietta. 'The parcel, ma'am?'

'Could that be taken to my room too?'

'Certainly, ma'am.'

As the butler left the hall, Charlotte linked arms with Marietta and they went into the drawing room.

'You've still got Thomas and Alice after all these years.'

'Faithful servants. I'd be lost without them. But you, Marietta – oh, I was so sorry to read about Richard.' Her voice faltered.

'I knew you would be.'

'But you aren't in mourning?' Charlotte showed her surprise.

Marietta gave a small smile. 'I know it goes against convention but it was Richard's expressed wish that after the funeral the family discard their mourning clothes. He hated them and thought they would detract from the happy remembrances we should have.'

Charlotte nodded, 'Thirty-six years. Marietta, you haven't changed.'

'Older. More lined.'

'But just as pretty.'

Marietta gave a little laugh. 'If only I was. But you, you are no different.'

They talked a great deal over tea, friends again. Those harsh words thrown at each other all those years ago in Whitby were never mentioned, allowed to drift away in the mists of time.

With tea over, Marietta stood up. 'I have something for you, Charlotte. If you'll excuse me I'll go and get it.'

'Turn right at the top of the stairs, and your room is the second on the left.'

Within a few minutes Marietta had the package unwrapped and was returning with Charlotte's gift. Her heart was racing a little, trying to anticipate her friend's reaction.

As Marietta came into the room Charlotte moved away from the window. 'A painting?' She could only see the back. 'One of Richard's?'

Marietta did not reply but turned the picture round.

Charlotte stared, hardly able to get her breath. Her heart was pounding. 'Where it all began!' she whispered. It was as if Richard had entered the room. She still saw what she had seen the first time she had looked at the painting – his love for her. 'Where did you get it? Father threw it out.'

Marietta told her of how Jacob Craig had found it and had taken it to Richard and advised him to hang it in his studio. 'Jacob always said it galvanised Richard out of the mediocrity into which he was slipping.'

'That can't be true,' protested Charlotte. 'Richard's talent would have surfaced no matter and it certainly would have when he married you. It was after that that his genius was recognised and his work was in demand. You must have inspired him with your love.'

'I hope I did. I know you did. You meant a lot to him. Don't misunderstand me. I loved him deeply and I know he loved me. He was a kind, considerate man; I could not have found a better husband nor could the children have had a better father.'

'I envy you your children,' put in Charlotte wistfully. 'Richard's children.'

'They gave us both much happiness.'

'You had the love of a dear and remarkable man.'

'Yes. I had. His love for me is ingrained in my heart.' She paused briefly. 'Nothing can mar the love we shared, but it was you he was always in love with. It is there in that portrait. You knew it, otherwise you would never have gone to Whitby. He was always open with me. He showed me the letter you wrote to him and he described his feelings on the cliff when he watched you sail out of his life. No one will ever know the sacrifice you made that day for British art.'

There were tears in Charlotte's eyes as she looked at the portrait and remembered the love which had inspired it.